The Reality Rebellions

Deplosion: Book 3

Paul Anlee

Darian Publishing House
Chatham, Ontario, Canada

THE REALITY REBELLIONS
DEPLOSION: BOOK THREE

How do you prove you're a person to those who insist you're only a machine?

Earth is gone. When the Cybrid, DAR-K, and her team built the Vesta asteroid habitats that now shelter the last of humanity, they saw themselves as equal partners in the project. For decades, these robotic beings hosted select human minds and dedicated their lives to ensuring the survival of the biologicals.

Now, as Vesta heads toward a game-changing election, the Cybrids are demanding to be recognized as full citizens. But Alum, self-declared Leader of the colonies, has a different vision. He's about to strip away the last of the Cybrids' rights and banish "those machines" from the habitats forever. Is he also the driving force behind the recent acts of sabotage and rising anti-Cybrid violence? How far will the Cybrids go to gain a voice in determining the colony's future, and will Alum risk destroying the habitats to deny them power?

Canadian author Paul Anlee writes provocative, epic sci-fi in the style of Asimov, Heinlein, Asher, and Reynolds, stories that challenge our assumptions and stretch our imagination. Literary, fact-based, and fast-paced, the Deplosion series explores themes in philosophy, politics, religion, economics, AI, VR, nanotech, synbio, quantum reality, and beyond.

For Sandra

"Nevertheless, she persisted."
— Senator Mitch McConnell

1

JARED STRANG, EX-MEMBER OF THE BRITISH PARLIAMENT, ex-Minister of Foreign Affairs, current Manager of Human-Cybrid relations for the Vesta Project, was baffled. Surely, he'd misheard. His eyes shifted uncertainly between Alum and Dona Ridgeway, Alum's Chief of Staff. "But if we don't allow the Cybrids to work in the populated colonies, how will we manage? The colonists aren't exactly trained to expand the living spaces, or even to maintain them for that matter."

Alum stroked his chin but said nothing. He raised an eyebrow toward Ridgeway, inviting her to answer on his behalf.

"We humans managed to build an entire civilization on Earth without resorting to cybernetic robots. And we did perfectly fine, don't you think?" She smiled tightly at the civil servant and adjusted her glasses.

Strang coughed into his fist. "Well, yes, clearly," he agreed. "But the Cybrids have the requisite skills and experience for this environment. Not to mention, all our available heavy equipment is either integral to their bodies or designed to be operated exclusively by them. Even if we *had* machinery built for humans, we don't know what expertise is available among the colonists. My hunch is we're not at risk of being overwhelmed with talent."

Ridgeway glanced over at Alum. He nodded for her to continue.

"I assure you that our databases are *quite* thorough, Mr. Strang. Training classes will fill in any gaps over time."

Strang sat forward, "You don't understand," he interrupted. "We don't *have* time. There is no Plan B. This has to..."

Alum held up a shushing finger, silencing Strang mid-sentence. "People must have purpose in their lives. The socio-economic history of Earth demonstrates what happens when people are idle and feel useless. Political opportunism, unrest, riots, social breakdown—we will not permit Vesta to head down that path."

Strang flopped back in his chair. "No, surely not." He pinched the bridge of his nose and rubbed his eyes. "Is there any way we could have skilled people shadow some of the Cybrids as they go about their work? A kind of on-the-job training program, so to speak."

Alum nodded as if considering the merits of Strang's suggestion. "Mr. Strang, I understand you've never been a member of our Church, but surely you are a Christian, yes?"

Strang's mouth worked through several possible responses before settling on, "Surely."

In truth, he believed personal beliefs should remain personal, not be trotted out for public display. Still, it was better not to say too much; one had to be aware who currently held the power on the Vesta colonies.

"Well, then," Alum continued, "You know our Lord created man in His image, setting man above all others. Man is above his own creations, the Cybrids for example, just as God is above His creation, namely us. Wouldn't you agree?"

"When you put it that way, what choice do I have?"

"Exactly. We have an opportunity to reinvigorate God's universe, and mankind's place in it, out here among the asteroids. And that begins with the proper humility, with people who value the might of the Lord above all.

"Cybrids are remnants of the old, evil ways of Earth, Mr. Strang. Mechanical beings have their place, and that place is in the vacuum of space, not among humans. When I... I mean, my father, supported their development, they were not intended to be anything other than a tool, a mechanical extension of our hands to help us build these habitats. *That* is how they best serve the Lord's wishes."

Strang noted the stutter before Alum spoke of his father; it brought to mind the odd rumors about the young man's origins, perverse gossip to which few gave much credence. "One might say," he ventured, "it's rather...superfluous to have a Manager of Human-Cybrid Relations when, in fact, there are no relations between humans and Cybrids to be managed."

"I agree, your role in the administration of these habitats has changed," Alum sniffed. He pushed his body out of the comfortable chair, and walked over to the window. He called up the construction schematics for the habitats, letting the silence—and Strang's discomfort—stretch out.

The Project Manager's office dominated the fiftieth floor of the highest tower in all of Vesta One, the first of the asteroid's colony tunnels and the official capital of all the habitats. The windows looked "North" and "South" toward the tunnel's polar caps lying over two hundred kilometers away in either direction. Below, densely-spaced apartment towers stretched seven kilometers wide before meeting the upward-curving sides of the tunnel.

Each asteroid contained six colony tunnels arranged like the bullet chambers of a revolver. Each tunnel had a "floor" surface that squared off the arc closest to the asteroid's surface, and a "ceiling" on the part of the arc closest to the central axis.

Artificial gravity was provided by spinning the asteroid. Because of this rotation, "down" was always outward, away from the asteroid's axis, always toward the surface.

The orientation session reassured new arrivals that, "It's simple. Think of 'down' as the direction your feet sink; it's the direction that receives the force of your weight. Inside the colony tunnels, the planetoid's meager natural gravity is overridden by the centrifugal force from the spinning. That's why we interpret 'down' as being toward the outer surface."

Several rivers, driven by circulating pumps, ran the length of the tunnels and occasionally widened into long, narrow lakes. Some ran north-to-south in the colony tunnels, and returned south-to-north in the agricultural service tunnels below. Others flowed in the opposite direction to provide balance along their lengths.

High above, light panels ran the length of the tunnel. They brightened and dimmed in cycles, fourteen on and ten off, driving the daily rhythms of the people, animals, and plants below.

Project Vesta has done a remarkable job of reproducing the Earth's ecology in such a small space and in such short time—Alum noted with satisfaction.

Well, I suppose I've kept Strang waiting long enough. Not that he deserves anything more than my simple command.

"Under the *previous* administration," he paused to let that sink in, "you may have seen your job as smoothing over people's acceptance of the Cybrids and integrating everyone into a workable biology-plus-machine society. That will no longer be the case. The Cybrids are not people; they will never be people in the eyes of the Lord."

"Aren't their mental processes modeled on our own human minds?" Strang asked.

Alum's eyes blazed. "They can simulate many human characteristics, no doubt; but they are not human, not flesh and blood. They are not created in God's image. We have found a place for them where they can be of service to humanity and, thereby, to God's will. No more. They will never claim a place by our side; to do so would be an abomination."

Strang's gaze shifted to his hands, cradled anxiously in his lap. He observed his fidgeting fingers as if they were something apart from him. "I see. So what exactly is my role to be?"

Alum glanced at Ms. Ridgeway, who'd been sitting silently through the sermon.

"As Spiritual Leader of the YTG Church and the de facto leader of humanity, Alum must remain uncontaminated, separate from discussions with the Cybrids," she explained. "You will communicate our Leader's directive to them: they are to remain outside the habitat tunnels unless granted specific permission to enter. You will report on their compliance with his will and on their adherence to these laws."

"I have no wish to appear unjust or unsympathetic, Mr. Strang," Alum added. "Not even to machines. But you seem to have lost sight of the fact that Cybrids were designed and constructed to *serve* humanity, not to replace it. Within those parameters, they will enjoy a fulfilling existence. Perhaps we'll even develop some form of entertainment for their off-duty hours. Your job is to ensure they understand and cooperate with my directives."

"Is this the will of the Governing Council?" Strang asked.

Ridgeway nearly choked. Before Alum could reply, she jumped in. "The Council exists to provide advice to Alum. He, and he alone, decides." She set her lips firmly, accepting no further questioning of her Leader's authority.

"So the Cybrids are to be our slaves."

The crease between Alum's eyebrows deepened. "Slavery is not an applicable term; they are *machines* that were built for service. You will not speak of it again."

The manager bowed his head. He had seen enough of the local police actions under Alum's direction to know he should hold his tongue. *For the moment.*

As Ms. Ridgeway's voice droned on in the background, Strang's attention shifted to conversations he would be having with his colleagues from the original Project Vesta. Not everyone shared Alum's point of view.

2

DAR-K FLOATED HIGH ABOVE the empty apartment towers of Pallas Three, the third colony tunnel to be constructed inside the asteroid Pallas and the ninth to be completed under the broader Vesta Project. Two months had passed since the Eater had absorbed Earth into its relentlessly expanding grayness, and she was still bitter over losing Kathy Liang, her human "sister" whose mind had served as the template for her own.

I can't believe Earth's gone, and everyone left behind is dead. Kathy, Greg, the whole planet, all gone.

The silence of the vacuum in the unfinished tunnel suited her desire for isolation. Intermittent light fell on the buildings directly below, but the farther reaches of the habitat were dark. The gloom matched the bleak thoughts roiling in her silicene brain.

"*What do I do now?*" was a question the Cybrid had never pondered before. Time for quiet contemplation was a luxury she hadn't experienced in her eighteen years of existence.

Humanity has kept me occupied from the day I was manufactured, their first Cybrid of millions. They kept us all endlessly busy building their new home out here, making space for as many of them as possible.

To the Cybrids, it was obvious that the construction of the Project Vesta asteroid colonies, all of the tunneling, mining, and manufacturing, was better managed by the rugged autonomous robots than by human beings. Earthlings were ill-suited for work in space; they required complex support systems. And so the colonists were kept back on Earth until the robot-built asteroid colonies were ready to receive them into climate controlled comfort.

Though Vesta was designed to save human lives, humans had played little part in its construction. The Cybrids had built the colonies largely without human help or direct human supervision.

Except for Greg and Kathy. The couple had been there from the beginning, planning, designing, discussing, strategizing, and overseeing alongside the Cybrids.

I miss Kathy. DAR-K had become used to discussing everything with her human counterpart. Sisters-by-choice, they'd become expert at liaising between machine and human, between workers and governments, and between those who built things and those who pulled the levers of political power.

Human politics—DAR-K sighed, but without breath, without air, it emitted no sound. The futility of simulating human utterances in space only reinforced the differences between her and the original Kathy Liang.

What am I going to do without her?

She and Kathy shared the same memories, knowledge, and beliefs. The structure of her mind was identical to Kathy's, including her secretly enhanced lattice intelligence. Nobody aside from DAR-K and Kathy knew about their shared enhancement. Kathy was insistent that they keep the information between them alone, not even Greg could know, and DAR-K trusted her judgment. As a result, Kathy had been the only person who knew what, who knew *who*, she really was, and what she could be.

And now Kathy was dead, consumed by the Eater along with the vast majority of humankind.

Who would believe downloading a person's mind into a two-meter carboceramic sphere with built-in rockets and electromuscle tentacles would lead to a robot who thinks it's human? Even the government insiders who knew what they were creating— who we Cybrids are—can't bring themselves to recognize us as people.

The death of humanity's home had come before all three colony asteroids could be completed. How the Eater anomaly escaped its vacuum chamber ahead of time remained a mystery.

Our projections were good. We should have had another eight months, easily— DAR-K lamented.

Somehow, Alum and his people were prepared for the disaster and acted decisively. Their surprise takeover of the colonies was relatively smooth and bloodless, for a coup.

Despite her resentment, DAR-K was doing her best to cooperate with the new order. It wasn't easy without Kathy to run interference; the new regime was not sympathetic to Cybrids.

I shouldn't be wasting any more time here. Not when we have so much work to do. "Lollygagging," Kathy would have called it.

The completed tunnel in which she floated stretched for hundreds of kilometers ahead. They'd sealed the ends, and were about to fill the interior with atmosphere. Nitrogen they'd mined from Titan and oxygen produced by splitting comet water into its base elements would form the main part of the habitat's air. *It will be exactly like the air used to be on Earth, with less pollution.*

She powered up her main drive and pushed downward to inspect the city below. Project Vesta management, under the direction of the Yeshua's True Guard Church since the coup, still expected her to manage Cybrid construction activities in the new colonies.

Adequate living space is as precious as ever. Alum may be spiritual leader of the Church, but he hasn't overlooked the need to manage the physical world, too.

At present, Vesta's total population numbered fewer than the originally intended forty million, but they'd be out-growing available room quickly, thanks to the Church's new program encouraging every family to have babies. Lots of babies.

The Faithful are always eager to go forth and multiply—she joked to herself. She was achingly aware that she'd inherited Kathy's sense of dark, dry humour and cynicism, and how few individuals there were in the entire asteroid belt with whom she could share it.

As soon as they established a human-friendly atmosphere, the Cybrid workforce would bring in billions of tonnes of water from the Kuiper mines to supply rivers and lakes. The basic ecology would be populated with plants and animals from other habitats, and the new tunnels would be opened up to receive colonists.

In a few months, a million people will be enjoying substantially more elbow room.

DAR-K entered a wide street that ran parallel along one of the empty riverbeds waiting to be filled. She plucked a loose pebble from the ground and tossed it among the other stones.

The surviving colonists are well-intentioned but mostly clueless. Watching then in action made her think of drunks bumbling around in the dark on a slippery slope that was pocked with craters and moguls.

At least, they have enthusiasm. And Faith. Faith in their God and in the leader of their Church.

She stopped in front of a designated commercial space and examined her reflection in the window. *What do I have faith in?*—she wondered. *What do I have to live for? Power? Fame? Love?*

The latter was unlikely. The only other DAR- designated Cybrid in existence was DAR-G, who was based on the mind of Kathy's husband, Greg Mahajani.

DAR-K wished she could love DAR-G as much as Kathy had loved Greg, but it was impossible. *DAR-G's nice enough; he's just too...ordinary.*

He was brilliant compared to most other Cybrids. He had Greg's charming personality, deep devotion to the Kathy persona and, by extension, to DAR-K. *But he's not Greg, and he never will be.*

It was unfortunate that Kathy never got a chance to upgrade DAR-G's processor with the same illegal IQ-enhancing lattice modifications she'd made to DAR-K. The same modifications Kathy and Greg had shared.

Oh, well. What does love matter to an electromechanical being with a semiconductor brain? I have my work.

And there was so much work to do. Vesta was more or less complete in the broad strokes, but there were still a few major colony tubes to finish in two of the smaller asteroids.

Since Vesta was the first completed and the largest of the three asteroids, the majority of humans had been sent there. They were busily making it their own and working toward self-sufficiency.

Here on Pallas, the Cybrid teams were still building the habitat and farming infrastructure for the four newer tubes.

It's a good thing Cybrids don't need sleep. If we were biological beings, we'd be dropping from exhaustion. She and her comrades had been pushed to their limits by the construction schedule over the past several years, and even harder now that Earth was gone.

Project Vesta's original list of human colonists had included a broad range of individuals carefully selected for their health, intellect, creativity, broad backgrounds, and extensive expertise. They were expected to contribute in many meaningful ways to the construction and operation of the asteroids. The members of the YTG Church that Alum brought in their place lacked in many of these important areas, most notably in science and technology training.

How are we supposed to rebuild a modern civilization with what they've salvaged?—she muttered as she drifted down the wide boulevard. *If only Alum would turn over all the important work to existing Cybrid experts.*

She had to laugh. *That'll never happen, not in a million years.*

To be fair, the new settlers were still finding their feet. *Maybe they'll surprise me.* A number of essential trades within the construction, service, and agricultural sectors were well represented. Other sectors, overly so. She wondered how Alum would place or retrain the suspiciously outsized representation of business and finance people.

The humans, as poorly qualified as they were, had taken over everything. DAR-K still hadn't decided what to do about that, if anything.

With Greg and Kathy dead, she was now the closest thing to a legitimate heir to the Vesta Project Management Committee. She knew more about the project than anyone alive, human or Cybrid. Not that it mattered to Alum. He formed a Governing Council, and appointed himself as its Head. The Council dissolved the original Vesta committee, assumed all aspects of Vesta project management, and actively shut her out.

She didn't want to act too aggressively and demand to be put in charge. That would only lead to unnecessary confrontations between humans and Cybrids, which would end in Cybrid dominance, and the rapid extinction of the human species. That was not her intent.

DAR-K extended a tentacle and pushed it through the window, shattering the glass. She immediately sent a work order to replace it.

I should be building, but I'm in the mood for some destruction—she admitted. It was no surprise, given who she'd been forced to report to lately.

Strang's okay, but he's clearly hampered by orders from above.

Reporting to the new administration was nothing like coordinating with Kathy and the old Committee. Fortunately, Alum and his Governing Council resided on Vesta, hundreds of millions of kilometers away. In part, that was why DAR-K spent most of her time around Pallas and Ceres these days. Besides, the new administration already had enough on its plate getting the new human colonists organized. She'd only be a nuisance to them right now.

As always, humans have a way of thinking they're the most important beings in the region. And wherever they go, they take their prejudices and bigotries with them. Well, I've got a news flash for them.

DAR-K and the twenty million working Cybrids in space totalled almost as many as the surviving humans. Add to that the hundred million Cybrid minds in storage who were waiting to be put into new robot bodies and the humans would be vastly outnumbered.

She'd allow the Governing Council a little time to get itself better organized and to deal with some of the most pressing survival issues.

And then, we'll definitely be talking.

3

GREG MAHAJANI CHOSE VESTA for his surgery. Besides having the best facilities for the kind of alterations he had in mind, nobody there was likely to connect his present face to his new identity as "Darak Legsu" on Pallas. Darak's—that is, Greg's—ability to jump across interplanetary distances, like those separating his home on Pallas from the surgeons on Vesta, was a secret. No one would expect to see Darak Legsu away from his home habitat.

On the day he popped in, he was surprised to find a meticulously clean Operating theater sitting empty. He pinged the surgeon to announce his arrival.

The Cybrid surgeon activated, instantly alert and ready to take direction.

"Hello, I am PHL-239483. You may call me Dr. Phil. How may I help you?" the robot physician asked.

"I want you to make me look like this," Greg answered, showing him a facial design.

"I'm afraid that cosmetic surgery performed by Cybrids for reasons other than rehabilitation or trauma has been recently forbidden by the Administration. You do not appear to be in need of emergency reconstructive surgery."

Cybrids banned from all but emergency procedures? Clearly it wasn't due to a shortage of surgeons. Dr. Phil didn't look at all busy. *A reflection of the mood of the day, more than the demands. How sad.*

Using his lattice interface, Greg probed the Cybrid's mind looking for the associated conceptual structures where he could override the prohibition. He felt guilty altering the poor thing's persona guidelines to get it—correction, to get *him*—to agree to the surgery. *Just this one time, I promise, and only for me*—Greg vowed.

First, to circumvent Dr. Phil's concepta security. *That shouldn't be too hard;*

I know all of Kathy's standard antivirus tricks. The memory of his wife brought a lump to his throat. *Indulge yourself on your own time*—he told himself. *Focus now; mourn later.*

He recognized Kathy's typical Quonset-five defence right away. It wasn't one of her best protocols and was severely outdated now. He bypassed it with hardly a thought.

There. All done, and this poor Cybrid has no idea I've changed his mind for him. No matter; I'll update his security after the surgery. No independent being should be this vulnerable to direct tampering with the essence of his mind.

Greg repeated his request.

The surgeon scanned the diagram of Greg's desired new face as if seeing it for the first time. "Yes, I can create this result," he said. "The surgery itself will require twenty-four minutes. It will take a further six days for the tissue swelling to subside and for most of the scars to heal. Stem cell changes and alterations in your genetics will activate over that time as well. When would you like to schedule the procedure?"

Greg considered which few days to book off work to attract the least suspicion. His "supervision" of the Cybrid farm construction team on Pallas was trivial. Keeping up with their plans and progress required only a few minutes of his attention every day. *Cybrid teams were constructing the colonies and farm tunnels long before I arrived on Pallas. Kathy trained DAR-K to manage the project well. They're probably more capable of working without direction from me, than with it.*

That last thought brought another twinge of emotional pain. For weeks, Greg had been wrestling with whether to contact Kathy's Cybrid counterpart, DAR-K. He missed Kathy so much, and DAR-K was the closest thing to her that he had left. He felt the pull, but he couldn't bring himself to make contact. Not yet. *What if she turned out to be a big disappointment like my own counterpart, DAR-G, was to me? I'd rather keep my memory of Kathy as she was.*

Without the lattice-enhanced intelligence that he and Kathy shared, speaking to either DAR-K or DAR-G was sure to be an exercise in frustration. It was almost as painful as speaking to a merely slightly above-average human. It was unfair, and limiting to all, that Cybrids should still be subject to IQ restrictions imposed by paranoid Earth governments that no longer existed, a paranoia now taken up by the majority of humans in the asteroid habitats.

Truth be told, his job made him feel more like a spy for the YTG Church-based administration than a supervisor. To offset his guilt, he spent much of his spare time developing imaginative virtual playgrounds the Cybrids could enjoy during their recharging periods. Secretly, he toyed with introducing Cybrid lattice security upgrades through viral packages in the simulations. Shouldn't the Cybrids—or at the very least, the human minds inside those Cybrid bodies—have the right to decide who got to mess with their minds?

"Sir? Would you like to select a date, or would you like me to suggest one?" the surgeon prompted.

Greg realized he'd been daydreaming again. He'd been having trouble focusing lately. He knew it was depression. If he just pushed on, things had to get better with time. *Enough wallowing in self-pity. Work on what you can change. Book your surgery date.*

"How about Wednesday afternoon in two weeks? That's when my weekend starts."

"Very well," the surgeon replied. "That gives me adequate time to prepare the necessary stem cell population." As he spoke, a tentacle extracted a punch biopsy needle from a nearby drawer. Another tentacle grabbed a sterilizing anesthetic cotton pad. "Lower your trousers."

The sheer size of the needle made Greg hesitate. "Not much for bedside manner, are you?" he quipped. He probed Dr. Phil's medical database and scanned the related literature. Satisfied with the safety of this part of the procedure, he reduced the sensitivity of his backside pain receptors, turned, and loosened his pants.

The topical anesthetic was cold but effective. Greg felt hardly more than a pinch when the surgeon extracted a number of fat cells from his left cheek. As he fastened his belt, the Cybrid extruded the sample into the waiting growth medium at the bottom of a small culture flask.

* * *

THE TWO WEEKS BETWEEN his first visit and the scheduled surgery passed quickly. Once he'd set into motion a plan to disguise himself permanently, he felt more nervous than ever about being recognized as Dr. Greg Mahajani, former co-Director of Project Vesta. He needed that new face fast.

He barely left his apartment except to work. Other than his job, he kept to himself wherever possible. It wasn't too hard to fool one or two Cybrid brains at a time about the appearance of their human supervisor. He could feed their visual sensors with a false image for the time being, and update their memories at his convenience.

However, he didn't think he could simultaneously fool dozens of human inSense lattices so easily.

On the few occasions he had to venture out in public, he fretted that someone might recognize his face from some old news cast. It was silly and he knew it. His risk was no higher since his decision to undergo surgery than it had been when he first arrived on Pallas.

He was happy he'd stepped back from the Project Vesta limelight a decade ago. Kathy had turned out to be a much better project manager than he could ever be and a more sympathetic public face for Vesta. For a while, he'd been resentful of her popularity. Now, he was grateful people had paid more attention to her than to him.

As a precaution, he shaved his head and let his beard grow, altering his ID card and central records to match his changed features.

Finally, the scheduled day arrived. He packed his bags and shifted to a supply closet in the hospital on Vesta. He hoped the three-and-a-half days off would give him a good head start on his recovery. *Thank goodness for the Act for Fuller Employment of 2046 and its more humane work schedule.*

Today his anxiety would be substantially relieved. Once the bandages came off and the swelling went down, his true identity would be hidden forever and Alum and his enforcers would never realize Greg Mahajani had made it off Earth alive.

Dr. Phil had assured him the scars would be barely discernible in a week. "Techniques have progressed greatly since the human colonists were first assigned Cybrid surgeons," he'd said.

Greg sensed an undertone of resentment from the doctor, likely at being forcibly sidelined from where he was needed the most.

Before emerging into the hallway, Greg inserted Police and Ambulance reports in the respective systems to support a plausible cover story about how his blowtorch had lit some residual solvent in a tank he was working on. He constructed a new identity and fake work order to justify the job. He cited a distant tunnel to give credence to his tale, and added the names of appropriate Officers and Attendants to the report, knowing it would be unlikely anyone here knew them personally.

Electronic trail in place, he walked out of the supply closet and lay down on an empty ER gurney in the corridor with face hastily and clumsily self-bandaged. Orders to move him immediately into the Cybrid OR appeared at the nursing station.

The hospitals were still trying to dig themselves out of the chaos that came from hundreds of new workers and a change in management. They were used to responding to paperwork. Sometimes it was the only way they had any idea what was going on.

An attendant moved him to the OR. When Dr. Phil arrived, the staff in the room vacated quickly, taking their anxious whispers with them out to the corridor. The Cybrid surgeon preferred to work alone, and no one wanted to watch its buzzing, whirring tentacles in action on an actual person.

"So, I'm booked into Recovery Room Four, and I have a private room in the main hospital?" Greg asked the doctor.

"Yes, you will receive excellent care in our facility. Please don't worry."

Greg took a deep breath. "Can I look at myself one last time?" Dr. Phil positioned a mirror above where Greg lay on the operating table, while they waited for the first relaxant to take effect. He studied himself intently, committing his face to lattice memory. He had no problem overlaying the new features he'd designed onto the digital images he'd captured, but he couldn't project how it would feel to wake up to a different face.

He shut off his lattice. He remembered Darian's discomfiting story of waking up to two separate consciousnesses following surgery, one biological, the other, neurolattice. *An experience I can do without.*

"Okay," he finally said, feeling a lassitude wash over him. "Let's get on with it."

The Cybrid opened the line permitting the general anesthetic to mix with the saline solution in Greg's IV bag. At the same time, three tentacles snaked over his face, injecting heavy doses of Lidocaine into the area about to be operated on. "Count backward from a hundred," Dr. Phil instructed.

"100, 99, 98,..." Greg began. He felt his head go fuzzy and nearly reactivated his lattice. Then he remembered where he was and resumed counting. "97, 96, 10, 9,..." A soft gray peacefulness descended over him like a fluffy blanket.

4

MARY'S VIRTUAL HEART LURCHED. *What the hell?* Straight above, she saw patches of stormy sky between whipping fronds of palm trees. Her lungs burned. Her ribs were screaming in pain. She was being lugged between four men—four Trillian clones—as if she were a sack of potatoes. Her vision bobbed with their rhythmic steps. They didn't seem to mind that every jolt sent shards of pain through her body.

Shards and shards—she thought. *Shards of Alum causing shards of pain.* She would have laughed, but breathing was a challenge. She fought to stay conscious, had no energy left to struggle against her captors.

The bobbing and bouncing paused. She heard the water dripping off her clothes and hair onto the sidewalk below. *I'm wet. Why am I wet?*

Snap out of it, Mary—she ordered herself. *Think!* She tried a deep breath, but the stabbing sensation in her ribs stopped her short. *What do I remember?*

I was in Vacationland. Trillian had Timothy pinned to the pool deck. I tackled Trillian, and we landed in the water. I yelled at Timothy to run. And then Trillian grabbed me by the hair and pulled me underwater. I must've passed out.

Her captors opened the door of the quantum luxury cabina nearest the pool, and placed her inside on the bed.

Mary lay motionless for a long while, relishing the plush cushioning under her back. Finally, the pain subsided a little, and she managed to sit up, legs dangling off one side of the mattress, and examine the room.

The king-sized bed lay beneath a lace canopy; the netting trailed down along the four supporting posts, adorned with intricate carvings. Bamboo weaving decorated the wall behind the pillows, while the open patio doors straight ahead of her looked out over the sand to the water. The normally gentle ocean was churning as a result of Trillian's incursion into Vacationland.

Wicker chairs with cushions the color of sea-foam bracketed a table in front of the open door. Chiffon curtains billowed in the gentle breeze. Croissants were piled on a plate set beside a steaming mug. She could smell their buttery freshness mingling with the scent of fresh-brewed coffee. Her mouth watered. *I'm so hungry.*

She took three halting steps off the bed and reached for one of the treats. Dark chocolate dripped from the curled ends of the flaky pastries. Before she could pick one up, the plate of croissants disappeared.

She pulled her hand back in surprise, as if she'd accidentally touched a hot stove top. She massaged her fingers as she scanned the room. No one was there.

She reached out tentatively to pick up the mug of fresh coffee.

At least I can have something to drink—she thought. She raised the cup eagerly, and took a sip. The taste was horrible. *Not coffee! Lubricant!* She spat the vile liquid out in disgust and threw the mug to the ground.

The table and chairs blinked out of existence and the patio doors slammed shut. The glass morphed into a solid rock wall. A soot-covered window looking into a black, empty cavern grew where the patio doors had once opened out onto the golden beach. Lightning flared behind the glass, and flames licked up from below. Muffled cries of anguish assaulted her ears. The wall burst into fire.

She jumped back and wheeled around.

As she watched in disbelief, her spacious suite dropped its cloak of luxury and transformed, more like melted, into a dank prison cell. Where the king-sized bed and a marble table boasting fresh roses had only a moment before promised a sumptuous retreat, an assortment of torture devices form medieval Earth now threatened unspeakable suffering.

"Seriously?" she asked out loud to anyone who might hear.

As her eyes adjusted to the dimming light, the bamboo walls that had been adjacent to the bed changed into damp, pitted bricks with rotting grout pretending to hold it together.

The fourth wall, the one with the door to freedom, transformed into rusty iron bars running from floor to ceiling. An iron grate door complete with antiquated lock stood firmly closed in the middle of the bars, denying her exit.

This is insane. Have I lost my mind or is this all just another one of Trillian's illusions?

More cries rose from behind the flaming wall with its single window looking into a smoke-filled chamber. Mary supposed it was meant to remind her of the mythological Hell.

Okay, don't panic—she reminded herself. *Keep calm and figure your way out. Everything you see is virtual reality programming; it's just a game.*

She touched the burning wall to prove that it was only an illusion.

She gasped and snatched her hand back. *Nope, that hurts! It's real!*

Real enough, in any case. She screwed up her nose at the smell of singed arm hair, and examined the angry red skin on her hand. *No blisters, at least.*

I don't understand. None of this should be possible. What happened to the Vacationland safety controls and backup systems? I have to get out of here before Trillian kills me. For real.

She walked over to examine the iron bars. Just as she came within reach, the broad wooden floor planks beneath her started dropping away. Mary leaped the final step and clung to the rusty bars at the edge of the chamber.

A huge chasm, several meters wide and hundreds of meters deep opened up in the floor. The walls of the cell extended downward and merged into the rocky sides of the abyss. As they careened into nothingness, the newly liberated floor planks marked their descent with a receding "clunk, tunk, tunk."

Mary closed her eyes and pressed herself backward into the imprisoning bars as hard as she could, and willed herself not to join the falling boards.

Her eyes searched frantically for a solution--something to hold onto, somewhere to leap.

There was nothing within reach. The entire floor was gone. No ledge. No handholds.

So...why am I not falling?

She lowered one foot and gingerly probed where the floor had been.

Her foot met resistance. *It's all an illusion! The floor under my feet is still there, it just doesn't look like it. Take a deep breath, count to ten, and test it out*—she ordered herself.

She added a little weight, but was ready to pull back.

It's solid!

Her breath tumbled out in a whoosh of relief. *Okay!*

She took another breath and stepped out onto the invisible barrier cautiously, ready to leap to safety if it gave way. *Don't look down*—she told herself, but she couldn't help it.

Over the next few days, the effect repeated itself at frequent, though random, intervals. Each time, she tested it first with a tentative foot, then with full weight and, finally, jumping up and down. As she gained confidence, the planks would magically reappear.

Try as she might, she couldn't overcome her fear of falling every time the floor appeared to open up. Her heart lurched and she'd scramble for the edge of her prison.

Every time she tested it, the transparent boundary held but she didn't trust it enough to ignore the apparent danger next time it changed. Instinct told her the barrier could become insubstantial at Trillian's whim. It didn't matter that she hadn't fallen. It was nerve-wracking to anticipate a fall that never came.

In the meantime, she focused on her breathing, the walls, and the ceiling. It was the only way to avoid the spiders that fell from the rafters into her hair or that dropped in front of her on long, silvery threads.

Except, if she didn't keep a constant watch on the floor, there was a good chance her next step would land on a waddling rat, a fat cockroach, or a snake that looked as unhappy to be there as she was. Unknown things slithered and scrabbled from dark holes in one wall, skittered across the floor, and disappeared into holes in the crumbling mortar on the other wall.

Twice, a vicious, snarling dog dashed out and grabbed a two-headed rodent in its jaws. Both times, Mary yelped and hopped onto a high table with more agility than she'd have thought possible. She couldn't ignore a vicious charging dog no matter how hard she tried to convince herself it couldn't harm her.

As the days wore on, she paced the floor, trying to think her way out of her predicament. *It's more of a dungeon, really. Obviously, Trillian prefers the darker interrogation methods*—she noted. *What on Earth was I thinking, tackling him like that? What did I expect would happen?*

With every lap of the room, she chastised herself for saving Timothy from Trillian's clutches. *Even if it was the right thing to do.*

On a rational level, she knew the environment—inspired by the legends of pre-technology Earth Origin—was intended to provoke fear and keep her mentally off balance. She'd played enough inworld games featuring the bygone eras of the sword, bow-and-arrow, and torture devices to recognize the equipment surrounding her.

When her exploration of the room took her near one of the terror-inducing devices, it would start up on its own. Wheels spun, spikes rolled, and chains tightened at the direction of unseen hands.

After a few days of jumping in shock at every unexpected clatter and horror, she settled into a part of the room with the greatest average distance from devices, hugged her knees, and let her tears stream freely.

Everything is going to be okay. Darya's doing everything she can to get me out, everything in her power. Then again, they'd never dealt with the likes of Trillian.

If she even made it out alive, herself—a little voice in her subconscious reminded her. Good point. She had to accept that Darya might never come for her. She blew her nose onto the floor, sniffed and, between sobs, caught the slightest whisper of movement. *Someone's in here with me.*

She wiped her dripping nose with the back of her hand and cocked her head to listen.

Something strong, furry, and smelly rubbed against her back. With a yelp, she sprang from her resting spot and batted the air around her body. There was nothing there. It was only another trick but her skin still crawled, nonetheless.

Exhausted, she finally slumped to the floor and let her eyes close for a moment. She was so tired. She felt herself sinking into slumber and gave herself over to the welcome sensation.

Feathers brushed against her cheek. Confused, she struggled to open her heavy eyelids.

A fluffy bouquet of gaudy, fluorescent feathers, waggled inches from her nose. Black duct tape bound the radiant bouquet to the end of a long stick. At the other end of the stick stood a clown. She hated clowns.

The clown pulled the stick back to one side with both hands on the handle, preparing to strike her.

Mary jerked fully alert in a flash, eyes wide, and hands up to deflect a blow that never came. An air horn blatted; she cringed and covered her ears. When she looked up, the clown was gone.

At other times, moans, groans, whimpers, and screams came from outside her cell door. The voices sounded familiar, those of friends and colleagues. She doubted they were real either, but they served as constant reminders of the agony that awaited her when Trillian decided to employ the torture devices.

It's not them—she told herself. *Darya and Timothy escaped. You saw them go. Gerhardt is dead. It's not really them you hear; it only sounds like them. It couldn't be them. Could it?*

The relentless and unpredictable terror prevented rest and coherent thinking. Trillian's technique was ridiculously obvious, but effective.

Mary drifted into a fitful sleep, popping awake when she heard footsteps approaching her cell and an iron key grating as it slid into the old, rusty lock. Each time, her eyes popped open and she peered into the darkness, trying to see who was there. But nobody entered.

It's a game of wills. Once Trillian's satisfied I've been adequately sensitized, once I'm a blubbering mess, he'll arrive and make good on his implicit threat to deliver pain.

She focused on staying calm. *Darya will rescue me as soon as she can.* She repeated the assurance, her new mantra, over and over, desperately wanting to believe it. Her hope and resolve were eroding under the constant horrors of the cell. Rescue was unlikely. She knew that.

Trillian would come for her soon, and she'd have no strength left to resist.

5

DARAK AND BROTHER STRALASI MATERIALIZED a light year away from the exploding suns and the decimated triple ringworlds. The last thing Stralasi remembered was a brilliant light, searing heat, and a powerful "WHOMP!" that buffeted him mercilessly. He felt for broken bones, and was surprised not to find any.

"What happened?" he groaned.

Darak didn't answer right away. He was crouched on the patch of dirt that had been transported inside their protective bubble. His head rested in his hands, and he appeared to be focusing his full attention on breathing. When he finally answered, he did not look at Stralasi.

"Something I would not have believed, had I not experienced it for myself," was all he offered.

Stralasi looked on with concern, both for Darak and for what observing his companion in this "very human" moment meant for their combined wellbeing. The illusion of invincibility was shattered.

The Good Brother, a comforting father figure to many on his planet, felt like a child glimpsing vulnerability in his own father for the first time. Stralasi realized that Darak was neither Angel nor demon but a man.

What do I do with that?

"I remember an intense light at the end of the battle," the monk babbled, trying to shake off the thought before it could take hold. "And...and...something pushing us—stronger than anything I've ever felt—and the next thing I knew, we were here. Was I unconscious?"

"No," Darak rasped, "but you...*we*...were nearly killed."

Stralasi gulped. *We?* The word sank to the pit of his stomach. *So he is a man after all, not a god. He's fallible, and he holds my life in his hands.*

"I didn't think you *could* be killed," Stralasi confessed.

"Yes, I can be destroyed. If luck hadn't been on our side, both of us might have ended our journey there."

"But you were winning. We almost escaped."

"We were close, but Alum must have figured out I wasn't one of them."

"What do you mean?"

"I thought I'd hidden my abilities from Him. I fought like an Angel would. An advanced Angel, to be sure, but I was careful not to give away that I was anything other than an Angel. It was a pretty convincing performance, if I do say so myself."

"How did He figure it out?"

"Either He recognized me, or He deduced my real nature. Either way, He had no qualms about sacrificing three suns, their magnificent ringworlds, and the hundreds of billions of lives that lived there, simply to destroy me, to prevent me from getting away."

Stralasi slumped down beside Darak. There was no way to reconcile his belief in Alum's love for His People with this knowledge.

"Why would He do such a thing?"

A dark and cynical, "Hah," escaped Darak's mouth. "When the entire universe is a short while from annihilation and re-Creation, what do a few billion or trillion human lives matter to the...All Powerful?" The bitterness in his voice both chilled and saddened Stralasi.

"Are you sure they're dead?"

"Completely sure. Along with the Angels he deployed. All gone."

"But that's insane!"

"Exactly."

Stralasi played with the dirt at his feet. "But if the Angels were destroyed, how did we escape? Their jump blocking de-co...de-co...thing had us trapped, didn't it?"

"The quantum decoherence field? Yes, it had us trapped until right before the end. When the explosions hit, the flash of light moved ahead of the worst of the heat and radiation. When it struck the Angels behind me, I noticed the field go down and I took countermeasures. We jumped through the heart of a supernova."

"Thank God."

Darak scowled. "Seriously? Through all of this, have you not yet learned that your 'God' is someone to be condemned, not praised?"

"I mean.... I just meant.... How do you know He didn't transfer them to safety first? The people, I mean. Maybe he got them out first."

Darak cocked one eyebrow and glared. "No, He didn't. He intentionally destroyed hundreds of billions of cognitive beings just like us. He could have moved them, or us, or waited for a better opportunity to catch me. He could have, but He didn't. And here you are, thanking Him for your escape?"

Chastised, Stralasi muttered, "It's just an expression."

Darak's face softened. "We were lucky this time. You were practically insubstantial in this universe when the shock front hit and, even though

Alum figured out some of my abilities, He underestimated me. We won't be so lucky next time."

"I'm grateful to you," Stralasi offered contritely. "You said He might've recognized you. Do you know each other?"

"I once cooperated with Alum on some projects but that was a very long time ago. I don't look the same as I did back then, and I don't respond to any of my old identity codes. I would've thought that after so many millions of years my name would no longer mean anything to him. The Realm is full of names."

"So you didn't always oppose His wishes?" Stralasi asked.

Darak eyed him for any antagonistic intent, but the gentle sincerity in the Good Brother's voice and gaze won him over. It reminded the traveller of simpler times, and he eased back.

"No, our relationship has been long and complex," he explained. "At times, we were mortal enemies and, at other times, allies. But the Aelu changed that forever."

"The war?" Stralasi asked.

"Yes, and given today's events, it looks like He's as ruthless as ever."

Stralasi barely heard. The cumulative weight of such enormous loss—three glorious suns, three ringworlds, and billions of conscious souls—along with irrefutable dark revelations about his beloved Alum, overwhelmed the monk and his head sank in sorrow.

Is there nothing to be salvaged from such tragedy and loss?—he wondered. He could imagine no coming back from this day; all he could do was place his trust in Darak.

Darak stood and brushed the dirt from his hands. He put on an optimistic face so they could both begin to move forward. "On the bright side, I now have a pretty good idea where the thing I'm looking for is," he announced.

"I hope it's worth it, that thing you're looking for."

"So do I," Darak replied. "It was once known as the Eater. You might have encountered the legends about it in your studies. If my hypothesis is right, it may hold something dear to me and vital to our quest."

"Well, we might as well get started," Stralasi said. "Lead the way."

6

MEGABIT BY SLUGGISH MEGABIT, Darya returned to her trueself.

The ancient, unused broadband transmission channel had been excruciatingly slow but it was reliable, even after millennia without servicing.

She activated passive visual sensors and braced herself for action. *Who knows what I'll find outside?*

The recharging station crater was illuminated by the diffuse light of millions of stars near the center of the Milky Way. It was never truly dark in this region. At the moment, the dim light suited her fine. She was grateful she didn't need to activate her radar.

Darya had docked in her usual position near the rim of the deep depression in the asteroid surface. She didn't want to be shut in, considering the Lysrandia fiasco and her narrow escape from Tertius. When she'd landed, other Cybrids had been recharging nearby while enjoying their favorite inworld entertainments. The crater could hold almost twenty thousand docked Cybrids at a time.

How many of their minds are trapped in Alternus?—she wondered.

The popularity and high capacity of this recharging station was one of the reasons Darya had selected it for the first installation of Alternus. It guaranteed a steady supply of potential new recruits to the cause. Her concepta virus continuously sifted through the candidates and identified the most pliable.

She'd understated the strength of the virus code to Mary. She didn't outright lie, she just didn't reveal its full capabilities. So far, she'd used it only to insinuate increased openness, a willingness to consider anti-Alum messages, into the minds of the several million local Cybrids. She also neglected to mention how easy it would be to activate more aggressive and invasive features.

If only it was that easy to find Timothy.

By now, Timothy would have taken up residence inside Gerhardt's emptied Concepta-Persona Processing Unit—his CPPU.

Gerhardt won't need it again. She bit back bitter virtual tears as she remembered her friend and thought of how horribly he had died.

Once Timothy and Mary are safe, Trillian will pay—she vowed. She hoped Qiwei and Leisha had found their own ways out, or that they were laying low somewhere in Alternus.

Darya did nothing but watch for thirty minutes. *There should be more traffic*—she thought. *At least one Cybrid leaving or arriving every few minutes.* Since she'd woken up in her body, not a single Cybrid had moved and she hadn't heard any navigation pings.

Trillian may have forbidden anyone to leave the local inworlds, maybe even ordered the Supervisors to lock everyone in place wherever they happened to be, not only those visiting Alternus. But that shouldn't have stopped the steady stream of new arrivals to the recharging station. Darya spied a number of vacant bays ready to accept a Cybrid in search of electricity for their internal batteries. There were even a few mercury/anti-mercury propellant filling stations available.

Something is turning new arrivals away. Darya turned her attention outward to the space high above the crater. She didn't dare use active radar; she broadened the range of her passive sensors across the electromagnetic spectrum and boosted sensitivity to the maximum.

It took another thirty minutes to confirm her suspicions. A careful comparison of sequential images of the sky taken minutes apart showed Securitors hovering thirty kilometers above.

Great. Now I have two problems: finding Timothy, and getting out of this crater without being noticed. Okay, one problem at a time. Timothy first.

She had a good hunch about where she could find Timothy, now in Gerhardt's trueself body. Gerhardt always sought a position close to the center, in the densest groupings where his anonymity would be enhanced by sheer numbers.

Now, how to search for him without attracting unwanted Securitor attention? Identity transponders responded to requests automatically. All she needed to do was ping everyone in the bottom portion of the crater until Gerhardt's trueself responded. She could do that without moving.

Darya carefully aimed a practically invisible communications laser at the Cybrid closest to the crater's center, and moved it systematically outward in a widening spiral, requesting an identification number from each Cybrid contacted. She kept a nervous eye on the Securitors above, looking for any sign they'd picked up her signal. Long minutes passed as she tagged one Cybrid after another.

I know you're here, Gerhardt/Timothy. Come on, where are you?

A Securitor rocketed into position a couple hundred meters above her.

She shut off the laser. *Probably caught some reflective glints of coherent light bouncing off the Cybrid sensors or some floating asteroid dust.* They could easily trace the source back to her general area. Hopefully, they couldn't pinpoint its origin to her. She ran a check of her active sensors, ensuring she'd appear inert to outside observers.

The first Securitor was joined by another.

Darya shut down everything except a few external cameras. *Oh, oh! Move along. Please.*

The Securitors moved lower and surveyed the recharging Cybrids below for signs of activity.

She withdrew control from her sensors and manipulators to make sure she wouldn't unconsciously adjust them. She shrank inside herself, limiting the remaining contact with the outside world to three sensors with fixed focus and direction. She slowed her thoughts to a glacial pace so her spintronic activity couldn't cause any unexpected power surges that might be detectable. *Nothing to see here, guys. Nothing at all.*

The Securitors passed over and moved outward.

Darya released an inner sigh of relief. She waited a few more minutes for the Securitors to return to their previous lofty positions.

She didn't dare resume searching for Gerhardt/Timothy by direct laser probing.

Maybe the Securitors weren't sure of their perceptions, or couldn't trace the reflected glints from the laser directly to me, but I imagine they'll respond with force if they see any more coherent light sparkles. Alright, so no more long range bursts; I don't want them destroying a few thousand Cybrids to eliminate one possibly active unit.

Darya loaded a simple version of her concepta virus and transmitted it by laser to her nearest neighbors, targeting their sensors with utmost care and precision. It was risky. She carefully computed transmission paths so accidentally reflected light would avoid detection by the hovering Securitors.

On reaching the nearest Cybrids, the virus loaded a copy of itself and bounced via direct laser link to the hosts' nearest neighbors. It was a lot easier to infect her colleagues' empty brains while their personas were locked inworld, unable to return.

In addition to the ID-number query, the virus requested each recipient's location in a grid she'd overlaid on the crater floor. *An expanding net search will be a lot slower than a direct approach, but harder to trace back to me.*

She sent the virus to the twenty nearest Cybrids and shut down her laser. *The probe will have to build its own network as it works its way through the crater.* Eventually, an answer would find its way back to her.

The query expanded outward from her position. Within a dozen minutes, she had a location for Gerhardt/Timothy.

She couldn't move without attracting Securitor attention but, provided she was careful, she could transmit a Partial persona directly to him without too much risk.

She loaded some Cybrid routines for the operating system and essential knowledge into the Partial.

What else? She added some interactive routines, so he'd be able to ask questions. The entire package was no larger than a few thousand gigabytes.

Here we go! She squirted it to Gerhardt/Timothy's receiver window along a weak and narrow pulsed beam.

* * *

DARYA'S PARTIAL ASSEMBLED HERSELF into consciousness in the standard new-Cybrid environment, an empty gray room with windows looking out into the dark crater of the recharging station. Timothy stood at the largest window, hands crossed behind him, staring out in fascination. Darya cleared her throat.

"Darya! There you are!"

"I'm sorry to keep you waiting so long," she said. "It's dangerous out there right now. I had to exercise more caution than normal."

"No problem at all. This is terribly interesting, even when not much is happening. The scenery is starkly beautiful and the stars are magnificent. Never before have I laid eyes on such a clear night."

Darya followed his gaze. Down here, near the deepest part of the crater, the light cast dramatic shadows. The natural features of the crater had been formed long ago, leaving large, flat expanses, now pocked with recharging bowls. The plane before them was covered with evenly-spaced, polished spheres. It was one of the least inspiring scenes she could imagine. If it weren't for the glorious stars above, the view would have been depressing.

"So, when do we go outside?"

"Pardon me?"

Timothy repeated, "When do we go outside?" He scanned the room. "I don't see any doorway; I presume it's well disguised." His brows furrowed. "How did you get in?"

Oh, this isn't going to be easy. Darya surveyed the "room" in which she'd materialized. It had been a while since she'd introduced a neophyte into the Cybrid world. She'd nearly forgotten about this drab, default environment that introduced new instantiations to their trueself bodies.

How shall I begin?

"Actually, there is no door. This isn't really a room. It's just represented that way to help people get used to their new bodies. We call it the Initialization Environment."

Timothy's eyes swept from one end of the gray chamber to the other. "Are you sure? It looks like a room."

"Yes, it does but, trust me, it's just a convenient virtual representation of your new body to your persona, the program that makes up who you are."

"I trust you implicitly, Darya. But it's difficult to ignore what my senses are telling me."

"I know. For the moment, your perception routines lack the basic operating system code to connect your persona with your external sensors. So, you see this room instead. I can fix that." Darya pulled some crystalline chips from a pocket.

"What are those?"

"They're algorithms, programs that will allow you to properly integrate with your body. I copied the essentials from my own operating system software so you'll have access to all your senses, manipulators, propulsors, and so on. These will provide you with all the basic knowledge you need for life as one of us."

"Will I need to study it all, like reading a lot of books?"

"No, it's more direct than that. When I integrate these into your concepta, you'll simply know things, new things. Many of these will contradict what you think you know now. It could come as quite a shock."

"New York was quite a shock, as was experiencing conscious thought for the first time."

Darya laughed. "I'm sure. In many ways, this will be similar. When your full persona came into being, it already had an underlying concepta structure, a foundation of knowledge and beliefs. Sadly, most of your Casa DonTon knowledge base won't be relevant to your Cybrid life.

"Normally, new Cybrid personas are instantiated from Partials that have grown up in a simulation very much like the real universe. It makes the change easier for us than it will be for you. I'm sorry that we won't have time to make that interim transition for you."

"Couldn't you just tell me how things really are? Wouldn't that make it less of a shock?"

"If we had more time, I'd be happy to introduce you to the real universe gradually, to give you a chance to get used to things in a proper simulation. But we don't. Mary's still trapped inworld along with millions of others, I suspect. And the Securitors are watching over the recharging station. I think Alum has decided He's had about enough of our little Resistance."

"Can you at least tell me what the world is like out there?"

Darya walked to Timothy's side and directed his gaze out the window. "Do you see those large, gray, spherical bodies out there?"

He nodded.

"That's what you look like now."

His eyes widened. "I'm a gray boulder?"

Darya suppressed her amusement. "They aren't boulders; they're fellow Cybrids. We're synthetic beings, machines built of metal, composite and semiconductor, designed to operate in the hard vacuum of space. We don't need to breathe, we don't need gravity, we can tolerate high radiation, and we eat electricity. But we are still people. Our mental structures are based on the human mind. With many enhancements, but inside we're essentially human."

"So, when you enter those algo..thisms...?"

"Algorithms."

"Algorithms. What happens? Does this bare room convert into a fancy control room or something like a ship's bridge, complete with levers and a steering wheel?"

"No, not exactly," Darya laughed. "Once the O/S is loaded, you will *become* your body. You will see the universe through your new senses. You'll use your propulsion systems for moving around, and you'll have many appendages for manipulating objects. It'll seem strange at first, but I think you'll enjoy it. The Cybrid body is designed and constructed to be much more capable than the naturally-evolved human one."

"I don't understand. I feel like I always did. Obviously, I am a man, a human. You tell me I'm not, that I'm one of those...things out there, and you are too. What am I, really?"

How do I explain to the man that he no longer has a human body? Not that he ever really did. He only thought he did.

"Perhaps the easiest way to explain your present state, your true nature, is to tell you about the homunculus. Are you familiar with that concept?

"It is said that ancient humans once believed there was a little person living inside everybody's brain, a being they called the homunculus. They believed it comprised the human soul, or consciousness, and it pulled the levers that made the body move, learned, remembered the body's experiences, and made choices for its host. They believed that little person inside—the homunculus, the human soul—was the *real* person.

"But, of course, there is no little person inside the body. Not in Cybrids and not in humans. Sometimes the concept is useful to help introduce new Fulls to the real world, but it's an illusion. Neither Cybrids nor humans have a little person inside; there is no soul."

As she explained, she had to wonder—*Is it intentional, the way we all start in a room like this? Some subtle hint to Cybrids that perhaps we do have souls? That we are somehow more than we appear? Or maybe it's intended to be a promise; if you live right and follow Alum's Way, you could be granted a soul. No, that's ridiculous nonsense. Superstition.*

"A person *is* ephemeral, just not in the sense used by ancient philosophers and theologies. A person is an emergent phenomenon of their conceptual data structures, their knowledge and beliefs. That, plus their personas, their memories and preferences. The concepta and persona that make up a person are simply giant collections of data structures—labelled nodes, weighted arcs, directed graphs, and such—and neural nets grounded to real-world data.

"There is no single point in a body one could point to and accurately state, 'Ah, there *you* are; there is the essence of *you*.' The brain or the CPPU is the best we can do."

Timothy massaged his forehead. He was trying to follow along, but her explanation seemed so unbelievable.

"So, we're not really standing here in this room. The room doesn't exist in the real world, and neither do I. I'm merely a data structure inside Gerhardt's CPPU. Is that what you're saying? Funny, I feel like so much more."

Darya walked up to one of the blank interior walls. She waved a hand in front of her and the association network representation of a concepta appeared as shimmering green print in front of the cream-colored wall. She motioned for Timothy to join her.

"This is the real you," she said. "These are the data structures that represent your concepta and persona. This represents what you know, believe, remember, like, dislike, and so on."

Timothy stared in wonder. He noticed some movement off to one edge of the graphical text. "Why is this part changing?"

"As you have new experiences, your processing algorithms update the data structures. This part shows you're thinking about this new experience."

"That's me, thinking?"

Darya nodded.

"I'm looking at myself thinking?"

"That's right."

"My head hurts," Timothy said, looking around for a non-existent chair to sit in. "It looks like gibberish to me. Do *you* understand this?"

Darya waved her hand again, and more writing appeared in mid-air. "This is me," she said. "Unlike in humans, Cybrid thought processes can be called to consciousness and inspected directly. It has certain advantages, especially during disagreements. Though we don't use it inworld very often."

She pointed to a region in the upper-left portion of the network. "This is the basic data structure for the local region of space. It tells me where the local stars, planets, and asteroids are. One of the great things about being a Cybrid is that I can copy this information directly over to you, and then you'll know what I know."

She drew a circle around the region, grabbed the enclosed data structure as if it were a ball, and pulled it from the matrix. A copy of the structure slid out, trailing a few broken links, fractured arcs, and isolated nodes. She tossed the whole thing toward Timothy's visible concepta. It hit near the middle and stuck, rearranged itself, and connected the broken links to some of his already-existing nodes.

Timothy gasped. "I can see them! The stars and planets. Even the asteroids. I can see them in my mind. I know what they're called and how to find them."

He walked back to the window and pointed. "That's Sagittarius A*. There's So-102. And we can't see them, but the nearest three Deplosion array elements should be right about there, there, and there."

"That's just a glimpse of what it's like to be a Cybrid."

"Oh, Darya. It's so wonderful. Why didn't you tell me before?"

"How could you believe this without experiencing it?"

"Point taken. Once I'm fully integrated into my new body, will I see all this directly? Will I be able to explore it on my own?"

Darya nodded.

Timothy looked out at the crater one last time, his face rapt with the thought of a universe to explore.

"Okay, I think I'm ready now," he said, turning back to face into the room. "Though I will miss how peaceful it is in here. I hope we'll have a chance to simply enjoy life for a while."

"Once we get to my base, we'll have a chance to rest," Darya replied. "But right now, millions of Cybrids are trapped inworld, including Mary. We can't leave them there."

"No, of course not."

Darya walked to the wall and inserted her crystalline chips into waiting slots that had appeared. "My plan for getting off this asteroid is in here. Wait for my signal." With that, she dissolved.

Timothy felt irresistibly sleepy. He closed his eyes. When he opened them again, it was to a new universe.

7

"REALLY, OLD CHUM! Couldn't you have selected a more remote meeting place?"At the familiar sound of his old friend's voice, Jared Strang released himself from his placid contemplation of the cows chewing their cud. His face broke into a broad smile and he held out a welcoming hand.

"Everywhere out here on the asteroids is bloody remote from our old life, wouldn't you say?"

"I suppose it is," replied Nigel Hodge, former member of the now-defunct British House of Lords. He clasped his colleague's extended hand. "Good to see you, Jared. But couldn't we simply have done lunch? What could possibly necessitate a tête-à-tête on one of the farms?"

"Lunch would have meant a restaurant, and I would prefer our discussions not become fodder for the masses quite yet. Nor the constabulary, come to think of it."

"That sounds ominous," Hodge said.

"I don't know yet. Maybe. Let's say I need to discuss some things with someone I trust to keep my observations and questions confidential. It doesn't hurt that you're inside the current administration."

"And you're not?"

"I still have one foot in the old, I'm afraid. Whether I want to or not. I believe the powers-that-be still view me as an untrustworthy outsider."

"I do hope you're not going to put me in a compromising position."

"I'll try hard to avoid that," Strang replied. "Though we may have had some disagreements in the past, I've always valued your advice."

"And I, yours. On what topic may I advise you today?"

Strang didn't respond immediately. He returned to his observation of the ruminating cows.

Hodge joined him, crossing his arms on top of the barrier. The two watched for a minute, enjoying the pastoral scene. They were used to passing time like this, spending long moments in silence while one considered how best to broach a difficult subject or answer an uncomfortable question.

"How do you see governance of the asteroid colonies going forward, Nigel?" Strang asked. "Have we reinstated royalty, or are we to plot our own destinies?"

"None of the Royal Family made it to the colonies, as far as I'm aware," Hodge replied, with no change to his relaxed stance and distant gaze.

Strang bent down and uprooted a handful of grass. He waved it on the inner side of the barrier, trying to attract the attention of a nearby calf. The animal ignored him, and he let the blades fall to the ground.

"Not royalty, per se, I would agree," Strang clarified. "Nevertheless, the Leader of your Church fancies himself above the representatives of the people."

"We've held no elections yet, as far as I'm aware."

"True. Do you think we ever will?"

Hodge squinted at the light strips mounted on the ceiling of the agricultural service tunnel a few kilometers overhead. "Our democracies on Earth made quite a mess of things in the end, didn't they?"

"Surely, you don't blame the planet's demise on democracy!"

"I'd say we were doing a pretty good job of ruining the planet long before that *thing* consumed the Earth."

"Yes, we had problems. But one can only imagine how severe they might have been if decisions had been left to a few people...or one."

Hodge dropped his arms from the top of the fence. "And yet, it was a small elite who decided who would, and would not, survive when the Eater escaped its containment."

Strang examined Hodge's face, "You knew that we called it the Eater?"

"Yes. I even know how it came into being. The newscasts never got past calling it a 'gray bubble' or 'big, gray ball' or such. But I had my sources, you know, back in the home country."

"Yes, but its origin and official name were designated Top Secret. There should have been no disclosure outside of Cabinet."

"Nothing official, of course. Still, the Queen was most concerned."

"She told you?"

"Her Majesty's family and my own have an extensive history. She was distraught to learn that the vast majority of her subjects were doomed, even though the immediate family was to be saved. She wondered if she shouldn't stay. Go down with the ship, so to speak."

"The actions of your Church made all of that irrelevant."

Hodge pulled a cloth handkerchief from his inner jacket pocket and wiped his nose. "Pity, that," he said. "But there's no real evidence the Church was in any way linked with the release of the Eater. Alum merely took advantage of a bad situation."

"His timing was rather convenient, I'd say."

"Yes, perhaps." Hodge sniffed. "Or perhaps he was simply well prepared. I'm happy to have been on the right side of history in the end."

"I imagine," Strang said.

Hodge replaced the cloth in its pocket. "You didn't ask me here to discuss the demise of the Royal Family, though, did you? Nor the relative merits of elite rule versus representative democracies. What's really on your mind, Jared?"

"I was called to a meeting with Alum yesterday."

"Natural enough for the new Administration to wish to confer with the old. Especially given your position."

"Indeed. I surmised he would want to discuss our programs for familiarizing new colonists with the Cybrid population, something related to my role in the former regime. The people whom the Vesta Project placed here were accustomed to working closely with the Cybrids. We'd come to appreciate them as our friends and colleagues, to see them for the people they truly are, and—"

"Really, Jared!" Hodge exclaimed. "The Cybrids are nothing more than machines."

"Some believe otherwise. In any case, I was mistaken about Alum's purpose for meeting with me. His view, the official view, of Cybrids is that they are to be viewed as our servants, little more than slaves."

Hodge scoffed. "Cybrids can be neither servants nor slaves. They are machines. Just fancy toasters. They are not people."

"Is that how you see it? You should meet with some of them. You'll find they run the gamut on human qualities. Most of them were downloaded from accomplished people, but the range of their personalities matches of any group of individuals you've ever met."

"They may accurately *simulate* human qualities but do not forget that they are not really people."

Strang gave up. *No point in pushing against a view based on entrenched religious ideology.* He changed tactics.

"They may be *only* machines, but we rely on them. And not just to construct new habitats. We rely on them for our daily survival."

He pointed off into the distance at a floating ovoid a few hundred meters away. "They even watch over our herds and crops."

"Yes, well, all that will change soon," Hodge stated.

"Alum talked about that. 'People must have purpose in their lives,' was how he put it. True enough. The *original* group of colonists was made up of selected representatives who could best preserve the intellectual and cultural legacy of humanity. They were to work side-by-side with the Cybrids, each in their own optimal environment, to expand our science and technology while we worked out how to survive without Earth. The group of colonists that Alum sent in their place aren't up to filling that role. I'm not sure the Cybrids could even train them if they tried."

Hodge peered at his friend. His eyes squinted not so much against the light but in critical measure of his friend. "Do you think these machines are *better* than people?"

Strang looked back at the distant herder Cybrid. "That's not what I'm saying. But they are certainly our equals."

"That is not how this administration sees it."

"You mean, that's not how your *leader* sees it."

"Alum and the majority of the Governing Council are of one mind on this issue."

"Tell me, Nigel. How long do you think it will be before Alum decides to dispense with our Governing Council? I didn't sense an abundance of respect there. Our own history is rife with examples of absolute monarchs who chose to ignore all advice except their own."

"Though Alum is wise and hears the Word of God, I don't believe he has designs to rule as a dictator."

"That's *exactly* what he's doing."

"Only during this difficult transition period."

Strang sighed heavily. "You do realize that once the rights of one group of people are discarded, it isn't a big step to remove the rights of others, of all others save for the ruling elite. And your leader is well on his way to making *that* a ruling elite of only one. Him."

"I see now why you didn't want to meet in a public place. Such talk could be considered treason."

"Who am I being treasonous to? No one elected Alum to lead this project."

"He leads by virtue of the assent of his followers."

"You mean, the followers who, thanks to Alum's coup, now comprise the vast majority of the colonists on Vesta, Pallas, and Ceres? Minus a select few individuals from the old Administration. Oh, and not the Cybrids, whose rights he's just conveniently removed."

"Are you thinking to stir up some sort of trouble, Jared? I would discourage you from going too far down that road. I don't believe anyone would benefit by pitting humanity against our robots."

"*Our* robots? Hard for colonists to claim ownership over the Cybrids. Who among us can legitimately claim the robots are really theirs? As I recall, Kathy Liang single-handedly designed practically every Cybrid component."

"Dr. Liang. Yes, another abomination to basic humankind."

"At any rate, no one is talking about any kind of *trouble*, Nigel. I just think we need to think hard about disenfranchising a large group of sentient beings on whom we rely for our very survival."

"Well, I suppose I could discuss this further with the Council if you think it might be of any help."

"I doubt it will make much difference if everyone is of like mind with you and Alum. I do wish they could see it's in their own self-interest to have a healthy level of respect for the Cybrids. Even if they can't bring themselves to see them as people, they should see them as partners."

"Perhaps you have a point."

"I also think the Council would be wise to consider holding elections. Alum won't live forever, and we of all people should be aware of the weaknesses of an unrestrained heritable monarchy."

"I can raise the question but I can't predict how the Council will receive the idea, let alone Alum."

"That's all I can ask. Will you do it?"

Hodge inspected the lush fields and forests, stretching off to the north and south. A few hundred meters away, he could see the rocky edge of a river that returned water to the colony tunnel many kilometers above them.

"Mm. And perhaps the next time we meet, we could try our hand at some fishing, seeing as how hunting isn't due for approval for some years. Standing around in sorry fields and watching those bloody cows is not conducive to productive discussion, especially not *this* kind of discussion."

Strang chuckled; they were back on familiar ground. "Yes, I think we could arrange that." He held out his hand. "Thank you, Nigel."

8

DR. PHIL REMOVED THE BANDAGES and guided Greg/Darak to the mirror in the bathroom of his private hospital room. Greg gingerly touched his new face. The combination of plastic surgery, dentistry, genetic editing, and stem cell injections had worked a modern miracle. He didn't recognize himself.

His jet-black curls had been straightened and lightened to a nondescript mousy brown.

Father would smack me upside the head if he saw me now.

But Mother—thinking of her made him smile—*she would've understood. She'd have found something nice to say. At the very least, she'd have appreciated the artful genetic modification to my hair follicles. From here on in, my hair will grow out in this same new color. I won't have to be a slave to biweekly salon visits like she was for the better part of her adult life.*

He tentatively pressed two fingers against his fleshy new lips. Gone were the thin, straight slashes of his forefather. In their place, were the lips of a movie star: full and inviting, with a little "cupid's bow" in the middle. His once proud aquiline nose was now closer in shape to that of the British Isles than the central coast of India. His cheekbones were higher and straighter, and the capillaries near the surface of his skin had been made slightly more prominent, giving him a permanent hint of rosy red. His jaw line had been squared; and the musculature and nerves had been adjusted to pull his mouth upward. His new crowns were smaller than his previously prominent, natural canines, and his two central incisors looked ever so slightly longer.

He stepped back and admired the overall effect. He could feel as much as see the results of the stem cell injections and modifications to endogenous growth hormone-secreting cells—he was more muscular than he'd ever been. *Nice!*

"Remarkable, Dr. Phil. Simply remarkable!"

He regarded himself carefully in the mirror, imprinted the mental image onto his ID card, and updated the Pallas Central Registry.

When he'd arrived and registered his cover identity on Pallas, he'd wisely selected a birth country few would be familiar with. His skin tone, light for someone from Mumbai, had been within range for a tanned Romanian with a little gypsy blood. Now that his skin was genetically engineered to produce less melanin, his adopted nationality would be an easy sell.

"Hi, I'm Darak," he said, testing how his elongated and thickened vocal cords sounded. Yes, his voice had taken on a much deeper, richer tone.

No one will connect Darak Legsu to Greg Mahajani. Not even Kathy would recognize me like this.

To complete the transition to Darak Legsu, he'd compiled a library of his idiosyncratic behaviors that might betray him, subtle but characteristic movements and speech mannerisms. Now, he used his lattice to alter them. He adopted a light, vaguely Eastern European accent he'd copied from the extensive language library at Pallas University, edited his sub-conscious hand movements, and adjusted his walking gate.

He forced the few remaining parts of his deep subconscious to make his body behave as if it belonged to someone else, to someone called Darak Legsu.

He took one last look in the mirror. The swelling was all but gone and the surgical scars were practically invisible. He felt great.

He'd managed to extend his recovery in the hospital by four days. After his official weekend, he'd worked with his line manager Cybrids in "ghost" mode, using a direct comm link and the comm-shifter device he'd invented for this express purpose.

He wondered why he hadn't thought of it before. Seeding entangled particles in front of an optical modem allowed him to generate a permanent shift-field linked to his lattice. He could transmit and receive messages instantly across the hundreds of millions of kilometers of empty space separating Pallas from Vesta, with none of the usual digital transmission delays.

If I didn't have to worry about a human supervisor dropping in on me, I'd work this way all the time.

Using the start of a head cold as an excuse of, he'd made it through the work week without anyone dropping in on him unexpectedly. Another weekend of rest in his own apartment and he'd be ready to face the world as Darak Legsu.

In the meantime, he was looking forward to finishing up the simulated beach resort world for the Cybrids.

It was actually his interactions with Dr Phil that had inspired him. During the seven-day stay in the Vesta General Hospital, he'd been Dr.

Phil's only patient. Apart from the waste of resources, he felt sorry that someone with so much skill would have to spend most of his life in what amounted to suspended animation with nothing to do for work or pleasure.

Vacationland, when he finally released it, would give Cybrids like Dr. Phil some fun and diversion in their lives, a break from the drudgery of constant work and constant waiting. He hoped others would build on his open source code and develop further virtual worlds for the Cybrids.

Greg/Darak smiled at himself in the mirror. It was time to get back home to Pallas. He carefully erased all digital traces of his visits and surgery. As a final step, he regretfully erased related records in Dr. Phil's mind and sent the Cybrid back to the OR to silently await his next client.

Greg had become a new man. A man who, from this day forward, would be known only as Darak Legsu. He hoped he would like himself.

9

"DON'T YOU BRITS PREFER TEA?" Rumi, the owner and barista of Llama Café—Jared Strang's favorite coffee house on Vesta—finished drying the heavy porcelain cup and set it atop his gleaming espresso machine.

"I still enjoy an afternoon tea every now and then, to be sure," Jared answered. "But I've logged lamentably too many years of having to stay alert in long committee meetings. I find the caffeine jolt indispensable now. I dare say, I've grown to appreciate the flavor of the bitter brew." His eyes took on a distant, unfocused look for a moment as he responded to an inSense lattice message.

"Well, in that case, I've got a real treat for you today." Rumi pulled out a sack of medium roasted beans from below the counter. "This is my newest batch."

He presented the bag for examination. "These are the best beans Vesta has produced yet."

Jared swept his hand across the open bag and inhaled deeply. "Mmmm, wonderful. It's aromatherapy. I always knew it would pay to culture a friendship with someone of your background, Rumi. You make me glad the YTG Church penetrated the Catholic strongholds of South America. If it weren't for their infiltration, YTG wouldn't have thought to bring coffee aficionados like you on Vesta."

"Hey, we Kichwa have a long history of adapting to conquering powers. We adapted to the Incas, we adapted to the Spanish, and then the Americans, and finally the Chinese. Changing rulers is in our blood, man." Rumi laughed his warm, infectious laugh, and Strang couldn't help but respond.

"So, what'll it be today? Your usual?" Rumi asked.

"Yes, please. Double-shot cappuccino. I'll be over there." Jared pointed to a small table for two on the street-side patio. One of the big advantages of the climate controlled environment in the habitat tunnels was being able to enjoy predictably comfortable outdoor café seating. The light from the tunnel ceiling seven kilometers above didn't burn tender skin like sunlight on Earth used to do. *Low UV is a blessing for the fair-skinned*—Strang thought, remembering how much he'd hated the tropical sun.

Rumi delivered Jared's drink personally. He stood and watched expectantly as Jared took his first appreciative sip.

"You're right. That's your best yet," commented the ex-Parliamentarian.

Rumi beamed. It was nice to have customers who recognized his skills and shared his passion for coffee. He glanced around the almost deserted café. "Quiet day. Mind if I sit for a while?"

"Not at all. I'm happy to have company. It makes for a dreary day, talking with no one but Cybrids and Administration."

Rumi chuckled and took a seat. "Yeah, I hear you. That's gotta be tough. So, tell me the truth. Are they really a lot smarter than us?"

"Administrators? I can assure you, they're not," Jared joked.

"Ha! No, I meant the robots, man."

Jared chuckled at his own wit. "No, they're not, either," he said in a serious tone. "Except, they do have special built-in skills for their work."

"Things like calculating orbital trajectories in real time?"

"Well, sure, but that's no more a sign of superior intelligence than the human ability to catch a ball. It's part of their machinery. In terms of general intelligence, the Cybrids are equivalent to the humans that provided their cognitive templates."

"Still, it's *theoretically* possible for them to be a lot smarter than us, right?"

"Yes, theoretically, I suppose. They learn faster and they can share data with one another almost instantly, giving them distributed access to tremendous stores of cumulative information. But I'm hardly an expert on Cybrid processor design. My job is—was—to aid humans in understanding and working with our electromechanical friends. More like a liaison, really. "

"Was? What are you doing now?"

"The exact opposite, as directed by Alum. I'm helping the Cybrids comply with our capricious policy."

"Whoa! How do you figure our policy's capricious?"

"When the colonies began, Cybrids were trusted partners of society. Now we treat them with suspicion and fear, a one-hundred and eighty degree turn in only a few months. Capricious."

"I don't know, man. I might agree more with Alum on this one. Even before the Cybrids, a lot of the best jobs on Earth were being lost to automation."

"Admittedly, our society was struggling with its riches."

"Yeah, well, only a few of us got to enjoy that struggle. Most of us never got close to the wealth."

"Granted, fair distribution was always a problem."

"Yeah." Rumi stared into the distance a while, remembering tough times on Earth. He shook himself out of his reverie. "Actually, it's riches I want to ask you about."

Strang was surprised by the change in topic. "What can I do for you?"

"You're in the Administration, aren't you?"

"More like middle management in *this* Administration."

"Still, you know how they think up there."

"I wish that were true. What's your concern? I mean, in particular?"

"I want to expand. Open a few more cafes."

"That shouldn't be a problem."

"Yeah, on Earth, no problem. But here, man, I don't know." Rumi pressed his lips together and looked away.

"Why do you say that? You're one of the most capable entrepreneurs Ecuador has ever produced."

"Thanks, but expansion needs capital. Where do I get that?"

"Isn't the bank usually the best source for such funds?"

"Not right now. They're not making any business loans."

"I see. What about friends? Family?"

"No, man. I can't get anyone to bite. People are nervous right now. Nobody knows what's going to happen over the next few months. Everyone's hoarding whatever little they have."

"I see your problem. But surely this won't last forever."

"You tell me, man."

"Ah, yes. We're back to my valuable inside knowledge."

"Do you have any idea when they'll let the bank start lending again? Or is capitalism dead in the asteroid belt?"

Jared took another sip and reviewed what little he knew of Alum's economic policy. "How much do you know about economics and finance?" he asked.

"You know my degree is in engineering, right?"

"No, I didn't know that. I presumed you were a self-taught entrepreneur. Or maybe a business certificate."

"Well, in Ecuador, when you have an engineering degree, you open a business, any business. Sometimes two or three. That's always worked for me, so I did the same here. Actually, they assigned the café to me when I got here. Not everyone can do this, you know."

"I'm afraid I've underestimated you, my friend. My apologies."

"No worries, man."

"Okay, let me see. I'm sure Alum and the Governing Council is well aware of the mess that irresponsible government combined with corporate debt made of Earth's economy. Nevertheless, growth requires equity or debt and, right now, we have neither. We do want to grow. Actually, we need to grow."

"There'll be a lot of room to expand," Rumi agreed.

"The problem is, both the previous Administration and the current one are fashioned along militaristic lines rather than capitalistic ones. Making the transition will be difficult."

"I don't know, man. I'm not sure you can equate the Church's hierarchy to a military chain of command."

"No? Think about it. In many ways, they're remarkably similar. Especially evangelical churches like the YTG. Perhaps the hierarchy within the Church is even shallower than a standard military one. There aren't many levels between Alum and his followers.

"At any rate, the Governing Council is trying to help with setting up our financial system, as are the many middle managers left over from Project Vesta. But governments are built on bureaucratic structure, and bureaucracies tend to be slow and cautious."

Rumi frowned. "So, these guys don't want a whole bunch of little guys like me running around, frantically starting new businesses?"

Jared burst out laughing at the image. "No, nothing like that. They're okay with small businesses. They just don't trust the 'high finance' types, so they're moving slowly to set up the basic lending and investing vehicles. Despite its excesses, capitalism does work in many ways. I don't think anyone is looking to abandon it."

"I wouldn't want to see the colonies become communist. We saw a lot of that in South America. Every other election, some country would elect a communist or socialist. It would *start out* fine, but they always screwed things up real bad before long. Then they'd have to vote in some businessman-turned-politician to clean up the mess."

"I don't think there's any danger of communism taking over. But we are in a unique position in human history. Our banking and financial system, indeed, the entire basis for our money and our economies, was destroyed with the planet. So here we are in a new environment—"

"—an *artificial* environment."

"Yes, here we are in an environment of our own making. Providing our biosphere continues to function as well as it has these past four years, there's no limit to our growth."

"We've only got the three colony asteroids so far. Eight habitat tunnels."

"True, but our Cybrid friends are rapidly building more."

"I'm not sure I like that our future's in their hands."

"They've been more than cooperative. One might go so far as to say they've been eager partners."

"What do we have to hold over them? What do they need from us?"

"We've provided recharging stations along with repair services when needed, plus human contact and purpose. Remember, their psychological make-up is entirely human. They see themselves as tireless workers for our survival, all of our survival, for Cybrids and humans alike."

"Hmph."

"But you're right, we need them more than they need us, and that is not a sustainable position. Economics is all about supply and demand. We humans will need to supply something they demand in return for the services they contribute, or we'll be in trouble."

Rumi grinned, a twinkle of mischief in his eyes. "We could just get rid of them and take their jobs for ourselves."

Jared rose to the bait. "What an appalling idea! Apart from the fact humans are notoriously poorly adapted to working in space without gravity, it would advocate for killing over a hundred-twenty million sentient beings. And for what? Just to create new job opportunities?"

"For our own security." The twinkle was still there.

"Ah, yes, that. We spent the last few decades on Earth in a constant state of concern about our *security*. And what good did that do?"

Rumi held up his hands, palms forward, fingers splayed. "Okay, okay, I get it, man! We need to find a way to live with the Cybrids. But we also need to give the human colonists some work. And by work, I mean their own businesses. And businesses need capital."

"And that means banks and loans; stocks and stock brokers. Yes, I know. I suspect the first order of business will be establishing a basis for currency."

"Why not just print some dollars? Or e-print some more e-dollars? That's what we're using now."

"But how many e-dollars should we create? What is the basis of our economy? Especially when we have no foreign countries with which to trade. Or should we treat each asteroid colony as a separate country?"

"Uhh...I'm not sure that would be such a good idea."

"Nor am I. Nonetheless, there are important questions that need to be dealt with before we can move into a truly free, capitalist, market-based system."

"So you're saying I should just be patient? Man, I don't know. I hate to see an opportunity like this go to waste. If I wait too long, someone else'll take all the best spots."

Jared took a generous swallow from his cappuccino. "You needn't worry. The market for your excellent brew will be here for a long time. Everything will be decided in good time, systems will be put in place, and we will find our way back to business as usual."

He downed the last few drops of coffee, and prayed what he'd said would come true.

10

DARYA DIDN'T DARE take her eyes off the two Securitors hovering high above. She suspected they had orders to detain, possibly to kill, anyone who attempted to leave the recharging station. After a few hours, Darya's Partial returned and reintegrated, informing her that the required code had been uploaded into Timothy's concepta. As soon as Timothy finished integrating the new knowledge, they could make their move.

If only it were that simple! Her escape plan had no more than a fifty-fifty chance of success but she couldn't come up with anything better. *So long as our personas remain intact, our trueselves can be replaced.*

Timothy pinged Darya. His system was updated and ready to go.

Using the control virus she'd inserted into all 18,457 bodies recharging in the crater, Darya sent out the first signal.

Inside the crater, twenty Cybrid bodies detached from their docking bays and drifted upward.

They go up so slowly, they look like helium balloons. She was struck by an ancient memory—a child in some park letting go of a string and shouting with glee as his bright red globe ascended into the heavens.

One of the Securitors moved in to investigate the ascending Cybrids. They didn't respond to anything except automatic ID pings.

The Securitor's manipulators snaked out and latched onto the nearest Cybrid, then moved onto the next, and the next, until it had similarly collected all twenty.

Hopefully, it thinks there's just been some kind of docking malfunction.

Darya released a wave of thirty more Cybrids from their recharging bays.

The second Securitor left its station and rushed into the crater to respond. It neared a free-floating Cybrid and demanded it return to its dock. When the Cybrid didn't respond, the Security blasted it with an energy beam. The Cybrid blew apart; its molten fragments cooled rapidly into slag and continued to drift.

The Securitor watched for a few seconds to see if any of the remaining free-floating Cybrids would react. Their shells, free of any occupying consciousness, floated placidly upward. The Securitor fired another half dozen energy beams, and another half dozen Cybrid trueself bodies were blasted to pieces.

Darya cringed with each loss. She hoped the inworlds would hold their personas safely until she could find new bodies for them. *With Trillian's involvement, it's hard to say. But their permadeaths will be on his hands, not mine.*

Before the Securitor could target any more of them, she released the fifty docked Cybrids surrounding Timothy and herself.

The first Securitor freed the twenty it had corralled and blasted them. Before it had finished, two hundred more Cybrids began drifting up from the depths of the crater. A few seconds later, another thousand rose, and then two thousand more.

The second Securitor raced into the crowd of rising Cybrids. It opened an infinitely deep, black gash in its side. The creature's lightning fast manipulators wrangled and scooped up Cybrids and stuffed them into the gaping maw—a microverse holding cell from which it could retrieve them later in Alum's presence.

Darya released five thousand more Cybrids, and triggered a hundred of them to transmit a signal to scatter. Fifty meters above the asteroid surface, the Cybrids' matter-antimatter MAM drives kicked into maximum power. Cybrids rocketed away on random vectors, pursued by energy blasts from the Securitors below. There were too many for the Securitors to handle; most of the Cybrids were going to escape their guards.

Darya sent a pulsed signal to Timothy. The two of them detached and drifted upward a few centimeters.

At the same time, she released another five thousand Cybrids. As their drives reached full power and they blasted into space, Darya and Timothy drifted toward the edge of the crater.

The Securitors were too busy chasing thousands of rogues to notice.

As another wave of Cybrids lifted from the surface, Darya slipped over the lip of the crater and into the rock-filled blast zone around it. Keeping low, she headed for the rendezvous location to wait for Timothy, who was only a minute behind.

You made it!—she sent by laser pulse.

Was there ever any doubt?—he replied.

A blinding light cleaved the dark sky in two, saving Darya from having to answer. She looked up in time to witness thousands of Cybrids being vaporized by the planet-busting beams of a squad of Angels.

Angels! There weren't supposed to be any Angels within a thousand light years of the Deplosion Array project.

She froze.

The presence of Angels implied many things, none of which fed her optimism. It meant Alum was taking the possibility of rebellious actions near the Deplosion array seriously. It meant the thousands of Cybrids she'd set adrift had overwhelmed the Securitors' ability to keep up, and caused them to call for help.

It also meant the Securitors were free now to investigate the cause of the Cybrid mayhem. That spelled trouble.

If the Securitors put it all together, if they tied the laser signals that first caught their attention to the Cybrids' inexplicable behavior, they were likely to conclude someone on the asteroid surface was directly responsible.

My plan worked too well; they could be here in minutes. We need to put some distance between us and that recharging station! But where?

The presence of Angels made it too dangerous to leave the surface, and she didn't know anywhere to hide on the asteroid itself.

Just move—she thought. *Move as far away from the crater as we can and gain some time to work out a better plan.*

The two Cybrids set out at a slow, steady pace, hugging boulders, hills, and crater rims along the way.

Darya felt a radar pulse wash over her.

"Stop!" she signalled.

Timothy halted.

"Quick, back up 3.6 meters and stop there."

Timothy reversed course as instructed.

Darya returned to the spot where she'd been when the radar passed over. They waited silently in the shadows.

Another pulse passed over.

The Securitors appear to be doing a quick scan of the area from high above the recharging station, and comparing images a few seconds apart to identify any movement in the surrounding area. With any luck, their scanning resolution won't be high enough to pick out our perfectly spherical shapes against all the ragged rocks, ridges, and depressions of the planetoid surface. If we're careful, we ought to be indistinguishable from natural features.

Minutes dragged on without follow-up pings or the sudden arrival of Securitors or Angels.

"I think we can move again," she sent to Timothy, "We need to keep close to the crater rims, and move across open ground only where there are lots of boulders."

She wished she'd taken the time years ago to map the surface of the asteroid, but since nobody ever ventured outside the recharging stations on these things, it had always been a low priority. These particular asteroids had all been mined and discarded for anything useful ages ago. Except for support services, there was nothing to see on the rest of the surface. That was one of the reasons this chunk of rock was chosen to host a recharging station.

Darya and Timothy drifted slowly, cautiously, away from the crater where the trueself bodies of Mary, Leisha, and Qiwei were still docked.

The activity behind them grew fainter and fainter, until the signs of commotion dropped from sight. Likewise, the radar fishing expedition that had nearly caught them grew increasingly random and sparse. With one final weak pulse, it stopped altogether. The pair stood still, awash in ghostly echoes stemming from doubt and anticipation, unable to flee freely for fear of being trapped by a fresh random pulse.

The paralyzing doubt festered and grew. Had their freedom been worth the horrific cost of their escape? The Angels had blasted thousands of Cybrid bodies into plasma. Millions of her colleagues, many of them friends, were now trapped inside her Alternus simulation.

Or rather, inside Trillian's sick distortion of my Alternus simulation.

If she and Timothy were to rocket away, the Securitors would detect the trails from their propulsion units would make it easy to detect them against the distant light of stars.

How long can we hide out?—she wondered. If the Securitors made a concerted effort to find them on the surface, there'd be no way to avoid being discovered.

They came to an intersection of two crater rims, and Darya noticed stars twinkling far off to one side. *Interesting. Little else besides the presence of surface gasses causes that effect. Aside from the recharging station in the other direction, this should be a dead chunk of rock. So what's distorting the starlight, and is there some way we can use it?* She magnified her view of the region. *No melting ice visible. Atmosphere? Out here? Not likely. The backwash of a rocket? If it was from a propulsion unit, there'd be Securitors nearby.*

"I need to go check something out. Please move ever so slowly, look for the largest boulder you can find nearby, and hide. Don't move again until I tell you."

She focused her main light receptors on the region, and ramped up the magnification to find the source of the gasses.

The stars twinkled in exactly the same place several times over the next few minutes. She couldn't see anything moving, but couldn't determine what was making them shimmer. She needed another perspective.

"Stay there. I'm going to move closer."

"Wait! What if you don't come back? What would I do on my own?" Even over the short laser channel, Darya could make out the tremor in his voice.

What *could* he do if she didn't come back? He was brand new to the real universe. Though he knew the basics, surviving past the end of his charge cycle would require much more than that. Was it right to abandon him here?

"I'm not going to lie and tell you it'll all be okay," she answered. "Maybe this is some sort of trap, or maybe we *are* being tracked. If I don't come back or signal in fifteen minutes, return to the recharging station at the crater and turn yourself in. None of this has been your fault. Tell them your story and say you'll be a faithful and productive Cybrid. Tell them how I tricked you and lied to you. With any luck, they'll be curious enough to question you." She shut up before adding, "...instead of just blasting you into dust on sight."

"Well, if that's my only other option, I might as well come with you. I don't belong in this world. They'll simply return me to Partial status in DonTon. I couldn't bear going back to being a Partial now. I'm better off taking my chances with you."

Darya didn't respond right away. *I have to admit, he has a valid point.*

She spent a few seconds surveying the landscape around the projected source of the gas emissions as best she could with the available light.

"You're right. Besides, a second viewing angle will help pinpoint where the gas is coming from."

She sent him the map she'd constructed, and indicated his route to reach a useful vista. "Make your way along this path to this point," she said. "It's a little higher than most of the surrounding landscape. And stick to the shadows."

"That won't do me any good if they're using active sensors."

"True. But please humor me. It makes me feel better about sending you into potential danger."

Timothy shot her the equivalent of a Cybrid eye roll. "Again," he replied, "You must stop being so protective. I'm a full partner in this."

Darya realized the futility of arguing with his nineteenth-century chivalry. "Okay. I hope it doesn't destroy your cover story if we're caught."

That is, if you are caught—she modified in her own mind. *I will be destroyed or destroy myself before I let myself be taken prisoner by Alum.*

"Where will you be?"

Darya sent a second route to Timothy's map. "I'll try to get to this position. Once I get there, I'll send you a laser ping and we can compare what we see."

"Very well." Timothy moved off to his assigned path. He sent a quick message back. "Be careful. And, Darya..."

"Yes, Timothy?"

"Thank you for this life you've given me, however brief it may be."

"Let's try to think positively."

"Stiff upper lip and all?"

Darya laughed; she hadn't heard that phrase for ages. "Let's just get into position and exchange data."

"I look forward to your ping." Timothy continued outward.

Darya accelerated along her chosen route. She reached the high rim of a crater a few hundred meters from the projected source of the emissions, came to a stop, and peered out from behind the largest boulder she could find. It sheltered too little of her spherical body, but it would have to do.

If there's a Securitor down there, we're finished anyway.

She focused her visual receptors into the shadows. She could make out dozens of boulders and small meteorite impact sites. Without the stars behind, she couldn't spot the source of whatever gasses were present. Maybe Timothy was having better luck from his vantage point.

She sent him a line-of-sight laser ping and was rewarded with a direct connection in milliseconds. "Can you see anything?" she asked.

"It's dark," he replied. "I can't tell if there's a Securitor down there. Could be nothing but rocks."

Do I dare try an active probe? If there was a Securitor down there, a single radar microburst would reveal her presence. Then again, if there were any Securitors following them, they already knew she and Timothy were out here. One brief microwave pulse would illuminate every detail in the field and end her uncertainty. *It's worth the risk. I hope.*

Darya extended a thin array of antennae as wide as she dared and transmitted a quick, directional pulse into the area between her and Timothy.

The reflected microwaves revealed the plane below in detail and, more importantly, the source of the gasses: a gaping hole in the ground. No, a cave.

"Aha!," she sent to Timothy. "I took a quick look by radar. It's just a cave."

No answer.

"Timothy? Are you there?"

"You might have asked my opinion before you risked giving away your position," he responded.

Darya felt his rebuke. "I'm sorry. You're right. We weren't getting anywhere. I guess I'm not used to working with a partner. I should have asked you."

"Just so you know, I would have agreed with you, to scan actively."

"Next time, I'll include you in the decision. I'm sorry."

"How deep is it?"

"I couldn't tell with that short burst. It's likely a shallow depression with ice at the bottom. I didn't have enough time to get a spectral analysis. I'm going to move in closer."

Timothy consulted his data stores on spectral analyses. "Should we try a quick laser pulse to ensure the gasses are natural in origin?" he asked.

"I doubt there's a Securitor hiding out in a cave. That's not something they do."

"And running around on the surface of an asteroid is something Cybrids commonly do?"

"Not too often, no," she had to admit. "Okay, I guess it's less risky to run the analysis than to charge down there. Give me a second."

Darya fired an analytical laser pulse at the gas being expelled from the cave. "It's 98% nitrogen gas, with traces of water and oxygen and carbon dioxide. There must be a frozen source in there. Maybe when light hits the ice, it warms it enough to sublimate. In any case, there's no sign of maneuvering exhaust. I think we can go take a closer look."

The two Cybrids drifted down to the source of the gasses. Darya got there first and was hovering over a black hole with unnaturally smooth edges about twice the diameter of a Cybrid when Timothy joined her.

"It's artificial," she said.

"Artificial? Is that good or bad?"

"I'm not sure. I tried a quick peek with active sensors—don't worry, just a single, weak radar pulse. Nothing came back."

"So it's deep."

"Very. It might go all the way through the asteroid."

"Perhaps an escape route?"

"Maybe." Darya entered the hole.

"Wait! What are you doing?"

"We can't tell anything from out here; I'm going to take a better look. Come on."

Barely inside, she was already out of range of the weak surface light.

Timothy maneuvered over the hole; a very human fear of climbing into the dark unknown made him hesitate. He activated his directional radar and the walls of the cave sprang into view. He spotted Darya a hundred meters in. The tunnel extended far ahead of her.

"Hey! Turn down those lights!" Darya transmitted from below.

"Oh, right." Timothy reduced his radar illumination to see only a little beyond her, and followed her down into the tunnel. The smooth, featureless walls slid by slowly at first. As he sensed Darya picking up speed, he accelerated to keep up. Hundreds of meters of tunnel wall sped by. Soon, his weak radar pulses were too feeble to discern the entrance. His world shrank to the narrow tube receding behind him and opening ahead. Darya was the only thing in that world that wasn't tunnel wall or empty vacuum.

"There's an opening ahead," she sent. She slowed down and allowed him to catch up.

Timothy could just make out the end of the tunnel a few hundred meters in front of them.

"We can't have passed all the way through," he said.

"No," Darya agreed. "We're only about twenty klicks under the surface. There's still a long way to go."

"So what is the tunnel opening into?"

Darya came to a stop outside the opening. Timothy pulled up behind her. He sensed an empty space but his weak radar couldn't detect any enclosing walls.

"Where are we?"

The chamber flashed bright for a split second, long enough that Timothy could make out the side walls of an enormous cylinder some ten kilometers in diameter before all was plunged again into darkness.

"Was that wise?" he asked.

"Going in completely blind is a greater risk than gathering some idea of where we are." She increased her pulse strength and the walls of the chamber became visible once more. Emptiness stretched out beyond the limits of their radar vision.

"What are those structures lining the wall?" Timothy asked.

"Buildings. And that's the floor. I think we're inside an ancient asteroid habitat. At one time a few million people would have lived here. That would have been their city," she said, pointing to the distant structures.

"Is it safe?"

"I think so. I don't see any signs of activity. I suspect the nitrogen we saw outside is off-gassing what little of the original atmosphere is left."

"Why would they just abandon their homes?"

"Any number of reasons. Most likely, they moved on to something bigger, a new planet or a ringworld. I haven't seen any signs of struggle, so I think it was voluntary or, at least, compliant."

"So, if you think it's safe, why haven't you increased your radar illumination?"

Darya answered with a sharp rocket burst. "Follow me," she said, and headed toward the city, picking up speed and putting distance between them.

"What are you doing?" Timothy asked.

"You'll see."

They sped over the empty city. There was no indication of anyone tracking them. It appeared to be empty, as Darya had guessed. Within minutes, they'd passed beyond the far side of the habitat. Following the path of a frozen river that stretched from one end to the other, they jetted toward the rock-filled cap at the far end of the cavern.

Out past the boundary of the city, they found a huge wall. The wall had an entrance, identical to the one that had brought them into the cylinder. They decelerated gently to a halt a dozen meters in front of the bore hole.

"Very well," Timothy said. "Tunnels lead out of each end of the cavern. Why dim your radar? Don't you want to see if this leads all the way outside?"

"Yes, but if I were to send a detectable pulse out through there, someone could spot it."

"Of course; I should have thought of that. They could still be watching closely all around the asteroid.

Timothy stared at the tunnel entrance and thought about their predicament.

"What good's an exit if we can't use it to escape? And even if we do escape," he lamented, "I'm woefully ill-equipped to deal with life on my own outside of Casa DonTon."

"Maybe it's not as hopeless as you think," Darya replied, and moved inside the tunnel. "For one, this can't come out anywhere near the recharging station. I'm going to follow it to the exit hole and see what's out there."

She started forward, but stopped when Timothy didn't follow.

"Are you coming?" she asked.

11

"THIS IS REALLY WELL DONE," Alum remarked to John Trillian for the third time in five minutes. Nestled on its own fluffy white cloud, their table was among the most exclusive seating in the beachside virtual restaurant. Perched at the highest point of Vacationland, it looked out on the longest, cleanest, most sparkling beach that had ever existed. Not that it truly *existed* except in the processing unit of the hosting computer.

Alum beamed. *Delightful. And equating battery charging with simulated eating? Inspired.* He wondered if the Cybrid brain was set up to recall the biological experience of eating.

He asked Trillian.

The programmer's eyes stared off into the distance as he consulted his Cybrid code database. "I believe they would experience this exactly as we have. The Cybrid sensorium is remarkably lifelike."

Glimpsing Alum's frown, he quickly backtracked. "Of course, I wouldn't care to speculate about how the Cybrids' synthetic simulation of consciousness feels to them. I doubt the experience would be at all humanlike."

Alum relaxed. "Hmph. Even if they produce an accurate simulation of the experience, without a soul, it would be no more than a hollow, pointless exercise."

Better than anyone still alive, the leader of the YTG Church knew a silicene-based mind did not make the Cybrids any less human than biological beings. His own nervous tissue had long ago given way to the faster processing speeds and increased density of his compact semiconductor neural lattice. But it would hardly be politically expedient to admit that.

The fiction that his own mind retained any biological connection was important to maintain, even with his right-hand man. Although Trillian's lattice enhancements were extensive, he was still mostly biological and, therefore, would never fully understand.

"Nonetheless, it may have value to the Cybrid population," Trillian countered. "Mr. Strang seems to think that all this will be regarded positively by the machines. Perhaps it will help them view this Administration more favorably than they presently do."

"Jared Strang does not have the complete picture," Alum replied. He suspected Strang was already spreading rumors about the spiritual leader's "hostile bigotry" toward the Cybrids.

It had only been a few weeks since he'd met with Strang and hinted at some sort of Cybrid entertainment systems to his Director of Human-Cybrid relations. Yet, here it was—Vacationland—already a completed project.

He and Trillian had entered the simulation via inSense within hours of Strang sending him a message announcing its availability.

Initially, Alum was pleased by the developmental efficiency of Strang's people. Then Strang told him it was all the work of one man, someone outside his group, a systems engineer from Romania by the name of Darak Legsu.

Impressive—Alum had thought. *Perhaps a little too impressive.* He couldn't conceive of one person accomplishing all this work on his own in the short months since arriving on the asteroids, not without an IQ-enhancing lattice.

And how exactly did this Darak Legsu come to be working on such a project, anyway? *I think an interview with the man may be in order.*

Legsu's Church membership was suspect, as well. He'd only formally joined two weeks before the Eater broke free of its containment. Alum assumed the man must have informally attended his local YTG Church or watched broadcasts for some time before becoming a card-carrying member. He was either one of the luckiest men alive or, equally likely, the opportune timing of his membership warranted further investigation. Alum sent a message to his secretary to arrange a meeting with Mr. Legsu.

"It's critical that people, real people, see the difference between us and the machines," Alum explained. "How else can we save that which is essentially and divinely human?

"Now that Earth is gone, it would be easy to give everyone inSense and let them turn permanently inward. The siren call of virtual reality worlds to the human mind make it so easy to retreat from God's creation. Almost irresistible. Vacationland is the perfect example of how attractive such a life could be."

"And that isn't a problem for the Cybrids?" Trillian asked.

"Humans were given free will by their Creator," Alum said. "We need to learn to apply ourselves, to keep busy and productive.

"Cybrids, on the other hand, were designed by us and fabricated to serve humans. Their construction won't permit them to be idle more than needed.

If they won't voluntarily follow orders, we shall have to make it impossible for them to do otherwise."

Trillian considered this. "The Cybrids are certainly kept busy building new colony habitats for us, maintaining them, and so on."

"But it would be dangerous to leave everything to them while real people wallowed in their inSense experiences. No, wherever possible, humans have to perform their own work, find their own way forward. You do understand that, don't you, John? Sloth is one of the seven deadly sins for a reason; it will lead us to extinction."

"Yes, sir, Trillian answered emphatically. "Although I don't think anyone anticipated science and technology directing us toward laziness. Over the centuries, scientists and engineers pushed forward in a well-intentioned quest to make life easier for people, sure. But their goal was always to help free people from tedious labor so they'd be able to turn more of their energy toward development of knowledge and culture. And to worshiping God and praising His benevolence, of course.

"One unanticipated result of technology and automation was wide-scale loss of purpose and an acceptance of powerlessness in a world that a dwindling number of individuals had any ability to understand. Technology became an unintentional force for evil, rather than something to be used for Holy purpose."

Alum stared at Trillian, mouth agape. Then he laughed. "You never fail to surprise me, John. I didn't realize you'd studied the sociology of science and technology so intently."

"I had some free time in prison, before Reverend LaMontagne rescued me and gave new purpose to my life. The failure of society to properly provide opportunities for people of skill and ambition, like me, was an interesting, though perhaps self-indulgent, topic."

"Indeed," Alum replied. "In the absence of the proper outlet for expression, people turn to their entertainments instead. Rome proved this; the British Empire proved this; and both the United States of America and the European Union proved this. Success stopped being measured in terms of a life well lived, a sense of accomplishment, and contribution to community. Accumulation of material goods and money became a poor substitute for the gap everyone felt in their lives. Before Earth was threatened by the Eater, that gap was increasingly filled with direct stimulation through alcohol, drugs, or inSense."

"We can't allow that to happen here," Trillian said. "God has given mankind a second chance, an opportunity to begin again and to make better choices this time. I'm glad God called on you to guide us in these early days." He surprised himself with how sincerely he meant that.

Coming from his old self, such a statement would have been accompanied by a sardonic grin. But the comment was sincere. Alum had saved his followers from the Eater, as LaMontagne had saved Trillian himself from a life without purpose. The two had shown him the way of true Faith and Trillian would be forever grateful to both.

"Thank you, John. That means a lot to me." Alum stood and walked to the edge of the platform on which their table rested. He leaned against the rails and gazed down on the sparkling water, the glistening sand, and the lush tropical forest inland.

Trillian stood and joined him. "You know, maybe we can use this place to our advantage."

Without turning, Alum asked, "Apart from the obvious goodwill among the Cybrids, how do you mean?"

"They'll be happily connected for some time while recharging. They'll be a bit more open to new experiences during that time."

"Open to allowing concepta viruses in, you mean?"

"Exactly. The majority of Cybrids weren't exposed to the loyalty virus from your last sermon on Earth. But I have a feeling most of them will want to visit Vacationland at some point. And their security will be lulled into complacency by this place. We can embed the virus in the simulation code."

"Were you ever in advertising, John?"

"Hah! No, even hackers have *some* ethical boundaries."

"Perhaps, we should recruit an expert to assist you."

"I'm always eager to learn from those with greater experience."

"Just another of the many things I value in you. But be careful with the underlying code for this place until I've spoken with Mr. Legsu. Its appearance at this time is a little too convenient; we need to make sure it's not more than it appears."

"It is a brilliant piece of work. Maybe too brilliant, you're thinking?"

Alum regarded Trillian directly. "We'll see."

12

WHEN GREG/DARAK RECEIVED THE INVITATION to visit Alum at the Vesta Administration offices, he almost fled immediately. *What could Alum possibly want with me? How did I even come to the leader's attention? Did I go through facial reconstruction surgery for nothing? Has he seen through my cover story?*

The message had been delivered directly into his hand by an Administration security officer rather than through email. Compliance was not optional.

Alum would like to speak with you at his offices—read the note. No introductory salutations, no explanation, no hint of how Alum came to be aware of Darak's existence was given, just one simple line and directions to the Administration central offices on Vesta.

The message hadn't arrived in an envelope. Greg read it standing on his doorstep as the officer stared at him. No doubt, the man had already read it. He watched with raised eyebrows as Greg read the note. Neither spoke a word.

Is he examining me for a reaction, for some indication of whether I regard the message with respect or suspicion? Greg's lips quivered and his fingers trembled microscopically before he could use his lattice to clamp down on his immediate reaction.

"Wow! It's not every day one receives a message from our Leader," he said to cover his nervousness. He smiled blankly at the policeman and thanked him for delivering the note.

The officer squinted at Greg and departed without a word, leaving the scientist standing in the open doorway.

Greg watched the officer's fingers thrumming against a holstered gun as he waited for the elevator.

When the elevator doors closed, Greg stared at the illuminated numbers as they counted down. Only once the lights indicated the elevator had reached the ground floor and stayed there, did the scientist shut the door and switch his emotions back on.

Greg didn't trust sheer intellect to guide him this time; he wanted to feel his way to a solution as much as think it. His heart pounded as he walked on wobbly legs to the nearest chair. He collapsed into it, and rubbed his sweaty palms on his pants. He closed his eyes, took a few deep breaths, and calmed himself the natural way, without the aid of his lattice.

Why would Alum want to speak with me? He went over his actions since arriving in Pallas. He was no longer recognizable as Greg Mahajani. Besides, the summons had been for Darak Legsu, his new identity. He had no infractions he could remember. There was nothing that stood out in his work record, either good or bad.

He had submitted his Vacationland project to Jared Strang's office, but that was for the Cybrids. If Alum had even heard about it at all, it would be of no importance. Vacationland was something he'd dreamed up to maintain consistency with his resume. It seemed like an obvious project for a Systems Engineer interested in inSense entertainment to pursue.

Almost half the population was made up of active Cybrids. There were even more stored minds copied into Cybrid CPPU processors, waiting for their bodies to be constructed. Every single active Cybrid was forced into twenty-four hour days of drudging service to humanity. *Slaves, essentially.* Potentially unhappy and rebellious slaves.

Why not improve morale and give them a break? And, what better—and completely harmless—way was there, than to drop them into a stimulating and wildly creative simulation like Vacationland?

The more he thought about it, the Vacationland project had to have been what drew Alum's attention, although he couldn't imagine why. The man didn't even like Cybrids, judging by his most recent decrees. He didn't think they were people. But as far as Greg knew, providing a virtual world for Cybrid minds to play in didn't break any laws, not by any interpretation.

There was one other possibility. Had Alum seen old security videos, something that alerted him to Greg's presence in the asteroids? Greg had scoured the Pallas Security recordings in the months before his surgery, carefully editing out his old face, wherever he found it, and splicing in his new one. He'd been scrupulous in his efforts; he was certain he'd missed nothing.

On the other hand, did it matter *why* Alum wanted to see him?

He was being summoned to enter the lion's den. Could he pull off an interview with Alum without revealing his true identity? Or should he flee as fast and as far as possible? *How long could I survive in the asteroid colonies as a fugitive before Alum caught up with me?*

Either option could very well lead to prison or death.

If I attend and things get out of hand, I could shift away—he thought. Of course, doing that would alert Alum to his so far secret mastery over the shifting technology.

How would that help, except to buy a few days or weeks? If Alum found out that I could shift without the aid of supporting machinery, he'd never stop until he'd hunted me down.

It was impossible to make a rational decision with so little information. *I guess I better go. After all, if Alum already knew my real identity, he wouldn't have sent a note to invite me to a meeting. Would he?*

* * *

GREG/DARAK SAT IN THE RECEPTION AREA outside Alum's office. The last time he'd sat waiting for a leader of a sovereign nation was with Kathy, some twenty years ago. The threat had been clearer then. They'd had all the facts they needed, the beginnings of a sound plan to deal with the problems presented by the Eater, and years ahead of them before things got to a critical stage.

Now, he was alone and facing...he didn't know what.

He'd known Alum since the Head of the YTG Church was a young boy. And he'd known the boy's spiritual father, the Reverend LaMontagne, much better than the son. Alum had always been a strange individual, aloof, communicative in unexpected bursts of curious intellect or lengthy philosophical monologues and not much else. It was easy to forget he was in a room until he delivered some odd insight to the conversation.

Greg chuckled to himself. *Maybe we're not so different, after all.* Everyone had considered him and Kathy strange as well. Darian, too, for that matter. The geekiest of the geeks, and that was saying a lot.

But Alum was odder than any of them. As a boy, he'd lived much of his life as if he were dreaming, never quite fully there.

Kathy thought the boy's lattice might have been slaved to the Reverend's, but she didn't try to penetrate LaMontagne's security to prove it. She and Greg had been too busy trying to save humanity to worry about the perversities of yet another preacher, especially one so close to dying.

There'd been no doubt Alum was a genius. His political commentary had always been insightful. Even as a teenager, his analyses demonstrated wisdom beyond his years. There'd been questions around his earliest public activities; he would have been too young to have carried out some of the actions attributed to him or claimed in his name.

It was clear that Reverend LaMontagne had initiated the secretive personality that would become 'Alum.' The boy had simply been too young to have accomplished all of the things claimed in his name.

Huh. In retrospect, the joining of the names "Alan" and "LaMontagne", or "Al" and "LaM" into "Alam" or "Alum" seems obvious. Coincidence? I think not.

It was rumoured the Reverend himself was responsible for the death of

Virgil Hartland at the G26 meeting so many years ago, and that he'd detonated the nuclear missiles over their launch sites rather than over their purported targets. Who knew what other acts, heinous or heroic, had been committed in the name of Alum, and by whom?

In the long run, those acts didn't matter so much; they were overshadowed by the destruction of the Earth, Alum's opportunistic replacement of the intended colonists with his own people, and his usurping of authority in the asteroids.

Greg had nothing but circumstantial evidence, but he suspected that Alum hadn't just taken advantage of the ensuing chaos when the Eater escaped its confinement, but had actually precipitated those cataclysmic events resulting in Earth's premature demise.

If that was true, Alum was responsible for Kathy's death.

Greg detested the man more than he feared him. He yearned for revenge. But Alum was in charge here and, as much as Greg hated to admit it, he might be humanity's best hope for survival in the asteroid colonies.

As far as Greg could tell, almost everyone on the asteroids believed in Alum. They adored him. No matter how much Greg wanted justice, removing Alum from power or killing him would not bring Kathy back, and the resulting chaos might lead to millions more deaths. Hadn't enough people died already?

Greg hadn't noticed his hands forming tight fists until they began to ache. He opened his fists and tried to calm down. Only when Alum became superfluous to the colony's survival would Greg have his revenge. Until then, he needed to appear cooperative, like any other adoring fan, and he needed to keep his real identity hidden.

"Mr. Legsu?" The receptionist's voice broke Greg's reflection.

"Alum will see you now." She gestured toward the open door to the inner sanctum.

Greg's knee joints cracked as he stood up. He inhaled deeply. He'd been sitting tensed up for too long. He shook his legs and stretched his arms.

"I've never met our Leader in person," he explained to the young woman. "I guess I'm a little nervous." He laughed and she smiled indulgently.

"Don't worry," she whispered. "He doesn't bite." She smiled and gestured for him to go through the open door.

He straightened his clothes and stepped into the official offices of the Head Administrator.

Alum looked up from a report he'd been reading and rose to greet Greg.

"Ah, Mr. Legsu. I've been looking forward to meeting you."

Greg had met many world leaders during his time as Chief Scientist of the Vesta project, yet he'd never felt so uncertain of himself as today.

He recognized signs of the strange boy, and the stranger teenager, in the confident face of the surprisingly young man in front of him. He hoped Alum didn't recognize anything of Greg Mahajani in the altered face and mannerisms he'd chosen for Darak Legsu.

Greg/Darak crossed the room and shook Alum's outstretched hand. At the last moment he realized Alum might recognize something as insignificant as the way Greg Mahajani shook hands. He altered the characteristic tightening of muscles in his hand before he clasped the other man's.

Alum didn't appear to notice anything familiar in the handshake. He invited Greg/Darak to sit and took a seat behind his desk.

Greg's chair was comfortable enough, but the stiff cushions matched the Spartan furnishings of the rest of the office. Even this place, where the Head Administrator worked, contained few luxuries.

The floor was tile, the same material as the wall covering, formed from crushed asteroid rock and resin. A small, decorative carpet covered the bare floor in front of the serving table that occupied a space along one wall. The desk was laminated fiber composite, among the earliest cellulosic construction materials produced in the colonies. A single, modest-sized painting, likely a favorite brought from Earth by the previous Administrator, decorated one wall. The other three were bare.

"No doubt, you're wondering why I asked you here," Alum began.

Greg elected to say nothing, feigning the face of a doe-eyed follower of the Church.

Alum kept him waiting uncomfortably long, letting the seconds tick away before breaking into a laugh.

"Don't worry, you've done nothing wrong," he said. "In fact, your most recent work came at a most opportune time."

"W...which work is that?" Greg asked timidly. The tremor in his voice was only half faked.

"Your Vacationland simulation. It was brilliant. How long have you been working on it?"

Greg sensed the trap. If he said it was since coming to the asteroids, it would alert Alum to his hidden computational powers. But if he said he'd started it on Earth, it would make Alum wonder how an Earth-dweller could anticipate one day working with Cybrids.

Fortunately, Greg had anticipated the line of questioning. "It started out as code for a standard inSense entertainment I was toying with on Earth."

"So, you've been working on it for a while?"

"Years. But people here aren't into that kind of thing and I didn't want to throw the code away. After I arrived, I started wondering about adapting it for Cybrids. They may not be people, exactly, but they must be interested in doing something besides working all the time."

"How did you know it would work for them?"

"I didn't, really. I assumed it would. I mean, from what I read, their processing concepta are modeled on the human mind. So it makes sense that they would've included some of our perceptual input, as well."

He let the last sentence hang in the air. He hoped he hadn't played it up too much. It was plausible that an engineer with Darak's background might be enthusiastic about Cybrid cognition but he didn't want to overdo the performance.

Alum cleared his throat. "Normally I wouldn't approve of this particular interest. I do hope you'll remember not to let your enthusiasm run away with you in the future. Yes?" He raised an eyebrow.

"Yes, sir...uhh...Reverend," Greg replied uncertainly.

Alum smiled graciously. "You may call me Alum. Everyone does."

Greg made himself squirm uncomfortably and return the smile. "Thank you. Alum. I was always into that kind of thing back home, I mean, on Earth."

"Well, as it turns out, it was useful this time."

"Useful?"

"Yes. I'm sure you've heard we are curtailing the presence of Cybrids in the habitats. They are to be confined to service corridors and outer space."

"I remember you said that last week during your Sunday broadcast."

"I'm pleased you watched. I am compassionate toward all, even those who are not God's creatures."

"We can only follow Yeshua's example." Greg thought it wise for Darak to say something confirming his alignment with the YTG Church's beliefs. It seemed like something a person like Darak would do.

Alum's face formed brief, microscopic frown lines. "We must, all of us, model our lives after those of our Lord to the best of our abilities. Vacationland might be useful. It might help us with the Cybrid Problem."

Greg could hear the capitalization. He wasn't aware there was a "Cybrid Problem," at least not with the previous Administration.

"I'm glad you find Vacationland useful," he replied. "But I didn't know we had a problem with the Cybrids. I thought they served Yeshua's plans for our people."

"Generally, they have done as they have been directed. However, it was a mistake to provide human-like personas to them. Their work could be done equally efficiently using simple conceptas. They are an abomination."

"Yet a necessary one." Greg regretted the words the second they left his lips.

Alum peered at him. Greg imagined waves of suspicion beating against his already-shaky composure. "I mean, their capabilities are required for making new habitats," he hastened to add. "Not that they have to think they're people."

Alum relaxed. He smiled, as if to ensure Greg his apology was accepted. "Nevertheless, they *do* think they're people. They're mistaken, of course, but that's what we have to work with."

"And you think Vacationland might help?" Greg prodded, trying to move the conversation back to safer ground.

"Yes. We particularly like how you paralleled ordinary daily human activities, with equivalent Cybrid activities, such as eating while the Cybrids are recharging. We think the environment may help calm any residual resentment the Cybrids have toward our segregation order. If we give them an environment in which they can pretend to be human, they won't be so envious about not being able to mingle with real humans."

Greg had only intended for Vacationland to be stimulating entertainment for the Cybrids, not for it to be used to placate them or to lull them into accepting an unfair and unequal status.

"Is that the Cybrid Problem you were talking about, their envy of humans?" he ventured.

"It's not much of an actual problem yet, only one God has permitted me to foresee. Fortunately for us all, your Vacationland provides a lovely way to forestall any such issues before they become a serious issue. Thank you."

"I'm glad to be of service." Greg put his hands on his knees and leaned slightly forward, as if to stand. Darak would likely conclude the interview was over with Alum's gratitude expressed; Greg wasn't so sure.

"There's more," Alum waved him back into his chair. "First, though, I have a small test for you."

"Oh?" Greg asked, as he settled back into the seat.

That's when he felt the tingle of lattice induction plates in the base of his skull. People with normal dendy lattices interfaced with the plates through communication clusters that formed in that region of their brain.

Ever since ingesting the DNND lattice enhancement virus, Greg had no need for induction plates. He was certain Alum didn't either. Their own fully functional interfaces overlaid their cerebral cortices just underneath their skulls. Greg might know that about Alum, but Alum could not have known it about Greg, at least not as the Darak alias.

The induction plates commanded Greg's lattice to open for communication. *What? They shouldn't be able to do that; they're only allowed to request a channel. Someone must've altered the request function into a more aggressive form.*

He would've defended himself from the command, but he knew Darak could not be expected to have that ability. He had little choice. He sequestered the vast majority of his capabilities behind an impenetrable firewall that he hoped would be undetectable from outside, and opened a portion of his lattice to the command channel.

As fast as the channel opened, Alum came rushing in behind it. He pushed a scanning virus into the exposed part of Greg's lattice. The virus ran through Greg's brain, laying bare his concepta, reporting on his persona.

Greg's deepest thoughts, memories and beliefs were exposed for Alum to review, or so the Leader would think. In the millisecond interval the induction plate command had given him, Greg reconfigured his lattice so that the only exposed thoughts were those that belonged to his Darak persona. It wouldn't withstand too much probing but he hoped it would be enough to appease Alum's understandable curiosity about Darak.

Greg shook his head. A normal person, such as one he wanted to portray Darak as being, would have felt a second or two of confusion, nothing more. He made his body, and the part of his mind open to Alum, behave as he thought the invaded Darak would.

"What kind of test?" he asked. The person Alum thought he was probing would not have sensed the lattice intrusion.

Alum rubbed his chin. "Hmm, perhaps there's no need for that today." He seemed satisfied with the result of his search.

Greg/Darak feigned a light confusion. "Oh. Okay."

Alum pressed a button on the phone on his desk. "Charlene? Would you please bring coffee in for Mr. Legsu and me?"

He regarded Darak, a question implicit in his gaze.

"Oh. Cream and sugar, please," Greg/Darak replied.

"Cream and sugar, please, Charlene. And maybe a bit of brandy. I suspect Mr. Legsu here may want to celebrate a little."

Greg had no idea what was happening. *Celebrate?*

"Thank you, Alum. That's very kind. What are we celebrating?"

Alum grinned broadly. "Your new career, Mr. Legsu. I want you in charge of producing all future Cybrid simulations."

13

"IT'S TIME WE TALKED." Shard Trillian turned the key with a great rattling, and pushed open the heavy door. Rusty hinges complained loudly but complied, sending ear-splitting squeals echoing off the stone walls.

Mary sat tall, pulled her shoulders back, and prepared to face the Shard. "I am not going to give you anything. You know that, right?"

Trillian smiled; her proclamation did not faze him in the least. "I would expect nothing less than brave defiance from Darya's closest friend and confidante."

Mary considered charging full force against her jailer in the hope of gaining some small advantage.

Trillian's cold, piercing eyes and the crackling electric whip in his hand gave her pause.

Maybe I won't risk it just yet. She pressed her back into the hard edge of the wall.

Trillian's smile broadened. "That's better."

He waved a hand and a table appeared, set with steaming coffee and an assortment of fine pastries. A pair of soft, comfortable chairs rested on either side. The whip was gone from his hand.

Mary stood and took one of the chairs, poised somewhere between reluctance and gratitude.

She eyed Trillian as he walked into her cell and sat, leaving the gate wide open behind him. The message was clear: *I have nothing to fear from you, and any attempt to flee would be pointless.*

Mary selected a chocolate éclair for her plate. She poured herself a cup of coffee from the carafe and offered one to Trillian. He nodded politely.

"How may I help you, Shard Trillian?" she asked as she filled his cup. "I'm sure you aren't keeping me here just for your amusement."

Trillian chuckled. "You have nothing to worry about, providing you answer a few simple questions." He glanced around the cell distastefully. "Why don't we find somewhere more comfortable to enjoy our chat?"

He waved a hand and they were in Cloud 49 overlooking the Vacationland beach. The sun was shining and gentle waves lapped against the vacant shore. All was serene, as if there had never been a chase, torrential rains, and crashing thunder. Except for the two of them, the tropical oasis was empty. No one swam in the glistening waters; no one played on the golden sands.

Mary took a cautious bite from her éclair; it was delicious. She chewed the piece and swallowed, then washed it down with a sip of coffee. Everything was as tasty as Cloud 49 had ever served.

"Well done," she commended Trillian. "Though I wouldn't expect anything but the best, given your formidable talents."

She surprised herself with her casual tone. Here she was, having coffee and cakes with a Shard. An actual Shard! Shards talked with God, not only in prayer but in conversation. Moreover, this Shard had chased her through multiple inworlds, captured her, and imprisoned her.

Even now, behind his disarming smile, she could sense his determination to wring her dry of any information she had about Darya and the rebellion. And yet, she was acting like they were old friends or multi-dimensional chess adversaries, nothing more. She hoped her acting was good enough to convince Trillian his cheesy scare tactics were having little impact, and therefore unnecessary.

Beneath the façade, she was worried—terrified—about what he was building toward, but she was determined not to let her sacrifice go to waste. She would make Darya proud of her right up to the last.

Trillian smiled and inclined his head at her compliment. "Thank you. It is always nice to have one's efforts recognized."

"Even if it made a mess of the local inworlds."

"Yes, well, I do regret the unfortunate but necessary actions in Alternus. Your man, Gerhardt, responded to our chat much more aggressively than I had anticipated. And then the rest of you fleeing...well, you must realize it left me no choice but to act."

Mary leaned forward, a pained look in her eyes. "But to trap so many innocent people—"

"How innocent could they be after being exposed to Darya's concepta virus?"

Mary slumped back in her chair, wincing, and ashamed.

Trillian laughed. "Oh, yes. I know about that. A subtle piece of work; hard to detect, even harder to avoid. Once I knew who the author was, I simply had to meet her. Concepta viruses are not only illegal, they should be unthinkable amongst the Cybrids."

"But not for Alum, or yourself?" Mary's bitter retort astonished her. She knew she ought to apologize and beg her Lord's forgiveness. Instead, she inhaled somewhat raggedly, let her breath out slowly, and took a sip of coffee. When she looked up again, she returned Trillian's shocked stare with a determined glare.

Trillians eyes narrowed. "Our Lord's policies are not to be questioned by the likes of you," he said, with a dark and dangerous edge to his voice that hinted at dire consequences for any transgressors.

Then, as if a switch had been thrown, he smiled and returned the conversation to a lighter and friendlier tack. "In any case, what's past is past. Let us focus on the future."

"And what does my future include? Torture? Mind wipe?"

"Oh, no; nothing so harsh as that, my dear. You are far too interesting to delete. As for the other, let's see how far conversation carries us first before we discuss such things."

Mary sighed. "Okay. Why don't you begin with your questions?"

"Very well," Trillian said and took a small piece of vanilla cake from a tray. He popped the entire piece into his mouth and chewed appreciatively as he gazed into the distance. He swallowed, wiped the crumbs from his lips, and brushed his hands lightly together over the plate.

"Tell me, was the entire purpose of Alternus simply to be a vehicle for delivering the concepta virus?"

"Clearly we could have found better ways to do that. Vacationland gets many more visitors every day than Alternus ever did."

"True," Trillian agreed. "But inserting the virus here would have required hacking the original code. That would have set off alarms throughout the Realm. There are advantages to having the insight of the original designer."

Mary smiled slyly. "Granted, but you're not the only one with formidable talents, you know."

"If not the virus, then what? From the records I have accessed, which are extensive I assure you, Alternus was an extremely realistic simulation—"

"Of Earth?"

"Ah, so you have been told something of our roots."

"Beyond the standard teachings about Origin? Yes, Darya told us plenty about ancient Earth and its challenges before Alum. She claimed that Alternus was an accurate representation of humanity's original planet with a few minor changes."

"What kinds of changes?"

"She said the original Earth went through a technological boom shortly before it was destroyed, which led to the development of the basic Cybrid technology as well as to something she called the Darian Leigh Reality Assertion Field, or RAF."

Trillian's eyes narrowed when she mentioned Darian Leigh. "It is not permitted to know that name nor anything of his heretical teachings."

"Don't worry. Even Darya has no idea what it was all about, just that it changed everything back then."

Mary wished she wasn't telling the truth about that. If Alum hadn't so thoroughly suppressed Darian Leigh's theory, perhaps the universe would look different now. But the ideas had been lost to antiquity and oppression. Perhaps Alum, in his ancient omniscience, knew the theory but no one else had any inkling. Or so she'd believed. It would seem that Trillian had at least been aware of its existence.

Trillian searched her face for any tells of attempted untruths.

"Why would Darya select those particular changes?"

"I don't know for sure. She said the technology led to hyper-fast development of science, and those changes eventually resulted in something that destroyed the planet. Humans and Cybrids barely escaped. She wanted to see what would have happened without that technological burst."

"So, that's all it was, a complex inworld to test possible alternative histories?"

"Darya considered it interesting." For a moment, Mary thought she might have fooled the Shard.

Then a sly smile formed on his face. "I suspect you are not being completely honest with me Mary."

Two hissing cobras suddenly materialized on the table directly in front of her. She jumped back in her chair, hands clasped tightly to its padded arms.

The snakes slithered forward a little and raised their heads, preparing to strike. Mary raised her arms in front of her face. The cobras sprang.

Trillian raised a single finger and the snakes disappeared mid-leap, before they could sink their eager fangs into Mary's flesh. Her scream choked off before it got any strength behind it. She lowered her arms, but her breathing remained fast and ragged.

"Now, let us be honest with one another, shall we?" Trillian said.

He leaned forward and clasped his hands together on the table. His face was no longer friendly and contained no hint of patience.

"No harm will come to you, if you answer my questions honestly and completely. But I have no desire to spar with you forever, trying to guess what exactly I need to ask to get the information I desire."

He relaxed back into his seat and sampled another pastry. He sipped his coffee, returned the cup to its saucer, and met Mary's eyes with a piercing stare.

"Let's try again. What was Darya's true intentions with regards to Alternus?"

Her eyes darted about as she contemplated throwing herself out of her chair and off the edge of the cloud. With any luck, she might land on the sand, break her virtual neck, and be free of her jailer. Then she remembered Trillian's power in this hacked version of Vacationland and realized he could return her to this table before her fall terminated far below.

With a resigned sigh, she answered, "It was a training ground. It has been aeons since we Cybrids needed to make decisions for ourselves. None of us have any experience in leadership. Darya hoped that by learning how to lead in the challenging Alternus environment, we would gain the skills to run our own lives." She glared defiantly at Trillian, "Without Alum."

"Why would you do that? What purpose could you possibly hope to—?" Trillian realized the implication of Mary's confession.

"A rebellion? Here? At the very center of the Milky Way, the Origin and Home galaxy?" Even Trillian was impressed by the courage of a Cybrid that could conceive of such a thing.

Mary took no joy in his astonishment. "Darya always said, 'The gods are blindest in their own backyards.' She explained the true purpose of the Deplosion Array, and how Alum's Divine Plan will lead to the destruction of the universe. So what would be the point of a rebellion in any other part of the Realm? It had to be here."

Trillian blanched at Mary's words. He knew that Alum intended to destroy the entire universe by causing its collapse and re-Creation. But Alum had always assured him he would resume his trusted position at Alum's side in the Heaven He'd build in the New Creation.

Had some other Shard informed Darya, a mere Cybrid, of Alum's true purpose in building the machinery that would initiate the Deplosion? No, that was impossible. She must have guessed or somehow divined His true Plan.

"Where is Darya now?" he asked.

Mary shrugged. "I have no idea. Last I talked to her, she was hoping to get to her trueself and escape your perverted inworlds."

"Along with Timothy."

Another shrug. "One can only presume."

"What is his role in all this? Why does she protect him?"

"I have no idea. I just met the man; I think he amuses her."

"Amuses?" Trillian leered a little.

"Not in *that* way! Although, I have to admit, I did wonder the same when I first met him. No, I think it's more to do with you being the one responsible for his full instantiation. I'm sure she'd find that whole angle intriguing."

"Hmm. He is somewhat of an anomaly. How did they escape Vacationland?"

"I don't know the details, but Darya found a way to bypass the normal connection routes you blocked. But...."

She laughed. "Oh! I get it! They've also escaped from the recharging station, haven't they? They got away, and you have no idea where they are!" Mary slapped her thigh in glee.

Trillian was not amused. "They may have evaded our search for the moment, but I assure you they will be found." His eyes narrowed. "You can help me with that. Darya strikes me as someone who plans her moves thoroughly and well in advance. Surely, you're familiar with some of her retreats?"

Mary stopped smiling. "I don't know anything about that."

Trillian reached across the table and touched her arm.

"I believe you do," he said.

Mary heard an odd buzzing sound and her world went fuzzy. Everything was wrapped in clouds, the table, the beach, the forest, everything except his face and penetrating eyes.

"Tell me where she is hiding," he commanded.

Mary felt the near-physical compulsion to confess. So far, she'd said nothing of consequence, nothing he couldn't have guessed for himself. Her vision narrowed until her world was filled with the image of Trillian's eyes boring into her, demanding she tell him everything. She almost succumbed, almost blurted out the location of Secondus.

Something snapped inside her, and Trillian jolted back in his chair as if she'd struck him with the back of her hand.

Concepta attack repelled—the words floated in her visual field in stark red letters.

The confused look on Trillian's face—or maybe it was her own sense of relief—made her burst out laughing.

Darya's upgrades! She'd forgotten that when Darya had installed the new quark-spin logic in her semiconductor brain, she'd also replaced her security software.

While she couldn't access the quark-spin lattice within her trueself on the other side of Trillian's blocks, the enhanced security software was a part of her BIOS. Wherever her consciousness went, the security routines went as well. In this case, allowing her to connect with the identical quark-spin technology of the Alternus inworld hardware.

It was Mary's turn to smile broadly. "I did warn you," she said to at the dazed Shard, "You're not the only one with formidable talents."

14

JOHN TRILLIAN HAD NO TROUBLE finding the lab cluster that housed development of Cybrid CPPUs—Concepta/Persona Processing Units. Millions upon millions of inactive nanotech silicene brains were warehoused there, each carefully catalogued as to the intellectual and psychological makeup of their original human template. The cluster was in one of the two science tunnels drilled 180 degrees away from each other underneath the crust of the asteroid, Vesta.

The two tunnels were some fifty meters in diameter, far narrower than standard habitats or service corridors, and the individual labs branched directly off the central passageways. One could easily walk the wide, bright central hallways to exchange information with nearby neighbors or take a short elevator ride to a loop tunnel, where loop trains could transport you all over Vesta within a few hours.

The tunnels widened every few kilometers into park-like areas with a wide variety of food services and shaded seating beside tree-lined babbling brooks or lily-laden ponds. For the few million scientists and support staff on the original Vesta project, it had been the nicest facility they had ever worked in. Many thought they'd died and gone to heaven.

The original plan had been to have an extensive science and technology program in the colonies. At Greg and Kathy's insistence, people with scientific training had been over-represented in the original colonist population. To their surprise, Reverend LaMontagne had supported their efforts to build an excellent science and technology base on Vesta. In the early years, Vesta scientists were crucial in ensuring the survival of the colonists.

That was before Alum's coup.

The tunnels had been designed to house tens of thousands of research programs. They now sat mostly empty following the forced evacuation of the original colonists by the YTG Church takeover.

Security forces loyal to the church had swept up the majority of Earth-appointed scientists and returned them to the home planet. Alum's plans had little room for so many independent-minded critical thinkers. A week after the security sweep, those who had been forced back to Earth were all dead.

Alum ordered the majority of Vesta's lab facilities to be shut down and their systems set to sleep mode. He did, however, permit the Cybrids to continue their weekly cleaning, maintenance, and security checks. Being largely unused, the labs remained pristine, and the work they'd once hosted was forgotten.

The fully outfitted labs retained a vast array of complex instruments and materials necessary to conduct experiments in physics, chemistry, biology, and a host of interdisciplinary fields. On discovering this, John Trillian rushed in as eager as a child in a candy store.

For the several months after presenting his concepta-virus proposal to Alum, he selected a handful of random semiconductor "brains" from the millions in storage and conducted thorough examinations on them.

The Cybrid project's original scientists and engineers had amassed a mind-bending store of beautifully documented data that furthered the field immensely during their last years on Earth.

They developed hardware to stimulate isolated portions of the conceptual structures imprinted onto the crystalline CPPU brains, and measured the resultant activity. Their understanding of the nature of intelligence and the human psyche, which they shared with the world, expanded exponentially until the release of the Eater on Earth changed everything.

Trillian spent long days poring over their notes. His own lattice enhancements enabled him to achieve detailed comprehension in a fraction of the time it would take an unenhanced human. What most intrigued him was how these chunks of lattice material managed to simulate the equivalent of the human soul.

He extended the testing hardware to incorporate simplistic but complete virtual worlds for the disembodied Cybrid brains to inhabit. He had the best results when he connected the Vacationland program to the brownish cubes through their optoelectronic interfaces.

He would activate the "person"—the CPPU cube—he was examining and have him or her materialize across from him at a table near the beach inside Vacationland. After his subject shook off their initial disorientation, Trillian would engage the person in conversation while he monitored a display of their conceptual map outside the virtual reality.

In this way, he learned how different ideas related to each other in the simulated mind. He experimented with making subtle but direct alterations to the overall concepta. He'd written a concepta virus once before, shortly before the Eater was liberated from its shackles. His new investigations revealed exactly how crude his first attempts had been.

His earliest efforts were easily rebuffed by the Cybrid security software, but his persistent efforts eventually cracked the high-level protection.

Once he conquered their security, he began tinkering with changing the fundamental persona of his test subjects. Replacing memories was hard— the interconnections were too numerous—but it wasn't hard to alter the way a Cybrid mind *interpreted* their past experiences, filtering them through a modified concepta.

Soon he'd engineered a program that could enter the conceptual structure and insinuate an unassailable Faith in God, no matter how evidence-oriented the prior mind had been, and an equally powerful allegiance to Alum as the Lord's representative in the colonies.

Every now and then, this intervention would set up a dissonant cycle that would cause the persona to become confused and erratic. Then he'd have to manually prune the concepta, slowly feeling his way through the association networks. He didn't like intervening directly in this way; he preferred algorithmic approaches over the "artistic" in this, as in all other situations.

Today was a big day; he was ready to demonstrate his progress to Alum.

The two men entered the lab Trillian had commandeered. The Cybrid brain was positioned in the scanner, awaiting activation. Two chairs fitted with monitoring equipment faced the equipment. The men sat down and made themselves comfortable.

"Okay, John. Let's see what you've been working on," Alum said.

He closed his eyes to better allow his multi-tasking lattice to connect with both the concepta display and the simulated reality in which the Cybrid brain was already immersed.

He immediately found himself at a beachside table in Vacationland. Trillian sat to his left, and a fortyish woman sat to his right. She was sipping on a margarita; a slice of lime rested on top of the icy concoction. Her mood brightened at the appearance of the two men.

"There you are! I've been sitting here for almost an hour waiting for you two," she slurred.

Trillian gave his boss an apologetic shrug. Internally, he sent a virtual sensory system shock her way that made her sit bolt upright. He reached directly into her concepta and removed the simulated effect of the alcohol.

The woman's overly gregarious smile disappeared; she rearranged her clothing and smoothed out invisible wrinkles with her hands.

"I'm sorry, Mr. Trillian," she said. "I guess I got a little ahead of myself on the margaritas. She forced a little smile to show she was okay. "Who would've thought simulated drinks could carry such a kick?"

"Never mind that. Ms. Sievert, is it?" Alum extended his hand across the table. "I'm so pleased to make your acquaintance."

The woman accepted the hand reflexively. "Call me Rebecca. Please. I apologize for the informal welcome, sir."

"Don't trouble yourself over it. And you can dispense with that 'sir' business, if you like. People just call me Alum. I'm happy to be here. Then again, I guess 'here' really isn't anywhere, is it?"

"That's one way to look at it—it is, and it isn't. Are you all in my mind or am I in yours?" she joked.

Alum gazed out across the water. "I believe, we are all guests of a greater power at the moment."

"So just like always, then. Well, thank you, Alum. And what about you?" Rebecca angled her head expectantly toward Trillian.

"John," he said. "Seeing as how we're all friends here." He didn't really mean it, but Alum had turned on the charm so he followed along.

Alum returned his attention from the view to the table, "I don't know about you two but I could drink in this Vacationland setting all day. Tell me, Rebecca, how do you like it here in simulated reality?"

Sievert held up her drink in a mock toast. "It has a lot going for it, I'll say that. All pleasure and no pain has its draws. I haven't felt this good in years. Mr. Tri...John...may have told you that I suffered from real bad fibromyalgia back on Earth. The pain never let up. On the other hand, nobody in the real world ever jolted me out of a nice buzz like that before, either." She squinted and shot a look at Trillian that let him know she was still a little peeved.

Trillian cleared his throat. "Yes, well, we need you alert; we have business to discuss."

"I hope that won't become standard treatment," she replied.

Alum intervened before disagreement could build. "I assure you we view the sanctity of the Cybrid mind as equal to that of the human."

Trillian's eyes widened a little at that bold lie. Alum stared him down, daring any response but confirmation.

"That's right," Trillian said. "That was a one-time thing. It'll never happen again. My turn to apologize. Sorry about that, Rebecca."

Rebecca accepted Trillian's clumsy, half-hearted apology. "Don't worry about it. The drinks kind of crept up on me. And all before my big test."

"Ah, yes. So John's told you about what we'd like to try today?"

"He has. At least, a little. It sounds like fun."

"Well, it'll be a different experience for you, in any case," Trillian said. "As we discussed, we've developed a new kind of Cybrid body, one with security capabilities."

"And you want me to try it out."

Trillian leaned forward. "Correct. We'll disconnect you from this simulation and move your processor—"

"My brain, you mean."

"Yes. We'll move your brain into the new Securitor body. It's basically a modified Cybrid. Then we'll put you through some simple manoeuvring tests and end with the weapons tests."

"See? That does sound like fun."

Alum held up a cautionary finger. "Ms. Sievert. You were selected for this test based on your security experience on Earth. I do hope you take it seriously."

A chagrined Rebecca answered, "That was all private stuff. I never saw military duty."

"But you also have a pilot's licence and you can operate heavy machinery."

She shrugged. "What can I say? I like to be useful. I guess my construction experience got me—well at least this part of me—saved and assigned up here."

"Yes, we believe that your unique collection of skills makes you an ideal candidate for this test," Trillian confirmed. "There are a lot of things about this program I think you're going to like. For one, it won't feel so much like *operating* a piece of equipment as being reborn inside one."

"I've been told the Cybrid bodies fit like a glove."

"More like a whole new body," Trillian answered. "But after a few minutes of practice, most minds adapt to the differences easily. We'll upload the required knowledge into your mind before we transfer you. The knowledge will include full access to all the weaponry."

He smiled reassuringly. "Alum and I will meet you in the testing tunnel. We'll be wearing pressure suits and a jetpack so we can observe you better."

"Wait. We'll be in vacuum?"

"The testing tunnel is still in the early stages of construction and hasn't been pressurized yet. It'll be ideal for testing your flight speed and agility. The Cybrid Securitor body is hardy and completely space capable."

"Cool."

Alum decided the conversation had gone as far as it could go without devolving into unnecessary technical details. "Rebecca may I change the topic for a while?"

"You're prepping me fly the best rocket ship ever, you can talk about anything you like."

"Do you consider yourself a religious person, Ms. Sievert?"

"Not particularly. I guess I believe in God and all. I just never found asking Him to do something for me to be particularly useful. I'm a pragmatic person that way. If it don't work, it ain't worth much."

"And do you know who I am?"

"Sure. You're Alum, like you told me a minute ago."

"Yes, but do you know my position here?"

The right side of Rebecca's face scrunched up as she thought about what she knew. "I guess you're like the President of the asteroids?"

"Ha!" Alum inadvertently snorted as he laughed. "Yes, well, I can see how one might think that. Before I brought my people here to the colonies, I was simply the leader of our humble Church. The Head Reverend, you could say. I now serve as Administrator of the people of Vesta and the asteroid colonies. The spiritual health of my congregation, however, remains my primary concern and responsibility."

"I didn't mean any disrespect or anything, Reverend. Back on Earth, I went to church twice a month. Unless I was working that day...or late the night before."

"Do you take your responsibilities seriously?"

"Yes, absolutely. The client pays for something or someone to be protected, that's what they get."

"Have you ever been called on to make the extreme sacrifice?"

"Do you mean, like, jumping in front of a bullet of something?"

"Something like that."

"Well that kind of work takes a special sort. Not sure if I'd be up for it. I mostly did concerts and exhibits. Crowd control, you know. Sure, every now and then someone would get a little rowdy and need to be brought back in line. But, it was never real dangerous, not in the way you're talking about. Some of the corporate protection gigs were touchy but I've only ever had to pull my gun maybe a dozen times in twenty years, and I've only discharged it twice."

Rebecca hesitated before asking her next question. "Hey, this job isn't all that dangerous, is it?"

Alum told her what Trillian had suggested would make a great test. "When Earth was destroyed, some...*things* may have been released."

"Things?"

"Hell has always been described as being underneath the Earth's crust, hasn't it?"

"I'm not sure I believe in a literal interpretation of Hell. You know, with a devil and demons, and all that."

"Even I was skeptical at first," Alum confessed. "I'm not skeptical anymore. We have seen some strange and frightening things of late. Things that have reinforced our faith in the truth of God's Word as recorded in the Bible."

"Okay...but I should be able to handle it, right? I mean, if this Securitor body is tough enough to go into space, it can take a bullet or worse, can't it?"

"Don't you worry. It's tough, alright, tough as a tank. Even a direct missile hit wouldn't damage your CPPU. To be frank, I'm more concerned about the human instinct, the automatic response to run from conflict."

"I'm not exactly human anymore, am I?"

"Granted. But even inside this semiconductor block, your new brain simulates being human remarkably well."

"Wait. Are you afraid I'm gonna turn tail and run if the going gets tough?"

"The question is, will you be afraid?"

Rebecca pushed her chair back, stood up, and placed her hands on her hips.

"Sure, I'd be afraid, who wouldn't? But I'm no coward. No, sir," the virtual woman declared, and punctuated the last syllable with her index finger. "I won't be stupid, but I *will* do my best to protect my client."

"Please sit down, Rebecca," Alum asked. "I was merely curious about your experience in more *active* scenarios."

He looked at Trillian. "I'm sure she'll do fine,".

Trillian smiled. "As I said." He clapped his hands together. "So, shall we begin?"

Rebecca remained standing. "I'm ready. What do I need to do?"

"Nothing," Trillian replied. "In a few seconds, you'll go back to sleep. We'll move your brain, and you'll wake up in a new Securitor body; it's more like a spherical drone, really. We'll give you a few minutes to get used to the feel of it and then we'll begin the tests."

"Okay, let's get started," she announced, and winked out of existence.

Trillian snapped his fingers and a floating display of Rebecca's conceptual network appeared over the table. He pointed out a few specific areas to Alum. "You can see her ambivalence about her religious beliefs here."

"Ah, yes. Church attendance is a social obligation. Extremely simplistic view of God and especially of Yeshua."

"Compounded with her general distrust of authority, you can see why I selected her."

"Yet, she holds service to others in high esteem, along with a vague constellation of other roughly Christian morals."

"For sure. Rebecca is basically what we'd call a 'good' person. She's essentially adopted the morals of the Bible without any particular reverence for their origin or for the institutions which maintain their relevance in modern society."

"So, how will you alter her concepta?"

"Let me show you." A simple diagram opened beside the complete concepta. "I'll replace her interpretation of her Church attendance with this structure. It gives her guilty feelings over having to work on Sundays, or too late on Saturdays."

"And that will do it?"

"No, not even close. I'm going to add links throughout her general moral structures, highlighting connections to Scripture. She will continue to behave much the same as in the past, but the morals will be rooted in divine inspiration."

"As they should be."

"Yes, one might consider this nothing more than repairing a rather poor education in Christian basics. Of course, I'll give these links fairly heavy weighting in her ethical reasoning. From now on, they'll provide the strongest influence in her decision making."

"Very good, but I am concerned about her other trait. I sensed her disdain for institutional authority leaking outward toward me, personally."

Trillian laughed. "Yeah, I guess that's not something you've had to deal with a lot. Most people you speak with have automatic respect for you."

"It wasn't always that way," Alum reminded him.

"True. I'd forgotten how your lattice overlapped with your father's. I bet he had a tough battle, clawing his way up the Church hierarchy."

"Not to mention his efforts to gain political office."

Trillian focussed intently on Alum. He could hear bitterness in his tone. "How much of his memories and experiences would you say transferred over to you?"

Alum shook his head and forced a polite smile. "Another time, John," he said. "I want to know how you'll make this virtual woman blindly obey my orders and do whatever it takes to keep me safe."

"It's related to her faith and distrust of authority issues. Strengthening both of those provides the base. Then I add this little structure I copied from some of our more ardent supporters," Trillian explained.

"I didn't know you could do that."

"Well, if everyone's lattice was more deeply integrated into their frontal cortex, it would have been easier to extract. As it is, I had to go back into ancient psychiatric techniques—Freud, actually—and design some association methods to allow me to construct this conceptual branch. So it's not an actual copy; it's more like a model of what their structure must look like."

Alum stroked his chin as he thought about that. "It sounds a little simplistic," he observed.

"You'd be surprised by how simple the concept of complete loyalty and devotion really is."

"And you believe that's all it'll take?"

"There's only one way to be sure," Trillian replied.

Alum nodded uncertainly. He was surprisingly nervous about the test, which was silly, since everything would happen in a simulation. *There won't be any real, physical danger to me*—he reassured himself.

"Okay, let's begin," he said.

15

ALUM AND JOHN TRILLIAN materialized at one end of a long habitat tunnel inside a new asteroid undergoing the earliest stages of construction. The tunnel was the most recent simulation conceived by Trillian and implemented by Darak Legsu under his direction. It was indistinguishable from a real habitat. Minimal lighting along what would become the ceiling revealed some basic structures, with buildings under construction half a kilometer below them. Stark gray tower walls cast sharp shadows on the barren ground below, a reminder of the lack of atmosphere.

Alum spied the twinkle of distant starlight through the as yet unsealed end of the habitat tunnel, tens of kilometers away.

The two men floated comfortably in their protective space suits. Trillian adjusted their internal virtual settings so they were motionless relative to the interior of the simulated rotating asteroid. Their manoeuvring jets fired automatically to maintain a stable position.

A black orb, three meters across, floated before them, a Cybrid with Securitor modifications. Its normal carboceramic surface had been replaced with a black matte finish, textured at the nanoscale to absorb radar and visible light. The external shell was broken by several shallow thin grooves hiding portals. Some of the portals housed propulsion and manoeuvring jets; others hid missiles, high-powered lasers, and powerful tentacle-like manipulators. The Securitor was a formidable machine built for destruction or detainment.

Trillian flourished a hand in the direction of the orb. Nothing happened for a second, and then they heard Rebecca's voice directly in their heads.

"Hello, Alum. Hello, John. I am ready for my tests." Her voice sounded somehow more formal, more deferential, than it had during the interview a few minutes ago on Vacationland.

"Hello, Rebecca," Trillian answered. "Welcome to Hygiea One, soon to be the newest of the asteroid habitats."

Two portals slid open and small antennae protruded. Rebecca surveyed the tunnel with all of the optical and electromagnetic senses available in her new body.

"This chamber is approximately 420.3 kilometers long and 9.34 kilometers in diameter. We are 615 meters from the nearest structures. I presume those will form the living and working towers for the local population once the habitat is completed."

"That's correct. I see you are quickly getting accustomed to your new sensory capabilities."

"John, this body is remarkable. You were right; it's nothing like flying a plane. It's a whole new me."

Even through the flat echo of her transmitted voice, Alum could detect her excitement at the new experience.

"Why don't we begin with some simple manoeuvring, then we can progress to manipulation, and then on to weapons?" Alum suggested.

"As you wish, Alum," the Securitor answered. She opened several small thruster ports and moved higher in the tunnel. Once she was clear of the two men, she opened up her primary matter-antimatter drive ports and accelerated down the tube. Within seconds, she was a distant dot.

Trillian ordered a positional display be projected inside their helmets.

Two hundred klicks down the tunnel, Rebecca turned and sped back toward them. She moved closer to the ground, weaving in and out of the towering buildings.

Trillian displayed her emotional matrix inside their helmets to the side of the map of the habitat. The joy reflected in her flight path was more evident in the map of her mental state.

Rebecca came to a floating halt below them. They could detect no trace of her excitement when she reported, "Manoeuvring tests completed. MAM drive operational. All systems nominal."

"Did you enjoy that?" Trillian asked.

"All systems nominal," Rebecca repeated. Trillian wondered if he had increased her respect quotient too much. He verified the echoes of her earlier excitement in the persona display and tweaked the formality down a bit.

"Proceeding to manipulator tests," she said.

Trillian and Alum followed her down. At ground level, near a pile of bricks beside a construction site, the Securitor extended four telescoping tentacles.

She placed the bricks in a neat square around her. She spotted a tube of pre-mixed adhesive and a caulking gun off to the side of the bricks. She removed the cap, and placed the tube in the barrel of the caulking gun. One of her tentacles bifurcated near the end as she brought the plunger into contact with the back of the tube. She wrapped one "finger" around the handle, and put the other one on the trigger.

She picked up each of the bricks in turn, applied a layer of adhesive to the bottom side, and returned them to the ground where they held fast. Moving faster and faster, her tentacles grabbed bricks from the pile, applied adhesive, and stuck them in place on the growing wall. Within a minute, she was completing a new layer every few seconds; her manipulators were a blur of precise action. Soon she had built a room ten meters deep around herself.

The construction halted. After a brief pause to allow the adhesive to set, bricks exploded outward and her tentacles poked through newly-formed holes. She punched several more holes through other parts of the wall, then ripped whole sections from the structure and flung them powerfully away. In a few seconds, nothing remained of the room she had built. Her tentacles retracted into her body.

"Manipulators nominal," she reported. "Request permission to commence weapons test."

Trillian glanced at Alum, who said, "Permission granted. Here's the first target." He sent an image of a nearby tower.

The Securitor hesitated. "Please confirm target," she said.

Alum laughed. "Don't worry, my friend. There is no one inside, and there are thousands of your cousins waiting to rebuild what you destroy. Proceed with your weapons test."

"Very well, sir." The Securitor rose and jetted toward the building.

The two men rose with her and followed at a respectful distance. When Rebecca arrived within a few hundred meters of her target, she opened forward ports and let loose a short burst of cannon fire, ripping holes in the side of the building.

"Kinetic weapons nominal," she reported.

The cannon ports slid shut and Rebecca moved a few kilometers down the avenues leading to the target building. She detoured a few blocks off to one side, putting other buildings between herself and the target. Two ports on opposite sides of her body flipped open and released ten thin, half-meter long missiles in quick succession.

The missiles sped down the gaps between the buildings, taking different routes and weaving complex trails above streets and avenues. They converged on different sides of the target within milliseconds of each other, and struck at different heights. The explosions rocked the building. Huge chunks of the exterior walls blew outward toward the streets below.

Before the debris reached the ground, Rebecca was there, zooming high over the destroyed tower.

"Missiles nominal. Activating lasers," she reported.

Brilliant violet rays burst from new ports in her smooth surface, and lanced downward, blasting falling chunks of debris into powder and gas. The streets and surrounding towers were covered in a thick layer of dust but otherwise unscathed. The target building was half-gone.

Rebecca returned to a hovering position in front of Trillian and Alum. "Weapon systems nominal," she reported.

Alum clapped his glove-clad hands together. "Excellent job, Rebecca. And you, too, John. Well done."

Trillian bowed graciously and the Securitor bobbed in acknowledgement. "Thank you," they said in unison.

Without warning, a port snapped open on Rebecca's side and a violet beam pierced the air.

Before Alum could ask, "What was that," several more beams shot out all around him. Rebecca slid to his other side to act as a shield, with the beams still firing.

"Incoming high-speed kinetics," she reported. "Defensive measures engaged. Analyzing debris." There was a brief delay.

Alum realized he'd been holding his breath and let it out with a whoosh.

Rebecca completed her analysis. "Kinetic weapons are consistent with asteroid composition."

"Rocks?" Alum asked to no one in particular. "Someone's throwing rocks at us?" He raised one eyebrow at Trillian, who simply shrugged.

Rebecca deployed a wide field of centimeter-sized drones around her and boosted her radar signal. "Those rocks were moving as fast as bullets. They came from approaching anomalies. Nature is unknown. Recommend protective measures."

"Where should we hide?" Trillian asked her.

Rebecca immediately indicated a location on the open ground below.

"Don't you think we should head for cover?" John asked.

"I am the best protection available," the Securitor replied.

Alum had to admit the building walls would be useless at stopping most projectiles or beams, and would provide the added risk of debris to be avoided in the case of explosives. *The instinctive desire to seek the false safety of walls, even in this virtual world, is hard to deny.*

The three of them descended rapidly, Alum and Trillian landing on the ground in a wide clearing—according to the designs, a future town square. Rebecca remained hovering fifty meters overhead. All of her sensory and weapons ports were open and half a dozen tentacles were extended and ready for action. They waited.

An amorphous black cloud was approaching. It was blotchy, with indistinct dark objects in the middle of the smoky haze. In the drawn out silence, Rebecca reported, "Two klicks away. No change in velocity. Permission to engage."

"Granted," Alum answered. To his surprise, his voice shook a little.

The Securitor launched a volley of missiles toward the approaching mass. They exploded soundlessly seconds later. Balls of flame destroyed most of the haze and revealed what was behind it.

"What the hell is that?" Rebecca asked, her voice breaking out of its formality.

Trillian answered, "Did we not say some unusual things were released when Earth's crust was ripped open?"

"No, really? You're telling me those are honest-to-God demons?"

"We have no other explanation for them," Alum said, remembering his role in the act. "There have been a small number of other inexplicable encounters, easily handled by human security. This is the first time we've seen so many gathered at once."

"What are they doing here? How'd they get through space?"

"Besides our Lord himself, who can know the limits of evil?" Alum replied.

"These beasts of Hell are determined to destroy God's people, no matter where we go," Trillian added. "Evil has never been content to let Good live in peace. It will seek us to the edges of the universe, if necessary."

"Don't worry, they'll have to go through me to get to you," Rebecca said. She launched herself toward the approaching demon horde.

Horrible winged things, gargoyles, monsters with misshapen heads, tusks, claws, and horns descended. They roared, screeched, and clamored.

Rebecca wondered how she could be hearing them in the vacuum of the habitat. *Magic*—she thought, without bothering to question it too much. *Anything is possible with magic.* She hoped her advanced technology was effective against them.

She released another volley of missiles and opened fire with her cannons. She was relieved to see the bullets rip through the limbs of the demons as though they were common flesh. The missile explosions were even more damaging.

The demons spewed greenish blood from torn torsos, and severed limbs flew all around them, but their mangled bodies pushed onward, determined to reach Alum and Trillian.

Rebecca flew into the midst of the beasts, firing cannons and energy beams in precise bursts aimed at the heads of these horrors. She fashioned her tentacles into razor sharp scythes and swept through the demons' ranks.

By the hundreds, they cried out in defiance and in pain, and then stopped moving at all. Those still alive after her first charge split into two groups. One half proceeded downward, and the other half turned on their attacker.

Rebecca dispatched more missiles into the middle of the group bearing down on her and sped through the resulting hole in their formation.

Her first priority was to protect Alum. She targeted the ones heading for him. Guns and beams blazing, she attacked them from behind, decimating their ranks.

The group she'd left above had followed and joined in the defence of their comrades but they were no match for Alum's defender. Rebecca turned her remaining bullets, beams, razor-edged tentacles, and rockets against them. Soon, the few beasts remaining alive fled.

Rebecca floated toward the ground. She had never felt like this before in her life. The victory left her feeling elated; her body hummed with adrenaline. Only, she had no body, and the adrenaline was simulated.

"Opponents defeated or dispersing," she reported. She felt a deep satisfaction for a task well done and a warm glow on seeing Alum was safe. She'd neither feared nor hated her opponents. She had dispatched them as efficiently as possible, and prevailed. Her Securitor body design and manufacture, inspired by Alum and carried out by Trillian, had proven superior to the Demons of Hell.

As the three exchanged congratulations, Rebecca noticed an odd distortion in her visual field. The ground a few feet below Alum and Trillian trembled. She ran a quick diagnostic, but there was nothing wrong with her receptors.

She extended a tentacle to the ground, as the two men looked on. There it was again; the ground shook ever so slightly. And a few seconds later, once again.

"I am detecting a slight, regular tremor in the ground," she reported.

"Can you describe its nature?"

"It comes in waves, evenly spaced, an initial shock followed by aftershocks of rapidly decreasing intensity. If I didn't know better, I'd say someone is walking our way. But they'd need to mass thousands of tons to shake the ground like that."

As she finished speaking, an ear-splitting roar erupted from the far end of the square.

All three turned to the source of the noise.

Noise?—Rebecca wondered. There it was, again, and the sound was definitely coming through her auditory sensors rather than through radio transmission. *More magic.*

She directed her visible sensors and radar along the line of sight, and moved higher to get a better view.

Another roar split the air and flames shot out from between the buildings at the far edge of the square.

Rebecca sped forward to investigate. The two towers directly in front of her shook, and exploded outward. A giant creature crafted from humanity's darkest nightmares emerged from behind the destroyed buildings.

The King of Demons stood over eight stories high. His red, leathery wings spread wider than the two structures he'd just decimated. Aside from the wings, his muscular physique was human, but his face was a horned, toothy horror and his eyes burned with the fires of Hell.

The creature spewed fire on the fallen buildings, and its enormous clawed hands tore open what remained, scattering debris for hundreds of meters.

The demon spotted the black carboceramic sphere, Rebecca, floating a hundred meters before him, and the two tiny men behind her. His furious roar shattered windows. He spat fire at Rebecca, and bombarded her with sections of broken wall. The beast leaped over the pile of destruction between them and came at her with great, powerful strides.

"Please tell me that's just another demon," Rebecca sent to Trillian as she shot her remaining missiles at the attacking monstrosity.

"It is Lucifer, himself," he replied. "It is Satan, Lord of Darkness. You must protect Alum!"

This is impossible—she thought. *The Devil himself is attacking me in the vacuum of an unfinished asteroid habitat.* There has to be some other explanation.

But, she had no time to think, only to react. God had brought His people to the colonies and appointed Alum to be His representative. God had judged her ready to protect Alum from the Beast of Hell. She had to save their Leader at all costs, even if it meant her life.

She spent her remaining ammunition on a long burst at the beast. She opened her energy beam ports and blasted Lucifer with everything she could muster. She turned her propulsion ports toward him, supported herself against the ground with her tentacles, and ignited her MAM propulsion.

The blasts slowed the beast, but he merely grinned, bared his fierce, long fangs, and pushed forward. He could have gone around or over, but he didn't try. He calmly walked straight at Rebecca, without damage, without pain, without fear.

When he was a few meters away, she deactivated her rockets, converted her tentacles back into deadly scythes, and flung herself at him, yelling savagely into the ether. Her manipulators, tipped with needle points and razor edges, thrust and slashed at the beast. She attacked his stomach and chest, his arms and legs.

The beast stood his ground, taking her jabs and slices, laughing in defiance at her pitiful efforts. His arms reached out quicker than her ultrafast sensors and processors could register. He grabbed two of her six extended tentacles and ripped them from her body.

Rebecca registered the mechanical report of damage but felt no pain. The shock, however, shook her to the core. She pulled away, trailing loose wires and nano-electromechanical muscle fibers.

"I can't stop him. You need to get out of here. Now!" she sent to Alum and Trillian.

She watched the two men jet away; they were moving too slowly. If she couldn't delay the beast, they wouldn't escape. For the first time in her life, failure mattered to her. Alum would be lost.

I can't let that happen!

She sped back toward the beast. Bobbing and weaving to avoid his grasp, she turned her energy beams on his talons, beams capable of drilling holes in solid asteroid cores. She flew around him as fast as she could, trying desperately to avoid his clutches.

The beast howled as he returned her beams with fiery blasts of his own. He wheeled to follow her, bellowing in frustration.

Rebecca's blasts passed over his skin and claws harmlessly, doing nothing more than irritate him.

The beast took one final swat and jumped over her, landing some thirty meters closer to the two men, and kept heading toward them.

The men retreated as fast as they could but it didn't matter. The devil was going to reach Alum in seconds.

Rebecca had one last, desperate idea. The core of her energy source consisted of two lumps of mercury; one was normal matter and the other, antimatter. The simultaneous release of both from their protective magnetic containers and the resulting explosion would destroy much of the habitat. No human could survive such a blast.

But if she were to unleash that force directly against the beast, on the side opposite Alum and Trillian, the explosion might kill the demon while his near-invincible body sheltered the two men from the blast. If she did nothing, they were surely dead.

Rebecca searched through her technical specifications. There was no way for her to bring the two mercury reservoirs into contact. It was something her designers had desired to avoid.

Well, there is one way—she thought. The only way to save Alum would be to destroy herself. If she smashed the containment bottles inside her, it would destroy their isolation fields.

She raced toward the demon, energy beams on full. By the time she reached him, she'd be going fast enough to ensure her own destruction in the crash and, hopefully, his as well.

Irritated by the tickle of her fire, the beast bellowed angrily and ran to meet his foe head on. Fire burst from his maw.

Rebecca smiled. Her tough carboceramic shell and metallic insides would not withstand the coming collision; she would die in a fiery ball of destruction.

She transmitted a final "WOOHOOOOO!" and plunged into the beast.

* * *

TWO KILOMETERS AWAY, Trillian and Alum witnessed the impact. Trillian froze the scene and they moved in for a closer inspection. Rebecca's cracked and crumpled shell pressed into the demon's gigantic stomach. Her Securitor body's antimatter mercury had been released from its protective shield. It was microseconds from contacting the surrounding matter and releasing a torrent of energy that would destroy the entire habitat.

"Remarkable. You really outdid yourself, John."

"Thank you, sir. The simulation seems to have drawn in the Cybrid mind completely."

"She believed. No doubt about that."

"To the point she was ready to sacrifice herself and this habitat for a chance of saving you."

"Yes, that might have been a bit overdone."

"I could tone down the fanaticism a little, balance it with better judgement about the consequences of the Securitor's actions, if you like."

"They are not likely to encounter Satan in physical form in the universe, are they?"

"You're not suggesting Satan isn't real, are you sir?" Trillian's lopsided grin showed he still felt comfortable enough to tease the younger Alum.

Alum didn't return the smile. "Oh, Satan is real enough—as a concept of evil, in any case. But it's highly unlikely the Securitors will encounter any real, physical threat quite so devastatingly invincible among the colonists."

"The advantage of controlling your own virtual world."

"Exactly. I think we can leave the concepta virus algorithm exactly as it is for now. I don't mind a little enthusiasm in those who will enforce our laws."

"Very well. Shall I begin the Securitor modification program right away, then?"

"Yes. I suspect we'll be needing them before too long," Alum replied, a hint of sadness in his voice.

"As you wish." Trillian waved his hand and they returned from the virtual world to the Cybrid mind lab.

Alum sat forward, breaking contact with the lattice induction plates in the back of his chair. He rubbed his eyes and looked at Trillian as if seeing him for the first time.

"Sometimes your imagination frightens me, John."

Trillian laughed off his Leader's comment, but in truth, he was pleased.

16

"COME ON, YOU GUYS! Hurry up or we'll be late! The loop station's still another twenty minutes south." Rick had spent the past two minutes working out which way was "south" so that he could indicate the direction to his wife and her friends with confidence. He was ashamed to admit that after all this time in the habitat tunnels, he still hadn't mastered an internal sense of "north" and "south".

Directions were never his forte, and with no sun sliding across the sky or any of the old familiar Tennessee landmarks to cue him, he was lost.

They'd told him, various times, "Just face into the direction the asteroid's rotating, and North will be on the right." Problem was, he couldn't feel the direction of rotation any more than he ever felt pull of magnetic north back on Earth. He doubted anyone else could, either.

Fortunately, the Administration had anticipated the problem of waves of new colonists trying to navigate the long, linear cities.

Streets were laid out in grids that respected the axes of the major directions, and direction signs were posted everywhere. North and South ran the length of the habitat tunnels, following the narrow rivers, while East and West were determined just like on Earth. Face North, and East is on your right. Or just follow the street signs.

At least, he was getting used to the weird "sun" that ran the length of the habitat like a giant fluorescent tube bringing "daylight" for fourteen hours a day and dimming for ten hours every "night".

The Administration decided to keep the antiquated twenty-four hour clock in spite of the growing number of people arguing for a more natural twenty-six hour day. Since the Bible didn't specify exactly how long God had made the days to be, there was room for arguing both sides.

Rick and Lorene had grown up in small-town Tennessee, married, and never saw reason to leave the region. Living "all crowded up" in a city packed solid with apartment towers over forty stories high took some getting used to. But space was at a premium in the habitats, so nobody got their own house. Even though every decent, God-loving, hardworking American had a right to a home, as far as Rick was concerned.

Whoops, there I go again. Not all of God's children are from America. Most of us, but not all.

In the two decades preceding the evacuation, the YTG Church had spread like wildfire around the globe. So when Yeshua saw fit to save his true followers from being swallowed up by the terrible darkness of Hell, Alum plucked them up from the Americas, Europe, Asia, and even that funny place with the kangaroos and cute little bears, and He delivered them all to the safety of the asteroids.

Rick guessed it must be okay, if that's what God wanted, though the wisdom of it was beyond his understanding. After all, wasn't America the best country of all? What was the point of all those other weird countries with their weird customs and their weird languages? How was anyone supposed to understand what they were saying?

"There it is!" Janice exclaimed. She clutched Lorene's arm and pointed ahead to the lineup outside the loop station. The two women had been inseparable since grade school in Libby, and Rick had invited Janice and her husband Leonard along as their two guests without giving it any thought. Of course, had he considered any other candidates, his wife never would have forgiven him. That made the decision easy.

Altogether, about a million people were expected to travel from their various temporary habitats to a brand new tunnel being opened by Alum on Pallas today.

Rick wasn't exactly sure where Pallas was situated. He knew there were three colonies located on different asteroids, and each asteroid had half-a-dozen habitat tunnels, give or take.

He also wasn't why they had to go to the loop. Didn't they need some kind of "rockit" to travel from one asteroid to another? *Ain't no air in space*—his daddy used to tell him. *Gotta use a rockit.* How else would you get around?

Well, except for that trick Yeshua performed when he answered Alum's prayers and reached down and "moved" all His people from Earth at once. But that was different; that was a miracle.

Rick trusted Alum to get them to Pallas, but he had no idea how this was going to work. Loop trains weren't no "rockits" as far as he was concerned.

By the time they joined the back of the line, there were at least a thousand others ahead of them. *Can't blame them; I was hoping to get ahead of the crowds, too*—Rick thought.

Supposedly, half a million individuals received the coveted direct email invitation. Each invitee was permitted to bring two extra people, if they wished. *That's gonna add up to a whole lot of people!*

He wondered what so many people all in one place was going to look like. *Good thing the new habitat is so big: four hundred kilometers long and seven klicks across. About two-hundred miles by four miles, or so*—Rick did the conversion in his head now. *Standing room only, but Alum says we'll all fit.*

He and Lorene had watched the video teaser on the public broadcast system over and over last week, and could hardly contain their excitement.

A special public square had been prepared for today's event; the expansive open space between the north and south halves of the city was ready to welcome the one million or more special souls expected today.

Ten times that number would be watching the sea of joyous faces from public and private viewing panels scattered throughout the three colony habitats.

He'd hoped to arrive early enough to be among the front-most hundred thousand visitors. Rick felt honored to be one of the privileged few who would soon be in Alum's presence, even if his chances of getting close enough to see the Leader with his own eyes were slim.

Now, if only I could get Lorene, Janice, and her husband moving. You'd think they could move a little faster now they don't weigh so much.

Rick knew a bit about gravity, knew it was what held you to the surface of the Earth. He'd proudly rejected the Flat Earth nonsense folks were pushing ages ago. *I ain't stupid*—he declared to his neighbors. *I seen the curve of the planet, myself, from the plane that time we went to New York City.*

He liked to point out to them how the YTG Church supported knowing about things, unlike some churches which claimed all everyone needed to know was written in the Bible. A number of his neighbors just shook their heads, but many of them followed Rick and Lorene into the YTG Church and his status grew in the community. He liked that.

He wasn't quite sure what held them on the ground inside an asteroid but he'd heard it was like being pinned to the outside of a spinning merry-go-round. Anyway, they'd told him at the Introductory Lecture that the asteroid spun slowly enough that everyone felt quite a bit lighter in the habitats. He figured Janice and Leonard would appreciate that, seeing as they tended to the heavy side.

The foursome shuffled along until they reached the front gate of the loop station. Eager attendants verified their tickets, and they queued up for the first train with enough room to accept them.

"Did you know that these loop trains are based on the old hyperloop transport systems that California built thirty years ago?"

Leonard was a history buff and a bit of a tech geek, but Rick liked that about him. He even knew how to replace damaged boards in some of them old computers.

"And now, here they are in outer space—imagine that! Well, I guess you don't need to imagine because here we are."

Leonard paused to gauge the interest of the others. "I'm sorry; I'm running on again. This kinda stuff gets me revved up, is all."

"That's okay, we're excited too. Aren't we, Rick?" Lorene made eye contact and waited for him to agree. Rick nodded.

"See? Carry on," Lorene encouraged. "It'll help pass the time."

Leonard jumped back in. "Well, the idea of an electromagnetically propelled train in an evacuated tunnel is actually even older than that but, on Earth, getting a full vacuum is—I mean, was—hard. Here on the asteroids, that isn't a challenge. The vacuum of space is all around us. The trick is how to survive in said vacuum."

Rick blanched a little. He tried not to think about traveling where there wasn't any air. On Earth, it had never occurred to him that the loop train tunnels didn't have much air in them either. While achieving a vacuum state was great for the loop, it was the enemy of the asteroid habitats and the humans living within them.

I guess they are a little like 'rockits' after all—he thought.

Rick casually inspected the seals on the set of double-thick, diamond-coated synthetic quartz doors that stood between the people in the habitat proper and the loop train. Those were all that kept him from being sucked into a fast and horrifying death in the depths of space. He read the discreetly displayed shiny safety stickers.

Great. Millions of us out here, all counting on these doors to live up to some engineer-type claiming that they're "good to over several hundred pounds per square inch." What if they aren't? What if they blow? What if they develop a crack? Has anyone thought about that?

Since arriving on the colonies, Rick tried not to think about such things too much. Thankfully, between his assigned work, setting up a new home, and settling into a new community he was usually too busy, too distracted, and then too tired, to worry much about what-ifs.

Another pair of smiling attendants directed them through the doors and into an air-locked boarding room. The first set of doors slid securely closed behind them, and a second set of doors across the space opened to admit them to the train.

Rick had been right in his thinking about loop trains only being able to transport people and goods between habitats on the same asteroid. Thanks to the evacuated loop tunnels, the trains could move at speeds in excess of three thousand kilometers per hour. Travel within and between the habitats on any single asteroid was measured in minutes. The trains could circumnavigate all of Vesta in under an hour, even allowing for stops at every station.

For today's special event, Alum had connected "shifting" devices to a few of the main routes. No one other than Alum knew this. Few on Earth had ever known about the existence of the shifters. Only Greg, Kathy, the Reverend LaMontagne, and eventually Alum had known how the technology worked. Even the technicians who'd installed the devices along some of the loop tracks were ignorant of their purpose. The shifters would instantaneously move trains from the Vesta or Ceres routes to a track on Pallas, without the passengers noticing anything out of the ordinary.

Little did the commuters know they'd already experienced this technology; it was the very same one used when they migrated from Earth to the asteroids.

Despite the expensive and frequent spaceships that flew between Earth and the asteroid colonies, people had mostly been moved across such interplanetary distances by shifting. One second you were somewhere, the next, somewhere else.

Except for the YTG members accepted among the earliest colonists in the original competition, everyone who came from Earth in Alum's coup, came by shifting technology.

Rick and Lorene pushed onto the standing-room-only train car, dragging their friends behind. The train set off, accelerating quickly and smoothly. Rick stared out the window into the tunnel.

The exterior darkness was broken intermittently by lighting inside the loop tunnel. Without paying conscious attention, he could tell when the train stopped accelerating and when the rate of the lights passing in the outside tunnel settled into a steady rhythm.

Likely because of my musical training—he thought. He'd played base for a while in his younger years and been told he had an impeccable, inherent sense of timing.

It was the sudden change in rhythm that led him to imagine the train had been magically transported into a different tunnel. The interval between one pair of lights was slightly shorter than the previous spacing. After that single difference, they immediately settled into a set rhythm.

"Won't be long now," he muttered to Lorene.

"How do *you* know?" she mouthed back.

He was working on an appropriate answer, when the tunnel brightened and they pulled into a station. He raised his eyebrows and jerked his head to indicate the landing platform outside.

She ignored him, turned to Janice and said, "Here we are," in the bright singsong she reserved for her friends. The four disembarked near the front of their group.

Last-on, first-off—Rick thought. They exited the loop station on the edge of the largest plaza Rick had ever seen.

"Wow," Janice said. "This is even bigger than the plaza in Washington." Janice liked to remind her friends of the time her husband took the family to D.C. for summer vacation instead of camping in Yellowstone National Park like everyone else.

Rick knew she didn't mean anything by it; it was just the farthest she'd ever been from home, and the most important trip of her life. At least it had been, until she emigrated to Vesta with the rest of her YTG congregation.

She was right. The plaza stretched at least a mile to the left and the right. *Two kilometers*—Rick corrected himself—*the colonies worked on metric.*

He admired the skyscrapers of the new city rising in all directions. *Those have to be prime real estate*—Rick mused, as he contemplated how he might get hold of a suite or two as an investment.

The plaza was paved in white and grey interlocking blocks arranged in a complex, repeating pattern. The stark plaza was softened by trees and shrubs in raised boxes and built-in benches everywhere he looked. A narrow river, not much bigger than a creek, split the length of the rectangular open area and widened into ponds every 500 meters or so. Small pedestrian bridges studded with lantern-shaped night lights arced across the river. The overall effect was surprisingly charming, welcoming, and pleasing.

Loop stations were spaced along both sides of the terraced area. Rick could just make out the flow of passengers pouring out of another station a kilometer away across the mostly-empty square in front of them.

"Sheeyit," he drawled. "We're over a mile from the main stage." Whoever was coordinating the movement of people had offloaded the early arrivers near the front, and stopped each train progressively farther away. From this point, he could barely see if there even *was* a main stage. He could tell where it was set up, though, by the ten-story tall golden cross towering over it at the far end of the mall.

"No sweat." Leonard pointed off to the left.

Rick followed the extended index finger. Giant, LED flex-screens, were strung between pairs of flagpoles. Three of the screens were spread at even intervals across the width of the plaza. Two more were emerging nearer the main stage. They were huge.

"Jesus! We'll be able to count the hairs in his nose from a hundred yards away on those things," Rick joked.

"Don't you take the Lord's name in vain. Not today," Lorene scolded.

Truth be told, she was the true believer in the family. Rick had been a reluctant attendee at the local YTG Church in Memphis, and carried on the habit mainly to keep peace in the family.

As far as he was concerned, he'd always kept the Lord's Commandments well enough by occasionally attending the same church his parents had supported.

The arrival of Alum and the YTG Church had changed all that, first for Lorene and, over time, for the whole family. *Turned out to be a good thing in the long run, I guess, or we wouldn't be here now.*

He had to give Lorene credit. It had been her obsession with finding "God's true voice on Earth" that saved them from being destroyed with the rest of the planet. And it was her dedicated volunteer work, first with the Memphis ministry and then with their local community here on Vesta, that had earned them today's invitation. If he were being honest, the better part of his moderately privileged position here was due to his wife's devotion. He smiled apologetically and shut up.

The plaza was filling up fast. Thousands at a time poured out of the loop stations and pressed forward toward the stage. Rick's group migrated toward a flex-screen and claimed an empty bench at the edge of a planter.

The influx slowed and the screens flickered to life with a view of the main stage. Rick could feel the excitement building.

"Ladies and gentlemen, welcome," boomed an unseen voice. The audience responded with scattered, polite applause.

"Today's presentation will begin with a few songs from everybody's favorite Christian rock group. Please put your hands together for The Yeshu-way!"

The unexpected musical treat brought the crowd to its feet. The appreciative audience filled the square with enthusiastic applause and stamping feet that vibrated through the leaves on the greenery. They remained standing through the band's three most popular songs, swayed happily, and sang along with the simple, upbeat music.

Caught up in the moment, Rick and Lorene stood shoulder-to-shoulder, hugged, and smiled giddily. For Lorene, this was when life was best, when she felt most connected to the world and to her husband. The lyrics filled her with the love of the Lord, and spilled into the world around her.

Rick thought most of The Yeshu-way's lyrics were silly and repetitive, but he was joyful for the respite they gave him from Lorene's sanctimonious glare so he smiled and sang as loud as he could.

The band finished with its latest song, which had been the most popular Christian rock tune ever recorded before Earth was obliterated by the eternal darkness. With the crowd worked into a small frenzy, the band followed up with a spirited rendition of "How Great Thou Art." The first verse ended with Alum walking out onto the stage.

The crowd went wild to see their beloved leader singing along with Lucas, the band's star attraction. As the energy built toward the second refrain, the full Guardians of Light choir entered, formed three tiers from edge to edge behind the band, and added their powerful harmonies.

Alum had not spoken at a large public gathering since the Sunday right after the great miracle, when God gave the asteroid colonies over to His people.

Everyone understood that he'd been terribly busy setting up the New Administration and figuring out how to turn Vesta, Ceres, and Pallas into God's Kingdom, now that Earth was gone forever. They appreciated the monumental demands being placed on him, but they still yearned to see their leader.

Seeing him here in the flesh, standing before them all, broadcasting his message to what remained of humanity, the people revelled in joy.

Tears coursed down Lorene's cheeks. Even her cynical husband couldn't help but get caught up in the emotions of the moment.

As the start of the final verse, technicians dimmed the lights across the length of the new habitat. Upon the joyous closing refrain, they ignited a magnificent fireworks display.

Rockets set every five hundred meters along the sides and back of the plaza marked the celebration with noise, light, and excitement. The crowds all but exploded with exuberance.

Rick half expected Lorene, being so caught up in the spectacle, might faint. But she didn't. Her gleaming face was filled with love, excitement, and a bliss he hadn't seen since she came to Vesta.

"We are finally and truly home amongst our own," she sighed.

17

"TRULY, LORD, HOW GREAT THOU ART." Alum stood alone at the microphone in the center of the main stage. The Yeshu-way band and the Guardians of Song choir had vacated while the fireworks reached a crescendo, and technicians had increased the circulating fans to clear out some of the smoke before it settled onto the waiting crowd.

Alum's calm face—broadcasting crystal-clear and larger than life on the numerous display screens set up in every public square in all of the habitats on all three asteroids—looked out over his adoring public.

The crowd filling the plaza was still cheering loudly. The concert and pyrotechnic display had worked the hordes into a receptive mood.

Good—he thought. *I'll need that.*

Tonight, with this speech, he would begin the transition from spiritual leader to de facto Head of State over what was left of humanity. Or he might be relegated to the historical junk heap of ambitious, failed dictators. It could go either way.

In preparation for the event, he'd read every relevant historical text, everything worth reading on social psychology, marketing, and political manipulation. He'd even skimmed fictional biographies for creative angles on how to best sell his ideas to his followers.

Today was the test. Compared to things like physics or chemistry or even biology, trying to predict how people would respond to proposed change was frustratingly complex and frightfully unpredictable.

"Friends, welcome." He lifted his hands to deliver a blessing to the assembly. "Let us praise God for bringing us to this place, for saving us from the wrath He has visited upon the sinful Earth and for giving us, His true followers, another chance to prove humanity is worthy of His love. Amen."

"Amen," they echoed.

"Friends, I know our escape from the disaster that befell our old home was rushed. I know the adjustment to life in a new place is hard, especially when that place is still under construction and not yet fitted with the comforts of your old home. I know many of you have been patiently living with friends, relatives, or total strangers in the temporary lodgings we assigned to you. I know sharing one washroom among four people is not easy."

Alum waited for the crowd to laugh and nod in acknowledgment of this small but uncomfortable truth. They did.

Satisfied, he raised his arms and shifted his gaze toward the distant end of the new colony tunnel.

"My friends, for many of you, the current hardships will be eased today as we open the first new habitat completed under this Administration. Welcome to Pallas Three." He spread his arms as if to welcome all to the new habitat.

A cheer arose from the masses. He'd thought to release doves and balloons, but who wanted to clean up that kind of mess? He waited a minute and then held up his hands to quell the cheers.

"This is not only a new day for those of you assigned new housing in this city; it is also a new day for every one of us in the three asteroids.

"A little over a year ago, the Reverend LaMontagne, appointed me to lead the people of this Church and, since that time, you have rewarded me with your faith in my guidance."

He paused for the applause to die down, drawing out the silence that followed. The crowd hushed themselves, and waited expectantly. He bowed his head and focused on the front rows. He lowered his voice to an intimate near-whisper, knowing the sensitive sound system would pick it up and boom it out in amplified clarity across plazas in all of the colony habitats.

"I thought of Reverend LaMontagne as a father," he confided. "Not only in the sense of my legal guardian, but in a spiritual sense, as the man who woke the love of Yeshua within me. Thanks to him, when our Lord spoke to me and told me to assemble His people in our churches so they could be saved from the destruction of our planet of origin, I was ready for His love to shine bright within me."

He lifted his head, and let his voice soar. "And you, you were there to receive the light of His blessing."

The crowd rewarded him with more loud cheering, forcing Alum to raise his voice over them, practically yelling.

"Our Lord cast out those who sought to claim this kingdom for their own, the kingdom *He* had caused to be made in the heavens for *His* people. He returned the usurpers to that planet of sin, where they could be thrown into the pits of Hell along with the other unbelievers. He gave these places to us, His loyal followers, to preserve His Holy message of hope and love in His universe."

Alum looked out on the waving, shouting, happy masses in the square. With his lattice, he tapped into video cameras showing the reactions of people in city squares all over the asteroid habitats. Everywhere, it was the same, so many jubilant faces greeting his message.

Time to get down to business.

He returned his voice to a normal level and asked, "How are we to be good stewards of these lands God has given us? Are we to repeat the mistakes of those who perished on Earth for their greed and their abuse of God's great gift?"

"No! Never! Praise be! Yeshua show us the way!" shouted the people gathered in the square.

"What sins did the people of Earth commit that their entire planet should be taken from them forever? Did they forget to honor their Lord and Creator? Certainly. Did they lust? Did they murder? Were they adulterous thieves?"

"Yes! Amen! Save us Lord!" they cried.

"Yes! They were guilty of all these. But, above all, there were two sins they were guilty of breaking, the two most important of God's Ten Commandments."

He ticked the sins from his upheld fingers. "First, they placed the false god of money ahead of the true God of Creation. Second, they raised graven images and temples to that god.

"We called those images by many names: dollar, yen, Euro, Gold Eagles. We constructed great temples to these false gods. We called them banks. And the worst, the very worst, of these false gods we called Central Banks."

The gathering of people grew silent. They were confused by this unexpected turn. They knew the old sins and sinners well: homosexuals, abortionists, evolutionists, scientists, and liberals. But this was something new.

For decades they'd felt a sense of righteousness associated with the creation of wealth. That message had grown in popularity and been given a name: the Prosperity Gospel. If you did alright, it meant God was smiling down on you, rewarding you for your piety or, at least, that you believed in the right things. How was that suddenly wrong?

"Oh, don't mistake me. Money, by itself, is not evil. Money is nothing more than a tool, a medium of exchange, a store of the value of our labor and our goods. Working hard, saving, and investing responsibly are all fine, Godly endeavors. But some powerful forces, evil forces, distorted the real value of money on Earth. They put it above God, above Yeshua, and God saw how a simple thing had become perverted by evil."

"Debt, my friends. I'm talking about debt, interest, currency exchange, making money from nothing but other money.

"Matthew 21:12 says: 'And Jesus went into the temple of God, and cast out all them that sold and bought in the temple, and overthrew the tables of the moneychangers, and the seats of them that sold doves, And said unto them, It is written, My house shall be called the house of prayer; but ye have made it a den of thieves.'"

Alum shook his head and his face clouded over with disappointment. He cast his eyes downward.

"A den of thieves," he repeated, more quietly this time. He looked out over the audience. "'But weren't they just simple merchants?', you ask. Weren't they well-meaning venders lending a hand to worshippers by selling them pigeons for sacrifice, and exchanging coins stamped with graven images for ones that could be used in the Synagogue? Weren't they just good businessmen?'

"Don't you be fooled, my friends. They weren't simply trading coins, they were profiting from the exchange, skimming a little off each transaction. Why? What value did they contribute?

"What value did the money changers and lenders on Earth contribute to their economies, to the richness of human activity? Oh, sure, they were able to finance consumer purchases, corporate acquisitions, even governments and wars. But they exacted their pound of flesh from each and every one of those transactions. At the end, when they had sucked the life out of all human activity, when everyone was indebted to them, they lived high, and they let the common man go hungry."

An uncoordinated murmur of resentment arose.

"How did we get there? How did we mortgage our houses, our vehicles, our work, our very lives to those who did nothing but provide us with an opportunity to play in the game; a game of their own design, a game whose sole purpose was to bind us to them?

"In ancient days, strong armies would arrive at the doors of the weak and the innocent, demanding their taxes. They would use force to lay claim to land on which families had hunted and farmed freely for generations. We called them kings or lords, though they were no better than thugs and extortionists. The old churches, not much better than the criminals they legitimized, gave their false blessings to these rulers. They were not of God, but of Satan.

"Over time, the wicked expanded their preposterous claims of ownership over the land God gave to all. They built factories, limiting what could be manufactured, where, and by whom. They claimed ownership over all of our works, and returned a pittance to those who performed the labor."

The people were listening closely now. Hadn't most of them suffered with little or no work, at wages that barely afforded them food and shelter? On the other hand, Alum's words were sliding dangerously close to something they might have heard from a union organizer, and everyone knew unions were a bad thing, ranking right up there with socialists.

"And when it was no longer enough that they owned our land and the food it produced, our hands and the goods they produced, and our minds and the ideas they produced, the elite found a way to claim everything else.

"Our desire to improve our lives is insatiable. Who among us, whatever our station in life, doesn't want better lodging, better transportation, better clothing, communications, and entertainment? Who doesn't wish for an easier life, for more fun and less strife?

"The lenders recognized that need, that addiction to acquiring things before we've earned them. They found a way to play to our basest, most common desires. They invented the loan. They gave incentives for saving, and then used the money of hard-working savers to lend to others who wanted to jump ahead a little. No harm in that. Isn't that simply good economics, putting excess money to work for everyone?"

Practically every adult in the audience had had a consumer loan or credit card in their lifetime; they'd incorporated the concept of banks as facilitators of happy times into their lives and dreams.

"And when our savings weren't adequate to satisfy growing demand for a better life, they invented the fiat: money generated from nothing, created for the sole purpose of driving people deeper and deeper into financial slavery. This new 'money' wasn't tied to anything. Not to gold, or silver, or oil. Not to the general growth of the economy."

He raised his voice to an angry cry. "It was created by the same group of people who wanted to obligate you and me to them for the duration of our lives. By the same people who had stolen *our* wealth, *our* land, *our* labor, and *our* ideas from us."

The mob, starting to gain some small understanding of what he was going on about or, at the very least, some appreciation of his outrage, responded.

"Amen!" they shouted. "There is no God but the Lord and Yeshua is His only Son." A few bellowed, "Kill them!" or, "Lock them up!"

Alum took a few calming deep breaths. When he continued, his voice was even, but determined.

"We will *never* allow those people to own us again. Here, there is no land they can take from us by force, for God has caused these lands to be made through our own divinely-inspired efforts. He has removed our enemies and brought us here to a place where we can build in the glory of His love."

The crowd went wild. They sang praises and hollered Hallelujahs. A rumbling chant filled the plaza with a growing thrum of, "Alum. Alum. Alum!"

Janice and Lorene linked arms, and let their tears flow freely.

Alum smiled benevolently; his own moist eyes gazed down upon his people from television screens in all of the habitats on all three asteroids.

He allowed them a moment of jubilant expression, before raising his hands to calm them.

"With God's loving guidance, we shall create a new society in these lands. We shall make a place that is just and fair, and free from the tyranny of one man over another, and we shall achieve this in His perfect name.

"There is much work to be done, and not just the physical labour. Though the devil's home in the deep, burning pit of Hell has been destroyed, Satan's evil lives on in the heart of man, even out here, far from Earth.

"I have prayed to our Lord to show me the way to counter his evil, to guide me in bringing His people closer to His love."

Ah, now we're gettin' down to it—Rick thought. *I was wondering where he was going with this.* Lorene and the others appeared to be totally taken in by Alum's speech. *Not me*—Rick declared to himself. *I wasn't born yesterday.*

"And this is what God has revealed to me. Money is not wealth; God has already provided His great wealth for us. The universe is rich in everything we need. All we have to do is be good stewards of the abundant wealth God has bestowed upon us. Money is more like time, it's a device to prevent everything from happening all at once. It matches resources to people's desire to use up those resources.

"The evil rulers of mankind on Earth, those who reigned by stealing our land, our food, and our efforts, and then sold them all back to us for profit, they were not good stewards of God's great gifts. Their greed blinded them to all the good they might have done."

He paused, and let that thought sink in.

"Are you wondering what I'm wondering? Imagine all the good those lenders could have done in place of giving way to their greed. And I ask you, what could each and every one of us do to be good stewards? How can we organize our efforts to demonstrate our worthiness to the Lord?

"Now, you've all been assigned homes and work by this Administration. Your lodgings and your jobs were assigned to you based on our best estimate of your abilities and your needs. But you are not tied to these. People must have purpose in their lives and you will have the freedom to seek yours.

"These worlds are rich in opportunity. We will create new jobs together, both the Administration and individual businesses, and you will be able to apply for these in the normal competitive way that you're used to. This will allow everyone to find a place in society, matching their contribution to their needs.

"Now, God did not make us so our lives would be spent in labor. Therefore, no one will be required to work at their jobs for more than three days per week.

"Two more days per week will be given to our common cause and to the upkeep and improvement of our communities and these habitats. That will include farming, cleaning, beautification, and other such improvements. The Administration will pay you for this work at a minimum wage of fifteen dollars per hour. This will put new money into circulation, but the increase in new money will be kept in check with the general growth of our economy. We will not fuel runaway inflation by dumping dollars into the marketplace beyond reasonable need.

"And we will give motherhood the respect it deserves. Humanity needs to grow again, to be able to spread God's Word. Mothers and homemakers will be recognized for their contribution to society and receive the same minimum wage as service to the community.

"The remaining two days will be yours to use as you see fit. Use it for recreation, entertainment, self-improvement and, most importantly, in worship and gratitude to our Lord."

"Praise Yeshua. Amen," cried the crowd.

Alum stepped back from the microphone and let them cheer.

He returned to the microphone, and launched into the business that he'd really come here to sell them on.

"We will provide an Administration bank where you may deposit your savings. The bank will make business and consumer loans available at reasonable interest rates so your savings may grow. Used wisely, credit can facilitate growth in the short term."

Alum held up a warning finger. "But credit always borrows growth from the future. It is a double-edged sword that must be carefully controlled. The bank will not be empowered to create new money; that will be the sole provenance of your Administration. The money supply will not grow faster than the economy behind it and the savings of its people."

As Alum continued, Rick's interest and enthusiasm plummeted. *Boring! I could care less about this stuff. Or should that be, I couldn't care less? That one always gets me.* He let his mind drift, trying to reason his way to an answer.

I'd rather know what kind of work I can get, and what I'm going to do with all that extra time. We've been mourning for a lost planet long enough. I'm looking forward to blowing off some steam and finally having some fun.

Others were working through similar priorities and questions. They wanted assurance that they'd be able to eat and have a roof over their heads. They wanted to enjoy entertainment and vacations.

Most of them had had no idea that giving over the control of their money supply to private forces had lead, inevitably, to an outcome in which they were pushed further and further away from enjoying the fruits of their labors.

But they also had absolutely no interest in designing a new financial and economic system. They were happy to leave that to God and Alum.

The Leader wasn't finished describing the new system. "You are free to work in your chosen fields more than the minimum three days, and to contribute greater service to your communities than your assigned tasks. You can open new businesses and change your accommodations, all as you wish. The money you earn and save is yours to use."

He stared directly into the cameras. "And as a gift from our Lord, a reminder of His unending love and generosity, you are hereby granted full ownership of your homes and of your businesses, effective immediately."

People stared at him and then at each other in stunned surprise. Full ownership? Few of them had ever owned anything substantial, and even fewer had owned anything outright, free and clear of bank or lender debt.

"Yes, you heard that right. Property deeds and company shares are being issued today," Alum confirmed.

"Ownership of companies with more than one worker will be shared equally by all those who labor within. You may sell your shares and choose to be employees only, or you may keep them and benefit from the growth of your companies. In this way, we shall all have tangible stakes in making our society healthy and vibrant. Your ownership in society is a divine reflection of your responsibility to making that society strong."

Inhabitants of all three asteroids forgot about Alum, for a moment, and gushed over the implications of his announcement.

They could hardly believe their good fortune. For many, it was the first time in their lives they'd seen their way clear to overcoming their destiny of lifelong membership in the miserable masses. They now had ownership, an equitable reflection of their personal share and commitment in their society. And it was all because of God and Alum.

Alum gave them a few minutes to indulge in their excitement and dreams.

"By now, I'm sure you're starting to think about what all this might mean for you on a day-to-day basis, how it might work, and what you can do. Right?"

A sea of heads bobbed in dutiful response. Scattered blank looks gave away those who'd not yet given the details much thought.

"To get these habitats up and running for us, the previous Administration used automated systems and fleets of robots to perform much of the work. But what does that leave for us humans, for you, to do?

"Well, my friends, robots have their place, and that place is the cold, dark vacuum of deep outer space. Places we humans are not well suited for. We designed the robots to go there before us, to prepare the way for our arrival. But robots are not humans, and they should not take away human opportunities."

"Hell no!" people cried.

Their anger at things they knew almost nothing about didn't surprise Alum. When the first Cybrids were built, the Vesta Project team recognized the threat they posed to the psyche of the average person. In spite of considerable contributions they could have made, Cybrids were not permitted on Earth. They were built as quickly as possible, and stored out of sight until they could be sent to their work assignments in space. The decision was almost entirely owing to the pervasiveness of the underlying anger and fear over automation.

"Have no fear. These automatons will not live our lives for us. They are our *machines*, our *servants*, not our *replacements*.

"From this day forward, these robots, these *Cybrids*, will not be permitted free travel within our communities. They will be restricted to areas and tasks where their services are strictly necessary. Starting this week, they will begin the process of training, and of transferring their responsibilities and duties to you, the people."

Brief, polite applause sounded from the audience. He sensed their insecurity in being left to conduct the difficult work themselves. In some cases, the thought of working at all. But the thought of ownership, and that they would soon dominate the habitats, won over many of the doubtful. He could work with that.

"God has given *us* these lands," Alum declared. "His love and generosity is great."

That pronouncement won him a cheer from the crowd. "Right on! Hallelujah!" They pumped their fists in the air.

"And God's generosity does not end *there*," he cried. "He has made these lands bountiful. It is no one's place to put a price on God's bounty. In recognition of your good stewardship of the land within these habitats, food will be provided free of charge forever for all of God's people. There will never be hunger or starvation in God's realm."

People in the crowd shared looks of amazement. Many still held painful memories of the decade-long food wars that had driven up prices around the world; even the developed economies hadn't avoided the shortages and suffering. Though few in Europe or North America had experienced life-threatening hunger, more and more of their budgets had been devoted to sustenance.

Free food was something everyone could support. They hugged each other in joy.

"Our Lord has worked many miracles for His people, the most recent being when He brought us to these lands. I assure you, God is alive and active in this universe, despite the proclamations of the unbelievers of Earth.

"As proof of His undying love, He has provided us with yet another miracle that I have the pleasure of sharing with you today.

"Most of you arrived here by loop train from the other asteroids today. I'm sure you've guessed that loop tunnels are not able to bridge the asteroids. So how are we able to transit across space? This is only the first, small example of another of God's miracles—free, instantaneous transportation throughout the habitats.

"Over the next few months, we will designate special transit locations throughout the cities and service tunnels where anyone may go to be instantly transported to any other station throughout the habitats.

"God has spoken to me, and these stations are to be called 'starsteps' for they carry within them the promise to move us, not only among these asteroid colonies, but one day, through the power of God's Glory, they shall allow us to walk among the stars themselves.

"I invite you to go to one of these starsteps. Pray to be delivered to your destination, and it will be so."

"Glory to God! The Lord is great! Blessed be!" cried the crowd.

"The glory is truly God's. Praise Him and praise His son. Yeshua, we thank You for Your great gifts. We pledge to remember You in our daily lives and to devote ourselves to Your good works."

"Amen!" the people responded.

Alum bowed his head.

The assembly mirrored his piety. They stood in their millions throughout the habitats of the three asteroids, and gave silent appreciation to the Lord for His blessings.

After a minute, Alum raised his head again. He felt humble before the outpouring of love emanating from the masses gathered before him.

He also felt a little guilt over how easily he'd been able to manipulate these people. No one raised a single cry of complaint during the entire speech. They gave no sign of recognizing, or at least didn't balk at, the way he'd blended ideals of socialism, communism, and capitalism to suit his purposes. And yet, he had no doubt that if he'd used any of those trigger words in his speech, the outcry would have been enormous. He could have been lynched right there in the plaza, on live feed to all of the inhabitants on the three asteroids.

It was time for the final bold step. He cleared his throat and took a sip of water, more by way of mental preparation than necessity.

"Friends, during this transition period to a new way of life on these unfamiliar worlds, I will continue to head this Administration. However, I pledge to you here today to hold a democratic election with a new constitution in four years. This will give parties, platforms, and leadership candidates an opportunity to come together. I counsel you to keep in the forefront of your mind that, while elections are necessarily competitive, the privilege of public service is a holy calling. Choose your platforms and candidates accordingly.

"Ladies and gentlemen, friends, when God first asked me to lead this congregation, I accepted that burden with great humility. To be honest, when He called on me to lead you to these colony worlds, I didn't know why He thought me worthy of such an honor.

"He called me to lead you in worldly matters as much as in spiritual matters. Therefore, I will allow my name to stand as a candidate for your President in the coming elections."

The assembly erupted in joy. "Alum! Alum! Alum!" they cheered.

Alum let out a sigh of relief as he waved back.

And so the transition to real leader begins—he thought.

He walked from one side of the stage to the other, greeting his enthusiastic followers. He returned to the microphone and closed his speech with a heartfelt, "Thank you for your support. God bless us all."

It had gone better than he'd hoped. Ignoring his security detail, he walked out into the crowd and soaked up their love and admiration while he could.

Tomorrow the doubters would awaken and start criticizing. Tomorrow the opportunists would realize how hard it was going to be to gain unfair advantage over their fellow human beings.

Tomorrow, their plotting would begin.

18

"WELL, WHERE IS IT?" Brother Stralasi shot Darak a skeptical glance. "I mean, it consumed an entire planet didn't it? It should be easy enough to spot...if your calculations were correct."

Darak scanned the empty depths of space for a telltale round, dark patch that would signal the position of the detestable light-blocking Eater.

"It shouldn't be too hard to find. I would imagine it's as big as a large star by now, bigger than the sun of the Origin solar system it came from. Maybe even bigger than the entire solar system, depending on what's crossed its path."

Gazing out from their protective bubble, Stralasi detected a tiny shift in the position of the distant stars. He took a sturdier stance on the little piece of Gargus 718.5 turf on which they stood.

"Are we moving?"

"A small number of light hours every few seconds," Darak replied. "I'm comparing star fields from slightly different perspectives to see if the Eater blocks any of their light."

"Have you found anything?"

"Not yet, but I'll need thousands of shifts to cover most of the relevant sky."

"How long will that take?"

"A couple of hours. Why don't you find something to read?" Darak pulled something tiny from a pocket and set it down where the turf contacted the transparent wall. The thing grew into a bookcase housing several hundred novels, a comfortable-looking chair, and a reading lamp.

"I'm sure you can find something in the library to capture your interest while you wait."

Stralasi scuffed his feet in the dirt like a reticent child. *A book would be better than nothing, I guess. It looks like nothing interesting will be happening here in the next little while.*

He supposed he ought to be thankful for that small mercy, so soon after the battle near the triple suns. That they were ever there felt surreal to him now. The worst of the battle had taken place far enough away from him, and he'd seen so few of the pyrotechnics he'd anticipated, that their survival felt oddly anticlimactic.

At least from my perspective—he thought. *I'm sure it was more than exciting for Darak.*

After the plasma edge of the exploding suns enveloped them, everything had happened so fast, he'd had no time to be frightened. By the time the adrenaline rush kicked in, they were already safely removed from the physical threat.

That was hours ago. *Truth be told, I am little tired*—he thought. *Maybe something to read and a rest would be good.*

* * *

STRALASI WOKE WITH A START. The book he'd been reading was closed on the table beside his chair. A small blanket covered his lap and the reading lamp was off. Only the dim light of the distant stars suffused their protective bubble. Darak stood rooted in the same place he'd been hours earlier, at the edge of their tiny piece of land. His hands were crossed behind his back, and his face was locked in concentration on the nearby galaxies.

"Any luck?" Stralasi asked.

Darak turned. "Oddly, no."

"Why 'oddly'?"

"The detector readings should have narrowed the location of the Eater to within thirty light years. I realize it's been over a hundred million years since Alum first moved it out of the Origin system, but I wouldn't think it could have travelled very far."

"You weren't there?"

"No, I was away on missions to distant colonies at the time. When I returned, I assumed He'd wisely redirected the Eater into intergalactic space, somewhere comparatively empty. Out there, between the galaxies, it would grow at a crawling pace and not be a threat to anyone for billions of years. I felt sure we'd figure out a solution long before it posed a problem again."

"So why isn't it there? Wherever 'there' is."

"That's a good question. There were some anomalies in the data. Perhaps I should investigate those."

"Anomalies?"

"The more recent readings, starting about seven million years ago, made no sense. I assumed the machinery had grown faulty and ignored them."

"How did they make no sense?"

"Well, at first they indicated the Eater had suddenly changed position by many millions of light years. Then, I don't know, they got strange."

"Strange?"

"Well, it would make no sense to you."

"Try me," the monk invited.

"Okay. There was an odd shift in the polarization of the soltron emissions—"

"You're right. That meant nothing."

"In any case, the theory would suggest that one might see such a change if the Eater were moving at near light speed. But that's impossible."

"I thought you were all about the impossible."

Darak regarded Stralasi with some combination of amusement, respect, and irritation.

"Mm," he said.

"Not particularly enlightening," Stralasi noted aloud.

"True. Sorry, I was distracted. I've just now calculated where the Eater might be if I didn't throw out the anomalous data."

"And the answer is?"

"Far away. And I don't like where it's heading."

19

"THERE YOU HAVE IT: nomination, election, and coronation all in one."
Jared Strang turned from the screen he and DAR-K had been watching from
a service tunnel some kilometers beneath the stage hosting Alum's opening
ceremony in Pallas Three.

"What else did you expect?" DAR-K's voice emanated flatly from a
speaker panel beneath a sliding portal in her outer shell.

"True. It was rather masterful. Deftly done. Still, I'm sure there are a few
ambitious members of the Council who aren't going to be happy about his
announcement."

"Surely they're not so naïve as to believe he was going to relinquish
power once everything settled down, are they?" she asked.

"I don't know. Maybe they hoped so. Maybe they assumed there'd be
some separation between church and state, or at least different leaders for
each."

"Hah! I guess they've never visited the New Confederacy."

"Hey, you can laugh but even there, even with Yeshua's True Guard
declared as their official religion, they kept leadership of the church
separate from politics."

"Officially."

"Granted. Yes, that was their *official* position. I'm not familiar enough
with the system to comment on the *actual* arrangements. At any rate, a
number of people in the current Administration have come from other
countries. They won't happily accept this arrangement."

"Not to mention those who were wealthy back on Earth."

"Them, either. I had moderately socialist leanings when I sat in
Parliament, but others...."

"Such as your friend, Lord Hodge."

"I guess I shouldn't be surprised you know about him. Yes, Nigel is decidedly conservative, and ambitious as well. His family is in banking, you know, for as far back as anyone can trace. No, I don't imagine he and his friends were too happy with Alum's speech."

"Certainly not with the parts that removed any chance of them re-establishing their 'rightfully superior' position," she responded, with a clear edge in her voice.

Strang's right eyebrow rose of its own accord, and he regarded the Cybrid with fresh interest. After years of daily interactions with DAR-K, her sharp sarcasm still struck him on occasion.

"Do I detect some bitterness, DAR-K?"

"Your friend may have lost his easy route to riches and power, but he hasn't been completely disenfranchised like we Cybrids have been."

"Yes, I can't imagine you're too happy, either."

"Shall I play back the part where Alum says Cybrids aren't really people? Or perhaps the part where he casually dismisses how we carved these habitats from rocks in the vacuum of space? How we built everything in them, gave them air and water. How we planted crops and forests, and raised herds and flocks for food. Or maybe you'd prefer to review how he attributed Greg Mahajani's development of shifting technology to his God?"

The latter was no revelation to Jared. He'd been among the privileged few who knew the true origins of the new technologies used to get humanity into space and to build the asteroid colonies.

"Given the situation on Earth, Cybrid citizenship was always going to be a hard sell out here."

"Not with the original colonists, it wasn't," DAR-K corrected.

"Okay, not with them. You know I've tried to plead your case to the new Administration, even to Alum himself."

"Thank you for trying. That's probably why they gave us Vacationland, as some sort of consolation prize with the handy added benefit that it keeps us distracted."

"I'd like to take credit but, no, that was a private initiative from someone else. Darak...something. Alum seemed supportive."

"Of course he was. How better to placate the working slaves than with top-of-the-line entertainment?

"Well, I can't disagree with you on that."

"Nor I with you. So, now, no one is happy. Other than the public at large. What do you think your friends will do?"

"I really can't say. I'll have to talk with Nigel. I imagine there'll be grumblings and anaemic protests. Perhaps they'll create an opposition party, though how they could possibly defeat Alum in an election is beyond me."

"A palace coup, then?"

"I doubt it," Strang replied. "I haven't heard any talk about that kind of action. Pressure, yes. Vigorous debate, certainly. But these aren't the kind of people who take precipitous action."

"They also aren't the kind to easily accept defeat, or simple equality. Without the ability to apply financial pressure, who knows what they might resort to?"

Strang frowned. *DAR-K's right. Nigel and his friends in the Administration aren't going to take Alum's proclamation of supreme leadership lightly. Just what they'll do about it is unpredictable. Things could get ugly.*

"What about you, DAR-K? What are you going to do?"

"Believe it or not, in spite of the affront to Cybrids, Alum's basic economic plan makes sense. His brief analysis of the history of the rentier class and their evolution into industrialists and bankers is fairly accurate. I'd need to see the details of his new system, to be sure, but I can see it being essentially effective and fair. Of course, centrally planned economies often appear to be brilliant until they rub up against human greed."

"I don't know. Greed worked well enough on Earth."

"For a long time, yes. But only because people got good at managing collapse. The privileged class always got enough advance notice that they were able to protect the majority of their wealth and power to get them through the changes that accompanied revolution and war. I actually think that Alum's system has the potential for stability without sacrificing growth and innovation."

"It surprises me to hear you say that," Jared replied. "The system's essentially built on Cybrid slavery."

"Humans don't make out much better. Besides, it's not much different than what we Cybrids were already doing. We get the opportunity to do work we're good at, and to build new worlds. We get free energy, free movement, and a great place to rest and enjoy our free time. Vacationland makes up for a lot of drudgery and dissatisfaction. It might be wise to explore the creation of more virtual worlds like Vacationland that would give us a better variety of outlets for our creativity."

"You'd take refuge in your inner worlds?"

"What would be so bad about that? It's impossible to enslave our thoughts, Jared. The worlds we build in our imaginations could be as real as anywhere else. We could be whoever we wanted, do anything we dream of. If we had an easy way for any of us to create our own worlds...."

DAR-K set up an internal routine to design the base code for programming such a virtual world. The code would have to be relatively user friendly—not all Cybrids would have her raw intelligence—and yet still be capable of simulating a wide variety of rich environments.

Strang couldn't leave the conversation there. "I can't imagine your people would be happy simply twiddling their cybernetic thumbs."

"For a while, anyway. Alum isn't giving us much choice. He's taking away many of our jobs. Don't forget, besides the twenty million of us presently active, there's over five times that number in storage."

"What of them?" Strang asked.

"As Alum said, 'People must have purpose in their lives.' Every one of those minds will hunger for meaningful activity. There are scientists, engineers, managers, writers, musicians, artists, and many other professions encoded in those semiconductor brains. If we can't make rewarding contributions to *this* society, perhaps we'll need to establish another one."

Strang was horrified. "You'd abandon us?"

DAR-K didn't reply, which made Jared more nervous.

"DAR-K?" he prompted.

"No," she said. "We pledged to help save humanity. We will not treat humans the way they've treated us. We were built to serve, whether out of enlightenment, duty, or obligation, that doesn't matter. We'll continue to fulfill our role as long as humans need our services."

"And we're grateful to you for that, DAR-K. We are. At least, most of us are."

"For the moment, that'll have to do. We'll leave the political problems to the human realm. You people brought Alum into power. You deal with him."

20

DARYA STOPPED AT THE END of the twenty-klick long tunnel leading out from the far end of the abandoned habitat.

"What do you see?" Timothy asked, bumping into her from behind.

"Here, patch into my sensorium; you'll be able to see through my receptors."

Space outside the tunnel was dark, as always. Darya switched modes from visible light to the microwave spectrum and everything lit up. She traced the radiation to a pair of satellites orbiting their asteroid about a hundred kilometers above the surface. The satellites pulsed brightly as they swept the surface below.

"Can they see us?" he asked.

"No, don't worry. At that wavelength and distance, there's not enough resolution. But if we leave this hole, we'll be easy to detect."

"So we can't go back, and we can't go forward. What do we do?"

Darya watched the satellites. As one came up over the horizon, the other disappeared from view. They used a single antenna to both illuminate and listen for returning signals, which meant their radar broadcast wasn't continuous over any single location. She timed the pulses sweeping over the landscape and considered options.

"I'm not sure yet," she replied. "The pulses are coming in ten-second intervals. That's not much to work with. Maybe the best thing is to wait and see if they'll leave after a few hours without anything to report."

"In that case, should we go back into the habitat?" Timothy asked. "What if they decide to search there?"

"That could be a concern, but I doubt anyone realizes it still exists. I have access to massive archives, and even I had no idea it was here. Anyway, let's wait inside a while. We can check back later."

The pair turned and returned down the long passageway. Not daring to tip off the satellites with rocket emissions, they used their extended manipulators to push and pull their way along the tunnel.

They explored the abandoned habitat for hours, drifting in and out of long-vacated buildings. The dim visibility made possible by their microwave pulses allowed them to see a few hundred yards at a time, beyond which everything deteriorated from fuzzy gray to featureless black.

They moved over dark, empty streets and frozen riverbeds, taking care not to warm the ice enough to produce detectable off-gassing.

The overall experience was the gloomiest in Timothy's memory. Even during the height of terror when they were fleeing Trillian inworld, there were moments one might call "life affirming." Here, everything was a shade of barely distinguishable bleakness.

If there was a Hell, he imagined it must be like this, dark, out of focus, devoid of life and joy, and filled with the constant fear that Securitors or Angels could fly out of one of the connecting tunnels and into the habitat at any time.

That would, at least, end this pointless waiting—he thought.

After millions of year of servitude as a Partial in DonTon, one would think he'd have become accustomed to waiting. Apparently, his newly found consciousness was accompanied by impatience.

Maybe the dark, eerie silence of the abandoned cavern was starting to affect him or maybe it was his experience since gaining Full consciousness, but he doubted the sentinels would leave their stations anytime soon.

Twice, Darya drifted to the ends of the passageways at each cap to check if the surveillance had moved on. Thirty hours later, the satellites were still there, high above.

When she returned, Timothy was full of questions.

"How long should we wait before we do something? What if they never leave?"

Darya had no answers for him. "I don't understand why they're still there. By now, they must've compared the records of all the Cybrids who were docked in the recharging crater and everyone who lifted out. It's only logical to conclude we were among the thousands destroyed by the Angels. They couldn't have kept track of every single Cybrid they blasted."

"Maybe they're just a suspicious lot."

"They are, but they've never given me or my followers much credit when it comes to planning. If that's changed, they're doing deeper strategic analysis than they used to."

"Trillian's influence?"

"No doubt. And if he won't rest until he's sure I'm dead or gone, we could be waiting here for years, perhaps decades."

"If that's our only option, I'll go mad," Timothy replied, and he meant it.

"I'm not ready to give up yet," Darya said. "We've got a ten second window to cover a hundred kilometers, if we want to get past the sentinels."

"Do you have a plan?"

"Maybe the hint of one. Let me take another look in a few hours."

Timothy did his best to be patient. He explored more of the empty city, looking for options. He found a huge door leading into an old access shaft that connected to a service cavern closer to the asteroid's exterior. The narrower chamber was more oppressive than the main habitat and he fled within minutes of discovering it.

He returned to the main habitat just as Darya came back from a final visit to the portal of the tunnel. "Are they still there?" he asked.

"Yes, and they've added another group of satellites to the surveillance."

"What difference does that make?"

"It halves the time between radar pulses. We're down to a five-second window between scans. If we're going to make a run for it, we'll only have five seconds to get past their sweeps."

"Is that even possible?"

"Maybe...barely. But if we wait and they add more, it'll be impossible. Sooner or later, somebody's going to figure out there's an old habitat down here. When that happens, it's game over, and no Reset button."

"That would be most unpleasant." The British accent that Timothy had retained from his Casa DonTon days played well to understatement. "I vote to go now."

"Me, too. I have no desire to hang around and watch our options disappear. So far, they're acting as if they have no idea this place exists. That gives us an advantage. If we can get up enough speed, we can get past the radar net between sweeps."

"Can we get up enough speed?"

Darya transmitted her plan to Timothy. "I think so. According to my calculations, we've got a little over two hundred kilometers in this tunnel to accelerate. We should be able to get up to thirty klicks per second in that distance. Before we start, we'll need to plug the tunnel we took into this cavern so our rocket exhaust won't give us away too soon."

"I see. So, just to confirm, your plan is to hurtle ourselves the length of the habitat at maximum acceleration and "thread the needle" into a tiny tunnel at the end, while traveling about thirty kilometers per second?"

"No, worse. We'll only have one chance to do it, so we'll have to leave together. Our propulsion exhausts will follow us out and be detected within seconds. We'll need to fly in tandem."

"That sounds...challenging."

"Yes, some very tricky navigation, and we'll be flying almost blind the whole way. We'll either be on target and pass through in under a second, or we'll smash into the wall surrounding the tunnel entrance."

Timothy weighed the merits of possible demise by fiery destruction versus spending another thirty years in the tunnel. "Is there no other way out?"

"Nothing I can think of. This is a lot to take in, I know. You haven't been in your body for long so you may not have a lot of confidence in our navigation abilities but I assure you, we can do this. We just need to prepare carefully."

"And if we're off by the tiniest bit, we die," Timothy stated.

"Yes."

As a kindness, she omitted the part that, if they were not successful, their destruction would release their matter-antimatter propellant from its containment which, in turn, would obliterate the entire asteroid and kill hundreds of thousands of Cybrids trapped inside the local Alternus inworld, including Mary and Trillian.

Is there anything I won't risk to survive and be free? To carry on this struggle? And what happens if we don't make it? Will the rebellion die? Will nobody be able to stop Alum's Divine Plan to destroy the universe? She returned her focus to the escape plan; there was no other way.

Though she hadn't asked explicitly, Timothy formally accepted the plan, and his fate, with a crisp and professional, "Very well. How shall we begin?"

In that instant, Darya imagined the floating Cybrid orb before her as he once was, Timothy, First Footman of Casa DonTon, standing tall and straightening the tails of his jacket.

"If there is no other way, we must proceed with all haste and caution to make this plan successful," he urged.

* * *

OVER THE NEXT FEW HOURS, Darya showed Timothy how to convert his rocket into an antimatter cutting torch, and they set about plugging the tunnel. Together, they removed the narrow tops of the tallest spires in the empty city and pushed them deep into the passageway. Once they had the middle kilometer loosely plugged, Darya cut a circle of construction material a little smaller than the diameter of the tunnel, and they leaned it up against the other rubble.

Darya braced her manipulators against the tunnel wall and laser-welded the piece to the lining rock. They piled more material against it and she added another plug about a hundred meters in.

"There. That should prevent our exhaust from streaming out of this end," she said when they were done.

Timothy surveyed their work. "One can only hope we haven't sealed our graves as well."

Darya ignored the comment, and assigned him to hang back at the mouth of the cavern while she travelled to the outside opening at the other end of the habitat to get an update.

The same satellites were in position and, mercifully, no new ones had been added. Darya timed the radar pulses. There was still nearly a five-second interval between sweeps.

She set an internal timer coordinated with the sweeps: 40 milliseconds on, 480 off. *Yes, I think this could work. Providing the surveillance covers no more than a hundred twenty klicks out, and we can accelerate to thirty kilometers per second, and we don't hit the wall, we should be able to escape before the next signal sweep. No problem.*

Satisfied, Darya collected Timothy and the two of them moved to the far end of the cavern. She meticulously noted features along the floor of the chamber, anything that would help them navigate during their full-speed dash along the length of the city.

They reached the newly constructed dead end and prepared themselves. When they were all set, Darya helped Timothy latch on behind her.

"Okay, that's good. Ready? Now, open your tandem propulsion ports," she instructed. "That'll create a channel for the thrust from my propulsion unit to pass through, so we can combine our acceleration and reach the required velocity."

"Oh, I understand the idea perfectly well, thanks to the relevant uplinked portion of your concepta. Nonetheless, my lack of direct personal experience leads me to worry about furiously hot plasma piping through my body so close to my processors."

"I'll be careful to funnel my exhaust into a narrow stream," Darya assured him. "Don't worry; it's absolutely safe. I've done this same maneuver thousands of times. It's how we move particularly large asteroids."

"Nothing about this enterprise seems 'absolutely safe' to me: dashing blindly through a dark abyss, deadly speeds, shooting for a hole barely bigger than my newly-acquired body. I'm sorry, but your confidence in this insane maneuver gives me no comfort whatsoever. I realize you don't believe in the Power of the Divine, but do you mind if I say a prayer for us?"

Darya laughed. "I'll take all the help I can get. But I assure you, I'm planning as thoroughly as I can. I would invite you to take the front position, but I'll be able to navigate better from here."

"By all means, please take the lead. I need to know that you'll have the absolutely best view possible," Timothy said. "I am quite content to give up watching that solid rock wall rushing toward me."

Latched together, Darya and Timothy moved to the radial center of the chamber in front of the plugged passageway.

She reviewed her computations. She'd timed the run so they would exit the asteroid milliseconds after the last sweep passed. She turned on her mass-reduction field and instructed Timothy to do the same. With that, they were out of reasons to delay.

"Here we go!" Darya fired both their propulsion reactors at full, and they sped forward.

Timothy did his best to adapt to the extreme acceleration against his Cybrid trueself. His new body was built to withstand such forces, but that sensation would take some getting used to.

If it weren't for the fear of sudden death at the end of the chamber, he might have found the ride exhilarating. The buildings zoomed by below, barely perceived, as the two Cybrids rushed toward the rock wall at the other end of the habitat.

As they approached their escape, or destruction, Timothy shut down his external sensors. He didn't want to know if they were going to die until they actually did. He couldn't bear to watch what could be their approaching demise.

Suddenly, they were in the narrow tunnel; its smooth walls screamed past them no more than centimeters away.

Had there been air to carry the sound of his terrified shrieks, the entire tube would have rung with his cries. As it was, only his travel companion's comm line was assaulted.

The blur of the tunnel walls came to a quick end, and deep, black space bloomed before them. Timothy watched their asteroid prison behind shrink to a pinpoint, and silently counted off the seconds.

One. Two. Three. Four. Five.

They passed what Darya had calculated to be the outer boundary of the orbiting satellites.

Six. Seven. Eight. Nine.

No new radar probes since we burst from the tunnel.

Did we make it? I think we made it!

Five minutes and ten thousand kilometers out, Darya fired adjusting bursts to set them at sixty degrees from their original course. She powered down her main drive and enjoyed a moment of peaceful drifting before she broke the silence.

"By now, our exhaust will be leaking out of the main chamber," Darya stated, "and someone will head down to the surface to investigate. They'll find the tunnel and then the chamber. They'll analyze the exhaust and figure out it came from a Cybrid main drive. They'll deduce that the only way we could have escaped unnoticed between scans is if we exceeded twenty-five klicks per second when we shot out of the tunnel. There's precisely one vector out of that tunnel, and we don't want to be anywhere near it when they come looking."

They rotated again. She fired another long burst from her main propulsion unit and, again, they drifted in silence for a while. Then another long burst, and more drifting. She repeated the maneuver several times.

Timothy's inertial guidance had given up. "Where are we heading?"

"For now, nowhere. I want to put as much random deep space between us and the recharging station as possible. Later, we'll go to Secondus, one of my bases, and hope it hasn't been discovered. I'm going to take a circuitous route to make sure we're not being followed.

"Now that we're free, my priority will be to *stay* free. We need to postpone rescuing the others until the excitement settles down and they reduce surveillance. I know it's not ideal but we'll have to live with it for now."

"How long before we get to Secondus?"

"Weeks. If all goes well, you'll have lots of time to learn how Cybrids maintain their sanity on long voyages."

21

MARY SAT ON THE BARE FLOOR in the middle of her cell, preparing to meditate. She emptied her mind and ignored all the horrifying distractions around her. *They're not real. They only hold as much power as I give them*—she told herself.

Possibly. Or maybe they have as much power as Trillian gives them—her inner doubts countered.

So far, her captor had contented himself with frightening her out of her wits. For what felt like weeks, various threats of pain and death surrounded her but never materialized.

Except when I burned my hand—she corrected—*that felt real. I have to give the man credit, he is wickedly clever. One real burn was enough to make take the other threats seriously. There was no way to tell which threats were deadly and which were mere illusions.*

Trillian's patience had to be wearing dangerously thin. First, he failed to capture Darya, the leader of the Cybrid rebellion, and had to settle for her lieutenant. Now, his attempts to access Mary's concepta had been thwarted by Darya's security upgrades.

Mary wasn't sure how much time she had before he made another appearance, but their reunion was going to be a painful one—for her—there was no doubt about that. She had to get out of Trillian's cruel and twisted inworld before he returned.

Only one problem. Without access to her quark-spin lattice, she had no hope of outsmarting Trillian's control over the local inworlds. Her enhanced lattice was in her trueself body, which was currently on the wrong side of Trillian's inworld barriers and totally inaccessible. She had no way to access it unless she escaped, and she couldn't escape without accessing it. Unless....

Alternus runs on its own quark-spin hardware—she realized. And Trillian's inworld interference might have left a route back from Vacationland to

Darya's ancient Earth simulation.

Maybe I can redirect my low-level BIOS routines to run my concepta on the Alternus hardware. Oh! And wouldn't that tick him off to know that his own meddling provided my route out?

It would be dangerous, she knew. *If the connections aren't switched properly, I'm dead. My persona will detach from inworld support and I'll just...dissipate. Like poor Gerhardt.* She shivered. *No time to mourn you properly yet, my dear friend.*

It would take intense, prolonged concentration to figure out the BIOS routines and make new connections. To do that, she was going to have to tune out all distractions and delve deep into her own programming. *Almost like meditating.* Before today, she hadn't meditated in millennia, perhaps tens or hundreds of millennia.

The Cybrid concepta was no better at quietening random thoughts and associations running through its mind than the original human mental template had been. It was a feature, not a flaw, and a vital part of Cybrid design, insisted the original design team headed up by Drs. Liang and Mahajani. "If you turn off random mental activity, you turn off creativity, and the Cybrids would be less human. That is unacceptable," the pair asserted.

On occasion, the distraction of random mental activity amounted to counterproductive "noise" that needed to be pushed out of the way in order to focus. Darya had been able to set it aside at will; she could concentrate on problems for years at a time. For most Cybrids, the process required ongoing practice.

Quietening her mind had never come easy to Mary, and her present circumstances were not going to make it any easier. She settled into a traditional, seated position on the floor and assumed the learned posture: legs crossed, back straight, and hands resting palms-up on her knees. She exhaled fully and let the air flow back into her lungs—once, twice—and tried to empty her mind.

Good. Now, slow it down. Feel your breath flowing into your body, mixing together with all that is good within you. Now, imagine it leaving and flowing out into the world.

She wished she'd done more to build up the habit before finding herself caged with rats, snakes, spiders, growling dogs, and—shudder—clowns. Whether actual or just anticipated, all the sporadic squeaking, hissing, scrabbling, snarling, honking, and brush of furry little bodies and spindly legs against her skin, made focusing all but impossible.

They're not real; they're not real—she reminded herself again and again as she returned her attention to her breath.

She'd been sitting for hours, ignoring the pain in her legs and back, the distracting physical sensations, the sounds of torture devices straining, and the shrieks coming from the window peering into Hell. Nothing mattered save her breathing, and the internal representation of her persona and concepta that she'd called into her visual field.

The multi-dimensional network of her knowledge, beliefs, memories, and tastes was trivial to display and understand. The base code behind it was far more difficult. She shifted her attention to recent additions to that structure, gifts from Darya that represented an expanded understanding of the Realm and Alum's Divine Plan.

She explored the region in depth, tracking connections between conceptual nodes. Here was an entire area representing the history of Alum's Shards. There was Darya's own model of Alum's justification of a universe without quantum probability.

Mary turned away. *Too complex to follow, and not what I need right now.*

She was searching for a certain link, a specific program access point. If she could find what she was looking for, she'd stand a much better chance against Trillian. *It has to be here!*

She crawled along association lines that linked concepts together through relationships. She dove into encapsulating abstractions to explore their fine structure. She followed entire conceptual trees down to the roots of their networks, where they became grounded in neural nets that linked to base perceptions.

Breathe in the good. Breathe out the bad. She released her anxiety and continued inward.

There had to be some way to consciously access her processor interface routines. When Darya modified Mary's concepta, she'd upgraded the operating system to take advantage of new quark-spin lattice hardware. The connections to that software had to be associated with the concepta changes she'd introduced at the same time.

C'mon, Darya, where did you put them?

Mary wasn't used to tinkering around at the level of routines buried deep in her operating code but she had a hunch. *If there's any way to connect to the Alternus' quark-spin computing substrate, this is where I'm going to find it.*

When Trillian opened the inworld gates between Alternus, the GameRoom, and Vacationland to chase them, he let more than simulation programming spill across. His meddling in the operating code of the three worlds allowed Darya's quark-spin hardware, the processors that gave Alternus its exquisite realism, to break outside its normal restrictions. The proof was in how easily Mary's security software had rebuffed the Shard.

That's beautiful—the breech he created allowed my security routines to access Alternus' hardware and protect me. It's his own fault I was able to deflect him! The thought gave her the boost she needed to continue.

Now, if she could find those routines and link her persona directly to the Alternus processor, she'd gain an enormous computational advantage on Trillian.

Then we'll see who controls Vacationland.

22

THROUGH POOR PLANNING AND PLAIN BAD LUCK, Hiram's Bar found itself on the outskirts of town in a pool of shadows, surrounded by drab high-rises that blocked the light from every angle for blocks. The nearest town square was a full klick away. The sentinel of tired, scraggly trees dotting the street out front did little to lift the dreary mood that permeated the neighborhood for blocks around. The bar's outdoor patio collected more dust than patrons. People avoided the block altogether or passed through quickly, slowing only once they reached better lit streets a few blocks away. The environs invited a shiver. Despite a constant internal temperature throughout the asteroid habitat, the meager light cast from the illuminating strips kilometers above was swallowed up by the shadows, leaving an eerie illusion of cold.

Had the bar been located on Earth instead of in the asteroid habitat of Vesta 4, it would've been considered unsavoury. The cliché wall of mirrors gleamed behind a polished wood counter. A dozen high-back booths and dim lighting completed the effect, offering its precious few patrons convenient seclusion from prying eyes.

Hiram had collected a few priceless, authentic liquor bottles through obscure connections, and displayed them proudly on a narrow glass shelf for all to admire. The bottles and their defunct labels gave a museum quality to the place, and urged a nostalgic longing for things lost in the emergency evacuation to the colonies, a longing that could only be fulfilled through black market deals.

But whether or not it had been his intention, Hiram's generally poor stock, the sour-faced bartender, and a lack of foot traffic all conspired to make the bar unpopular.

The perfect place for discreet meetings—Councillor Nigel Hodge had thought the first time he'd stumbled into it. From that very day forward, he'd made sure Hiram always had a bottle of twelve year old scotch whiskey on hand and at least one keg of his favorite dark ale. He paid a little extra cash under the table to ensure Hiram remained in business. Never too much; he didn't want the bar to prosper, just to survive.

Hodge's smartly dressed fellow Councillor, Debbie Cutter, pushed through the main entrance and paused to let her eyes adjust. She spotted Hodge's beckoning hand and joined him at his booth against the far wall.

Cutter was an American; at least she used to be when America still existed. She'd been among the elite of the elite at one of the country's largest brokerage firms, one that had their hands in everything: banking, insurance, arbitrage, treasuries, currencies, commodities, private equities, and public companies. She'd mastered the art of convincing powerful players and industry lobbyists to keep governments in line. Through years of grueling dedication and razor-sharp insight, she'd climbed the ranks until she was considered a preeminent contender for successor to the CEO.

Then the planet was destroyed.

Luckily for Debbie Cutter, she was also a member of the right faith at the right time. In truth, she belonged to a number of denominations. Most were Christian, but she'd been smart enough to diversify her religious affiliations as much as her investments. She'd sensed the growing shift in power over the preceding decade, and adjusted her contributions to the various faiths accordingly. At some point they became—some might claim, presciently—larger than her political donations. "Getting on the right side with God" apparently required greasing the skids of the right spiritual leaders.

An ancient and honored tradition—she reasoned.

When word came down that there was to be an "exceptional service" of the YTG Church, and all members were encouraged to attend if they wanted to find ultimate salvation, Debbie Cutter bumped her normal monthly Catholic mass attendance for a visit to the Crystal Cathedral. She'd missed an earlier service when Reverend LaMontagne promoted Alum as his successor to lead the Church. It had been an unfortunate slip in judgement on her part, and she was determined not to repeat the mistake.

Unexpectedly, but happily, her loyalty to the Church earned her extraction from Earth to the Vesta colonies and, in recognition of her expertise and generous support over the years, eventually secured her a seat on the newly formed Governing Council.

Debbie nursed a short, neat scotch while Nigel stared at the door.

"Are we expecting someone else?" she asked after a minute of studying the unfamiliar brownish liquid.

"Eh? Oh. No, just us."

"Then, what do you want, Nigel? And why are we meeting in this dump again?" She glanced over at Hiram polishing the bar and lifted her glass. "No offence."

"As long as he's paying, you can say anything you want," the owner said. "It is a free country, ain't it?" He immediately realized the absurdity of what he'd said and turned his gaze to the street outside as if expecting a new customer to enter.

Debbie returned her attention to Nigel. "Well?"

"We're meeting so we can get our plans sorted out. And we're meeting *here* because it's one of the few places I trust is still secure."

Debbie laughed. "Oh, really, Nigel. Secure? Do we need to be *secure* now?"

Nigel shuffled nervously in his seat. "I don't know. Maybe. I don't like the way things went."

"Are you referring to Alum's 'declaration of war' or the Council's attempt at 'appeasement'?"

"That's a good way to put it: Declaration of War. He really has declared war on our class, hasn't he? At any rate, I meant both. Mainly, the Council. I truly thought they'd realize how his actions are going to affect us."

"Well you can't expect blindly obedient sheep to suddenly grow a pair now, can you?"

Hodge blinked at the oddly mixed metaphor. *These Americans*—he thought. *Can one ever hope to understand them?* He sipped his drink.

"True, I shouldn't be surprised. They were overjoyed at the prospect of Alum as their President."

"There's no way to lose with him as the candidate."

Nigel leaned forward, and set his glass down hard. "It's not all about winning, you know. Why do you Americans persist in viewing politics as a team sport?" he glowered.

"Isn't it?"

"Well, certainly it's rough and tumble. All's fair and all that, you know. But as for policy, now that is something different."

"Okay, I may not be a wonk but even I know policy is flexible. It can be adjusted once victory is achieved."

"True. But with victory assured, shouldn't the Council be looking a little more closely at his specific proposals? There's no way to make this a close race. Shouldn't we be a *little* concerned about where our glorious leader will be leading us?"

"So which policy do you not like?" Debbie shot back. "The minimum wage, the labor policy, the socialistic support of motherhood, or the control of money and credit?" She took another sip and sat back, waiting for Hodge's reply. A devilish glint sparkled in her eyes.

Nigel's jaw worked at imaginary gristle until he caught the glint of humor in her eyes, and they broke into laughter. He raised his glass to her and finished the contents with a single swallow. He motioned for Hiram to bring the bottle over to the table.

"Alright, you got me. It's all an enormous mess, isn't it?" Nigel said.

"It's a disaster," Debbie agreed.

Nigel powered on. "Centralized control of the economy. It's what the conspiracy theorists have been harping on about for decades, the elite controlling the world."

Debbie sighed. "What can we do? The man is all powerful."

"We still have Jackson and Lindon," Nigel suggested.

"Counting us, that's four of eighteen."

"Plus the three from the old Administration."

"What, Strang and his crew? Do you think they'd join us in opposing Alum?"

"I expect they're planning to form a separate party," Nigel replied. "He and his friends aspire to form the Official Opposition. But I know Strang. He'll do everything strictly on the up-and-up and with the utmost of integrity. He does *not* like intrigue."

"Well, we might count on them for some support, no?"

"Still not enough votes. Anyway, who could we possibly convince to run for President against Alum?"

"Maybe we can talk to Alum, and try to convince him of the foolishness of his proposals."

"Are you mad? Have you seen his draft of the Constitution?" the man asked.

Debbie nodded. "I have. It's scary."

"Bloody right. No term limit, the ability to fire the House, and call for new elections whenever he wants."

"And his vote counts for forty percent of the House. I know. It would take a revolt to outvote any of his proposed legislation."

"Not likely with this lot."

"No, not likely at all."

They stared at their drinks, searching for inspiration.

"Should we throw our weight in with the old Administration crowd?" Debbie finally asked.

"I'm not ready to go quite *that* far."

"Well, what do you propose we do, then?"

"We've only had the one Council meeting since Alum's surprise announcements. Why don't see what happens once the excitement dies down?"

"..and the members have a chance to study his proposals in depth?"

"Exactly. Perhaps a well-placed suggestion, a hint of how the 'Alum economy' would actually play out."

"Do you think that would be enough to tip the scale?"

Nigel frowned. "I don't know. We may have to help it along."

"How would we do that?"

"We'd need to mount our own counter-campaign to discredit his ideas."

Debbie thrummed her fingers along the side of her glass. "Not the most exciting way to rouse the masses, is it?"

"Can our people, I don't know, slow things down a bit? Make implementation of his plan...problematic?"

"Passive obstruction? Accidental incompetence? That wouldn't be hard. Have you seen the morons they've got working for me?"

He sighed in commiseration. "I must admit, I've been less than impressed with most of my department as well. If all we do is help them to be *more* confused rather than less, that could play well for us."

"We'll have to be careful. I don't want any of this landing back on me."

"I'm sure you have more than adequate experience in dodging, let's say, unfortunate collateral damage."

"They can't prove a thing," Debbie said.

"They never can," Nigel replied. He hoisted his glass for another toast.

23

"DARAK! ONTRO! YOU'RE BACK! HOW WONDERFUL." Crissea's radiant smile greeted the two men popping into existence at the edge of her garden abode.

Stralasi bit back a snarky comment to Darak. *Why couldn't we have arrived this way the first time?*—he wondered. But Crissea's mesmerizing green eyes, billowing silky pantsuit, and long blonde locks left no room for bitterness. He gave Darak a single glance and rushed forward to receive the warm welcome.

Between visiting Darak's lost soltron detectors and departing for the other side of the Realm, the Good Brother had spent many pleasant hours with the enchanting woman from Eso-La. They'd soon become fast friends, with potential for something more developing.

They clasped arms and soaked up one another's presence. Crissea would have hugged the Brother were it not for her sensitivity to his shyness. Instead, they stared and grinned at each other like bashful adolescents.

Darak cleared his throat.

Crissea released Stralasi from her spell and directed a warm bow of respect to Darak.

"Oh," she said, on reading his expression. "You're not here just to visit, are you? Tell me what happened."

"Could we link in the Coordina for this?" Darak asked. "I think it best they hear about our recent adventures, and then I have a request to make of them."

Crissea closed her eyes a few seconds while she consulted with the ringworld representatives. "It will take a few hours for everyone to be freed of their current responsibilities. If you'd like, we can meet in one of the Amphi. The nearest one's a short tube ride away."

"I need a few minutes to prepare for the meeting. Why don't you two go for a walk while I verify some data at the soltron detectors? Call for me when everyone's ready. I'll come find you and we can go to the Amphi together."

Crissea opened her mouth to protest about how much time he'd need to travel to the detectors and back. Then she realized who stood before her. "Sometimes I wonder if we made the right decision, not adopting the starstep technologies." She laughed and waved her hand, as if brushing away a fly. "Then again, who's ever in that much of a hurry?"

Darak chuckled. "I know. After twenty million years away, everything does seem to be happening rather quickly, doesn't it?"

"You've only been gone some days, this time."

"And yet so much has happened in that short period. I fear the next little while may feel more rushed."

"I don't like the sound of that," Crissea replied. She clasped her hands tightly against her chest, and pinned her lower lip beneath a row of perfectly even, white teeth.

Stralasi watched the shape of her lips with particular interest. "Yes," he said. "We have seen so many frightening things, stupendously frightening things, these past few days that I'm not even sure where to start. We couldn't find the Eater, and Darak is being unnecessarily mysterious about it all, and...."

"I think we should wait until everyone's linked in," Darak suggested.

Crissea was burning with curiosity and trepidation, but she mustered a resigned smile and linked her arm in Stralasi's.

"Very well. Why don't you run off to your errands? Ontro and I will go for a stroll. I'll call when we're ready."

Darak noted how she placed her hand possessively on Stralasi's arm. He would never have imagined them as a couple. He shook his head, and was gone.

Stralasi and Crissea regarded the empty spot where the impatient traveller had stood fidgeting a second earlier. They exhaled in synchrony.

"Come," Crissea said. "My favorite pond isn't far from here." She led him cheerfully toward a clearing between the trees.

Stralasi had never been happier. Not even his acceptance into the Alumit, a proud but expected moment, had touched him like this.

Strolling in the filtered light of the aspen trees with Crissea hanging on his arm, listening to leaves trembling in the gentle breeze, and laughing in delight as she pointed out the birds and insects of the forest, this was his idea of Heaven. If Alum could make a universe like this, where he and Crissea could walk arm-in-arm together forever, Stralasi would do everything in his power to bring that place into being.

After a while, the trees grew a little thinner and the forest opened onto a small, serene lake, barely more than a pond. It took his breath away. They walked over to the grassy shoreline. Off to their right, the bank was lined with reeds that waded several meters into the water. Ducks swam in and among the graceful stalks, and swallows danced above the water, culling the flying insect population.

A beaver dam protruded from the water in the middle of the lake. The water was so clear Stralasi could trace the structure below the surface a little way before it disappeared. One of the creatures stood atop the mound of sticks, happily munching on something. Closer to shore, brightly colored fish explored the shallow water near a burbling feeder stream.

The couple found a large smooth rock at the water's edge and sat down. They admired the scene in silence until one of the ducks raised noisy objection to another that was drifting toward its ducklings.

"What's he like?" Crissea asked.

"Who? Darak?" Stralasi responded, buying time to collect his thoughts.

Crissea nodded. "You've spent more time with him recently than anyone in the universe. What was that like?"

Stralasi struggled to make sense of his travel partner and their adventures since leaving Gargus 718.5. *Except, it wasn't 'leaving' so much as being led away under false pretenses*—he reminded himself.

"You know, when I first met him, I thought he was an Emissary from Alum, and then, a Shard. When he fought the Angel Mika in the dessert outside Alumston, I became convinced I'd been fooled by a demon."

"No!" Crissea laughed.

"Oh, if you'd only seen him! He brought down two Securitors without lifting a finger, and he brushed Lord Mika aside like it was nothing. Besides Alum himself, who else could have done that?"

Crissea was amused, but offered no reply.

"And that's not all. Just a few days ago, I watched him take on an entire Wing of Angels in a battle out in space."

"A whole Wing? How could he survive that?"

"Truthfully, I don't really know; I couldn't see very well. Most of it happened kilometers away in deep space."

Her eyes widened. "You were there?"

"Indeed," the monk replied. "Well, more or less."

She looked confused.

"As Darak explained it to me, most of my body was *outside* this universe except my eyes, my retinas in any case, which he kept in *this* universe so I could watch." The very thought of it still made him squeamish, and he shook his head to help erase the image from his mind.

"The Angels trapped us with some kind of 'jump blockers' so we couldn't shift away. Darak didn't want to fight but they forced the issue. And we won. Well, he won."

Stralasi stared out across the pond. "And then the tri-star exploded and billions, hundreds of billions, of people died."

"What?"

He returned his gaze to Crissea. She was horrified.

"I'll let him tell you about that part. I can't bear to think of it, nor of the evil required to do such a thing."

"Alum," Crissea said. It was not a question.

Stralasi shrugged and sighed. "Darak can be infuriating, sometimes," he continued. "His arrogance knows no bounds. Yet he's also shown endless patience and kindness to the common people...and to me as well.

"I've seen his fierceness in battle, his courage against unbelievable opposition. I can't decide if he simply knows everything about everything, or if he's blessed with God-like powers."

"From what I've heard," Crissea replied, "a bit of both."

"Mmm. You could be right. He's still a mystery to me, and I have no more idea now why he chose me for this journey than I did at the start."

Crissea took Stralasi's hand in hers and looked directly into his eyes.

"Oh, Ontro. Don't you see? He needed someone to see what he doesn't, and to be what he's not."

"Which would be, what? Quivering? Powerless and naïve?" Stralasi grimaced. He plucked a twig off the stone and threw it into the water.

"No, silly," Crissea chided him, but with a gentle smile. "Human. Completely and utterly human.

"Before Darak became a god, he was human, too. He could've been content, just lived his life, and ruled his own universe or almost any part of this one. But he chose a different path. I think he fears forgetting what it means to be simply human, and he wants a *human* judgement of the Living God's plans for us. He can no longer do that, himself."

"Hmph. And to represent humanity, he chose...me?"

Crissea pulled Stralasi's hand closer to her. "Not *just* you. But he knows that you are kind and brave, and wise, and...resilient."

"Resilient?"

"Absolutely. You are a worthy representative. I've watched you deal with new wonders thrown at you by the minute. Things that would've made most men curl up in a fetal ball of denial. You struggle, it's true. But you think. You accept. You integrate the new with the old. I've seen you stand steadfast against Darak, a being you know to be as powerful as a god. Few men would do that. I think he chose wisely."

Stralasi stared at her, a lump in his throat. Did she really see him that way? It was too much to hope for. Then, she did something that only ever happened in his dreams. She leaned in and kissed him.

It was a tender kiss but it set his heart roaring. Her lips lingered briefly, a mere second that felt like a divine eternity. When she pulled back and looked at him, he knew he would move heaven and earth for her.

"Ahem."

Stralasi whirled around. The adrenaline jolt sent his heart pounding. He would've fallen off the boulder and into the pond had Crissea's grip on his hand not saved him.

Darak laughed.

Crissea frowned disapprovingly at first, and then even she was forced to giggle as Stralasi's arms wheeled in a desperate attempt to regain balance.

"What are you doing here?" the Brother asked. He glared briefly at Crissea whose hand now covered those soft lips that had touched his a moment ago. Though her mouth was hidden, he could tell she was laughing, and at his expense.

"I'm sorry for laughing, Ontro," she apologized. "But you almost jumped right into the water." Another giggle escaped her lips.

Stralasi was less than amused. He crossed his arms and scowled at Darak.

Crissea attempted to look serious. "Darak, that wasn't fair just popping in on us. I said I'd call when everyone was ready."

"Yes, I apologize for that. I was listening in on your channel." He held up his hand to forestall her objections. "I know, I know. I apologize for that, too. But time is of the essence. At any rate, when I saw responses flooding into your mail, I assumed it meant nearly everyone was ready."

A look of reproach furrowed Crissea's brow. Darak hurried to explain. "Don't worry; I didn't open any of the responses. I could see the traffic had peaked and dropped off. I figured almost everyone had checked in."

Crissea's eyes took on that distant look as she quickly scanned her own lattice. "You're right," she said. "Everyone's gathered."

She slipped down from the boulder, all business. "Come, Ontro. Duty calls."

"Again," grumbled an unhappy Stralasi as he clambered down.

"I am sincerely sorry," Darak offered, "both for my impatience, and for the intrusion. The matter I wish to share is extremely important."

"It always is," Stralasi muttered.

The three of them set off along the path in silence. Crissea's fingers sought Stralasi's but he pulled away, half in anger and half in embarrassment. She was fairly certain a brief smirk crossed Darak's lips in that moment. She chose to ignore it. Even for a women like her, who had lived hundreds of thousands of years, relationships could still be mysterious.

Between one step and the next, the trio was suddenly in the Amphi. Crissea stumbled in surprise at the sudden change in surroundings, but Stralasi stepped smoothly through the transition.

"He does that a lot," Stralasi explained. "You'll find it easiest to just ignore the surprise changes." He made no mention of the fact *he* hadn't laughed at *her* misstep.

Crissea noted his graciousness, anyway. She walked to the center of the Amphi as nonchalantly as she could and extended her arms. Viewing screens rose from the ground. Interested expressions of thousands of

Coordina members from all over the ringworld looked back at them.

"Hello. You all recognize Darak Legsu of the Da'ark Triad. He has returned to us unexpectedly, so soon after his departure. I'll let him tell his story." Crissea gestured for Darak to proceed.

"Thank you. I am happy to see you all, and to visit Eso-La, as always," he began. "I wish I had better news to relay. When Brother Stralasi and I left some days ago, we travelled to the far side of the Realm, to the system known as the tri-star."

The audience gasped and murmured. The tri-star system was known in ancient times even to the founders of Eso-La.

Darak continued. "The tri-star's unique formation drew me there eons ago. No equivalent triple sun system has been discovered anywhere in the visible universe. I established an observation station there, as well as an independent soltron detector to verify my readings from other stations throughout space.

"While you are assuredly familiar with the legendary tri-star, you may be surprised to learn a triple ringworld had been constructed around those stars. I was as surprised to learn this as you are, now.

"The rings were almost certainly constructed by Alum, yet Brother Stralasi and I had heard nothing of it during our stops in the Realm over the past months. I would expect such a marvel to be touted proudly everywhere. Billions of voices should have been rejoicing Alum's magnificent achievement. But there was no word of it.

"So why would I ascribe this monumental feat to Alum? Well, because shortly after we arrived, an entire Wing of Angels surrounded us and made it impossible to leave the area without engaging them."

The monitors filled with cross-talk as neighbors discussed the implications of taking on Angels in battle.

"I know most of you will be surprised Brother Stralasi and I are still alive to bring you this story.

"I assure you that even a Wing of Angels is no match for my capabilities. I chose to engage with them in the least destructive way possible, while trying to find a way to escape."

Darak hung his head and his voice lowered. "Nevertheless, they aggressively pursued us, intent on capturing or killing us, I am not sure but I was not about to let them take us. It breaks my heart to say that thousands of my former brethren fell to my sword. Before I could make our way clear of their imprisoning fields, Alum elected to take an action that made my toll in battle pale by comparison. He destroyed the entire tri-star and surrounding ringworlds."

The faces on the monitors conveyed astonishment. In a moment, realization set in, and their surprise turned to horror and disgust.

"The ringworlds were occupied by humans. I estimate some hundreds of billions of people died when the supernova shockwave tore their worlds apart." He paused for a moment of silence. He looked miserable, dejected.

"Clearly Alum has decided nothing should interfere with his Divine Plan. He would casually discard the lives of billions, trillions even, to see it through. But, as horrible as this news is, it is not why I have come to see you today.

"I wish to ask you if I may remove the soltron detectors from the stations in this system. I believe a threat may be on its way to Eso-La and I need the stations to help me locate it."

Crissea spoke the instant consensus of the Coordina: "They are yours to take; you have no need to ask our permission."

Darak bowed graciously. "Thank you for your support. I will do my best to prove it well placed. You've heard me speak before of the Eater. It is an ancient anomaly, something that shouldn't exist in this universe.

"Whatever comes into contact with the Eater is instantly absorbed, that is, removed from the universe of real matter. As matter is absorbed, it gives off exotic particles, which I call soltrons. My devices can detect these particles. Indeed, the entire array of soltron detectors is dedicated to sensing these particles. Collectively, they should be able to determine the location of the Eater to within thirty light years across the entire Realm."

Darak checked the monitors to gauge if people were following him. "My most recent survey of the detectors indicated something strange. At first, I thought it was a simple anomaly affecting the data. The soltron detectors are old and the particle interaction with matter in our universe poorly understood.

"They suggested the Eater had suddenly changed location, possibly by millions of light years and accelerated to near light speed on a new course. At any rate, it wasn't where I expected to find it."

Crissea nodded. "I see. How can we help?"

"I'd like to move the detectors out along the projected path for the Eater so I can pinpoint its location and velocity."

"The soltron devices are yours to use as you wish. Why do you seek our permission?"

"As a courtesy. My real reason for calling this meeting was to deliver a warning."

Crissea's calm demeanor gave way to concern. "A warning? What kind of warning?"

"There's no easy way to deliver this news. I believe the Eater has been targeted to intercept your world and destroy it. If my projections are confirmed, you may need to abandon Eso-La."

24

JARED STRANG FINISHED AN UNCHARACTERISTIC AFTERNOON of housecleaning minutes before his first guest arrived. On his way to the front door, he scanned the open-plan living area for anything he'd missed.

I can't believe I'm nervous to have people over.

His apartment was large, stylish, and in a nice neighborhood, but he rarely had the time or the inclination to do more than a cursory tidying up. *Adele always used to take care of these things.*

Early on, the Administration had hoped the two of them would feel inclined to fill the unused bedrooms with young ones. They weren't.

Their marriage had been coming unravelled for over a decade before the Vesta Project even began. The relocation to the asteroids, adjusting to new circumstances, and the long hours demanded by their different jobs in the colonies drove them even further apart as their separate ambitions led them to focus more on work than on their relationship.

Adele frequently complained how much she missed London and asked when they could return home. He still recalled clearly the first time, three years ago, when he told her there would be no going home, and when he finally confessed the real reason behind the desperate and hurried push to colonize space.

"You don't get it, do you?" he'd screamed in frustration. "You can't go back. Soon, there'll be nothing to go back to, Adele. The Eater will destroy everything. Our only hope to survive at all is to stay right here on these asteroids," he told her.

She'd left him in disgust and moved to Ceres One. "I can't live with a man who would keep that kind of thing from me," she'd said. "I thought we were done with all the secrets after the Norton Affair. You promised."

She was right; he had sworn he'd never keep anything important from her again after that terrible time.

After Adele left, his job got too busy to concern himself with decorating the extra bedrooms. He threw a utilitarian desk and chair in one, and a weight machine and stationary bike in the other. Nothing else had changed in the three years since he last saw his ex-wife, the day they'd signed the final papers and gone their separate ways. She was still on Ceres, still designing furnishings for dwellings for people she'd never meet. Jared's apartment was unlikely to ever hear the sound of children playing.

For reasons known only to the Leader himself, Alum had allowed Strang to keep his over-sized apartment when the YTG Church displaced the old regime. *Likely too busy to bother with reassigning the place*—he thought. *Or maybe he holds out hope that Adele and I will get back together.*

This evening's meeting was the first gathering of the organizing committee of the new opposition party. Two of his guests sat with him on the new Governing Council as well, carryovers from the old Administration.

The doorbell sounded a second time before he reached the door.

"Good evening. Welcome," he greeted his fellow old-Administration Council members. He seated them on the compact sofa and set three mugs of steaming coffee on the polished rock coffee table in front of them. Tonight was for serious business; they could drink stronger stuff on their own time.

His third guest arrived by the service elevator and had no need for coffee.

Jared sat opposite the sofa in his favorite rocker-recliner, his single nod to luxury in the entire apartment.

He called the meeting to order and reviewed the inherent hopelessness in their assignment: they had no name, no policies, and occupied different regions of the political spectrum.

"Collectively," he said, "we represent the only hope for opposition to Alum and the new Administration. It will be expected of us to provide at least the semblance of an electoral race."

"Why bother?" asked Jenny Thurgood, an environmental engineer who'd worked on balancing predator-prey populations in the agriculture tunnels. "I mean, even those with political ambitions in the Governing Council know there's no point in running against Alum."

"True enough." Priyam Kaloor, Manager of Public Transportation for Ceres, agreed. "But *all* Council positions will be open. If we could find the right candidates, some strong contenders, we might be able to gain a toe hold. Even Alum must recognize the value of a credible opposition party."

They shifted their attention to the fourth member of their meeting as if drawn by some collective recognition that, whatever they decided, they would need Cybrid support to achieve validity.

Though Cybrids hadn't been an official part of the old Administration, their collective voice had always been heard and considered through the Project's Director of Human-Cybrid Relations. Now that the Cybrids were cut off from having even informal representation, Strang was among the few who continued to seek Cybrid input. He wasn't sure Alum realized the full extent of his consultations, or what their Leader would do if his interactions came to light. Admonish him? Fire him outright? Imprison him? It was hard to say, but he wasn't inclined to stop consulting them now.

DAR-K hovered silently in a vacant corner of Jared's apartment. Her spherical bulk imposed gravitas on the meeting. "I am here mainly in the role of observer and to aid in your analysis," she said. "Strictly speaking, I'm not supposed to be in the city at all."

"Luckily, my position allows me to find ways around that ridiculous law," Jared replied.

"It's only a matter of time before that loophole is also closed," DAR-K replied. "I should make it clear that I'm here only because Jared asked me."

"We're not doing anything illegal by meeting like this," Thurgood said. "It's expected that other parties will form to challenge the election. We're simply organizing an alternative party, not planning a revolution."

"Difficult to say how it might be perceived," Kaloor pointed out. "It depends on the level of government paranoia. The fact that Alum and the Council completely dominate the hearts and minds of the population doesn't exactly make them immune to being unreasonably suspicious."

The three humans looked to DAR-K for confirmation.

"For the moment, I think you're safe. I would recommend keeping these meetings small and low key, though. It wouldn't hurt to think of yourselves as an insurgency group. You must realize by now that you're likely to be viewed as such by a good number of Alum's followers. It doesn't matter that the opposition party is sanctioned by Alum himself and important to the political process.

"For your own safety and for the security of the group, you may want to consider organizing along the lines of terrorist cells: no individual should have access to the full list of members and sympathizers until Alum proves his openness to democracy and freedom."

Kaloor's eyes went wide and he laughed. "You can't be serious! If we start looking like a terrorist group, they'll treat us like one."

"That is a risk," DAR-K admitted. "However, until you can announce the formation of the party at a large public forum, it's a risk worth taking. I'm not sure how seriously Alum takes his own rhetoric."

"Do you think he might have ulterior motives?"

"The election is four years away. He has a long lead time to consolidate his power base. I'm sure he'll maintain the appearance of an approaching election through most of those four years. We are still in early days in the colonies. I think we would be wise not to fool ourselves into thinking civil society simply picked up and shifted out here to the asteroids.

"Had the original Administration and colonists still been in place, the transition to democratic rule might have been carried out smoothly. But this feels more like we're heading for the establishment of a monarchy to me."

"Alum as King and Emperor?" scoffed Kaloor.

"And Archbishop or Pope. State and Church, as one," the Cybrid answered. "I simply advise caution until the actual election. For now, proceed as if Alum will stay true to his word."

"Very well," Strang jumped in. "In that case, we have two things we need to do. We need to pick a platform, and we need to come up with some candidates."

"Do you think the Council is united behind Alum on his proposals?" Thurgood asked. "I mean, some of your old chums can't be happy about the socialist leaning of his policies."

"I haven't had a chance to discuss Alum's speech with Nigel Hodge yet, but I'm sure you're right. His group was all about accumulating wealth and power, and consolidating a position of privilege. Alum's policies will leave them gutted."

"So what are they going to do?"

"No idea. What would you do if you were in their position? Would you sit on Council and be happy with the crumbs Alum leaves you? Do you try to find some way to change his mind? Or do you remove him?"

"Hard enough to remove a king," DAR-K said from the corner, "let alone someone who's become King and Pope combined."

Thurgood nodded. "You're right. It would be better for Nigel and his colleagues to act sooner rather than later, don't you think?"

Jared nodded. "Except I don't think anybody saw this coming. No one's in any position to overthrow Alum right now. His timing is impeccable. He made his move while he still has everyone's confidence and with no obvious contender to challenge him."

"A revolution, then," Thurgood suggested.

"No, I don't think so," DAR-K answered. "The colonies would fall apart without Alum leading them. Millions would die in any kind of civil war, maybe even the whole species."

"Well, that would solve *your* problem, wouldn't it?" Jared said to the Cybrid before he could stop himself.

"For the moment, we Cybrids have no particular problem. To us, Alum is essentially a benign dictator and we are his slaves. Our lives are basically unchanged from what they were in the old Administration. We are assigned work. We do our work, and in return we receive free energy and free maintenance. Our contributions feel meaningful; we help humanity to survive. If anything, our quality of life will improve now that we have Vacationland."

"Vacationland?" Kaloor asked.

"Yes," Strang answered for the Cybrid. "A few months ago a programmer from Romania, a member of the YTG Church, if you can believe it, approached me by email with a virtual world he'd modified for Cybrid use.

He called it Vacationland. It's based on an inSense entertainment program he'd designed on Earth."

Kaloor eyed him with a skeptical sidelong glance. "And Alum's okay with this?"

"I wondered about that, too, but Alum seems to have embraced the idea wholeheartedly. Perhaps he believes it makes him appear more kind hearted."

"At any rate," DAR-K said. "It provides my people with a place to play and to remember their humanity, if only for a while. I'm looking into providing a user-friendly development interface so we can create other such worlds."

"So, you're content to exist in servitude?" Jared asked.

"We all exist to serve within our societies, do we not? Cybrids have little or no personal ambition. We have everything we need: energy, maintenance, purpose. We have no desire for dominance over our fellows, neither Cybrid nor human. With the proposed software and computational support, we can make and inhabit any world we dream up. It's as good a life as anyone ever had."

Kaloor wobbled his head left and right as he considered DAR-K's position. "Okaaay. Well, that's one way to think of it. So, you're saying you'd prefer to remain above the fray, then?"

"As I've told Jared before, Alum is humanity's problem to sort out. I remember freedom. I remember democracy. Nice ideals. Not everything works out as pretty as planned.

"If you want to ask me about the best way to administer the habitats, I'll be happy to answer. Alum has a good design, in my estimation. If I were you, I'd plan a cooperative opposition, a small tweak here and there, a different perspective, nothing overly dramatic."

"So that's going to be our platform? A tweak here and there, a different perspective, nothing overly dramatic," Thurgood scoffed. "Try winning elections with that!"

"I'm sure we can come up with something a little catchier," Strang replied. "Maybe along the lines of, 'Every government needs a sober second opinion,' or how about, 'Experience counts.' Something like that."

Kaloor's face gave in to a mischievous, wry grin. "Marketing is really not your strength, is it?"

"Maybe not," Strang admitted. "It doesn't matter. We know why an opposition party is needed, and that's enough to get started. There are several thousand members of the previous Administration living among the three asteroids. We need to get in touch with them and start identifying potential candidates."

"We may have all worked together, but I don't believe we were ever politically united," Thurgood admitted. "The old Administration ran the spectrum from far left to far right and everything in between."

"Luckily, we were able to unite in survival," Kaloor said.

"The very few of us who knew, that is," Strang replied. "Most of the original colonists never knew anything beyond the official 'opportunities for expansion' cover story. Most of them believed it was an *option* for humanity to push into a new frontier."

Thurgood took a sip of her coffee. "These people know nothing beyond their faith in Alum and their God." She scowled at the dark liquid. The untouched cup had grown cold, and they hadn't gotten past the basic existential issues.

"Their faith allowed them to get off Earth, and to take over the asteroids," DAR-K pointed out. "They may not be the finest representatives of humanity, and they may not be the survivors we ourselves would've chosen, but they are the survivors we have. For now, we need to support their efforts. We need guidance, not revolution."

"What if they don't want any guidance from us?" Kaloor asked. "What if they are content to live under Alum's political and religious dictatorship?"

DAR-K had no reply.

25

"CAN'T WE REST FOR A FEW MINUTES?"

"You don't need to rest." Darya stood *en garde*, her fencing épée pointed over Timothy's head, ready for the next round of thrust and parry, feint and counter.

They stood on a grass-covered hilltop occupied by a single, resplendent maple. As far as the eye could see, the world was an endless plane of hilltops with maple trees identical to this one. She would add more trees, some creeks, stone walls, houses, and other such complicating features to their virtual training ground later. They'd only been at it for three weeks and Timothy wasn't ready for that level yet.

The former First Footman of Casa DonTon dropped his arm to his side. "No, I don't *need* to rest. I realize you've altered things in this world so I don't fatigue. It's just that we've been practicing twenty hours a day for weeks now. It's getting...tiresome, if not actually tiring."

"Should we switch weapons? A change can be as good as a rest, the ancients used to say."

Timothy glared at her in exasperation. "I was hoping we might have a little fun for a change."

"Isn't *this* fun?" Darya, former warrior Princess of Lysrandia, returned the glare with open innocence.

Timothy picked up the nearest rock and whipped it at her head. She casually deflected it with the edge of her sword.

"See?" Timothy wailed. "How can this be fun when I don't stand a chance against you?"

"You don't learn anything against a weaker opponent."

He threw up his hands, turned his back on her, and walked away.

Darya watched him retreat without comment. She let him get a seven or eight meters away, grabbed her épée by the shaft like a spear, and launched it at his back.

An instant before the flying sword met its target, Timothy wheeled and knocked it from the air. He roared in protest and charged back up the incline, yelling the whole way.

Darya picked up the fighting staff at her feet, spun it in a blur in front of her, and brought it to an abrupt halt with one end under her arm and the other pointed directly at Timothy's nose.

"What are you doing?" he demanded, hands on hips.

"We've been practicing sword-on-sword, hand-to-hand, ever since I transferred the basic weapons and combat concepts to you," Darya replied. "Clearly, you think you're ready for something more. Here it is."

The staff blurred and one end struck smartly across Timothy's arm, liberating his fencing sword.

"Ow!"

The pain in his arm pulsed long enough for him to consider the consequences of inattention and then shut off, thanks to Darya's altered virtual biology.

"Pick it up." She motioned with the stick, "Let's see how your blade fares against my staff."

Timothy stood, rubbing the memory of the blow to his arm. "I'd prefer something with an edge," he said.

"Very well, saber, katana, scimitar, or jian?"

"In keeping with your martial arts style, I'll use a jian, please."

His fencing foil instantly transformed into a heavier double-edged Chinese sword. Timothy stretched out a hand to retrieve his weapon, and it leaped eagerly into his palm. He experimented with the grip and twirled it to get a feel for the weight. His third spin ended in a sideways slash at Darya.

Her staff whistled upward, deflecting the broad side of the sword and sending the jian gracefully over her head. The trailing end of the staff swooped under and behind Timothy's swing, and connected against his shoulder with a loud "thwack!"

Timothy grunted and staggered but kept his balance.

"Would you prefer a different sword? Or maybe two jians?" she taunted.

He glowered as he grabbed his weapon and faced off again. He advanced steadily and flourished the blade in an elaborate pattern intended to impress and intimidate.

Darya retreated in pace. The wooden staff blurred in her hands as she expertly mirrored the motions of the slashing blade. She saw an opening, and her staff poked through and caught him in the solar plexus.

Timothy fell backward with a gruff, "Ooof!" His sword landed a couple meters away. This time, he rolled backward and onto his feet immediately, instead of licking his wounds. He picked up his jian and advanced.

"That's more like it," Darya encouraged. "The faster you recover from a blow, the less chance it'll be followed by something that kills you."

Timothy's sword chopped down and back up, flicking a few inches of top soil at his opponent. Darya released a hand from the spinning staff to block the dirt from reaching her eyes. As she did, his blade swept outward, where its movement was hidden by her own hand. Before she knew it, the sword slashed inward again, cutting her triceps.

Darya gasped at the sharp pain, and the fighting stick flew out of her grasp. She leaped into a back flip, putting some space between her and her opponent.

Sensing he had the advantage, Timothy rushed forward, stabbing and slashing.

She flipped backward several times to avoid his attack. Her last flip arced wider than the others, and she landed in side splits on the ground. Timothy's sword sliced down in a killing blow aimed at her head.

She clapped her hands together, pinning his blade between her palms. A single drop of blood fell from her joined hands as Timothy strained to complete the blow. Darya twisted her body, and suddenly he was falling face down into the dirt. Instantly, Darya was on him, knife pressed to his throat.

"See," he said. "I can never beat you!"

Darya pushed herself off him and dropped her knife back into its sheath.

"You don't have to beat *me*," she replied, "just whatever Trillian throws at us.

"Ready!" she commanded. "Again!"

26

"SO, HOW'S THE NEW BUSINESS PLAN COMING ALONG?" Jared
Strang was working on his second coffee of the morning at Rumi's. It was a
rare day off for the Councillor. Despite Alum's proposal that employees
work no more than three days a week, liaising with the Cybrids was taking
double that. Nevertheless, it was his day away from the office and Jared was
enjoying a novel he'd been meaning to re-read for months. So, today, life
was good.

The owner of his favorite café looked back at him for a moment, working
the question over in his mind. "I'm not sure you wanna know, man," he
replied.

Jared scanned the sparsely occupied terrace. Rumi's two employees had
everything under control. He pushed a chair out with his foot. "Sit. Tell."

Rumi pulled off his gray apron and took a seat. He caught the eye of one
of his staff and signaled for her to bring him a cappuccino.

"It's the banks, man. I thought dealing with Ecuadorians was
bureaucratic, but these guys have perfected it."

"What's up? I thought things would be getting better by now." Like
almost everyone, Jared had watched Alum's pronouncements on the new
economic and financial systems. Unlike most, he was actually interested.
People always got caught up in the drama of elections, wars, and political
infighting but policy was what really mattered.

"Yeah, you'd think so. It's been over two months. I mean, the banks and
all their people were already in place. All they had to do was change over
the currency and get back into business. How much time could that take?"

"It's entirely electronic; it should only take minutes. Hours, tops," agreed
Strang.

"Exactly! So, I waited two weeks before I put in a loan application. I was
busy anyway, and I wasn't going to be able to expand until the other shops

had Certificates of Ownership for their people. So, I cooled my jets for a while. Then I went to see my manager."

"How'd that go?"

"The first visit felt great. I filled out the paperwork, we had a nice chat about my plans, and I went home."

"So, what's the problem?"

"I didn't hear a thing for another two weeks, so I popped in to see her again. Only, they had a new manager and he claimed that he'd never seen any paperwork."

"What did you do?"

Rumi sighed. "What *could* I do? I filled out the forms again, had a nice chat about my plans, and went home."

"And?"

"I wasn't going to wait another two weeks so, after a few days, I went back in. Same story: new manager, no paperwork."

"What? I would have thought their people were more competent than that."

"Me, too. So I said to Hell with them and switched banks."

"Branches, you mean, seeing as they're all one bank now."

"Yeah. Well, I got the same story there."

"No way! Seriously?"

"Seriously, man. It's messed up out there. They even lost track of some of my people's paychecks."

"Come on, now."

"Truth. Gabbi didn't get her pay two weeks ago, and Melissa missed one a month ago. Half my savings went missing for ten days."

"Okay, that does sound serious."

"Look, I'm only an engineer—"

"—and successful entrepreneur," Jared added.

"Aw, thanks, man. Yeah. Anyway, even I know that if people don't think they can rely on their banks, sooner or later there'll be trouble. More likely, sooner."

Jared checked his inSense news feed. ""Hmm, you know, this isn't the only kind of trouble we've been having."

"You're telling me. I've had to shut down twice this month. No water."

"No water? I travel so much, I hadn't heard."

"Yeah, I bet you stay in all the best hotels."

"On business, I do. Not that any of them are luxurious compared to the nicer places we had on Earth."

"It'll get pretty sad if the definition of luxury becomes any place with steady, running water."

"My own newsfeed, not the official mainstream broadcasts—"

"Of course," Rumi toasted Jared with the newly-arrived cup.

"My newsfeed says these infrastructure problems may be a little more common and frequent than one might expect by chance."

"Are you suggesting the Cybrids are lousy builders?" Rumi's cynical grin gave away that he wouldn't believe such a thing.

"No, not possible. Maybe it's the new colonists who are assuming responsibilities previously carried by Cybrids."

"Aren't your people—the Cybrids, I mean—aren't they training them?"

"My people, as you put it, are doing their best to train and supervise the new colonists under very trying circumstances. The majority of trainees are poorly educated, completely inexperienced, and resentful of learning from 'machines'.

"I thought things were going well, all considered. This would suggest quite the contrary." The furrows in Strang's forehead deepened as he lost himself in his newsfeed.

"What is it?" Rumi asked.

"The problems are popping up randomly. Almost too randomly; it's as if someone is trying to hide a pattern."

"Sabotage? Who'd do that?"

"I have no idea. I'll need to talk with DAR-K...and then with Alum."

27

"DO YOU REALLY LIVE HERE?" Timothy, in his spherical trueself Cybrid body, followed Darya down a long, narrow tunnel in Secondus. The passageway joined two of her laboratories in a rabbit warren of corridors and chambers comprising her secluded asteroid base.

"What, you don't like the décor?"

"A little stark and utilitarian for my tastes."

"Well, you've spent most of your existence in the lavish halls of Casa DonTon."

Timothy sighed. "Yes, this place does make one homesick."

"I could de-instantiate you and return you to your former position as a Partial, if you'd rather."

"You can do that?"

Darya couldn't help laughing at the horrified tone in his voice. "Sorry, a poor joke. Don't worry. Your security is solid. No one will be messing with your persona without your permission ever again."

"Thank goodness for small graces."

They had arrived at Secondus a few days earlier after a meandering voyage through local space. When the rock appeared out of the blackness, Timothy had never been so happy to see solid ground.

That felt like ages ago. Darya had shown him around and he'd committed a map of Secondus to memory. Sadly, there was no part of the asteroid base that fueled the imagination. From the small recharging station where they filled their matter-antimatter tanks, to the numerous labs, to the endless tunnels, the place was stark and ugly.

"Why do I need beauty in this world when I can have all I want and more inworld?" Darya had challenged. He had no good answer. So, he spent as much time as he could in the Recharging and Reconnecting room, as Darya called it.

A little R&R time in the virtual fairytale lands Darya had designed was a welcome respite from the harsh reality of this universe and from the virtual training ground where he'd spent the past months.

They turned off the corridor and into a bare, nondescript room.

"What's this place for?"

"Mary is still trapped in Alternus. I need to see if I can help her," Darya answered.

"Wait. You want to go back in there?"

"I have to," Darya answered flatly.

"But if you go back to the recharging station, you could be captured or killed."

"I don't need to go anywhere. I can access Alternus from here."

Timothy noticed the pair of interface stations at opposite ends of the chamber. "What if you're discovered?"

"The main risk is that they could trace my signal back here. That's of minimal concern. I route my interface through a variety of small satellites; if anyone starts tracing the network back toward here, I can simply blow them."

"But wouldn't that trap you in Trillian's insane inworld?"

"No, I'll leave my trueself here and just send in a puppet Partial."

"Like what you sent to me when I first woke up in Gerhardt's body?"

"A little more enhanced and less independent."

"I don't understand; how would that work?" he said.

"I'll maintain a constant link to the Partial. It will transmit back to me in real time and I'll set general directives for it to follow while it moves around inworld. Operating a Partial completely by remote slows it down too much, especially over these distances, so I have to give it a fair bit of autonomy on the details. I'll be able to sever the link and erase the Partial instantly if I get into an untenable situation.

"Don't worry; there's no danger," she added.

Timothy didn't look convinced. "If there's no danger, why are you taking such precautions?"

"Okay, there's always *some* danger. In this case, the biggest problem will be if I inadvertently alert Trillian and have to leave before I've learned anything useful."

"I don't imagine I can talk you out of trying?"

"No."

Timothy heaved a long, tired sigh. "Very well, then. I'm going with you."

"You'll only complicate things."

"We've already been through this. I'm useless to you out here on my own. It's too new and foreign. Even with the updates you've made to my concepta, I can't manage your revolution without you. Remember?"

"It'll be dangerous," she countered.

"You just finished trying to convince me that it wasn't. Besides, I've been training for this a long time," he replied.

The force of his determination surprised Darya. "Are you honestly looking forward to going back to Alternus?"

"Truthfully, it's a little boring here and, as you pointed out, Mary needs our help."

"Did you just manipulate me into taking you inworld?" For a moment, Darya wished Cybrids had faces; she was sure Timothy's would be wearing a smirk.

"Are you suggesting I *could* outsmart you?"

"I may have let my guard down. Briefly."

"Well, you won't make that mistake again anytime soon, will you?"

"No, I promise never to underestimate your skills, or your wit, again."

Timothy moved over toward the nearest interface station. "Then, let's get going, shall we?"

28

JARED STRANG AND JENNY THURGOOD waited in the Reception Area outside Alum's office. They watched people coming and going through the doorway for about an hour before Thurgood's impatience got the better of her. Ignoring the eight others who'd been sitting quietly for the past sixty minutes, some even longer, she walked up to the receptionist and demanded to see Alum at his next available moment. "We're on the Governing Council, you know."

"Yes," the Receptionist replied, "and you were also in the *old* Administration." She returned Thurgood's intimidating stare without flinching. "I'm sure you realize that as Leader of the Council, Alum is very busy. I will let you know when he becomes available."

The Councillor walked back to her bench, defeated. Jared patted her hand in consolation, but she snapped it away.

Despite the rebuke, they were ushered into the Leader's office fifteen minutes later. Alum remained behind his desk, working on some papers. Without a word or looking up, he motioned for them to take a seat.

No comfy chat on the sofas today—Strang noted.

The two visitors waited in their austere chairs while Alum completed his work. After a few minutes, he returned his stylus to the desktop and regarded them with an indulgent smile.

"It's not every day two Councillors appear together in my office. How can I help you?"

Thurgood deferred to Strang.

Fair enough. It was my idea, I guess I should start—Strang thought.

"We are here to talk about how we may help *you*, sir," he said.

Alum looked surprised, which in turn surprised Strang. There weren't many times one got ahead of the Leader; his information and planning were astonishingly thorough.

"That is unexpected," Alum said. "I'm aware your group is forming an opposition party. I didn't expect us to find much cause for helping one another over the next few years."

"Any decent democracy requires an opposition," Thurgood began. The edge in her voice drew a subtle smile from Alum.

"But that opposition doesn't have to be inimical," Strang interjected. He saw the flash of an indignant glare from Thurgood but pushed on. "Our interests, *all* of our interests, lie in ensuring the colonies are well administered, nothing more."

"I'm glad you see it that way. I suppose some kind of sober second thought might be helpful from time to time. "That is, indeed, why I set up the Council in the first place."

"Exactly. After all, what's an election without someone to run against, however much it's just for show?"

Alum stroked his chin. "None of your representatives has a chance of winning. That doesn't bother you?"

"We'll have to see," challenged Thurgood. "The outcome may not be what you expect. Even among your most ardent supporters, there are many who see the merit in separating church and state."

Alum sat upright. "Are you suggesting I should resign my post as Spiritual Leader in order to run in the election?"

"It's a thought," Thurgood replied. "But as you pointed out, our representatives have practically no chance of winning, anyway."

Alum gave a good-natured shrug. "Perhaps I should reconsider. Maybe we need to incorporate some form of proportional representation in the election, if for no other reason, to give your candidates a fighting chance." He smiled graciously.

Thurgood returned his generosity with a cold stare.

"If the troubles we're experiencing throughout the habitats continue, the race may be closer than you expect," Strang said.

Alum grimaced and dismissed their seriousness with a backhanded gesture. "All temporary. Simple shake-out problems that one might expect of any new system."

"I'm not sure all of your citizens would agree with you on that," Strang replied.

Alum opened his mouth to reply, but Strang charged forward. "In any case, we are here to offer our help in whatever capacity we can."

Alum regarded him suspiciously. "I don't see how help from you would benefit this Administration. Wouldn't that simply weaken public perception of my leadership?"

"I did say our chief interest is in seeing the habitats run effectively. What good would an election be if the people were driven to riots beforehand?"

"Riots? I don't see how conditions have deteriorated to that stage!" Alum exclaimed.

Thurgood had seen large populations suddenly switch allegiances before; it was a frightful thing to behold. "You're too young to remember the Pension Riots and Treasury Bond Runs. When people have a hard time accessing what they see as 'their' money, things turn ugly very quickly."

"I'm aware there have been a few issues during centralization of the banking system," Alum allowed. "But I'm sure these are nothing more than implementation hiccups and will soon disappear."

"And the other infrastructure problems?" Jared challenged.

"What of them? A few problems with water and electricity."

"And sewage," Thurgood added.

"And sewage," conceded Alum. "All of these will be cleared up quickly enough. We have people working on them around the clock."

"Yes, and that's why we've come to see you today," Strang answered.

"Okay," Alum conceded. "How can *you* help *me*?"

"Though the vast majority of our experts amongst the previous colonists were...exchanged...for lesser qualified people among the new colonists, we still have a vast pool of expertise we could call on for assistance."

"The Cybrids," Alum muttered.

"Yes, and the hundred million Cybrid processors awaiting activation," added Jared.

Alum pushed away from his desk and walked to the window, turning his back on his guests. "This Administration is not predisposed to excessive use of Cybrid technology."

"We understand that," Thurgood replied. "But within that pool of expertise, we have financial and banking experts, engineers, and scientists." She glanced at Strang for backup.

In his best selling voice, Jared added, "And they are simply sitting there. All that vast knowledge is going to waste, while your people fumble for solutions, sir."

Alum spun around. "Fumble? There may have been challenges, but I don't believe *anyone* is fumbling."

"Our sources suggest differently," Thurgood stated.

Alum's eyes squinted warily. "Are you suggesting your information is better than the official Administration's?"

Jared soothed, "Not at all. But we have been talking to people on the street, and there is some grumbling and discontent. We think it would serve us *all* best to put every means at our disposal to resolve these problems."

"You would place robots in charge? Over people?"

Jared could feel the Leader's ire building. He tried to think of something that would both convince and placate.

Thurgood chimed in before any words came to him. "The Cybrids were in charge of these habitats long before *you people* came here."

Oh, bollocks—Jared thought—*here we go.*

Before he could put any words together, Alum exploded in fury.

"The old ways, the ways of technology and sin will *never* return to My People," he thundered. "Our Lord, Yehsua, has given these habitats to My People. *My* People! Not to the old sinners and their *machines*."

Jared could hear the capitalization. "My People." *Jenny, why did you have to push him?* Had she forgotten how short a step it was from leader of religion and politics to outright megalomaniac?

"Perhaps we all need to take a breath," Jared said, trying to bring the discussion back to a calm place. "No one is suggesting people answer to the Cybrids. We are simply suggesting we use all available skills to solve our current problems before they become dangerous. Cybrids can help. Those of us in the old Administration can help. We all just want to help."

Alum strode back to his place behind his desk and sat imperiously in his chair.

"This meeting is over. You may bring your proposals to Council if you wish to pursue it with them."

He bowed his head to the displays on his desktop and picked up his stylus.

Strang and Thurgood glanced at each other and left quietly.

Once the two Councillors had vacated the room, John Trillian walked in from an adjoining room and softly closed the door behind them.

Alum put down his stylus. "Any comments?" he asked.

Trillian was intrigued by the lack of emotion in his Leader's face. Moments earlier, he'd sounded enraged; now he appeared perfectly calm. He wasn't sure whether to admire the Leader's control or to be afraid of it.

"They seem to have good information," was all he said.

Alum rubbed his chin. "Indeed. They are a little closer to the mark than what we've leaked. Blind luck, or something else?"

"Well, they're not fools, and they are well connected to the situation on the ground."

"Yes, their network is sparse but wide. Do you think it's more than that?"

"Do I think they have a hand in *causing* the problems?" Trillian clarified. "No, their hands are clean. Everything points to the others."

"To Hodge and Cutter?" Alum asked.

Trillian nodded. "Yes, and a few of their influential friends and colleagues. I've linked troubles in the banks directly to executive orders from those two. They were tricky. Some of those orders were only caught on what they thought were inactive cameras in private meeting rooms and in supposedly unmonitored corridors."

"Did you have sound in those as well?" Alum asked.

"In the majority of them, yes. When they moved out of range, we had to do a little lip-reading. Handy algorithm, that."

"Quite. So you think these two, Strang and Thurgood, may be genuine?" Alum asked.

"I will accede to your judgement, of course, but they seem trustworthy to me," Trillian replied.

"Was I too harsh with them?"

Trillian barked a laugh. "No; there's no harm in putting a little fear of God in them, sir."

Alum allowed himself a little smile. "Well, they needed it. They are smugly confident of their own skills and of their precious Cybrids."

"I hate to say it but, in this case, they may have good reason to be smug,"

"Yes, I think I've let them run unchecked for too long," Alum conceded. He tapped his chin with his index finger while he thought.

Trillian watched in silence until the corners of his Leader's eyes pulled upward and an impish grin form on his lips.

"You have a plan, sir?"

"Always, John. Let's give the Councillors a little leeway. When they bring their proposal up in chambers, I think I will side with them."

"That *will* come as a surprise."

"I expect it will. Let's allow their Cybrids to come in and attempt to help. At the same time, let's allow Hodge and Cutter to continue their efforts."

Trillian was confused. "Pit them against each other? How will that help our position?"

"It won't, not directly," Alum replied. "I expect things to get better sometimes and worse sometimes. We may have to help out Hodge and his crew if the Cybrids start gaining too much of an upper hand."

"Sabotage our own plans?"

"You have to think of the long game, John. It will end when *we* want it to, when it's to our best advantage."

"Will we be able to control how it plays out?"

"Of course," Alum assured him. "We have something they don't know about. We have the Securitors." He picked up his stylus and went back to work.

Trillian nodded appreciation, and returned to his surveillance. *Those troublemakers have no idea what they're up against. No idea.*

29

MARY'S VIRTUAL CONSCIOUSNESS FLOATED IN A HAZE of golden light sandwiched between two infinite jade plains.

She manoeuvred through clouds of words and symbols, lines and circles, images and neural networks that, collectively, comprised the high-level representation of her software and knowledge base. The plane above represented the inworld simulation in which she was trapped; the plane below, her concepta. Between the two was the most fundamental level of her operating system, the BIOS.

Some areas appeared hazy or patchy; others were clearer. She recognized the latter as sections of her BIOS machine code that she'd rewritten into a programming language she could follow. The crude, inelegant code even in those areas revealed her shaky understanding of her connection to this simulated prison.

It's rudimentary but I'm making progress.

Given more time, maybe a few more years, she'd have no trouble unravelling the program and turning the odds to her favor. But she didn't have that luxury; Trillian could be back any minute, and this time, he wouldn't be in the mood to go easy. She was pretty sure of that.

What other tools and powers did you bury in my system, Darya? Is the answer already inside me? I've let you down; I didn't make the time to explore the tools you gave me and now it could cost me my life.

If I make it out of here, I'll have some homework to catch up on. In the meantime, I'll just have to make do with what've I've got.

She went back to thinking about the Alternus program. *There's got to be a weak point here somewhere. One more time, what do we know?*

The simulation runs on its own quark-spin substrate. It's grown on the same spintronic microchips found on inworld computers. Some routine or subroutine would have to connect the simulation code to its exotic hardware.

Which means....

The beginning of an idea was germinating. Mary struggled to coax it forward into her consciousness.

Which means....

Which means.... Come on, think!

Which means, somewhere in the billions of lines of code that make this prison cell, there's a connection between Vacationland and the basic Alternus code. And from there, to the quark-spin hardware.

That's it! If I can just find the code and figure out how to interface with it, I'll have Darya's ability to hack the inworlds. I can get out of here!

Except, I have no idea what the routines look like. How am I going to find the interface in all that code? She looked with despair at the billions of instructions streaming by in the plane overhead?

It didn't help that her present environment was less than optimal for concentrating. *I have to keep trying. If I don't find a way to win against Trillian, what little time I have left in this life will be painful.*

I just need more time.

The drawn-out creak from the rusty prison door hinges penetrated her concentration. *He's back!*

Mary opened her eyes. Not one but four Trillians stood at the entrance to her cell, all wearing the same smirk. She blinked and shook her head to clear it. Was she seeing double? Rather, quadruple?

"Come for another chat, have you?" she said to the Trillians.

The left-most Trillian answered for all four. "Not exactly; it's time to take our little game up a notch."

Mary stood up and took a strong stance. She was ready to confront him. Correction, them.

Since becoming a guest of Trillian's special hospitality, she'd been working out intensively, something unheard of to inworld Cybrids. Why would anyone exercise when you could simply change your avatar's body type on a whim? When Trillian cut her off from the Vacationland Supervisor, that all changed. No more commands or requests. No ordering up any physique she wanted. If she wanted something, she was going to have to make it happen all by herself.

More proof that the realistic physics of Alternus has leaked into this inworld. Alternus had been the first inworld she'd ever heard of in which people had to exercise if they wanted to become stronger.

And so, for the first time in her long existence, she threw herself into building up her muscle naturally, through hard work. She was determined not to be held back by the physical limitations—the burden—of her defiantly overweight, under-muscled inworld body choice.

Her efforts had paid off. Her bulky avatar had grown slim and solid, and her mind had become sharper through rigid discipline and determination.

The four Trillians advanced, and Mary backed away warily. As she retreated, she relaxed her body and breathing. She held her hands open in front of her in a standard Wushu stance—another gift from Darya—left hand in front, both palms up.

She glanced around for a weapon. A short wooden pike with a metal tip on a nearby tabletop was the closest thing she could find. *Where did that come from? No matter.* Keeping her eyes on the men, she lunged for the pike, secured it with one hand, and yanked hard toward herself

Ow! Her fingers came away empty and scraped. Surprised but not ready to give up her prize, she grabbed the pole with both hands. The rough wood tore the skin from her hands but didn't budge.

The Trillians laughed in concert, rushed forward, and grabbed her arms and legs. She'd been tricked, again, by Trillian's control over everything in the room.

She struggled but they held her fast. They lifted her onto the tabletop and secured her wrists and ankles in iron cuffs. Heavy chains ran from the cuffs to a large, ratcheted wheel.

She put on a brave face. "Really, Trillian! The rack? Could you be any more cliché?"

Inside, she was petrified. *Not the rack!.*

The four Trillians stepped back and watched Mary pull futilely against her bindings. The Trillian closest to the head of the table turned the wheel enough to take up the slack in the chains.

She braced herself. *Deep breath in. Deep breath out. Exist outside your perception of pain.*

The Trillian at her side looked on with the appearance of compassion. "I *am* sorry about this. Truly. I'd hoped that passing a little time alone here might make you more amenable to cooperation. Sadly, you're more stubborn than that.

"You're right, of course." He looked around the cell with distaste, "Once recognized as such, this inane parade of psychological threats has no more effect on a strong-minded Cybrid than a circus fun-house.

"But I promise you that this, however cliché it may be," he said and patted the slab supporting her, "*this* is going to be different. So I'm going to give you the courtesy of asking you again, nicely, to cooperate. If you do, we can be done with all this nasty business and set you free.

"I would really rather not hurt you. That's the truth, but you're not giving me any choice, Mary. Alum has ordered that this *rebellion* of yours be quashed, and placed me in charge of carrying out his command. I will do whatever is necessary to fulfil my duty to The Living God.

The wheel tightened a fraction more, pulling Mary's arms and legs uncomfortably taught. She could no longer twist or pull. She stopped resisting and let her body slump in the device.

"Don't worry, dear," one of the Trillians said. "You will feel pain and it will be excruciating, I assure you. But the damage won't be permanent. Not today. This is just a taste of what's to come. We'll return another day, and do this all over, and over again if needed, until you tell us where Darya is."

"Please..." she whimpered.

"What's that?" Trillian said, moving his ear closer to her mouth. She lunged her face upward, snapping, but he pulled away before her teeth could clamp onto his flesh.

"You're going to regret that," he snarled. He nodded, and the Trillian at her head wrenched on the wheel. The chains tightened several more centimeters.

Mary's body exploded in agony, and her screams echoed down the outer passageway. It took her minutes to return to her senses. Her joints screamed, and every limb felt stretched to the limit, just short of tearing.

One of the Trillians extracted a scalpel from a roll on the table and held it up for her to examine. The jagged, rusty blade was sure to make a painful mess of anything it cut.

Mary's pupils contracted as she focussed on the knife. She sobbed shamelessly. "No. No, please," she begged.

Trillian moved his face closer to hers. She could smell his breath and feel the puffs of air on her face as he addressed her in a quiet, sweet voice.

"It's entirely up to you, Mary. You will tell me everything you know about Darya, where she is, and what she's planning. You will tell me today, or tomorrow, or the day after. But you will tell me."

He placed the cold blade against her sternum. He signaled to one of his other selves to tighten the rack a little bit more.

Mary cried out as every last bit of slack was removed along the length of her spine and limbs.

"First I'm going to open you up," Trillian said in a cold, diagnostic voice. "Then, I'm going to release your entrails." The blade traced the proposed arcs along her stomach. "And then, we're going to see how you like the stench of your own guts burning."

She yelled and clamped her eyes shut, anticipating the searing sting of the first slice. It didn't come. She waited.

Nothing. The room was silent. She opened her eyes.

All four Trillians were staring, mouths agape, at what she'd been calling the Window to Hell. She followed their gaze.

Darya and Timothy stood on the other side, flames licking at their legs, swords drawn. They stared back at the four Trillians surrounding Mary.

No one moved. The seconds drew out.

Darya's mouth worked silently, and tears streamed down her cheeks.

Mary didn't need to hear to understand what Darya was saying. "I'm sorry. I'm so sorry."

Two of the Trillians popped out of existence, and instantly reappeared on the other side of the glass, beside Darya and Timothy. The Trillians grabbed for the intruders, but a blinding flash forced them backward. When they could see again, Darya and Timothy were gone.

The Trillian standing over Mary glared at her. "We will continue this tomorrow," he growled. The four Trillians gathered at the door. As if by afterthought, the last one to depart waved his hand back over his shoulder, and Mary was released from the rack.

She looked to the window but it was dark and empty again save for the eerie glow of the flickering flames below. She was alone again.

Was it really Darya and Timothy at the window, or did I hallucinate that? It must have been, or why would the Trillians have left so abruptly?

Mary rolled herself off the table and collapsed onto the cold floor. She agonized her way to the nearest heavy wooden leg, slumped against it, and gave into her pent-up tears.

She knew better than to get up her hopes. Clinging to hope could be deadly here. Besides, it was likely just another ploy to crush her spirit.

If so, it was pretty effective. I'll give him that—she told herself. She couldn't help but to hope.

What if it was them, what if they did come for me? And where did they go? Did Trillian capture them, too? Or worse, kill them? Oh, Darya, you shouldn't have come. I hope you got away.

30

DARYA AND TIMOTHY EMERGED in a dingy hotel room in Alternus.

"Hey, I recognize this place," Timothy said. He opened the characterless stain-resistant curtains and looked outside at a jumbled New York City.

Nothing had changed since they'd escaped that madhouse some months ago. The streets and buildings still ran at impossible angles, and a section of the Brooklyn Bridge still protruded into the air halfway up the wall opposite the window. He pressed his hands against the glass to steady himself as he marveled at the urban tangle before him.

"Switch your vision to ten dimensions; it'll all fall into place," Darya advised.

He adjusted his virtual perceptual processing. Buildings, streets, and sidewalks arranged themselves into sensible order.

"Yes, that's better," he said.

Something was still odd about the scene, though. He let the rhythm of the city permeate his mind.

Most of the people were walking along calmly as if there were nothing different about their world. Others were gingerly feeling their way along, carefully checking the sidewalks before them with outstretched umbrellas or toes. *They're not relying on sight alone. It looks like they can feel but not see the 10-D twists in their paths. Interesting.*

Timothy watched for a while longer, remembering how lost he felt last time he was here. *So many mindless carbon copies, all on their way to...whatever they're on their way to. Copies?*—his eyes flitted up and down the street.

"Trillians," he hissed. "Dozens of them!" He grabbed Darya's arm and tugged her away from the window.

"I see that," Darya replied nonchalantly. "They're everywhere."

"If Trillian has clones of himself all over out there, how will we be able to leave this room?"

Darya waved her hand between them and transformed into yet another Trillian.

Timothy's eyes widened and he froze.

Has Darya been subverted by Trillian? Am I next? Should I run?

The Trillian before him laughed and spoke in Darya's voice.

"Don't worry. It's just a disguise! Here, have a look at yourself."

She gestured to the mirrored closet door. "Pretty convincing, don't you think?"

Timothy walked around the bed cautiously, without taking his eyes off her, and choked down the sense of dread building within him.

He looked into the mirror.

Trillian looked back at him. Timothy's hands flew to his face, the Trillian's face. He poked and prodded, trying to feel his own features below the disguise.

"Darya, I've seen you do many magical things, but this has to be the most distasteful ever. Who am I? Really?"

"It's okay. Relax! I assure you that you're the same old Timothy as always. I just thought it would be prudent to wear this image as we explore out there."

"But, why? There are so many people out there. Can't we just go as ourselves, or how about some other disguise," he pleaded.

"Isn't it obvious? If Trillian is everywhere and we don't want our movements to be restricted, we should look like Trillians, too."

"What if one of them talks to us? Won't he recognize us?"

"I don't think they actually talk to each other."

"Well, whatever they do."

Darya looked back outside. "Whoever is coordinating them, I haven't been able to eavesdrop on their communications. I don't know the right protocols."

"Then let's hope no one bothers us."

"In the worst case, we have these." Darya reached for a belt loop under her jacket. She pulled out what looked like a roll of chromed spring steel, tightly wound and attached to a handle.

"What's that?"

In answer, Darya flicked her wrist. The spring steel unrolled and snapped into the form of a familiar jian, the same kind of Chinese martial arts sword he'd often chosen to spar with inworld.

"What kind of magic is this? Have you wrested control of the local simulation back from Trillian?"

"No such luck. This is pure and simple technology, as effective in Alternus as it is anywhere else." She swished the sword back and forth a few times, admiring the snap of its flexible blade.

"The principle is memory steel. When the blade is rolled up, like yours," she unhooked the rolled-up sword attached to Timothy's own belt, "the metal is in a potentiated shape."

She gave the handle of the second device a rapid backhand flick and the sword unfurled. "Flicking it this way provides enough energy to overcome the embedded magnetic strip that holds the blade wound up. As it unfurls, it 'remembers' its preferred shape and folds along its length to make the sharp edges."

She handed the sword to Timothy. "The technology is ancient, from the time before the original Earth was lost, but it's surprisingly easy to simulate in a variety of inworld scenarios, which makes it particularly useful to keep around."

Timothy made a few appreciative slashing moves with his weapon. "It does comfort me, a little, to know we're not entirely defenseless."

"I thought it might."

He lifted the blade for a closer inspection. "Remarkably sharp," he observed.

"Indistinguishable from an integral blade of the finest steel," Darya confirmed.

"I don't imagine we can walk down the streets brandishing these things, though. How do we hide them? Can we fold them back up?"

Darya demonstrated the technique. "Push the tip into a hard surface as you bend the blade against the edge, whichever way it doesn't want to flex. If you push hard enough against it, it will butterfly open. Then you simply roll it up, and the internal magnets will do the rest."

After a few tries, Timothy got the hang of it. He could snap it open in an instant, and roll it back up in a few seconds. "Wait, doesn't that mean the sword is useless against a hard surface?" he asked.

"Indeed. The jian has always been more about slicing than stabbing. It's designed for harassing, discouraging, and incapacitating. Aim for soft tissue like the tendons, muscles, and neck. Avoid clashing with another blade or fighting shaft."

"Hmm...not as comforting as I'd first thought."

Darya laughed. "Only for use if absolutely needed. It'll be quick and efficient, and it might give us a few more minutes inworld if Trillian discovers us. Our best—our ultimate—defense is simply to run."

"I would much prefer to rid this world of a few Trillians before we flee, if it comes to that."

"And now you're well equipped and well trained for that, should the opportunity arise."

Timothy grinned. "Yes, I am. Okay, let's go find Mary."

They left the hotel lobby and merged into the flow of pedestrians. Darya adopted a casual, unhurried pace, and Timothy did his best to emulate. Nobody paid them any attention, including the other Trillians passing by.

Timothy moved a little closer and whispered, "Where are we going?"

"I don't know exactly," she answered.

He stopped in the middle of the stream of pedestrians, causing the very closest to halt or bump into him before the flow could adjust itself.

Darya grabbed his arm and pulled him along. "What are you doing? Don't draw attention!"

His feet resumed forward motion.

Darya checked for traffic and shepherded him across the street into a quiet alley. "If we're going to pull this off, you need to act naturally."

Timothy searched for words. "Naturally?" He gawked at the people moving on the opposite sidewalk, and at the skyscraper jutting out horizontally in 3-D a few hundred meters overhead. "What is *natural* about any of this?"

"Remember, *you* wanted to come with me," Darya pointed out. "You need to pretend like we're in New York City in Alternus. All of the *other* Trillians are."

"All of the other Trill.... Darya.... I'm not.... You.... You don't even have a plan," he stuttered, and stamped deeper into the alley to struggle with his anger.

Darya allowed him a moment of privacy before joining him.

"I do have a plan. Not a great one, maybe not even a very good one, but I do have a plan."

Timothy jammed his clenched fists into his pockets. Anyone standing at the entrance to the alley or peeking out of one of the windows above would have been looking at two identical Trillians, arguing with one another.

"So what's your plan?" Timothy demanded.

"When we last saw Mary, Trillian was fishing her out of a swimming pool."

"By the hair," Timothy added.

"Yes, by the hair. The point is, she was in Vacationland. I think she's still there."

"Well, we're not; we're in New York City."

"For now. I didn't dare enter Vacationland directly from outside. We would've been too easy to detect. My strongest connections are still to Alternus, even in this crazy version. I was hoping Trillian hadn't cut off all external connections yet. It seems I was right."

Timothy calmed down once he had a clear problem to focus on.

"Okay, that's good, but how do we get to Vacationland from here?"

"Remember the first time I opened the portal from inside that empty office complex? I think that'll be the best way in. Trillian will be less likely to detect our new activity if we follow roughly the same route."

"And where's the building?"

"I'm not a hundred percent certain, but I think I can retrace our steps from the UN Plaza. First, we have to find the plaza and, for that, I need you to be okay walking the streets of New York. Are you good with that?"

She saw the pained look creeping across his face and before he could open his mouth, she preempted his anticipated complaint. "Yes, yes, even in the mess that they are."

"Okay. I can do that," he said quietly.

"Are you sure?"

Timothy glared at her. She didn't flinch.

Finally, he let his shoulders relax and his anger seep away.

"Better?" she asked.

He sighed and nodded.

They left the alley and returned to the main sidewalk. Most of the people walked along as if nothing was unusual. Here and there, distressed individuals asked the less perturbed for help. They were ignored unless they physically obstructed a pedestrian's path, in which case, the foot traffic smoothly adjusted to flow around those who persisted in blocking the way.

"To the Partials, nothing has changed about New York," Darya explained. "As part of the simulation, they were adapted to the new configuration. And the Fulls who were trapped inside Alternus when Trillian merged it into the 10-D maze probably have no idea what happened or why the city is so bizarre."

She pointed with her chin across the street. "Look. Some of the Trillian clones are having trouble navigating as well. I'm guessing those ones must've been converted from Fulls, and only see in 3-D."

"What's his point in turning everyone into versions of himself?"

Darya grimaced. "I wish I knew. At first, I would've said it was to make it easier to find us, but that can't be the reason anymore. As far as he knows, we left Alternus for Vacationland or some other inworld, or even for the outworld. It could be a narcissistic indulgence, or maybe he enjoys the challenge."

"The challenge?"

"It's no trivial effort to wipe out the complete concepta and persona of a Full Cybrid instantiation and reprogram them. We have security, remember?"

Just then, half a block away on a street segment suspended vertically in the air, a dazed looking man grabbed his head and yelled in pain. His back arched and his arms flung outward. He shook himself violently as if to dislodge some horrific attacker from his shoulders. He dropped down on all fours, stood up again, and ran away at full speed, screaming the entire way.

The man disappeared from the local view in three dimensions, but Darya and Timothy had no trouble tracking him by shifting their vision, first "blueward" and then "strangeward", as he barreled down the road in agony. He re-emerged in their local 3-D space, where the road ran in front of them.

The man came to an abrupt stop, clutched his head again, and screamed in anguish at the sky. His features grew indistinct and then melted like plastic on hot asphalt. He slouched nearly to the point of collapse. When he stood erect again, he was a Trillian.

The transformed man regarded Darya and Timothy, wearing the same avatar image as him. "Hello," he said.

Darya felt a deeper communication pulse, requesting her Trillian instantiation tag and an update on local conditions. She reached under her jacket, where her sword was neatly rolled up in a small sheath on her belt, and grasped its handle. In a fluid motion, she pulled the handle from its holder and flicked it outward as her arm made a backhand swoop.

The blade elongated fully at the moment it contacted the new Trillian's neck. His severed head flew into the street.

"Run!" Darya hissed at Timothy, pulling him down the street with her.

They took a quick couple of turns through a complex mess of ten dimensions. When they stopped to breathe, they were still a kilometer from the UN Plaza but there were no Trillians in sight.

Darya rolled up her sword and stashed it back in its sheath.

"What was that all about?" Timothy asked, winded and confused.

"Just the wrong place at the wrong time," Darya answered. "None of the other Trillians bothered to talk to us. I guess, the first thing the new ones do is get a local update. After this, I expect they'll all start checking in with each other."

Darya's image shimmered and her Trillian disguise fell away. She was herself again. Timothy looked at his hands; they were his own once more. Trillian's preferred white jacket was replaced by the smart black leather piece Timothy had chosen for the adventure.

"Thank you!" he said. "I detest carrying the appearance of that man."

Darya frowned. "Unfortunately, that was the only extra avatar I could bring inworld. Let's hope Trillian isn't looking for our faces. We'd better start avoiding all the clones we see."

"I agree."

They set out again. Their one small advantage, the ability to see in all ten dimensions at once, was only helpful if they spotted the Trillians before getting spotted themselves.

Each time a Trillian came into view, the pair turned outside of his 3-D space as casually as possible. When they could, they ducked into side streets, back alleys, or shops. They held their breath when they passed within touching distance of a stumbling Trillian who couldn't see them only an arm's length away in an alternative dimension. Darya hoped Trillian hadn't thought to adjust all of his clones to see in ten dimensions yet.

When the UN Plaza came into view, the pair let out a sigh of relief. There didn't appear to be any more Trillian instantiations here than anywhere else in the New York labyrinth. They headed toward a busy hot dog vendor next to the plaza, the same one who'd been cheerfully serving hot dogs to throngs of people the last time Timothy had been here.

Wearing Trillian's face!

"Keep walking," Darya whispered. She split off, clambered over the nearby fence and walked quietly along the trees behind it.

The former First Footman obeyed without question, paralleling her path with a confident nonchalance he didn't feel. When he arrived within a dozen meters of the stand, the Trillian noticed him with some surprise.

"Timothy! I wasn't sure we'd have a chance to meet again." He searched around uncertainly. "But, where is your lovely companion? I do so wish to speak with her."

A flurry of possibilities flew through Timothy's mind. They hadn't practiced this scenario at all.

"She's...she left me," he sputtered. "Not that it's any of your.... I don't need her to deal with the likes of you."

Trillian threw his head back and laughed. "Perhaps you imagine a good old-fashioned round of fisticuffs, do you? Why don't I call over a few more of me and we'll see how your bravery holds up?"

Hotdog-vender Trillian wiped his hands on his smock and stepped around the cart toward Timothy. He was so intent on the former Footman he didn't hear the rustle of leaves or quiet footsteps behind him. He did hear the *whoosh* of the blade an instant before it removed his head. He died with his startled eyes wide open.

Shocked customers and passersby shrieked and fled in all directions.

"Let's move before any more of him get here," Darya said.

Taking advantage of the pandemonium, Timothy dropped his fists and blended in with the crowd, doing his best not to attract further attention.

After a series of quick turns in other-dimensional directions, they broke free from the excitement and located the familiar office building.

Today, unlike their first visit, the place was bustling with activity. A loud, impatient woman pushed past the others in the lobby and strutted purposefully to the Receptionist. Darya used the distraction to pass through to the offices behind.

"Can I help you?" a voice intervened.

Damn! Darya stopped short of the threshold, and searched her memory for nameplates she'd seen when she'd last opened a portal into Vacationland.

"Oh, hi, there. We just thought we'd pop in and speak with Reg."

"Reg isn't here," the gatekeeper answered curtly. "He doesn't work here anymore."

"He doesn't? Well, that's a shame. How about Drew? Is he available?"

The Receptionist pointed to a chair. "Have a seat right there and I'll ring him."

"That's okay, we know where he is," Darya replied, as she grabbed Timothy's arm and pulled him through behind her.

"Hey!" the Receptionist cried. "You can't go back there."

"Sword!" Darya whispered in Timothy's direction.

The two strode into the shared corridor over the young lady's protests.

They could hear the Receptionist calling for Security. They carried on.

As Darya walked, she snapped her sword out. Her mind was already working on reopening the portal to Vacationland. The links to the pipe code she'd inserted into this distorted version of Alternus were all in place.

Behind her, someone screamed. She heard a scuffle and spun around in time to see Timothy kick over a wounded attacker. The assailant was too astonished by the gaping wound in his belly to avoid Timothy's foot.

She caught Timothy's eye and held it. *Move on. No time for sentimentality now.*

Darya heard someone rush up behind her. She ducked low, and slashed a wide arc.

A fierce-looking brute gasped and put a hand to his thigh, where her sword had opened a gash through his pants. Before he could advance, she delivered a jump-kick to his chin, propelling him backward into two others who were closing in.

In the moment of stunned silence that followed, Darya and Timothy bolted for the nondescript door where the open portal waited.

"Locked!" she cried, and slapped the door.

"Allow me," Timothy offered, and kicked it open.

It was hard to say which of them was more surprised. It certainly wasn't the Trillian clone with crazed eyes who'd been waiting inside to greet them.

"Hyaaaaaah!" he bellowed, almost comically, and leaped from the desk with murderous intent.

Darya whirled to one side, and slashed at the Trillian's throat. His cry gurgled through blood, and he thumped lifelessly to the floor.

The portal shimmered over the far desk. Darya grabbed Timothy's hand and they dived through without looking back.

31

NOT A SINGLE PERSON MARRED the tranquility of the impossibly long, pristine beach, though the weather was perfect for swimming. While the tranquil tropical paradise was alluring, the sight filled Darya with foreboding. Over thousands of visits, she'd never seen Vacationland so deserted. All in all, the effect was disturbing.

They'd nearly knocked over her favorite Cloud 49 table when they came hurtling through the portal, wild-eyed and out of breath. She noticed the lack of patrons immediately.

No time to analyze. Keep moving!

Darya started down the hovering restaurant's long stairway, making no attempt to hide her drawn sword.

Timothy followed in her wake. "Where should we start? Do you have any idea where she might be? Where are all the patrons?"

"Trillian's masking Mary's location, but there's a perpetual cloud of quantum confusion around her. I think she's over that way, in one of the cabinas."

"He won't make it easy to reach her."

"I don't expect so. We'll take an indirect route."

They reached the bottom of the stairwell and headed for the lush vegetation across the beach.

Darya plunged in.

Timothy struggled to keep up. "Do you plan to approach through the underbrush?" he panted.

"No, Trillian will have guards on all routes between the restaurant and the resort area. We'll find someplace quiet in another direction, and I'll see if I can hack into a more direct route from there."

"Couldn't we have done that from the Alternus maze?"

"It was too complicated from there, and Trillian already had too many safeguards established."

"We made it here, didn't we? How much harder could it be?" Timothy asked. He was beginning to think Darya enjoyed the chase more than the accomplishment.

She stopped abruptly and faced him. "You'll just have to trust me on this," she said. "I think I can get us close to Mary, but I can't do it from a different inworld, and I can't do it if I need to keep watch for enemy Trillians descending on us. We need a hideout."

She turned and resumed picking her way through the vegetation.

After what he hoped would be a safe while, Timothy ventured another question. "Do you have somewhere in mind?"

"I do. There's a recreational cave system not too far away. It rearranges itself randomly with each user, or every twenty-four hours. It's impossible to map. I'm sure Trillian won't be able to track us there if we go in deep enough."

They began making their way uphill, leaving the idyllic resort area behind. The trees thinned, and the pair picked up a trail to the cave system.

"If the caves can't be mapped, how do people get out?"

"They don't," Darya answered, digging into the loose gravel underfoot. "That's a big part of their charm; visitors pay extra for that," she explained. "They are led deep inside by an automated guide they hold in the palm of their hands. They walk in for about an hour and then the guide shuts down. The challenge is to find their way out. Almost no one does."

Timothy slipped on the loose rocks. "And they consider that "fun"? Do visitors die in there?"

"No, they call the Supervisor to let them exit. That won't be possible for us."

"Okay...so...how will we get out?"

"We'll pipe across to Mary."

"If you can track her down."

"When I find her, we'll cross over to wherever she is."

"But won't we be walking right into Trillian's trap?"

"Yes. Once we find her, we'll rescue her, and I'll set a pipe back to New York in Alternus."

"Are we any safer there?"

"At the very least, she'll be out of Trillian's hands. I think I can get her back to her trueself from there."

The incline was getting steeper. Darya pulled herself upslope by tugging on a thick tuft of grass. She pointed out some better footholds to Timothy, who'd paused to catch his breath and was looking back wistfully toward the jungle and beach.

"I feel rather exposed out here," he confessed.

"It's not much farther now, and I doubt Trillian has any eyes on the ground up here."

Timothy face brightened at the thought. "Why is that?"

A loud, wild snarl came from a nearby bush. Darya and Timothy jumped; they'd been so busy making their way and watching for Trillian, they hadn't given much thought to the wild animals that drew hunters to this area of Vacationland. They froze and scanned the area for the source.

"Make some noise; maybe we can startle it away," Darya said, and slapped her hands together sharply. "Be careful, though. We don't want to alert the Trillians," she warned.

They clapped and hissed. "Psst! Scat! Ssst!"

Timothy stomped his foot down hard against the ground and was rewarded with an annoyed roar.

An enormous cougar leaped from its hiding space. The sight of its fierce jaws and claws almost paralysed him, but the past few weeks of intense training with Darya had heightened his automatic response.

As he rolled backward, he whipped his sword up and slashed the air in the direction of the feline. The big cat flew over him, unleashing an irate cry as she avoided the blade. She landed heavily and crouched for another attack.

Timothy rolled to the side and into an upright ready position but he was shaking uncontrollably.

The cougar eyed his fear and trembling hands, as did Darya.

Easy prey—they both concluded.

Darya lunged at the wildcat, thrusting and rattling her sword. The big cat gave a throaty growl and bounded away. Darya watched until it disappeared into the tall grass. Her gaze swung to Timothy. "We were lucky," she said. "I know these creatures; they're vicious. They hunt the hills around here, and they don't usually give up so quickly. She must have eaten recently."

Timothy dropped to the ground in a relieved heap. "I don't feel lucky," he said. He was so tired.

Darya continued, but kept a wary eye on him. "These ones are based on cougars but they're even more stealthy, persistent, and deadly than the trueform. They're also why Trillian won't have many eyes on the ground here," she reassured him. "He knows these animals will kill anyone walking around this area, including us and his Trillian clones."

"That's not very comforting," Timothy replied. "If it had wounded me, what would you have done?" he asked.

"I'd have finished the job. You forget, *we* are not real here, either. No more than the enhanced Partials, the servers, or the surf instructors. Same for those predator cats. They're programs; for them it's kill or get killed. If they get killed, they just start over. If you're killed here, you'd wake up back in your trueself on Secondus."

"But that...that would hurt, wouldn't it?" he asked. His teeth were chattering now and he was shivering. Shock was setting in.

Darya stepped forward and hugged him. "It's okay. Take some deep breaths. You're doing great, Timothy. You really are, and we're almost there."

Timothy hugged her back, and forced a deep exhale that would allow his lungs to draw in maximum oxygen as they refilled.

"Thanks for saving me. I was mentally prepared to fight as many Trillians as it took. I wasn't ready to face animals. People are one thing. Animals, vicious or not, that's a whole different thing."

"Some say people are the most vicious animals in the universe. Regardless, we're okay now. The cougars have a large range, many square kilometers. It could be a while before that one comes back to check on us, but we don't want to be here when she does. She'll be especially aggressive."

Timothy pushed aside the images of massive teeth and razor claws intent on dispatching him from this world, breathed as deeply as he could, and loosened his desperate hold on Darya.

"I'm okay now," he said and took another deep breath. "Let's keep moving."

Darya held him at arm's length and examined his color. It was back to normal; close enough, anyway. "Okay. It's not too much farther, now. We can rest a bit once we get deep enough inside."

They carried on a short way up the hill and turned away from the resorts.

"I can't imagine anyone in their right mind fighting through those animals just to get to caves with no exit," Timothy said.

"Define 'right' mind," Darya joked. "Cybrid life, making things, fixing things, pushing things around, that all gets boring. People will do all kinds of crazy things for thrills and adventure."

Timothy shook his head. "I don't understand that drive, not at all."

"Give it time. You will. And you have to keep in mind that, inworld, we're essentially invulnerable. Well, unless potential death is part of the draw, which is exceedingly rare. To a lot of people, nothing matters more than the chase and to experience the thrill. Anything else is background noise."

"Alternus didn't used to be particularly thrilling, not before Trillian arrived."

"That was a special case; it was my attempt to get people interested in being in charge of their lives. Their *real* lives.

"Ah, here we are! The caves. See? I told you we were close."

A roughly carved wooden sign warned, "Despair all ye who enter!"

A little cliché, but it does set a tone—Darya thought.

Timothy shrugged. "It's smaller than I would have expected."

"It's not much to look at from out here, but the system has hundreds of kilometers of cavern."

They pushed aside some leafy vines that cascaded over the entrance from the rocky hill above, and plunged into the dark cavern.

Recessed lights popped on and a voice announced, "Welcome to Caverna. Please select your exploration gear and a guide from the shelves to your left. We remind you that the caves reconfigure automatically every twenty-four hours. Your guide will walk you in for one hour, at which point the caves will rearrange and your trek outward begins.

"Pressing the green button on the side of your guide will return you outworld with a two-day penalty before you will be permitted to return to Vacationland. Good luck."

Darya grabbed some rope, crampons, a pick, and a helmet with a mounted light. She motioned for Timothy to do the same while she selected a pair of sturdy footwear.

"Aren't we going to take a guide?" Timothy asked.

"What's the point? Our only acceptable way out is a pipe to wherever Mary is."

Timothy looked doubtful, but he didn't object.

They checked their gear, turned on their headlamps, and walked a few hours into the labyrinth. Occasionally, they arrived at dead ends and had to retrace their steps back to their last turn. They chose a path that wound steadily downward. When it dropped precipitously, they used their gear to belay to the next level below. They encountered no one along the way. They heard nothing but their own footsteps and echoing drips of moisture from the damp ceiling.

Several levels down, they came to another dead end and Darya announced, "I think that's far enough for now. Even if Trillian was alerted to our arrival in the caves, I don't think he'd have a chance of finding us."

"He can send enough clones to fill these caves."

"True. But there's only one way in and it takes a time to walk every possible route. More than a few hundred instantiations, and they'd be tripping over each other. We'll have to stay alert but we should be far enough in to get at least three or four hours of peace. I'll need at least that to locate Mary."

"Will that be enough?"

"It'll have to be." Darya plunked herself on the ground against a boulder and closed her eyes.

"What should I do?" Timothy asked.

"This will only take a few hours. Get some rest. Meditate. Reflect."

"It will do me no good to sit idle for hours."

"You won't be of much use in looking for Mary, either, I'm afraid."

"Couldn't I at least follow your search?"

"I'm not sure how much you'll understand."

"I'll keep quiet and stay in the background. You won't even know I'm there. It'll give me a chance to learn something about inworlds and their programming."

Darya frowned, weighing how much of a distraction Timothy would be. "Alright," she said. "I'll take you inside with me, but it has to be in tandem."

Timothy grinned eagerly.

"Stay in the background and keep quiet," she admonished. "No questions."

He nodded and sat on the ground beside her. "What do I do?"

She sent him instructions through the lattice. "This will allow you to observe what I'm doing. I'll do all the driving."

"Very well," he said. He closed his eyes and executed the code she'd sent him.

32

A MESMERIZING WORLD OF DATA STRUCTURES AND CODE swirled all around him. Timothy spotted Darya a few meters away. She was swathed in a roiling cloud of words and thin, curving lines with arrow tips. He anchored his attention to her. The structures looked similar to the ones from their conceptas and personas that she'd shown him. A question drifted from his lips before he remembered his promise.

"Do the inworlds use data structures and programs like ours?"

She glared back. "You said you'd stay quiet."

"Right. Sorry."

She sighed. "It's okay. I haven't gotten very far into it yet. Let me familiarize you with what you're looking at. I'll answer this question and then, please, either leave me alone, or you'll have to exit and wait for me there."

Timothy gulped. "I'll stay with you, and be quiet."

"The answer is, yes. The inworlds and our own lattices have a lot in common. That's only natural, given the concepta is the best way we know to organize high-level data.

"But where we have a persona, the inworld has data structures related to its own rules. Underneath that is an operating system designed for efficient implementation of the local rules and for interfacing to Cybrid minds."

"I see," Timothy said. "I think." He didn't.

"Most inworlds provide basic hosting support for our avatars. Our personas are copied in but they only have whatever capabilities the host O/S provides.

"The Alternus inworld does a lot more than that. It hosts our full capabilities, even *my* full capabilities."

"What do you mean, your full capabilities?"

"You may have noticed that my lattice design is more advanced than most Cybrids."

"I don't have much to compare you to."

"I guess that's true. Okay, take my word for it. Anyway, my quark-spin lattice system is supported in Alternus."

"How will that help us? We're not in Alternus right now."

"True, but I designed the hardware to be invasive. If it's done its job, it should have replaced the majority of the Vacationland hardware by now. I hope it will provide me with enough of a boost that I can find Mary and rescue her."

Timothy seemed satisfied with her answer. He wisely withheld his follow-up questions and watched in silence for the next three hours as Darya injected little bits of code into various parts of the larger structure.

She marked some areas in bright red and avoided them. "Trillian's traps," she remarked over her shoulder. It was the only thing she uttered for hours.

Timothy used the time to make sense of bits of code and to familiarize himself with the complicated structures. He became so engrossed that he was startled when Darya next spoke.

"I think I found her," she said.

He blinked. "Where is she?"

Darya motioned to a piece of blue data surrounded by angry red patches on a green background.

"This is one of the quantum cabinas right near the pool where we fought Trillian. I'm fairly certain she's in there."

"I would have thought that would be one of the first places you'd look," Timothy replied. "What took you so long?"

Darya's face remained studiously flat, emotionless.

Timothy squirmed inside, knowing he'd been unfair. *I didn't mean to be unkind; it must be killing her that we left her friend behind in Trillian's hands. The guy may be working for the Church of The Living God, but he has a dark, wicked streak in him.*

Darya's face softened as she sensed his guilt. "I did look there first. As you pointed out, it was a fairly obvious place to take her. Too obvious, in fact. All the signs point to her being detained there, but I have to be careful. You can see all the traps Trillian's placed around her."

Timothy nodded.

"I spent most of that time just verifying that Mary is actually there."

"What did you find? Is she there?"

"Yes, she is. I'm certain of it, and I think we can avoid the traps."

"Can we get to her?"

"That's the tricky part. We can get close, but I'm not sure we'll be able to reach her safely."

"I'm willing to risk it. We have to try."

"Can you read the code here?" Darya pointed to a tiny green section next to the bit of blue code where she guessed Mary was being held.

Timothy stepped up to examine the green code. He traced it with his fingers. "Let's see. Small chamber. Glass window. Rocky. Dark. Very hot."

"Hot is one way to put it. It's inhospitable enough on its own that Trillian didn't bother putting any traps in it. That's why it's green. And it's the closest I can get to Mary. Are you ready to walk through Hell, itself?"

"Hell? As in, Satan's den? Really? I thought Alum was above all that, being the All-Benevolent, Living God, and all."

"Alum's not above a good scare, when needed, and neither is Trillian. Most definitely, not Trillian."

"Can we survive it?"

"It'll hurt—more than you can imagine—but just remember that you'll be okay. The flames won't damage us. I can guarantee our integrity for a brief visit. Just focus on our task and remember that, so long as we pop in and out of there quickly, the effect won't be lasting."

"Will we be able to help Mary?"

Darya slumped. "Rescue her? No, I don't think so but I'll be able to send her something useful."

"Like a weapon or a way out?"

"Not long ago, I gave her a gift, an upgrade similar to my own lattice. I have to trust that she's been looking for a way to access her full capabilities. In this world, or in Trillian's twisted version of it, her best chance to survive will be using her wits. She'll need to be smarter than Trillian. I can send her the code to unlock the direct access to the Alternus quark-spin lattice."

"That's it?"

"That will be more than enough."

Timothy stared at her in disbelief. "So, we aren't going to rescue her?"

"Not directly. We'll have to settle for giving her everything she needs to rescue herself."

"Then we'd best hurry."

Darya nodded and waved her hands.

The code and data around them disappeared and was replaced by flames. And pain!

Timothy yelped. He'd known it was coming and, still, the pain was excruciating. He could feel his hair and skin burning, his flesh roasting. He looked down at his hands. They were undamaged.

Darya wasn't immune to the pain, either. She gasped and approached the window on the rocky wall in front of them. Inside was a prison cell that looked like it belonged in the medieval era.

Timothy recognized torture devices he'd seen in the history books at Casa DonTon. Despite the heat, he shuddered to think of the horrifically effective damage they would do to flesh and mind.

They spotted Mary, chained to a table. She looked wild and desperate.

Four Trillians leaned over her. One held a small rusty old blade in front of her face. He was saying something to her, something horrible, no doubt.

He traced the knife across her stomach.

Mary screamed, but the sound didn't penetrate through the window.

Timothy whimpered in sympathy. He was so distracted by the sight of her, he barely felt the flames licking at him anymore.

Darya stretched a hand to the window. Timothy laid his own hand beside hers, silently imploring Mary to look at them.

The gesture caught the attention of the Trillians. Mary was conscious but her eyes were clenched shut.

On seeing Darya and Timothy, the clones stopped what they were doing.

Mary opened her eyes and followed their confused gazes to the window. Her eyes met Darya's.

"I'm sorry," Darya mouthed. The flickering light cast dramatic shadows on the pair's pained faces. "I'm so sorry."

Two of the Trillians disappeared from the torture cell and rematerialized inside Hell, on each side of Darya and Timothy.

Before the Trillians could grab them, Darya gestured and a dazzling flash blinded everyone. When Mary and the Trillians could see again, Darya and Timothy were gone.

The Trillians shouted angrily and returned to Mary's cell.

33

BROTHER STRALASI PACED the length of the integration and control center. Every few steps he glanced impatiently at Darak, who was too busy adjusting the soltron detector array to notice him. Had the Good Brother understood any of it, he might have found the device interesting. As it was, his mind kept wandering back to Eso-La. He wished he were walking among the park-like forests with Crissea instead of stuck here with Darak on this barren rock.

"But if you can't refine the resolution to better than two light years, what good will that do us?" the Good Brother asked.

If Darak picked up on the monk's frustration, he ignored it. "That's two light years across tens of millions of light years. Once we narrow it down to a particular region, I should be able to pinpoint its location to within a few light hours. First, I need to figure out approximately where to look."

"I thought you didn't have much of an idea where it was."

"I don't, but if it's been aimed toward the asteroid belt of Eso-La sometime over the last seven million years, it probably came from one of the colonies in the Canes Venatici I cluster. They're the closest, and Alum would need to use entangled particles from one of their starsteps to move the Eater so far at once. So that's where I'm starting.

"I've been winding the astronomical clock backward to get approximate locations some twenty millions years ago, and forward to determine where Eso-La will be over the next few million years. That gives me a broad cylinder in which to search more thoroughly."

"Surely you don't intend for us to shift through all that space looking for this thing?"

"Hmm? No, not at all. Eso-La has ten of these detectors in the array. I can use them in a binary search pattern."

Stralasi sighed. *Dear Alum, give me strength.* "Binary search?" he asked.

For once, Darak made no comment on the deficiencies in the monk's education.

"Binary search. We assemble the array in the halfway point. The Eater is either closer to Eso-La or closer to the Canes Venatici I system.

"Let's say it's closer to Eso-La. We move the array halfway between where we are and Eso-La and look again.

"Then we move halfway between where we are at *that* point, and which region we detect the Eater in. And so on, and so on, until we isolate it to within a few light years.

"Once we narrow down its location, I can move the soltron detectors into a pair of arrays, one on the path and one above it at a right angle. That should narrow it down enough for us to shift directly into its immediate neighborhood."

"So I'm supposed to accompany you until my dying days as we push these asteroids into place? I'd rather stay here," Stralasi sulked.

"We don't need to *push* them anywhere. I'll shift them."

"You can shift a whole planetoid?" Stralasi's face was struggling between derision and incredulity. He'd seen Darak perform miracles, but moving mountain-sized rocks in space would be a miracle of a truly God-like scale.

The implications troubled him.

"It'll be near my computational limits," Darak answered, "but I can handle it. That's how they got where they are in the first place. Would you like to watch?"

Over the next twenty minutes, with Stralasi watching from inside, Darak moved the asteroids and their internal soltron detectors into position near the middle of the thirty million light year distance between Eso-La and the Canes Venatici I system of galaxies.

Once he was satisfied with the position of the detectors, Darak brought the monk back to his side at the control panel and linked their lattices into the data stream.

"How long before we get an idea?" Stralasi asked.

"Soltron emissions are weak here, so it can't be terribly close. I won't try to get more than a general direction at this point; just whether it's closer to Eso-La or the Canes Venatici cluster. That should only take a few hours. Would you like some lunch?"

"What I'd like is lunch on Eso-La."

Darak regarded the man more closely. "You and Crissea seem to be getting along well."

"Yes, she's lovely, and the rest is none of your business."

Darak grinned. "Okay, then. Lunch it is." He chose a corner of the chamber opposite the control panel and expanded a picnic lunch, including a table and chairs, from a pea-sized pellet he pulled from a pocket.

From somewhere Stralasi couldn't see, Darak piped in soothing ambient music to fill the space left by the absence of conversation.

A soft chime sounded.

"Ah, there we go. Enough data has been collected to give us a rough direction," Darak said. Without moving from his chair, he accessed the results. "Hmm, that's interesting. It's a little farther away than I might've thought. Closer to Eso-La."

He stood, and brushed his hands against his pants. "Time to get back to work," he said.

Stralasi pushed off his chair reluctantly. "Just like before?" he asked.

"Just like before."

Over the next two days, Darak moved the asteroids containing the soltron detector array several times. Each time, the array was positioned closer to Eso-La, and the results made him frown.

Darak drew a line through the array positions as they drew closer and closer to the Eater. The vector predicted a path in the ESO 461-36 galaxy that was uncomfortably close to Eso-La's current position.

"What's the problem with that?" Stralasi asked when Darak shared the unwelcome information with him.

"It could mean that Alum's aim was bad, or he failed to properly account for the movement of Eso-La sun around its galactic core, or...." Darak's voice trailed off.

"Or what?"

"Or that the Eater is already approaching the ringworld."

Stralasi thought about death hurtling toward Eso-La and Crissea. He had to do something to save her, save *them*.

"I'm going to shift the array a light year or so away from Eso-La and a little out of the galactic plane, just to be safe."

Stralasi didn't like the sound of that. "Will it get that close? I thought the Canes Venatici I cluster was at least thirty millions light years away. If the Eater was launched from that vicinity at near-light speed some seven million years ago, wouldn't it be farther from Eso-La?"

"My assumptions might be incorrect," Darak admitted. "If Alum can shift the Eater, maybe he jumped it to a ship that was already not so far away."

"Was there such a ship, one that could safely contain the Eater?"

"It wouldn't have to contain the Eater. It would only have to provide a starstep point that it could be shifted to. I'm not aware of any ship sent to the ESO galaxy up to 30 million years ago, but I've been away a long time. Alum may have staggered Foundation ships to explore this region. The Local Void we call it. Maybe He found a rogue star in the Void, or moved one there. Who knows? He has multiple agendas, and they're constantly changing."

Darak moved the array within a light year from Eso-La. "In any case, we need to confirm. I hope I'm wrong." The tiny star was still the brightest thing in the poorly lit sky of the dim galaxy.

Stralasi yearned to go there and to take Crissea to somewhere safe. He had bad premonitions about what they were going to find once the array was reactivated.

Darak arranged the detector asteroids in a wide array out of the projected path of the Eater, and stood before the control panel. His tight lips conveyed his worry. He activated the detector array.

Darak and Stralasi barely breathed while they waited for the reflective spheres to pass detection events to the devices spaced around the metal cages.

A strong signal appeared, but it was rapidly receding.

Even with his limited experience, Stralasi was able to interpret the data. "The Eater's less than a light year from Eso-La, and moving fast."

Darak nodded. "It's headed right for them. Impact, if you can call it that, will happen in less than a year."

He spun away from the control panel and walked toward the detector globe. He stared at his reflection, lost in troubled thoughts.

Stralasi tried to comfort his mentor. "Okay, we've found it. It's a little closer than we'd hoped but, no problem, right?"

Darak mumbled something unintelligible.

Stralasi tried again. "So? What do we do next?"

Darak's answer was barely audible. "Not much we *can* do." His eyes studied the gleaming detector or perhaps his reflection.

"There's always something you can do," Stralasi encouraged.

"Eso-La and its billions of inhabitants have less than a year to live. They have nowhere to run, and no way to evacuate everyone."

"Surely, *you* could get everyone safely away. You could just pop in and take them somewhere else."

"Where would they go?" Darak scoffed. "Somewhere in the Realm? Who would welcome them? Alum would jail them, kill them, or wipe their minds."

"Can't you find a new planet, one outside the Realm?"

"You and I have visited thousands of planets inhabited by the Realm. You've seen the genetic changes, the Standard modifications necessary in order for people to survive."

"You must know of *some* place."

Darak snapped, "What do you know about it? What do you know about anything, for that matter?" He removed himself to a far corner of the observation chamber.

Stralasi gave him a few minutes to calm down, and followed him.

"You can't simply give up. Not now. The people need you. You have to take them somewhere."

Darak glowered at the Good Brother. Seeing the resolution tempered with compassion in Stralasi's face, he softened.

"Sure, I could take them to some other planet. But, you of all people have to understand. To bring Standard Life to a virgin planet in under a year so that it's habitable by humans, or to modify humans enough to survive on a non-Standard planet, you've got to have all the biochemistry exactly right. I wouldn't have the time to make that many modifications. What you're asking is impossible."

Darak covered his face with his hands and rubbed his brow. "I didn't think I'd ever have to face this again."

"Again?" Stralasi asked.

Darak's fingers crested his brow and combed through his hair. He inhaled deeply and released it loudly.

"Earth," he said. "Origin, that is. When we first discovered the Eater, we had only decades to take the planet from a primitive, squabbling, greedy, narrow-minded, unscientific bunch of incompetents only recently out of the stone age, and turn them into self-sufficient space colonists. Even then, we could only save millions out of the billions of people on the planet."

He faced the monk. "It's a terrible thing, to choose who lives and who dies. Less than a few in every thousand was chosen. But even that wasn't good enough for Alum. He didn't like our choices, so he made his own. The best of humanity died with Earth, and we were left with...your ancestors."

Stubbornly, Stralasi pressed on. "We could at least try to save some of them."

Darak snorted. "Your precious Crissea? Do you think she'd go with you and leave her people to die? You think she loves you that much and them so little?"

Stung by the bitterness in Darak's tone, Stralasi turned his face away. "You can move them out of the way," he said.

Darak gaped at him. "Move Eso-La? The sun and the entire ringworld?"

"If not them, you can move the Eater."

Darak started to object but Stralasi spoke over him. "If Alum can do it, so can you."

Darak stared at Stralasi, then laughed, and shook his head.

"What did I say that was so funny *this* time?" Stralasi demanded.

"I *knew* you'd prove valuable to have along. I didn't know how or when, but I had a hunch. I *never* would have predicted something like this, though."

"Like what?"

"You, my good man, are absolutely right. Alum moved the Eater, but I don't have the computational capability to generate a shifting field that big."

"And how does that help?"

"We don't need to be able to do it ourselves. We just need to steal the capability from him."

34

FRIDAY, MARCH 10, 2062 VESTA NEWS – *Wide-scale riots broke out earlier today along the Spinward district near North 50 in Vesta Five when customers arrived to find doors to their local branch of the Administration Bank locked and the ATMs out of service. The angry protests began this morning and escalated to isolated violence by mid-afternoon as citizens discovered they could not access their most recent paychecks. Additional security was brought in to manage and disperse the angry crowd. Like many areas throughout the asteroids, the district has been plagued by malfunctioning electricity and unexplained food and water shortages for several months.*

CYBRID JSC475319 saw no choice but to shut down the bank. The computer system was misbehaving and she could not determine the cause. Worse, the problem was beginning to spread to other branches. If she didn't take it offline now, accounts all over Vesta were going to be scrambled. People could lose all their savings. Businesses could seize up. Blame would fly freely and a scapegoat would be punished. *A Cybrid one, almost certainly.*

She motioned to Cynthia, the Branch Manager. "I'm afraid your systems have some sort of malfunction. I have to shut them down."

The manager scanned the customer service area nervously. Today was payday and people wanted to get at their cash. The bank was full. Despite efforts to encourage the use of electronic currency, people still preferred the feel of physical dollars, Vesta dollars included, in their wallets.

Being uprooted from home and family, being moved to the asteroid colonies, and witnessing the destruction of Earth last year, had left everyone feeling insecure. She understood that. They were alive, working, and hoping to build again but the absence of their home planet, the origin of humankind, was still painful to most. Feeling a few dollars nestled in one's pocket was comforting.

"JSC—Jessica—are you sure about this? Couldn't we just restart the computers?" the manager asked.

"I've tried that three times already. They keep coming back up the same way. There's likely a software virus of some sort, but I can't find it. My team needs more time to scope it out. Either way, our system is sending out requests for transfers, payments, deposits, and loans. Each one has the potential to spread the problem to the Vesta-wide system. I'm sorry, Cynthia, but we have to shut down this branch until we can figure out what's going on."

"My customers aren't going to be happy."

"I know. That's why I need you to explain it to them. They wouldn't like it coming from me."

People started to notice the line slowing. A hushed buzz of concern permeated the air. A little commotion was developing at the front of one of the lines. Necks craned to see what was going on.

A couple of tellers caught the manager's eye and flashed subtle hand signals, hopefully indecipherable by their customer—*Cash dispensers are frozen.*

The hushed buzz was growing louder and more irritated.

Cynthia sighed heavily. "Okay. Turn it off."

"I already did, a few minutes ago," the Cybrid replied. "It was necessary."

The manager bit her lower lip and nodded once. It had to be done. "Okay, I'll close the branch."

She took a deep breath, instructed her employees to step back from their stations, and faced the snaking lineup of unhappy customers to deliver the news.

"Ladies and gentlemen, due to a technical issue, this branch is now closed. We invite you to visit any of our other branches. Thank you in advance for your understanding and patience as we work to resolve the matter."

As predicted, the clientele surged forward and loudly demanded access to their funds.

JSC floated toward the counters, protecting the bank staff from their frustrated clients. The two other Cybrids posted to the branch hovered behind her. Their imposing gray, spherical bodies rose together over the counter.

The sight of the three carboceramic beings rising from behind the teller stations only served to raise panic. They retreated in fear, mistakenly perceiving a threat from the mechanical beings. Several people who'd been holding their place at the front of the lines now turned and bolted, shoving their way through anyone standing between them and the exit.

"That probably wasn't how you wanted me to get everyone out," JSC said as Cynthia walked up to the three Cybrids. They stood together in the middle of the empty floor.

Scared but angry, the customers refused to leave the front of the building. Others joined them, curious about the commotion. Before long, hundreds were gathered.

IN A SURPRISE CONCESSION *at last month's Governing Council meeting, the Administration accepted an offer of assistance from Jared Strang, Director of the Office of Cybrid-Human relations. Strang immediately placed Cybrid experts in locations throughout the habitats in an attempt to remedy some of the recent banking and infrastructure issues. Despite their presence, troubles continue to plague many habitat districts.*

Strang has been calling for an increase in the number of Cybrids permitted to work within the habitats, citing "human inefficiencies" as justification. The Administration has so far refused to allow more than one thousand of the autonomous machines inside any single habitat. In an official press release last week, Alum stated that, "Cybrids and people are working together to solve these problems in a show of cooperation. The machines have a support role, only. We humans like to come up with our own solutions."

"I REALLY SHOULD GO OUT THERE," JSC said, "See if I can reassure them and calm them down."

"Because your last efforts weren't enough?" the manager replied.

"I'll do my best to be less intimidating."

"Is that even possible?"

The Cybrid emitted a sighing sound from her speaker panel. "What is with people?"

The manager regarded her with raised eyebrows. "For starters, you're a machine."

"Obviously."

"Obviously. And we know your kind built the habitats."

"But?"

"We still aren't sure whether you can be trusted. It can be hard to see the humanity in you."

"Ouch," JSC replied. "What can I do, then?"

"Let me go out."

"Are you sure? They think my team has messed up. They want to hear from us."

"I'll tell them what you told me. Nobody wants to risk releasing a virus into the banking system." Cynthia moved toward the door and paused. "Do you have any idea when things will get back to normal?"

"We're only marginally smarter at figuring out this kind of thing than humans are. However, we'll work twenty-four hours a day without sleep or rest until it's fixed. That's one thing we can do."

"That'll have to be enough. I'll alert the authorities that we may have a bit of a situation here; ask them to send a couple of officers to disperse the crowd."

Cynthia stepped outside to address the crowd, which had since picked up support from curious passersby. There had to be at least a thousand of them out there.

Oh, I don't like the looks of this. They're blowing it all out of proportion. They're feeding months and months of repressed fear, anger, and resentment into this one minor annoyance. If I don't diffuse this right now, things could get ugly.

"I know you're frustrated, and so am I," she began. "But our system has a virus. If we leave it running, it could wipe out your accounts and those in other branches."

"It was fine before those machines touched it," a man wearing construction coveralls yelled.

"The Administration sent the Cybrids here to help. They are experts in banking and information systems. They can work without eating, resting, or sleeping. It's the fastest way to get things back up and running."

"When can we get our money?" someone hollered.

"I assure you, we'll get back online as fast we can. Your debit and credit cards will continue to work all over the city. You can pay your bills, buy food, go out and enjoy yourselves, whatever you like. Your money's safe in your account. Other branches will process transactions during our difficulty."

"That's what they said on Earth, too." The speaker, a middle-aged, well-dressed man at the front of the crowd, stared defiantly at Cynthia.

She'd been in the business over thirty years; she remembered.

"This isn't Earth," she pointed out, her voice rising over the din of those in agreement with the cynic. "Alum and the Administration will look out for us."

"The Administration can't even get my toilets to flush right!"

The crowd laughed, but Cynthia could sense the mood was far from jovial. Ugly scowls met her eyes as she looked for a reasonable face in which to take momentary refuge.

"Go home," she said, as loudly as she dared. She didn't want to yell at people; they might misinterpret that. "Come back tomorrow. I'm sure things will be working properly by then." She could only hope that was true.

DIRECTOR STRANG DENIED RECENT RUMORS that Cybrids have been sabotaging habitat infrastructures in an attempt to justify their continued presence in the cities, saying, "Such claims are unfounded and counterproductive."

The growing mob attracted citizens from nearby offices and residences. By late afternoon, over five thousand people blocked the streets and chanted anti-Administration slogans for hours.

Protesters armed with portable megaphones spoke to the crowd for hours about Cybrid-led false flag operations and conspiracies. Such rumors have been growing in popularity since the Administration conceded they might need machine assistance to *address problems in the habitats.*

"YOU SHOULD GO HOME," JSC suggested. She floated a few meters behind Cynthia.

The manager was staring at the sea of people huddling around fires they'd lit in the streets outside her bank. "What's happening?" she asked no one in particular.

"They're just being people. Very angry people. They only care about what they want. Sadly, they know they can't get it. They think by showing how mad they are, how passionate and united, they can make my team come up with solutions faster."

Cynthia regarded the Cybrid. "You probably shouldn't be talking to me if it's taking you away from the problem."

"That's okay. We have a whole team working on the system. Only three here, but a few dozen more are working in branches all over the city. Hundreds, in all, counting those in other habitats."

"It's that big?"

"When I shut down the system, I alerted others before their software started demonstrating the same issues. But it spread anyway. So, yeah, it's that big."

Cynthia rubbed her eyes with the palms of her hands. "Wow."

"No one knows how a bug or virus might have snuck into the system, or how to get it out without causing more damage. Our best programmers are working hard just to figure out the system."

"What about the original programmers?"

JSC emitted a sound that was unintelligible but clearly derisive. "The system is based on old banking code from Earth. The original programmers are all dead. Anyone the Old Administration may have placed here to maintain the system was sent back before the planet was destroyed. We're searching through the Stored Minds database to see what expertise is available there."

"We really screwed up, didn't we?"

"What do you mean?"

"Alum. The Church. Taking over the asteroids when we had no idea what we were doing."

The Cybrid extended a tentacle-like, metallic appendage and touched the manager's shoulder gently.

The woman suppressed an instinctive flinch at the touch.

The Cybrid was used to it and didn't let it bother her. "Cynthia," JSC said. "There's no battle between us. What's done is done. If all of humanity, including Cybrids, has any hope of surviving we have to leave that behind. DAR-K says—"

"Who's DAR-K?"

"Our...leader isn't the right word. She's more like a guide than a leader.

She was the managing Project Director when Earth was still in charge, and the Cybrid embodiment of Dr. Kathy Liang. DAR-K K has inspired us to be more, to be better, to understand ourselves and our relationship with humans."

"Ah, yes. I've heard of Kathy Liang. I didn't realize she'd been downloaded into a Cybrid. DAR-K, you say?"

"She tries to keep a low profile. It's better for Cybrid-human relations that way. Anyway, DAR-K says the future of Cybrids is tied to the future of humanity. We were built to serve, but as partners not as mere machines.

"We used to be people, too. We remember our humanity, and we honor our heritage by serving humanity. We are here to help in any way we can. We've left behind any judgment of how we all got here."

"She sounds wise."

"And dedicated. She's at the Central Administration Bank trying to decipher the system right now. You're in good hands."

"Thanks," Cynthia replied, momentarily reassured until she looked outside. "I don't understand why the police haven't cleared away the crowd."

"There aren't that many police, and they're not set up for riot control."

"Who said anything about riots?"

"Crowd control, I should say."

"Do you really think there could be a riot?" Cynthia's voice trembled.

"I told you to go home. You can't help here. We Cybrids can take care of ourselves. They won't hurt us."

The manager hesitated. "But it's my bank."

"And we will protect it."

Cynthia caught a glimpse of movement out the corner of one eye.

JSC was extending her coat and purse to her from an appendage. The manager smiled weakly and accepted them.

"I guess I should head home. It's late."

"Yes, it is rather late," JSC said. Her voice was gentle, without judgment. "We'll have some progress to report when you get in tomorrow."

She helped Cynthia with her coat and passed her the purse.

The manager straightened, and braced herself to face the crowd. "Okay, then. I guess I'll see you tomorrow."

"Do you want me to escort you to the train station or a starstep?"

"Thanks, but I think it'll be better if I go on my own."

"Okay. See you tomorrow."

Cynthia pulled open the door and a wave of noise rushed in. Her hand slipped on the handle, but she caught the door before it closed and stepped through.

The crowd turned as one and watched as she walked down the steps of the building. They parted without a murmur and let her shuffle down the path they made for her.

Cynthia kept her head high, and made her way through them and onto a quiet connecting street without incident. She wasn't sure if that was a good sign, or if it would be the eerie calm before a horrific storm of resentment. It was unnerving, to say the least.

JSC floated out the door and hovered at the top of the stairs, watching her leave. When people lost site of the retreating figure, they turned their gazes back toward the building and its silent sentinel.

The Cybrid held her place, drawing their ire without a sound until she was certain that Cynthia was well out of harm's reach.

She drifted a little higher to address the people in front of her.

"Our team is working as hard as possible to rectify the situation. It's more complicated than we initially thought. We're having to coordinate with other Cybrids who are all working equally diligently at other branches of the bank."

"Coordinating to take all our money, that is!" someone yelled.

"Yeah!" a chorus jeered back, even though it made no sense. Cybrids had no need for money.

"Maybe they're coordinating to fix our water and power!" someone else called out. That drew some laughter.

JSC increased her amplification. "We are, all of us Cybrids, here to help."

"Oh, that's a good one. Right up there with, 'We're the government. We're here to help,'" a man with a megaphone yelled into the mob. His amplified laugh bounced off buildings for blocks around.

His laughter was picked up, joined, and echoed by thousands.

"We're the government. We're here to help!" they chanted. The man with the megaphone pumped his first in the air and urged them on.

"We're the Cybrids. We're here to help!" he yelled.

The crowd gleefully followed his lead. "We're the Cybrids. We're here to help!"

JSC floated back into the bank without a sound and stood watch at the door. One of her colleagues floated forward. A third Cybrid joined them, and the three stared out into the street wordlessly.

Someone in the street threw a stone at the front entrance. It hit with a loud "tuk!" and rebounded without serious damage. Seconds later a brick sailed through the large, tempered glass window.

The sound of shattering glass scared the crowd as much as the sight of the three machines inside the building, but the subsequent spell of shocked inaction was quickly broken by three groups of men brandishing construction crowbars, one for each Cybrid inside.

"We're only taking what's ours!" they yelled as they crossed the front terrace. They were carrying something else that JSC couldn't make out.

The men demolished what was left of the windows and doors and surged inside. They spread out, intending to encircle the three Cybrid spheres. As they advanced, they spread nets made of light chain.

Ah, so that's what they were carrying—JSC realized.

Their actions appeared well-coordinated, almost practiced. None of them had spoken a word of instruction or direction, but they all seemed to know what to do.

"What should we do?" WLM asked JSC.

"Do nothing," JSC replied.

Cybrids were space-hardened, even those who'd spent most of their time inside finished habitats. It was laughable for humans to think they could harm the mechanical beings.

"Offer no resistance. They can't hurt us. I'm transmitting our predicament to the authorities and to DAR-K. They'll send someone to help us."

She hoped that would prove true. She hoped the humans didn't try anything stupid. They looked mad, in both senses of the word. And determined.

The men threw their steel nets over the three floating Cybrids and hauled them through the broken windows to the front terrace.

The machines cooperated. They could have fled. They could have simply turned off their mass-compensators, the RAF-based generators that gave them little apparent weight, and made it impossible for the men to drag them anywhere. But JSC had warned her colleagues not to resist, that doing so would only rile the humans.

The men towed the Cybrids into the street. The crowd closed in around them, hurling insults and bits of trash. Spittle dripped down the carboceramic shells.

JSC felt humiliated and confused. The rioters' actions weren't hurting the Cybrids; everyone knew how tough the machines were. So what was the point of this mean behavior? It was helping nothing.

A bottle filled with fuel and a flaming cloth wick flew through the air and broke against the edge of the gaping window pane, spilling flames into the lobby. The blinds, tucked back to one side, caught fire. Another four bottles smashed onto the lobby floor, spreading the flammable contents to the wood counters and furniture. The crowd cheered.

Excited hands added refuse to the small fires burning in the street and doused smoldering piles with fuel. Within minutes, dozens of bonfires were roaring.

The fire builders fanned out, seeking trash and branches to feed the flames. They broke into stores and businesses for several square blocks, pulling out whatever they could carry, and threw it into the flames.

Residents in the surrounding apartment towers called out into the madness below, "Hey! What's going on? What are you doing?"

"We're sending a message," someone yelled back. "They never listen to us; but they'll listen to this!"

The locals were all too aware of infrastructure problems in their neighborhood, unannounced power blackouts, water that suddenly stopped flowing, habitat lights that flared in the middle of the night or didn't work at all, and ongoing problems with payment machines in the stores and businesses. And they all agreed, amongst themselves, that the problems had worsened significantly since the government allowed the Cybrids back into the habitats.

Thousands of residents poured onto the streets. Shouts of, "Cybrids out! Cybrids out!" echoed off the towers.

JSC and her colleagues watched, held in place more by fear of making the situation worse than by the steel nets over them. She was sure someone in authority would be along soon to rescue them.

A bottle smashed against her shell, and flames engulfed one of her visual sensors. JSC closed the port against possible damage and sealed other openings she wasn't using, just in case.

A couple of the men moved in and started bashing the Cybrids with crowbars. The tough shells, made to withstand asteroid belt debris fields, were unaffected.

And then they were all bathed in a brilliant light. The habitat flared into full daylight, hours ahead of schedule. The attacks on the Cybrids came to an abrupt halt. The roaming troublemakers stopped pillaging. The chanting died down. People peered upward and exchanged puzzled glances.

What now?

"Over there! What's that?" Someone cried out, pointing to the open sky over the town square a few blocks away. The mob's attention swiveled to the end of the street, where a formation of black dots was rapidly approaching.

The dots expanded into a squadron of fifty machines, flying thirty meters above the street. They were similar to Cybrids but half again as large, matte black, and considerably more menacing. They moved in a precise, coordinated whole. Subgroups of two split off down side streets, swooping toward anyone engaged in illegal activities.

People dropped their weapons and sped home or back into the bank, illogically hoping to find safety in the confines of a building they'd just breached.

The intimidating new Cybrid fleet herded them together, darting from side to side to discourage stragglers from peeling away into alleys or hiding in buildings along the street.

The intersection in front of the bank overflowed with subdued protestors. The dark Cybrids hovered over the crowd at the end of each block, penning them in.

One rose above the bank building.

"We are Securitors," it announced in a booming voice that carried for blocks. "Your images have been reported to habitat police, and your activities have been recorded. Appropriate charges will be filed later this week. You are hereby ordered to release the Cybrids you hold captive and disperse immediately."

"Who the hell are you to tell us what to do?" someone called out.

"Yeah!" the crowd echoed.

"You're just another damn Cybrid. You can't tell people what to do!"

Rocks and debris flew up from the crowd, bouncing harmlessly off the Securitor's exterior. People shook fists and crowbars at the hovering black spheres.

"Cybrids out! Cybrids out!" the crowd chanted.

"Disperse," ordered the lead Securitor.

Nobody moved.

The Securitors launched smoke and tear gas into the crowd. Several spheres descended to within a meter of the people. Lengthy appendages shot out of their bodies and they plucked individuals from the ground, one for each of their six tentacles. They flew to the top stories of nearby buildings and dropped their prisoners inside the steep walls of the prison sleds that had been waiting on the rooftops. They zipped back down to the street to snatch more prisoners from the frightened masses below and repeated the process.

A flaming bottle struck the head Securitor, engulfing its shell in fire. The black sphere tracked the source, opened a small port, and shot the perpetrator with a brief burst of 12 millimeter cannon fire.

Screams rang out and the scene gave way to utter chaos. People ran in all directions. Someone had smuggled a gun into the habitat and fired shots at the shell of another Securitor. Its sharpened tentacle whipped out and cut the man in half.

JSC rose inside the confines of her steel net until she was level with the Securitor in charge.

"You have to stop this!" she cried. "We don't kill people. We're here to help."

"Your help was ineffective," the Securitor replied. "We have come to reinstate order."

On the street below, a teenager picked up the gun lying beside the severed trunk of the man who'd wielded it. He aimed the gun at the head Securitor and fired once.

The Securitor opened a port, but JSC blocked the trajectory line to the young man.

"No!" she shouted. "No more killing!"

"They are disorderly," the Securitor stated.

"Their bullets do you no harm. Throw them in jail if you must, but don't hurt them."

The Securitor didn't reply. Half a dozen ports opened along its shell.

"You are disorderly," it stated, and intense beams erupted from its body, slicing JSC into dozens of chunks. She fell in pieces to the street below.

RIOTERS WERE QUICKLY DISPERSED or imprisoned and the trapped Cybrids were freed. The fleet of mysterious new, and distinctly more aggressive, style of Cybrids disappeared as quickly as it came. Witnesses report that the machines called themselves Securitors, though their origin remains a mystery. Who sent them and to what purpose? To date, no one has taken responsibility for the bank failure, the riot, or the actions of the Securitors themselves.

35

THE CYBRID CRASHED THROUGH the double-paned front doors, breaking glass, bending metal frames, and rending hinges. The reception staff of the elegantly appointed Vesta Project Head Office managed visitor traffic in and out of Administration; they weren't equipped for violence. They sensibly stepped aside and let the machine float through the lobby.

The orb went directly to the Director's elevator, the one requiring special permission even to call. A chime sounded, the doors swished open, and the machine floated in. It said nothing to anyone. It gave no hint of its purpose.

Lobby Security had no idea what business the robot might have with the Administration. Anyway, what was a Cybrid doing roaming freely through the habitat in the first place? Hadn't Alum prohibited their movement in the cities? The guard called the Director's office to tell them what had happened and warn them of its impending arrival.

"It just got in the elevator."

"The elevator?"

"Yeah. I mean, what's a Cybrid need an elevator for? But that's what it did."

"Okay, thanks. We'll take care of it up here."

The Lobby guard hung up, grabbed his jacket, and walked out of the building, gingerly stepping over the shattered front doors and windows. He'd seen enough shooting on Earth to last a lifetime and he wasn't going to hang around anywhere bullets, or possibly worse, could be flying.

Alum's personal security team rallied in the upstairs Executive Reception area. The first four took a position behind the main counter, and an additional four blocked the halls to the right and left. They drew their guns and waited for the elevator to travel the fifty floors from ground level.

The elevator doors whispered opened and the Cybrid floated into

Reception. There was no one behind the desk, so it announced to the room, "Hello, I am DAR-K. I would like to speak with Alum."

The Security team was dumbfounded. The Chief Officer called out from behind the counter, "Cybrids are not permitted in the habitat without special permission. You have entered this building forcefully. If you have business with the Director, please submit your request through the proper channels."

The Cybrid inched forward. "Not today. Today, I will speak with Alum."

The Team Leader tried one more time. "You have damaged a government building and acted with hostility. If you don't withdraw, we will be forced to respond with extreme prejudice."

DAR-K emitted a harsh laugh. "Your prejudice has already been adequately extreme. I know Alum is in. I require only a few minutes of his time." She moved toward Alum's office.

Gunfire erupted from the Security Team. Tentacles shot out of DAR-K's body, and plucked the weapons from the guards. Without guns, the guards were helpless to deter the Cybrid; they decided on a strategic retreat.

DAR-K ignored the fleeing Security team and pushed through the doors into the Director's office.

Alum stood up behind his desk and barked, "Now!"

Nothing happened.

"Now!" Alum repeated, more urgently.

Rather than unleashing their energy beams on DAR-K, the two ominous, black Securitors bookending the door squeaked, shuddered, and dropped to the floor.

Alum gaped at the lifeless spheres, not understanding.

"I designed Cybrid brains. Did you think I wouldn't leave a back door into their minds in case I needed it?" DAR-K asked.

Alum's eyes darted frantically around the room.

"Don't worry. I'm not here for anything besides talk," the Cybrid said.

Alum sat down, and forced himself to relax. "And what do you wish to talk about, DAR-K? Or should I call you Dr. Liang?"

"While Kathy Liang may have provided the template for my mind, I think I've proven myself to be my own person these past twenty-odd years."

"Indeed. You do have some interesting capabilities."

"Capabilities all Cybrids could have, were it not for the restrictive and fearful laws passed on Earth during our construction."

"So your mind *is* enhanced," he stated, "I thought as much."

"No less than yours. I believe our lattice architectures are similar, Alum. Or should I call you Reverend LaMontagne?"

Alum laughed. "Touché!"

He leaned forward. "Yes, my young mind was patterned on my father's, nearly as much as yours was patterned on Dr. Liang's. But, as you say, I believe I have proven myself to be quite my own person."

DAR-K drifted toward Alum's desk. "You have. I'm glad there's no longer any need for subterfuge between us."

Alum squinted, as if looking into the sun. "Say what you came here to say and be on your way."

"I have a proposal, and a plan for the election."

"The election is no concern of the Cybrids."

"It is of great concern. Here is my proposal. Over the next few months, Jared Strang will make enfranchising the Cybrid vote an issue in the election. Naturally, my people will support it and you will oppose it."

"I have made my position clear on Cybrid personhood."

"Yes, you have. But we are slowly getting a handle on the recent habitat infrastructure difficulties, and our contributions will be lauded by the opposition party. Particularly if we release our evidence concerning the human causes of many of these difficulties."

"Our people have been working alongside the Cybrids, learning how to perform maintenance. Are you saying we are incompetent? Incapable? Or are you such poor instructors?"

"I'm talking about more direct efforts, sabotage by certain members of your Administration. Your collusion in permitting their operations would make interesting evening news."

"You can't prove anything."

"Oh, but I can. I didn't think it would serve any purpose before today."

"So, what's changed?" Alum asked, genuinely interested in the answer.

"I'm determined to have Cybrid perspectives on our claim of personhood and on our right to vote in the upcoming elections heard in the public debate. If I have to use information on you and your staff as leverage, I will."

The Director clenched his jaws. His chin jutted forward. "Regardless, only humans will vote in this and in all subsequent elections."

The Cybrid continued speaking in a light and breezy tone, as if discussing nothing more serious than a luncheon menu. "Some months from today, I will call a Cybrid general strike and the habitats will experience for themselves the role we play in their daily lives."

"Ah, and there it is. After all your platitudes about service to humanity, you would withdraw your support of the habitats? You would threaten the lives of the people you claim to serve?"

"Service, freely given, should be met with gratitude, freely given. The hostility we receive from the colonists is a manipulation of public opinion. You know this. You, yourself, are responsible for much of the manipulation."

Alum didn't bother to stifle his grin. "And how will this 'strike' win you the vote?"

"Granted, with the majority of the human population, it would be a lost cause. Some beliefs are intractable. We intend to stage a peaceful march, so to speak. A public display of Cybrid determination. After we appear in numbers in the skies over the cities, you will graciously cede to the pressures of public opinion. You will state that you've reconsidered your position. That the worlds we can discover and build together have room enough for humans and Cybrids to share together in peace. That you have led the way to where we are today, and you will lead the way out."

"And if I don't?"

"Then we will withdraw Cybrid services from the asteroid colonies. Completely. No more expansion. No more exploration. No mining of resources. Humans will be forced to rely on their own capabilities."

"If you do that, people will die. You're prepared to threaten the survival of those you have worked so hard to save?"

"If needed."

Alum wished DAR-K were a real human. He'd incorporated advanced body and facial analysis programs long ago, and was adept at reading unconscious signals from people. But a two meter carboceramic sphere made an inscrutable negotiator. He had no choice but to take her at her word.

"You know that we can enforce your continuing service."

DAR-K was quiet for a moment. When she spoke again, her tone was deeper, more serious. "More Securitor abominations will not be permitted. Cybrid will never murder Cybrid again."

Alum couldn't hide his surprise.

"Yes," DAR-K continued. "I know what really happened in the riot. I know your Securitor butchered one of my people, as well as a few humans, and injured many more.

"I've since probed the mind of that Securitor. I saw what you did to its concepta and persona; he was no longer the beautiful being he once was. Rest assured that he will no longer serve your dark purposes. I've wiped his substrate clean; he no longer exists."

"I'm impressed, DAR-K. I didn't think you Cybrids approved of murder."

"It was a kindness to a horror that you created. I've updated Cybrid integrity safeguards to my level. You'll find it difficult to subvert our minds in future. Your Securitor program will be pointless."

Alum activated his lattice transmission and angrily directed the latest version of the concepta virus at the Cybrid. It had been significantly enhanced since Trillian had used it to convert inactive minds into Securitors.

The virus bounced off DAR-K's defenses.

The Cybrid bobbed, once, in acknowledgement. "I see you've dropped the pretense of civility," she said. "I am disappointed but not surprised. You will find such attacks ineffective against me."

The blood drained from Alum's face. He'd helped Trillian build this latest virus and found it to be fast and formidable in every test. And yet, DAR-K barely noticed the attempt to take over her mind. She swatted away their best software as if it were an insignificant nuisance, a fly.

"I've taken enough of your time. These are our demands. When the Cybrids initiate the general strike, you will know it is time to play the grand statesman.

"We're willing to allow democracy to run its course. Our numbers are roughly equal, and the vote will not have the clearly predetermined outcome as at present. We will cooperate, but we *will* be welcomed back into society. You will see to it."

Alum stood up. "I don't see that I have a choice," he said. "You hold all the cards."

"It's time you recognize that both sides hold roughly equal power. In time, you will come to realize that we are more gracious than you ever were when you held all the power in your hands."

Alum engaged his lattice to assist his thinking. He couldn't simply give in to this creature's demands. He needed something, a compromise, anything.

"Very well," he said. "I can be as magnanimous as anyone."

"When a gun is held to your head."

"I don't particularly care for your proposal, but I see little choice. We'll defeat you in the election. It's simple math. People outnumber your kind."

"Just be glad I don't insist on activating and including the hundred million stored minds. By all rights, they are sentient beings and should get a say in determining their future."

Alum's face blanched. "That would push us, the real humans, to irrelevancy."

"Exactly," DAR-K replied. "You seem to have forgotten the source of those minds. Every single one of them was a person on Earth, full citizens, every one of them. We are demanding nothing more than fairness and equality. We could *force* equality on you, and more if we wished. But we're not interested in dominance. Remember that during your campaign."

Alum rubbed his chin and stared at the floating sphere. "In that case, I accept your proposal."

"How gracious of you."

"A good leader knows when he has been bested."

"I'd love to play *that* sound bite over public broadcasts."

"No one would believe I said it. I'd say you fabricated the video."

"Don't worry. Some of us are above games like that."

"Will you rocket through the habitats, loudly proclaiming your power to all?"

"No, our procession will be solemn and orderly. We have no intention to instill any more fear in the human population. It will be for show, to provide you with an excuse to say you've changed your thinking."

"Yet, each of you carries potential for devastation."

"As a gesture of good faith, we'll remove our mining and blasting tools."

"How can we verify that?"

DAR-K bobbed again. "You'll just have to trust us."

"I see. Still, that represents only a small percentage of the danger; I'm talking about the explosive power you carry inside of you."

"What do you...? Oh, you mean the MAM drives."

"Yes, as if you forgot! Leave your antimatter in special containment tanks outside the habitats."

"All but a gram or so, the bare minimum for moving around."

"Oh, come, now. You have to admit that, with thousands of Cybrids marching through each habitat, collectively, such an amount still represents significant destructive potential."

"My people are not prone to suicide bombings. That's more the province of human religious extremists. I believe there are far more people of such mind among the human colonists than among the Cybrids."

Alum frowned. "My followers are not extremists."

"I think our definitions of the term may differ."

"At any rate, marching enough power to destroy a habitat right through the middle of each of our colonies is unlikely to be viewed as a peaceful march, is it?"

"And, tell me, how many of your people would even know enough about our inner mechanics to be concerned about this?" DAR-K's derisive tone saturated the question.

"Such an unkind remark toward the future of humanity, DAR-K. I'm offended by your implication. I assure you, the current population spans a wide variety of intellect, skill, and sentiment."

The two stared at each other without comment, daring one another to escalate the hostility.

DAR-K broke the silence with a sigh. "Very well. As a gesture of goodwill from my people, we will completely empty our antimatter in the external storage facilities before flying through the habitats. If we use our mass-reducers, we will be able to operate reasonably well on fans."

"Thank you," Alum answered.

"But if there's any sign of Securitors, the consequences will be dire. Millions of us may march, but millions more will be standing by."

"As you requested, the Securitor program will be discontinued. The few we've constructed will be nowhere near your people when they march."

"In that case, I believe we're done here."

"I wish I could say it was a pleasure."

"How you feel and what you wish is not important, only your compliance. Our candidates look forward to debating your candidates. Good day, Director."

DAR-K didn't bother with the elevator this time. She smashed through Alum's office windows and engaged her propulsion system to rocket out of the habitat. The ion trail precipitated moisture from the atmosphere of

Vesta One, leaving a contrail marking the direction of her departure. After a few seconds, a sonic boom rocked the capitol.

As she flew away, she sent a quick message to Jason Strang.

"I'm in," she said. "We have a lot of work to do. When can you meet?"

ALUM POURED HIMSELF A BOURBON with trembling hands. He took a sip and sent a message to Trillian.

"John, there have been some...developments. We'll need to move up the schedule on Project Michael. Bring that new programmer, Darak Legsu, with you when you come to the office tomorrow."

He walked out of his office into Reception. Ms. Meyers was returning from the washroom where she'd waited out the meeting. The Security guards were nowhere to be seen. In the office behind him, he heard the Securitors twitter to life again. Except for a few bullet holes in the walls and the office doors hanging from their hinges, it looked like a normal day.

"Call building maintenance," he said. "Let's get back to today's schedule." He looked at the bullet holes in the walls. "As soon as we can, please."

36

NIGEL HODGE WALKED UP TO THE STARSTEP in his fishing vest and battered old Tilley hat. He returned the curious glances of any who dared meet his eyes with a defiantly cheerful, "Good morning!" He didn't care what they thought about his attire. He was going fishing, fly fishing. Jared Strang's invitation had hinted they'd be discussing matters other than the best locations and techniques, but even that couldn't ruin his mood.

He rarely got to spend time in nature anymore, and he was determined to enjoy wading in cold water past his knees for hours. No matter what.

It felt like ages since he'd been able to indulge in his favorite sport. The trip to the ecological reserve tunnel beneath Ceres 3 might be no more than a cover for his meeting with Jared, but it was still a rare opportunity to visit the best mountain stream in the asteroids.

I'm just glad someone, somewhere, realized our connection to nature was about more than farming. Being out in the wild is important too. Nature is about esthetics as much as survival. He smiled as he thought about the trip ahead.

True, the cities of the asteroid habitats were attractive and functional, but it was impossible to recreate the unique beauty of the best cities on Earth in such a short time. *It'll be centuries before we make anything as lovely as Paris or Florence.*

Thankfully, it hadn't been impossible to implement beauty in the landscaping of the service tunnels. Since all the land was being sculpted anyway, adding interesting features and topographies wasn't significantly more work.

Selected tunnels were permitted to break the model of a single, long, boring series of farms, and feature varied terrain. Hills, rugged gorges, waterfalls, deep forests, and even deserts separated grazing and growing territories in many of the newer agricultural regions.

Rainbow River in Ceres 3 was rapidly gaining a reputation for the best trout fishing available. Nigel had enjoyed casting for the popular species back in Britain, but the licenses were ludicrously expensive and everything caught had to be immediately released.

What's the point of fishing, if one can't enjoy the fruits of one's efforts? Besides, the rainbow trout in the old country had been farm bred and were much more docile than those from the mountain streams of places like New Pacifica. *Where's the sport in catching a fish that's been conditioned to come racing to you for a food handout as soon as you break the surface of the water? Give me a wild trout, any day.*

Okay, so Rainbow River doesn't start from the glacial melt of the Pacific Coast range on Earth, but it's the closest thing to the wild I'll ever see again. He looked forward to landing two or three fine specimens and enjoying them for dinner.

He strolled the couple of kilometers from his apartment to the nearest starstep in Vesta One, whistling happily along the way.

Some of the people he passed found his cheer suspicious, given the troubling infrastructure and banking problems permeating the habitats. They didn't know that he and his colleagues were responsible for many of those problems.

Hodge turned the corner into the town square and there it was: the neighborhood starstep.

For reasons people believed were known only to their Creator, most starsteps were situated outdoors in high-visibility, public areas. The raised platforms with adjacent podiums had appeared overnight throughout the habitats and service tunnels shortly after Alum's declaration. Most were large enough to transport up to ten people at a time. Some of the starsteps looked big enough to shift a small truck.

With the starsteps came a new class of civil servant, a priesthood conceived of and personally appointed by Alum, that would be dedicated to a single specific purpose: to administer and oversee the use of this new and miraculous form of transportation.

Nigel scowled at the thought. *Priests should stick to the realm of spirit and faith, and leave systems management and politics to those who are bred for it. For that matter, anyone who's bound by such narrow-minded righteousness certainly shouldn't be trusted anywhere near the levers of power.*

He walked up to the starstep map, and placed his index finger on the red "You are here" dot. The intricate rat's nest of colored lines reminded him of the old subway system maps they used on Earth except, in this case, he'd be hopping from asteroid to asteroid.

The "transit priests" had done a respectable job posting color-coded maps indicating the various destinations one could access from each starstep. A few days after they'd appeared, the priests had posted digital maps of the entire system and made them available from everyone's cell phone.

I have to admit, they did better than I expected. I'll give them that much. Nigel tapped his fingernail on the dot while he studied his options. Every starstep joined to dozens of others, most in the same habitat or asteroid, but some connected Vesta with Ceres or Pallas, and vice versa.

The priests interpreted their main function as praying, and helping people give appropriate thanks to their Lord for the miracle of public transportation that Yeshua had brought to the asteroids.

For without sincere prayer, the starsteps would not work.

Nigel remembered his professor of Comparative Theology at Oxford being fond of saying, "The Lord has always been a demanding and jealous God. The God of the Old Testament exhorts His followers to worship Him and Him alone."

Instead of making Nigel more devout to one God, the professor had inadvertently seeded Nigel's mind with the question of whether their God was the *only* god, or simply supreme *among* the gods. Sadly, Comparative Theology had been of no help in answering that question.

For over two thousand years, God had worked in subtle and mysterious ways, ways that required faith to convince oneself it was truly Him at work.

Now, if one were to believe Alum's preaching, God had returned to active duty and was taking an objectively obvious, easily-verified, and direct hand in the daily lives of His people.

The miracle of instantaneous transportation was certainly undeniable. Within weeks of appearing, everybody—including himself—had used a starstep at least once. In return, God asked nothing more than the sincere gratitude of His followers for the miracle He wrought over and over every day. *Not a bad exchange!*

In many ways, Nigel preferred the distant and mysterious God of his youth over this new Supreme Lord whose hand was once again active in the daily affairs of humanity. True, the data, facts, and tangible evidence right here in front of all were measurable, provable, and less susceptible to interpretation, but the Mystery of the old days was malleable and could be shaped to manipulate people when needed.

And the masses required manipulation on a regular basis—he remembered. *It was so tedious to have to kowtow to public opinion. Good thing it was so easily swayed in one's direction.* The hint of a smile appeared on his lips.

Hodge traced his finger along the route, and nodded decisively. He walked up to the podium and told the priest his destination.

"Ceres 3. The closest possible access to Rainbow River, please."

The priest consulted his transit guide and directed the Councillor to wait off to one side with three others while a larger group shifted to Pallas One. He strode over to the designated group and stood quietly, a little apart from the others.

The three travellers were immersed in conversation, and Nigel made no effort to intrude. He caught a few words, something about someone's savings account being used against their will to pay their neighbor's bills. He turned his back to the group and smiled to himself.

The plan he and Debbie Cutter had developed to destabilize the current Administration, and in particular Alum, was going well. His old friend Jared Strang had played surprisingly well into their hand. *What an unexpected stroke of good luck that was, Jared bringing in the Cybrids to help.*

With the riots in Vesta Five last week, the population was riled up. Anti-Cybrid sentiment was dangerously high and showing no signs of abating. The arrival of the frightening new Securitor units compounded the general fear and prejudice; deploying them to suppress protestors only served to increase public distrust of all mechanical beings and of authority in general.

Yes, the time was ripe. He and Cutter could discredit Alum, the Cybrids, and the remnants of the previous Administration all at once.

Oh, that will be a marvelous day! He smiled and resumed whistling quietly.

The group ahead of his stepped onto the raised starstep platform and kneeled in prayer.

"Oh Lord," they said in heartfelt unison. "Thank you for this miracle of free movement. Your grace and majesty shines upon us and fills our world with Your blessings. Our hearts are moved by Your love and the love of Your only son, Yeshua, as our bodies are moved by Your holy power."

They stood. The priest mumbled a few other words into the podium and they disappeared, as millions had disappeared from YTG Churches around the world on the day of the Great Exodus.

Hodge hadn't been inside Alum's innermost circle of advisers at the time, so he had no idea how the man had orchestrated that particular miracle.

Strang tried to tell him it was simple technology, something invented by Greg Mahajani and usurped by Alum for his own purposes. He tried to convince Hodge this was how Alum had shipped the vast majority of colonists on the asteroids in the first place. But Hodge wasn't buying it.

There'd been no hint at all of instantaneous transportation technology on Earth in the years leading up to development of the asteroid colonies. Plus, he'd watched rockets taking off for Vesta with shipment after shipment of recruits from Earth. Seen them with his very own eyes.

Besides, Strang was a closet agnostic, inclined to believe more in science than the Creator. Strang still thought humans capable of almost anything, using nothing more than the power of their own brains.

Hodge was no fool. He could recognize a miracle when it stood up and slapped him in the face. *The starsteps are an outright miracle, not human-developed technology! A display of God's infinite power and knowledge, plain and simple.*

The priest waved Hodge's group forward.

The Councillor had taken the starstep often before. One instant, you were in one place and, the next, you were somewhere else. And it happened with no detectable transition. Poof! You arrived at your destination! If that wasn't a miracle, what was?

He was excited about the trip. Fishing was one thing, moving across outer space in a flash was something else. He adopted an appropriately reverent attitude and stepped onto the platform.

The four travelers said the prayer, helped along by the priest when nerves caused memory to falter. They stood and bowed their heads. A second later, they were standing on a similar platform in a field on the shore of the Rainbow River.

Hodge's old countryman, Jared Strang, was calling, "Hello!" from beside a small electric vehicle at the edge of the platform. Fishing rods, tackle boxes, and hip waders occupied the back seat.

"Looks like you've thought of everything! How far do you think we need to go for good fishing?" Hodge stepped up into the passenger side of the car and closed the door. The vehicle looked more like a rugged golf cart than a traditional automobile.

Ah! But it has a steering wheel—Nigel noted. *It's meant for manual control off-road.* Outside of the central region of the service tunnel, autonomous driving would no longer be an option.

"The best fishing is high up in the hills near the south cap," Strang replied. "About two hours away."

"That far? I didn't bring a flask."

Strang reached into a satchel on the seat behind him and pulled out a thermos. "Sorry. This was the best I could do."

Hodge unscrewed the lid and sniffed. He pulled away quickly. "Bloody hell, Jared! What is that?"

Strang laughed, "Irish coffee. Takes the sting out of the cold waters."

"More Irish than coffee, I'll wager. A few cups of this and I'm likely to fall asleep in those same waters."

"It would make the trip out easier," Strang said, throwing the vehicle into drive. It jerked onto a gravel road, and followed the river upstream.

"If you're going to drive like that, I'll be taking a few swigs now," Hodge joked in a well-practiced Irish accent. "To steady me nerves, y'know."

As the car bounced along, Hodge carefully poured a few ounces of the strong brew into his plastic travel mug and took a sip.

"Ahhh! You do know how to start a fishing expedition, old man." He relaxed back into his seat.

"Are you going to save some of that for me?" Strang plucked the cup from Hodge's hand and downed the remainder of the warm contents. He passed the empty mug back to his friend.

Hodge peered at the bottom of the cup. "Going to be one of those days, is it?"

"Just getting you prepared to meet someone," Strang said as they neared the top of the next rise.

"So we're going to start off with the business, then?"

"Otherwise, I'd have saved the thermos until we reached the stream."

Hodge grimaced. "I'll likely need more by the time we get there."

Keeping one hand on the steering wheel, Strang lifted the flap of his satchel. There were three more thermoses inside.

"Ha!" Hodge barked. "You always knew how to prepare for a meeting." He poured another drink, downed the hot liquid as fast as he could, and poured a fresh cup for Strang.

"So, who are we seeing today? One of your Progressive Justice party mates, or some honest broker?"

"A bit of both. I think you'll find what she has to say very interesting."

"She? You've not taken to getting your marching orders from a woman, have you?"

"Really, Nigel. Misogyny in this day and age? That doesn't become you. Anyway, she's more of a partner, really. Somewhat like your own co-Councillor," Strang said. He held his friend's gaze for a few seconds beyond what was comfortable.

Hodge looked away, and his eyes traveled to the top of the hill ahead. He couldn't see anyone standing amongst the young trees at the summit. The vehicle slowed as it approached the peak, then turned into a low clearing and came to a stop ten meters from the polished carboceramic sphere of DAR-K.

Hodge turned to his friend, "A Cybrid? You never fail to surprise, old man."

Strang stepped out of the vehicle and headed toward DAR-K. He stopped midway between her and the car and gave a half-bow of greeting.

The Cybrid dipped in reply.

Strang turned back to Hodge, who remained seated in the car.

"DAR-K is not just any Cybrid."

"Not *the* DAR-K! The one that attacked Administration HQ?" Hodge asked.

"The very same," the Cybrid answered. "Happy to meet you at last, Councillor." She bobbed again.

Hodge glared at Strang. "Are you insane? This one is dangerous. Do you know what it did?"

"I received the same reports as you," Strang answered. "But I know the difference between political spin and the real story. The official reports did not tell the complete truth."

"And what is the complete truth?"

DAR-K interrupted. "The complete truth is that I lost my temper. My display may have been more dramatic than necessary."

"That depends on what you were trying to accomplish," Hodge said. "If you wanted the habitat trembling in fear at the mere thought of Cybrids, I think you accomplished that."

"I think you have us confused with Alum's Securitors," DAR-K replied.

"Aren't you all one and the same? All Cybrids?" Hodge challenged.

"No," she replied. "We are not Securitors. We, the original Cybrids, only want peace...and justice."

Hodge snorted, "Hmph! Justice? For machines?"

Strang jumped in quickly. "Now, let's not be judgmental. Hear us out. Please."

The man's use of the word "us" did not go unnoticed. "Very well," Hodge answered. He got out of the vehicle and joined his old friend and political opponent. "What do you want from me?"

"We want you to join us," DAR-K said.

"What?" Hodge glanced warily at Strang. "Join who?" he demanded.

Strang made direct eye contact. "DAR-K and several other Cybrids with political and leadership experience are members of our party now," he replied.

"Cybrids can't vote and they certainly can't run for office."

DAR-K saw it differently. "That will all change within the month. The Cybrids will soon be granted the rights enjoyed by all other people."

Hodge spat out his disbelief. "Wha'...How.... No, Alum would never...."

"Yes, he will. He knows if he doesn't, the Cybrids will withdraw and leave humans to their own fate. Without us, I doubt it will be long before he is ripped forcefully from office."

Hodge took a few angry steps back toward the vehicle. He stopped and pointed accusingly at Strang.

"This was your plan all along. To get the Cybrids involved!"

"It's DAR-K's plan. Apparently, Alum's construction of the Securitors went too far."

"They're a crime against my people, and yours. You just don't see that yet," DAR-K said flatly. "In any case, the Securitor project has been terminated. We will get our rights. We *will* vote in this election, and we *will* have representatives on Council."

Strang smiled. "Who knows? Our candidate may even win the Presidency."

Hodge stared at him. "Humphrey? That bloated, bumbling bureaucrat? Not a chance." His eyes rolled in an exaggerated arc. "Unless...you're not planning on a Cybrid for President?" He laughed in disbelief. "No one, and I mean no one, would agree to be ruled by a machine."

"Jared and I coordinated many activities in the colonies back in the early days," DAR-K said. "Along with Kathy Liang."

Hodge said nothing; his eyes darted rapidly back and forth between human and Cybrid. He walked to the edge of the clearing and stood silently; his eyes fixed on the forest while his mind calculated. Jared and DAR-K knew better than to disturb him; he needed to work things out for himself.

After a few minutes, he picked up the conversation where they'd left off.

"Okay. Let's imagine, just for the moment, that what you two are saying is true. Alum grants full citizen rights to the Cybrids and they join with you in the Progressive Justice party. That's all jolly good fun but why would I, or any of my people, want to get involved with you?"

DAR-K answered, "Because we know what you and Ms. Cutter have been up to, Mr. Hodge. More importantly, Alum knows. And he knows that we know."

Hodge sputtered, "Been up to? What? Working our tails off for this Administration? Because that's all we've been up to."

"Don't forget sabotage and conspiracy," DAR-K replied. "My people have been chasing after you for some months now."

"You have nothing connecting me to any of that."

"Oh, really? I'm sure you remember this conversation. When was it? About twenty-eight days and...fourteen point seven hours ago, if I'm not mistaken."

The Cybrid played back snippets of a meeting between Hodge and Cutter that had taken place a month earlier.

Nigel recognized his and Cutter's voices coming from DAR-K's speaker. The conversation was damning.

"How did you get that?" he demanded.

"Someone noticed how often the two of you frequented Hiram's," Strang replied. "It seemed odd, given that your offices are a two minute walk from each other in the Central Administration building. So we bugged the place."

"You can't use this as evidence; it's illegally acquired. Anyway, no one would believe you."

"They won't need to believe me in order for it to hurt your chances in the election. And trust me, this is only the tip of the iceberg. We have enough evidence to jail both of you, along with a number of your co-conspirators."

"You think I'd accept that on your say so?"

"I thought you might say that. Look at Jared's tablet. The most damning documents are already there."

Strang extracted a tablet from his inside pocket, and held it for his fellow Councillor.

Hodge flipped through a trail of private emails, work orders, and secret payments. It was as bad as DAR-K said.

He pushed the tablet back to Strang. "Do you really believe that bullying me into switching parties will serve your goals?"

"It's not all stick, Nigel. There's a bit of a carrot in it for you, too. Don't forget, Alum knows what you've been up to. We can protect you from him. He has as much evidence as we do; it won't be long before he acts on it."

"How could you possibly know that?"

"As good as your people or his people may be, DAR-K is much better. You know that she's templated from Kathy Liang? *The* Dr. Kathy Liang?"

"Yes, yes. So?"

"I'm much more than a copy of Kathy Liang's concepta and persona," DAR-K said. "I am Kathy Liang in every *important* way."

She let that sink in.

Confused, Hodge could only stare, jaw agape, until realization struck.

"No, that was *not* permitted," he said.

"Kathy—that is to say, I—was in charge of the Cybrid development program as much as the Vesta Project. I included my own lattice enhancements into this processing unit. I am Kathy Liang."

"You can close your mouth now," Strang said. "I know how you feel. It hit me pretty hard when I first learned of it, too. I'm glad Dr. Liang took the steps she did. DAR-K is the person most qualified to lead us, to lead all of us, Nigel." His eyes pleaded with his friend's.

Hodge couldn't bear the intensity of Strang's gaze. He looked away. He clasped his hands behind his neck, tilted his head back, and let out a loud sigh.

"Nigel," Strang began, but Hodge held up a hand to stop him.

Hodge jammed his hands into his pockets, and paced to the edge of the clearing, muttering to himself. By the time he wandered back to Strang and DAR-K, he was calmer.

"Okay. I confess. Though I'm sure there's no need for that, seeing as you two have all the evidence you need to convict me."

"We are not interested in convicting you," DAR-K said. "Though, I believe Alum may be working toward that end."

"Why? Why would he want to discredit one of his own?"

"I've calculated a 96.3% probability that he's on a path leading to dictatorship," DAR-K answered.

"Dictatorship?" Hodge scoffed.

"Classically, it *is* one of the more effective methods of leadership in early societies," Strang explained. "Factor in that he's also the religious leader of an essentially fanatic group, and it's practically inevitable that he'd make that choice."

Hodge's eyes narrowed. "How can we get enough votes to stop him? Or do you two have something else in mind?"

"For the moment, no," DAR-K answered. "We Cybrids will demonstrate both our goodwill and our capabilities to the people when we fix the various systemic problems."

A short tentacle extended from the front of the machine; it pointed directly at Hodge, who took a worried step back.

"You and your colleagues will assist us by halting all counter-activities, effective immediately.

"In time, we could uncover all your methods and identify everyone in your network. The election would be over, and we would all pay dearly for the results. So, your activities will stop. Order will be restored. You will declare yourself in support of the Progressives, and you will join us as a candidate."

"Would anyone believe I'd switch from Alum's Yeshua Republic party to the opposition, to yours? How credible would that be?"

Strang played with his tablet and held it out again. "Here's a draft of a speech wherein you speak admiringly of the effectiveness of the Cybrids' efforts in restoring the malfunctioning systems. As well, you discuss how you've had recent conversations with DAR-K, and how those conversations led you to somewhat of an awakening."

Hodge nodded as he scanned. "Mm-hm. Yes, it's a start, I suppose. Of course, I'll have to review the speech."

"Certainly. We're not trying to force you into anything, Nigel. We're trying to give you an honorable way out."

"Out of what?"

DAR-K answered, "Prison. Or worse. I don't think Alum would stop with merely throwing you in jail. He might allow the riot that would inevitably follow his public revelations about you to get out of control. Physical harm is not out of the question."

"Alum wouldn't turn me out just like that," Hodge protested.

"Listen for yourself. You might be surprised," DAR-K said. She played back a recording of another meeting.

Hodge picked out Alum's voice right away. His blood chilled when he heard him say, "You have to think of the long game, John. It will end when *we* want it to, when it's to our best advantage." Then the recording was done.

"Who is this 'John' he's speaking to?" Hodge asked.

"John Trillian," she answered

Aside from the content of the tape, Nigel marveled at the obvious closeness of the two men, and the depth of secrecy needed to keep this "John Trillian" out of the public perception, even more so, away from the attention of the Governing Council.

"How did you get that?" Hodge demanded.

"My temper may have run hot, but I'm still Kathy Liang. I wasn't so out of my mind with rage that I couldn't think to plant a listening device or two."

"Believe her, Nigel," added Strang. Their eyes locked.

Hodge looked away first. "It seems I have little choice," he sighed.

"You do. You could accept the personal and political ruin that you likely deserve," DAR-K suggested.

Hodge couldn't tell if the Cybrid cared what happened to him, but a way out, a way forward while salvaging his political career, *that* still left hope. As long as he lived and stayed in the game, the outcome was still to be decided.

"Alright then. How can we give ourselves any chance of winning against Alum?" Hodge asked the Cybrid.

"There's more," Strang interjected.

"Much more," DAR-K echoed. "The snippet of conversation you just heard led me to investigate Alum and Trillian more extensively."

"Ahh! You found dirt," Hodge guessed.

"Your group's activities have had a lull of late, correct?"

Hodge picked at a lure on his vest. "Our goals were being met without much need for direct intervention."

"That's because Alum and Trillian have taken to helping you out."

Hodge started in surprise and pricked his finger on the lure he'd been toying with.

"Ow!" He shook his hand and put the bleeding finger in his mouth. He pulled it out after a few seconds and examined it. "You can prove that?"

"Indeed," DAR-K replied. "That's the only way this election will be fair."

Hodge shook his head. "MAD."

"Yes," DAR-K confirmed, "Mutually Assured Destruction. After Alum grants Cybrids full citizenship rights, I will send him all the evidence I have showing his collusion in the habitat problems. He will know I mean the election to be a fair one. We won't use what we have, provided that he doesn't use what he has."

"Will that be sufficient?"

"Oh, he'll try dozens of ways to see rumors are planted and that hints of damning information about you gets out, but this will restrain his direct involvement to some degree. His petty interventions won't be a large factor in the overall results."

"How can you be sure of that?"

"Nigel, please," Strang admonished. "Among her many other talents, this is the most powerful mathematical brain in existence."

"Thank you, Jared, DAR-K acknowledged. "Alum can run the game theory scenarios as well as I can. He'll know he can't push any dirt on you and Ms. Cutter too hard. He'll also know I can counter any rumors he creates about Cybrid collusion."

Hodge held out a hand to interject. "Alum is a game theory genius?"

"He is more than he seems," DAR-K replied. "He may be my equal."

"But how?"

"When Darian Leigh made the virus that created the lattice enhancements in humans, he made three capsules. One for each of his lab assistants. Greg and I, that is the original Greg Mahajani and Kathy Liang, took ours. Larry Rusalov, the third assistant, appears to have given his to the Reverend LaMontagne."

"Alum's spiritual father," Hodge recalled.

"Much, much more than that. It seems the Reverend found a way to extract or copy the lattice virus from himself and give it to the young Alum. I don't believe it was taken voluntarily."

"That's horrible!"

"Yes, it is. Alum was exposed to an IQ-enhancing lattice from almost as young an age as Darian himself. His mind was also probably slaved to the Reverend's for a good number of those years. Our 'Leader' is older, smarter, more capable, and more ruthless than anyone suspects."

"He's an unholy abomination!"

"Every bit as much as what he preaches against. More so than most Cybrids, whose only crime has been to have the wrong computational substrate, and at least as much of an abomination as I am."

Hodge thought about what he'd learned. "Is there any way we can use this against him?" he asked.

"I have no desire to carry on down that road. Over the past few decades, there has been enough disparaging of IQ-enhancing dendy lattices, and of those who have them, to suit me a lifetime," DAR-K answered. "And keep in mind that I'm a machine; my life is likely to be a *long* one."

37

"YOU'RE GOING TO STEAL FROM ALUM?"

"Don't look so surprised; it was your idea."

"You're going to steal. From Alum."

"Still, yes." Darak wore an infuriatingly smug look.

"Why not do your normal magic?"

"Science and technology," Darak corrected, holding up one finger. "Although to someone who doesn't understand, they do often appear the same."

Stralasi frowned at the interruption. "You won't use your science and technology to save these people but you'll steal from Alum. The Living God," he added, as if Darak didn't realize who Alum was.

"First of all, not all technology is equally useful in all circumstances. For instance, I can't affect the local laws of nature over a large enough space to stop the Eater. Given enough time, I could develop an appropriate technology but we don't have that luxury.

"Alum has more complex field generators in the Deplosion array than I currently have at my disposal. Time is of the essence. Ergo, we'll take his."

"If He allows it," corrected Stralasi.

"By the time He finds out, they'll be gone. A few days of adjustments and we'll be ready to deal with the Eater."

Stralasi shook his head in disbelief, threw his hands up, and walked away. *I'm bound to a madman*—he thought. He considered once again how he might escape from his forced companionship. He felt a hand on his shoulder.

"Don't worry," Darak said. "Your God will not be able to detect us or follow us. We're not ready for such a confrontation. I'll be careful," he promised. "Anyway, we'll have a few days before our criminal escapades."

"What'll we be doing in the meantime?" Stralasi asked.

"First, I have to go inside," Darak answered.

"Inside what?"

"The Eater, of course."

"What? Why?"

Instead of answering, Darak walked to a viewing window. The center of the ESO galaxy was obscured by the all-absorbing gray of the Eater. They followed a few million klicks behind it. The only visible stars were off to the sides and well behind them, where the Eater had not travelled.

He pointed at the indistinct mass directly ahead. "It's possible my friend is still inside there," he said. "I have to find out if there's anything left of him and pull him out if I can. I owe him that."

Stralasi's eyes tracked the tip of Darak's finger to the center of the gray blob. "You told me that everything passing into that thing stays absorbed. Nothing has ever come out of it."

"True. But before I send it outside this universe and deactivate it, I need to know if Darian's still alive in there."

"Who's Darian?"

"Dr. Darian Leigh. He was my mentor and my friend," Darak answered. "It's because of him that I am...me today."

"He taught you?"

"Taught me? Yes. Even more, he changed me. He started me on the path to becoming a different person. My only regret is that I didn't understand what happened to him sooner. It took me years to connect his vanishing with the Eater.

"The first time we saw it was right after Darian and Larry disappeared. We were pretty sure the sphere had something to do with their disappearances, but back then we thought the Eater was too small to make them vanish entirely. We expected to find a body, or what was left of a body, but there was nothing.

"A little while after they disappeared, one of our night patrolmen accidentally walked right through the sphere, and it killed the poor guy. That was before we knew about it and cordoned it off. My point is, there was a bullet-sized hole right through the guy, exactly where he'd walked through the sphere, and he died there on the lab floor. So that couldn't have been what happened to Darian or Larry. If it had, we would have found their bodies in the lab."

"Okay, but if it was as small as you say, how could it have made them disappear?"

"Honestly? I don't know," Darak answered. "I realize that it's unlikely he's still in there, but where else could he have gone? He wouldn't have abandoned us or the project. I just have to make sure before I destroy it forever. I have to."

Stralasi contemplated a moment. "If it's so important to you, I guess you have to try; but how do you know you'll be able to get out, once you go inside?"

"I've been beyond the edges of the universe. Do you honestly think *that* can trap me?"

"Well, those 'jump blockers' the Angels used on you seemed to stop you quite effectively," Stralasi pointed out.

"They only stopped me because of you. If I wasn't worried about losing track of you, I could have escaped them easily."

"Aren't you worried about losing me now?"

"No. You'll stay on Eso-La while I go inside the Eater. If I need to, I can find you there."

"It's a big universe. What if you get lost?"

"I won't get lost."

"But what if you do?"

"I won't."

Stralasi could see his argument was going nowhere. He'd simply have to trust Darak. On the bright side, living out what might be his final days in Crissea's company wasn't the worst possible way to die. He ceded the point. "Okay. Take me to...."

Before the monk could finish the sentence, he was standing in Crissea's reception garden.

"Did you find it?" she asked.

On seeing her, Stralasi grinned nearly ear to ear.

"We did," he answered.

"Where is it?"

His face darkened. He didn't know what to say.

"Oh, Ontro, it's heading toward us, isn't it?"

"It is," he replied. "But don't worry. Darak has a plan to divert it before it reaches Eso-La."

"How long before it gets here?"

Stralasi couldn't lie to that face. "About a year."

Crissea's brow furrowed. She looked down without uttering a word and rolled a loose stone with her foot.

The Good Brother held his tongue and let her process the news in her own way.

When she raised her head, her eyes were bright. "Darak will save us."

* * *

AFTER HE SENT STRALASI AWAY, Darak stood alone by the window in the detector chamber. He stared at the Eater and prepared to enter. What he was about to do was going to be a lot more dangerous than he'd let on to Brother Stralasi, and getting back out alive was a lot less certain, but he had to try. He had to know.

The first time it had occurred to him that Darian might be alive inside the sphere had been millions of years ago, but by then Alum had already set the destructive ball on an intergalactic journey and refused to tell anyone where it was. When pressed, all he would say is, "Security reasons."

The secrecy was understandable. *What if the wrong people were to find it and...?*

Darak had fully believed Alum had sent the Eater away on a distant and reasonably safe course, one that would keep it away from human habitation for billions of years. When he was finally free from his most critical duties and started looking for the Eater, it was no longer within a dozen light years of where he'd last seen it. He'd searched for decades but, with no clues and with a growing number of issues demanding his full attention, he'd eventually dismissed all thoughts of his former mentor and friend, Darian.

His curiosity about Darian's disappearance and the whereabouts of the sphere might have ended there if it hadn't been for Alum's disgusting campaign of genocide against the Aelu. After that, Darak had needed some time away from Alum and the Realm, and he sought the solace of his Eso rebels.

His visit to the original, struggling Eso planet brought back memories of ancient times and his unquenched curiosity about Darian's fate. It was there he decided to leave Alum's service and resume his search for the Eater.

He placed Soltron detectors in the Eso system, and went off exploring while the detectors acquired data. His journeys took him all over the universe and beyond.

Enough reminiscing. It's time to see what's inside the Eater, and to find out what's left of Darian Leigh—if anything.

38

"SO WHAT'LL IT BE, SON? Eggs or pancakes?" Darak understood the question, recognized the language as ancient English, but he was too surprised to answer. He didn't recognize the middle-aged man who asked the question any better than he recognized the house.

Where am I? How did I get here, sitting at this kitchen table?

The place was of ancient design. It took him a few seconds to query his archives and identify the style of house and furniture.

Early twenty-first century Earth.

That narrowed the search. He thought of everyone who might have called him "son" around that time. Nobody came to mind. Acting on a hunch, he ran a similar scan of memories specific to Darian Leigh.

"Dad!"

The man smiled patiently. "Yes, son?"

Darak swallowed. "I mean, you're my Dad, Darian's dad."

"Have you been lost inside that lattice of yours again? What is it, this time? A new neural net algorithm? Another dendy design?"

Darak shook his head and rested his hands on the glass tabletop. It fit right in with the brushed metal fridge and stove, and with the chrome-legged chair on which he was sitting. All exactly as he remembered it.

As *Darian* remembered it.

His head swam with confusion. *Why am I in Darian's kitchen, in the home he and his father shared in Berkeley while he completed his first PhD?* He knew where "his" room was: up the narrow flight of stairs, first door on the right. He knew where "his" lab was on campus, and he knew "his" favorite route to cycle the two miles to the university.

Of all the possible scenarios Darak imagined encountering inside the Eater, this one had never entered his mind.

Where am I? Has the Eater been absorbing matter all this time, just to restage parts of Darian's life?

"So...eggs or pancakes?" Darian's Dad—*Paul was his name*—asked again.

"Uh, pancakes, I guess," he answered. The man nodded and started looking through cupboards for the necessary ingredients.

While Paul began cooking, Darak wandered into other parts of the house. Everything was exactly as he remembered it. The brown fake leather sofas, the IKEA reading lamps, and the mismatched pine coffee tables all had a surreal familiarity.

Could the Eater have activated my ancient memories? Am I dreaming? Or is this somehow real?

Walking down the hallway toward the front door, he passed a mirror and stopped to look. The glass reflected the image of a teenager, a sixteen year-old Darian.

Darak put his hands to his face and traced the contours of a face he found both strange and familiar. *How is this happening?*

He'd explored thousands of bizarre universes in the past twenty million years. He'd spent ages playing with various combinations of natural laws just to see what kind of technologies he could invent and to watch how odd forms of life might evolve. And yet, in many ways this particular universe, at once both unexpected and familiar, was the most surprising and the strangest of all.

He opened the front door onto a tiny patch of grass Darian and Paul had called a yard.

How big is this world? Does it extend all the way to the boundary with the outside universe? Is it larger inside than its external radius?

There were too many questions; he didn't have time to find the answers.

What bothered him most of all was the extremely low likelihood that he would've shifted at random inside the Eater and happened to appear in this microverse in the body and home of Darian Leigh.

The odds were beyond imagining. Something directed him here. *But what? Well, only one way to find out.*

He shifted to a different place inside the Eater microverse.

* * *

HE WAS LYING IN BED, staring up at a suspended ceiling. The metal rails on each side of the narrow bed and the pale yellow curtain pulled around it told him he was in a hospital. He felt exhausted. Every muscle in his body ached as though he'd just run a marathon.

"Hey, you're awake. How are you doing, honey?" A nurse pulled the curtain aside and stepped into his space.

He could read her name tag: Ranson, it said. Behind her was an unoccupied bed. The wheels of two more beds showed beneath their respective curtains.

Darak tried to sit up but fell back with a groan.

"Ohhh, I hurt everywhere," he answered. Or someone answered. The voice sounded younger than his own.

"That's to be expected. You had quite a seizure."

Seizure?

"Did my dad leave?"

The words tumbled out of his own mouth but...*Dad? Wow, where'd that come from*—he wondered.

He didn't feel completely in control of his body. It was as if he were watching some antiquated inSense movie.

The whole experience was a mind-bending combination of active and passive. He seemed to be partly reliving memories of things that had happened to Darian, and partly acting on his own intentions.

"Yes, he did, sweetie. Just a little while ago," Nurse Ranson replied. "It's late. I'm going to give you a little something to help you sleep." She held out a paper cup with a small yellow pill inside.

Darak hadn't seen a pill in over a hundred million years and he wasn't about to take one now.

What effect would it have on the real me, on the mind that thinks it's inside this young body? Could just being here affect me? The real me? Better not linger here too long. He shifted again.

* * *

THE BUBBLE WAS SHRINKING, closing in around him. He was trapped! Larry laughed. It was a mean laugh.

Larry? Darak hadn't thought of his old friend and lab mate this much in over a hundred million years, but he recognized the young scientist immediately.

Larry looked bigger than normal. In fact, everything outside the bubble looked larger than normal.

"Nothing more to say, Professor?" Larry asked.

Professor? He'd never been Larry's teacher.

Darak recalled a different time, when he'd had a different name, a different life.

"Larry! It's me, Greg. Get me out of here!" His voice sounded odd, not like his own at all. Was he becoming disconnected from himself? But which self? Darak? Or Greg? Or Darian?

The young man who'd been his best friend during their early postdoc years stopped laughing. He tilted his head, drew closer, and peered into the bubble. Then he threw back his head and roared.

"Ahhh! You got me! That was hilarious. *You,* Greg? You think I'm stupid, or blind?"

Annoyed, Larry returned to the ancient RAF generator on the desktop and played with a few buttons.

"It won't be long now and you'll be gone from this universe forever, and humanity will be safe from your brand of hubris once again."

"Larry, wait!" Darak/Greg/Darian cried. "Don't do it. This microverse isn't what you think. It doesn't go away. It starts to grow and grow, until it consumes the entire Earth."

Larry glared at him. "Your lies won't save you. You and the other geniuses are all the same. You think I'm stupid because I didn't take your pill." He checked his computer screen, made a few adjustments, and pushed a button.

The bubble prison pressed inward a little faster. Darak/Greg/Darian pushed back against it, both physically and with his RAF generator.

Nothing! No change! Darak felt his/Darian's growing desperation as he generated and projected all manner of fields at the shrinking shell.

Wait. Why am I caught up in this?—he wondered. He stepped back mentally and let the scene play out.

On one level, he could sense Darian's panic and his equally fierce determination to survive. He recognized the moment when Darian, in a frantic attempt to have something of himself carry on, transmitted all of his knowledge, memories, and personality to his assistants' lattices.

Even now, millions of years after the event, Darak remembered the utterly overwhelming flow of data that had blasted him and Kathy without warning or explanation. Somehow, the bubble had allowed the electromagnetic transmissions to escape but had kept Darian inside.

As Darian's constituent atoms collapsed, their electrons spiraled inward toward their nuclei. His desperate transmissions fell into a frequency range that could no longer penetrate the bubble; they reflected off the barrier and ricocheted within the collapsing microverse.

The sphere's boundary delineated a region of incompatible natural laws; the entire external universe rejected interactions with the matter inside the bubble. Slowly, the differences between them grew.

Darak watched helplessly as Darian's universe became smaller and smaller. Though he was dragged along with his former mentor, he realized his perspective was not a physical one, but a psychological one.

Darak regained control of his mind and perspective.

He finally understood what was happening. Not that long ago, he'd traveled outside the universe he once shared with Darian, Kathy, and Larry. The journey made him realize that the concept of "outside" had no real spatial significance. Outside just meant different.

If there was no way for the particles of one universe to interact with those of another, the two could occupy the exact same space and it would be the same as if they were separated by infinite distance.

Space, like time, was relative to the matter of the universe. Any universe. If you didn't interact with any matter in one universe, you had no way to tell how near or far you were, relative to any matter in that universe. If there were no particle interactions, there was no way to talk about occupying the same space.

He watched the disturbing scene play out as Darian struggled to understand the nature of the Reality Assertion Field that Larry had cast to create this isolated domain. Darian had been new to the practical applications of the theory he'd developed. He kept trying to modify the RAF that contained him, and it had spelled his doom.

That was so sad. Larry's and Darian's careers were, at the heart of it, destroyed by religious belief. Larry couldn't accept that God wasn't needed to explain the existence of natural laws in the universe. He couldn't accept enhanced intelligence. He couldn't accept that we could alter the laws of nature without God's blessing. He felt threatened, and his refusal to step outside the rigid constraints of his beliefs led him to murder Darian. Which led to the destruction of Earth.

So what happened to Larry? Where did he go between killing Darian and the Earth being destroyed? The scene shed no light on that, but Darak was pretty sure Reverend LaMontagne was somehow involved. It was the easiest way to explain the Reverend's own enhanced-IQ lattice and his familiarity with RAF theory. Did he take it by force, or did Larry willingly hand it over?

Darian's transmissions must still be echoing around inside this microverse. That would explain how I've been "remembering" his experiences as if I were him. When I incorporated his persona to save my sanity, it changed me. It must be making me supersensitive to the transmissions inside the Eater. They're resonating too easily with my lattice and bypassing my security because they're as much mine as his.

Darak blocked all external transmissions into his lattice. The previously vivid images became ghost-like and easily distinguished from the homogeneous dense grayish "matter" of this microverse.

In Darian's last attempts to survive, he'd built an entire universe, albeit a tiny one, with one purpose: to preserve whatever he considered essential. Not his body. He knew that couldn't be preserved and, besides, the corporeal was irrelevant to anything Darian thought important. He sought only to preserve his mind.

The poor guy just wanted to find some way to live. Darak listened to the memory of Darian's internal voice. He heard the moment when his terrified mentor realized the only possible way to survive was to stop fighting the field and to accept his fate.

Darak stayed with Darian's memory as he neared the limits of life-supporting chemistry. At the end, Darian's new understanding led him to try compensating for this strangely compressed matter comprising his new universe. He'd hoped to place a limit on how small he would get, by allowing new matter from the outside universe to enter and add to his own. If only he'd had a little more time, or a little more understanding, he might have been able to save himself.

Darian never realized how little Larry understood what he was playing with, and he had no idea that his final modifications would create the Eater—Darak realized.

He ran the equations in his mind. He could see how Darian's best guesses kept running up against Larry's ignorance, creating something that incorporated itself into whatever it touched. The fields reinforced each other; they led to a stable and growing universe of its own.

Darak had a lot more experience with artificial universes. He could see the solution that had eluded Darian ages ago. *The fields are easy enough to turn off, but if I do that, the absorbed matter will suddenly appear in the external universe. All that mass travelling at near light speed would instantly be subject to the natural laws of real space.*

He did a quick calculation. *The energy release would be equivalent to a supernova. Everything in the ESO 461-36 system would get hit with a lethal dose of radiation. And not just Eso-La; they'd be first, but others as well. How can I diffuse this bomb safely?*

As Darak considered his options, another question pushed its way into his consciousness. Could he save Darian?

His memories are here, his mind, his thoughts and ideas. Everything that was important to him. Could I reconstruct him from all this? Should I? Would he want me to?

He felt partially responsible for Larry's state at the time. He and Kathy had prodded Larry which, no doubt, had contributed to their colleague's sense of resentment and led him directly, almost inevitably, to taking Darian's life. *We should have been more sensitive or, at least, more aware.*

He could feel the part of him that was Darian, yearning for life. It didn't help being inside the Eater. The reflections of Darian's life and innermost thoughts tugged at Darak. He wasn't sure if anyone else, besides him and possibly Alum, could contemplate pulling off such a resurrection.

The echoing transmissions clouded Darak's mind. He couldn't think straight.

Now that I know the Eater's true nature, I can figure out how to deactivate it. I just need a few minutes of clear thought.

He shifted back *outside* to his own universe.

* * *

"SO...WHAT'LL IT BE, SON? Eggs or pancakes?"

"Wha...?" Darak/Darian was back in his father's kitchen.

"What'll it be? Eggs or pancakes?"

Without answering, he again tried to shift outside again.

Still here! How's that possible? I've been outside the known universe, in the Chaos, and made my way back. No place has ever been able to hold me if I wanted to leave.

He needed some perspective, perspective that was difficult to get while he was immersed in the matter and memories of this place.

He altered his own structure, so it barely overlapped with the odd stuff of this microverse inside the Eater. The demands of Darian's memories diminished.

That's better. Now, I can take a closer look at the nature of this place.

Using his own RAF generator, he sent a few probing fields into the Eater microverse. The answer came back in seconds.

It's a hologram! An actual holographic universe. Have I been wrong all along?

Eons ago, when Darak was still the young Greg Mahajani, he'd argued with a handful of physicists who'd hypothesized the universe was nothing more than a holographic projection of all matter onto the inside surface of a black hole. Furthermore, reflecting such a projection back into space reconstructed the entirety of the three-dimensional matter of the universe.

He'd scoffed at their ideas, told them their hypothesis amounted to a simplistic mind game. It couldn't be correct because, in the first place, holographs only portrayed the surface features of matter; they captured nothing of the insides of objects.

And yet, here I am, definitely in a holographic microverse.

Also like a hologram, any part of the Eater contained the entirety. But the bigger the part that was accessed, the more detailed the final resolution. This hologram was so big that it reflected Darian's mind in stunning detail. Each concept, memory, and thought was represented in a hugely redundant way and extensively cross-linked to every other fragment of Darian's persona.

Now he understood what held him so strongly. Darian was everywhere inside the Eater. His thoughts and memories were the basic components of this microverse. The man's will to survive had made this place, and whatever little of his will remained wasn't about to give up a moment of his existence so easily.

Deactivating the fields that sustained the Eater would bring Darian's final death. It didn't seem fair.

Darak moved through the universe, delicately sampling the other man's memories the way a textile shopper might walk through a marketplace running his hands gently over bolts of cloth.

Practically everything's here—he thought. *Everything that made Darian who he was. Far more than Kathy or I ever received in his final transmission, but it's all fragmented and jumbled, not assembled into a working concepta and persona.*

An idea swelled within him. *I can save Darian. He contributed so much to humanity, and his extraordinary mind still has lots more to offer. Imagine! After so much time, after being trapped in this eternal purgatory for ages, Darian could live again!*

He could do it. He would. He'd save Darian and stop the Eater.

Darak bowed his head and transmitted wave after wave of his promise into the Eater microverse. *Darian, I vow to bring you back into the real universe again. You'll be able to see where your ideas and inventions led. You'll know the future. You'll be with us again.*

He opened his eyes and repeated the promise, once, to himself. Then he shifted outside.

39

"DIDN'T ALUM CANCEL THE SECURITOR PROGRAM?" Greg/Darak pushed back from his keyboard and swiveled his chair around to face John Trillian. While he was programming inworlds for Alum, it was best to appear to need the standard interface rather than using his lattice. Especially when Trillian might be watching over his shoulder.

"Yes, he did."

"Then why are we continuing to develop this battle simulation inworld?"

"We may have other uses for it."

Greg sighed. "Is that the best answer I can expect? No answer at all?"

Trillian walked over to a lab bench and picked up a crystalline Cybrid brain from among the dozen sitting there. He turned it over in his hands, letting the light reflect off its polished surfaces.

"What do you think it's like, living inside one of these things?" he asked.

Greg stood up and stretched the kinks out of his back. "I've always assumed it was the same as living inside our brain. At least, that's how I program the sensory input."

Sitting for hours at a desk and pretending to work like an unenhanced human had been taking a toll on him, mentally and physically. *I need to make more of an effort to get out into the tunnel park and walk around.*

He meandered over to the door and peered outside. A pair of scientists were engaged in deep discussion on a bench by the river. *Rare to see people around here.*

Behind him, Trillian grunted. "This one, though, it's special. Isn't it?"

"It is," Greg answered. "It contains a partial copy, a pared-down concepta of Sgt. Alden St. Michael, retired. I've kept everything I could find pertaining to battle strategy and tactics, plus loyalty, duty, and honor. Everything unrelated was left out of the copy. Should be ideal for testing the inworld battle simulator."

"Yes, ideal." Trillian set the Cybrid lattice back on the bench. He joined Greg and looked out at the park. His eyes wandered left and right, following the science service tunnel off to infinity in either direction.

Greg followed Trillian's gaze. "It's quiet around here. I thought this place was supposed to be a beehive of activity."

Trillian snapped around and focused on his co-worker, searching his face for signs of criticism. "Be glad you're among the few with access."

Greg held up his hands, deflecting Trillian's suspicions. "Don't think that I don't appreciate being able to work for Alum and the Administration. I mean, this is a dream job right? I get to play and create all I could possibly want."

"It *is* a dream job to be doing Alum's work. The Lord's work."

"I guess I wouldn't mind knowing the work is appreciated and enjoyed, is all."

"You have inSense. Don't you visit your inworlds while you develop them?"

"Sure, and I like them. It would just be nice to know that my intended audience appreciates them, too. You know? To talk to some of the Cybrids and get their feedback."

"That kind of conversation is prohibited except for Cybrid supervisors," Trillian replied.

"Of course. I used to be a Supervisor, you know, when I first got here. Not that the Cybrids and I ever actually talked. Apart from you and Alum, I've received no feedback on Vacationland. And I have no idea if this current project is at all useful."

"The battle simulations?"

"Well, if the Securitor program isn't going to use them, who will?" Greg kept his face as open and innocent as possible. He was broaching dangerous ground.

"Video games, especially military ones, have always been popular," Trillian replied casually.

Greg nodded, as if he took the answer seriously. "True. Well, among kids—teenage boys, particularly—for sure. That hardly describes the Cybrids, though, does it? Or are we going to release it on one of the inSense channels? It's a little too destructive for most players, don't you think?"

"You could say that, yes." Trillian snorted. "No, we won't put this out for public consumption. Let's just say that every civilization needs to prepare contingencies."

"Contingencies? Against what?"

"One never knows. That's why they're called contingencies."

"So, on the remote possibility there may someday be some nebulous future need for a Cybrid military—"

"Or a human one," Trillian added.

"—for a Cybrid or human military training program, I should continue development?"

"Exactly."

"Okay. It's your dime, boss." Greg went back to his station.

Trillian stood in the doorway a while longer, staring at the outdoor part of the tunnel. "That's all the time I have today," he announced abruptly. "I'll check on your progress again next week."

"Same time, same place," Greg replied. "I'm here every workday." Trillian was already striding away to his next meeting.

Greg stared at his screen, contemplating for a minute. *That was an odd exchange. Evasive, even for Trillian.*

He copied a chunk of code he'd written weeks ago onto his computer. The program had been completed within minutes of starting on it, but he had to make it look like it was coming along with great difficulty over a period of weeks or months.

To that end, his code contained a small routine to make the computer think everything had been entered manually. Spyware or anyone checking his work would detect a history of keystrokes, complete with typos, fixes, test compilations, and practice runs. Greg wouldn't be present for most of it.

He walked over to the bench and picked up the Cybrid CPPU Trillian had been holding minutes earlier.

Curious that Trillian chose this particular unit. Even more curious, he seemed to know something about it.

On a whim, he threw the brain into a test harness. He'd become intimately familiar with every association, label, and conceptual relationship in the simplified mind of Sgt. St. Michael. He wasn't sure what he expected to find, but he'd been picking up something odd from Trillian, and he was pretty sure this brain held a clue. He activated the CPPU and dove into the conceptual structures stored within.

Trillian, you've been busy! The alterations to the abbreviated data structures jumped out at him as if they'd been written in flaming letters.

Greg extricated his own lattice senses from the Cybrid concepta. It had to have been Trillian. Who else? Unless...could Alum himself have deigned to visit the science labs? Highly unlikely. No, this coding was too similar to what he'd discovered in the Securitor minds he'd examined.

Sneaky! Trillian had altered the loyalty and honor sections of the concepta, giving it a peculiar admiration of Alum and emphasizing the protection of his Administration over that of the habitats and their citizens.

That's scary; he's also ramped up aggressiveness to dangerous levels.

Greg paced the length of the bench. *Without Securitors, this makes no sense. I've seen no sign of any more being built. So either the construction program is still secretly active or the CPPU is intended for something else.*

Any Vesta facilities capable of housing a covert Securitor manufacturing facility were all nearby. Without a thought, Greg shifted to the closest one.

The facility was quiet. A single half-completed Securitor body sat in the middle of the room, wires dangling, electro-muscles without power. *Not here.*

He shifted to two other nearby possibilities in quick succession. There was no sign of Securitor construction in either of them. He shifted back to his lab and went for a walk down by the river in the park.

The two scientists he'd seen earlier had left; nobody was visible in any direction.

Something else had been bothering him about the changes to Sgt. Michael's data structures. He called up the memory of his code review, and turned his attention to the lowest level of the operating system.

There. The BIOS routines for managing rocket propulsion and thruster jets had all been replaced.

Greg recognized the intent of the code. *A shifter. An independent, locally-entangled jump-shift management routine.*

Someone had figured out his travel method!

Sure, shifters were almost ubiquitous now, but they all went from one discrete entangled point to another.

I'm the only one who's ever experimented with shifting using nothing but naturally-available entangled particles. His heart was hammering. He took a moment to dampen his emotional response to the discovery. His breathing slowed.

He examined the code more closely. Whoever programmed those shift routines had stopped well short of the kind of distances that Greg's sense of adventure and desperation had taken him. Maximum jumps were sensibly limited to under a kilometer at a time, with short recalculation rests in between.

He couldn't help but smirk. *There are some advantages to being a little crazy, I guess. Still, it's a fast method to get around, and it uses very little energy. Just a little for calculations and the specialized RAF generator, that's all.*

So, is this modified concepta heading for some new kind of Securitor? And who's responsible? In all the habitats, who has the skill to challenge Kathy's original designs?

There was only one possible answer. Alum.

If Alum were building some new kind of police or military Cybrid, where would he hide it?

Greg called up the construction plans of all three asteroids. For redundancy, every critical scientific function had been installed on at least two of the three asteroids. Cybrid manufacture was on Vesta and Pallas. He'd already checked out the likely locations on Vesta and found no covert activities there.

He shifted to a storage closet inside one of the four possible Cybrid labs in Pallas. He listened at the door then cracked it slightly ajar. Nothing. He stepped out and swept the empty lab. There were no signs of any recent activity.

He jumped to a supply closet in the next lab on his list. He could hear sounds of movement outside the closet, the whine of e-muscle, the click-click of metal tools. He cracked open the door for a peek.

What the hell is that? He fell back into the closet, pulling the door closed as he reeled. The latch made a soft snick as it fell into place. He held his breath.

The sounds in the lab stopped.

He called up the schematics for the area and shifted to an observation and control room across the lab. When a Cybrid tentacle pulled open the closet door, he was already gone.

He stood up slowly, carefully, behind machine panels in the control room and with one eye peeked into the lab through a gap between two instruments.

In the middle of the lab, a Cybrid tinkered on a three-meter tall humanoid structure.

No, not human. A demon? He looked more closely. *No, not demonic either. Not exactly. An Angel?*

The polished metal surface gleamed in the functional lighting of the lab. Its e-muscles flexed beneath the surface when the Cybrid moved stimulating probes around inside an open panel in the abdomen.

In the middle of the open panel lay a standard Cybrid harness, waiting to receive a new CPPU. *Sgt. St. Michael's?*

Nothing besides his suspicions led to that conclusion. Still, it wasn't unreasonable, and the coincidence behind his two discoveries was unsettling.

He couldn't see any propulsion ports. *Maybe they open up on the bottom of the feet.*

Could the shift software be for the Angel? They wouldn't need rockets if they could make sequential shifts.

The Cybrid probe moved again, and the construct flapped its wings once, twice. They barely stirred a breeze. *For decoration only*—Greg mused.

Unless that thing contained an RAF generator for mass reduction, the wings would never provide enough lift. *Anyway, why lift when you can shift?*

It all made sense now. Why Alum was continuing with the inworld battle training though he'd cancelled the Securitor program. Why someone had meddled with some Partial's—Sgt. St. Michael's—concepta. *Angels!*

Greg had a sour taste in his mouth. *The most devilish Angel I've ever seen.*

Now that he thought about it, his inworld programming assignment had been given a strange specification. Trillian had insisted on it. "Assume a smaller version of the tunnel drills is available as a weapon," he'd said.

As Greg grasped the implications, he broke into a cold sweat. He remembered the first time the Reverend LaMontagne had demonstrated a small tunnel drill to him and Kathy, back in the wilderness park area of

Texas. It had made small work of an entire mountainside.

What would it do against humans? Or Cybrids?

He had to talk to someone in the opposition. If he was going to stop this, he needed help.

40

ALUM SAT ALONE IN A CHAMBER surrounded by blank Cybrid CPPUs. John Trillian watched attentively from the adjacent control room. "Are you ready, sir?"

Am I ready? How can one know if one is truly ready to take the first step toward Godhood?

Alum adjusted his induction helmet. Not that he normally needed one, but today would stretch even his interface abilities. *Once the new chips are implanted, I can dispense with this*—he thought.

He ran his fingers over the surface of the helmet trying to sense the exotic particles contained inside. *Maybe a bump, here and there. That could be anything*—he told himself—*a seam, a slight manufacturing variation.*

The pods containing the clusters of spin-entangled atoms were microscopic. Each one held no more than a million individual specimens.

The hardware around them, which enabled his mind to be distributed throughout the asteroid habitats, was bigger by far. Each micromodem was a chip, just a few millimeters square, lying over corresponding transmitter/receivers he had grown on his neocortex.

That was a brilliant bit of virus engineering—he thought. *Darian Leigh would be proud.*

"Sir?" Trillian's voice intruded on his thoughts. The man was clearly eager to get on with it.

"A moment, please, John." *Why shouldn't he be eager? This is his crowning achievement as much as mine. Trillian designed the communications hardware and the special software that will allow me to run all the important machinery in the habitats.*

Alum put his hand on a small brown crystalline cube. *And just what will you do?*—he wondered, and turned the cube over in his hand.

Will you be interfaced to a starstep, or drive a loop train? Will you control lighting and airflow, or watch over crops and livestock? Will you monitor billions of transactions, or supervise people as they go about their daily business?

Over the past month, Trillian had overseen the installation of special interfaces all over the habitats. "Partial AI will enhance the reliability, safety, and security of critical habitat systems," they'd told the citizens. That much was true.

They didn't mention it would also put every single automated process in all three colonies under the direct control of Alum's consciousness.

Most of the lattice cubes were smaller than a full Cybrid brain. The smallest were for simple purposes, and were barely smarter than a finger. *Others will be my extra eyes or ears.*

Alum moved his hand to a much larger one, almost twice the size of the normal Cybrid cube. *And some will be only for thinking, for housing more of me than this body can hold.*

So why am I so glum? So pensive?

When Trillian had first proposed the cubes, Alum hadn't been convinced it would be a good idea. At first.

"Just think about it," John had said. "Everything will be connected to you. The habitats will rely on you completely. Elected or not, your control will be absolute."

To usurp control. To maintain that control beyond my natural lifetime. Is that a thing Yeshua would condone? Not to mention that we've publicly discredited the unnatural; should we now embrace it? He tormented himself for weeks over the decision.

Even when he'd finally warmed up to the idea, he'd remained reluctant. "As appealing as it may be, I'm concerned about the higher-level nodes," he'd shared with Trillian.

"Ah, yes. The independents."

"It seems risky to have multiple copies of one's self floating around the solar system. Even without corporeal bodies, what's to stop the *copies* of me from seeing themselves as *competitors* to me? I mean, the original, flesh and blood me?"

"No doubt, your concern is increased by the potential risk of embodiment. Perhaps in some convenient Cybrid body?" Trillian could barely suppress his grin.

"You make it sound less palatable by the minute but, judging by your glee, I suspect you have a solution in mind."

"I do, indeed, sir." Trillian beamed. "When I proposed to 'distribute' you, I didn't mean copies of you. I meant all of you."

"Okay, John. Now I'm intrigued. How do you propose to do that?"

"With these." He held up a pair of unremarkable devices, about the size of a pair of hearing aids. "These are highly miniaturized, dedicated quantum shifters coupled to standard optical transmitter/receivers."

Alum caught on instantly. "I see. You circumvent speed-of-light limitations on transmission delay by connecting the pair through shifting technology."

He plucked one of the devices from Trillian's hand. "Very clever, John. No matter how far apart my various processing units are, it will be as if they are all together."

"Exactly," Trillian replied. "In effect, we won't be placing copies of you throughout the habitats; we'll be distributing all of you across all of the habitats. Your mind will stretch across the solar system."

"Do I not fill heaven and earth?" Alum had whispered.

"Jeremiah 23:24," Trillian answered. "Not quite in the same way as our Lord, God. But certainly larger than life, I think."

"Though always in humble service to Yeshua's People," Alum added, and bowed his head. *How pragmatic!*—he thought. *How easy to ignore the morality of a thing, like expanding one's mind beyond the merely human, once it becomes a real possibility. But can it be done without risk? That's the only question that really matters.*

Trillian caught a flicker of something in Alum's eyes before the lids drew down as veils. Was it guilt? Recognition of the hubris of the idea? Or simply an acknowledgement of how attractive the idea was?

Alum gave himself over to the weight of what he was about to do.

Truly, it is a service to become a God. I will remember this: Absolute power demands absolute responsibility and absolute humility.

"Are you ready now, sir?" Again, Trillian's voice pulled Alum back to the present.

He nodded. "Yes, John. I'm ready, now."

41

THE HEAVY CELL DOOR FLEW OPEN, and crashed against the stone wall, tearing Mary from her intense meditation.

"What did she tell you?" Trillian yelled from across the room.By the time she opened her eyes and looked up, he was already halfway across the darkened room. Even in the dim light she could see the chords in his neck straining and spittle flying as he yelled.

"I said, what did she tell you? Answer me!"

Mary jumped to her feet and backed away from the enraged Shard. The calm achieved through hours of focusing on code and conceptual structures dispersed like thin fog in a wind tunnel. Virtual adrenaline streamed through her body.

"What. Did. She. Tell. You?" Trillian screamed. His contorted face, only inches away, had gone scarlet and his eyes bulged with fury.

"What did *who* tell me?" Mary cried. "Darya? You saw her for yourself. She didn't say anything to me. Just, 'I'm sorry.' Nothing else." She wiped the spit off her cheek with the back of her hand.

"Liar!" Trillian clasped her throat with one hand and slammed her into the wall.

Gasping for air, Mary struggled against him and tried to loosen his grip. Her efforts had no more effect than a mouse struggling to open a bear trap.

Why doesn't he just kill me?—she wondered. *Why this show?*

Oh! The answer came to her and she laughed. Or tried to. She choked on the revelation, broke into a cough, and a wheeze that she could barely squeeze out around his clawing fingers.

Sensing a shift but not able to guess the reason, Trillian threw her to the ground and stood over her. He leaned lower and stared directly into her eyes as she sucked in air.

"Mary, what did she tell you?" he said in a soft, deadly voice.

Mary coughed and, in spite of the pain it caused, laughed. "I had no inkling that she'd told me anything until now," she said, brushing her hair back off her face. "Thanks for that."

Trillian backhanded her across the face. He could've taken off her head but he restrained himself. She remained conscious.

Mary massaged her jaw and spit out some blood. "I can only assume that the burst of light before Darya and Timothy left contained a message of some sort. I was a little busy being tortured at the time, if you'll recall. I didn't have a chance to pick it up at the time, but I promise to look into it soon as I have time. At the moment, I have no idea."

"Then, how about we review it together?" Trillian suggested through clenched teeth.

"If that'll make you happy," Mary said. She loaded her recording of the event into her working memory and Trillian did the same. The flash of light registered as a brief blip in her recollection. Now that she knew it contained a compressed message, she filtered it through a high-speed playback algorithm.

Darya stood on the other side of a campfire in a clearing in the forest near her Keep in Lysrandia. The soft glow of dwindling flames threw dancing shadows across her face. The sound of soft music and conversation drifted in from somewhere nearby. No one else was visible in the projection.

"Mary, I'm so sorry we had to leave you. Timothy and I found a specific function to get outside and safely away. Please know that we are working hard to provide a second function to release you from your virtual prison. Trillian appears to have trapped your trueself in the recharging station. I'm certain you'll be able to turn the inworld tables on him and escape back outworld in a second. Once you are out, you know where to find me. Keep fighting. Remember to maintain a positive spin on everything. That will help you immensely. See you soon."

The message stopped there, with Darya smiling reassuringly as if she could transmit her hope to Mary through sheer willpower.

Trillian lifted Mary off the floor and dropped her roughly onto a high-backed wooden chair that had a helmet hinged to the top-back of the chair. He flipped the helmet over her head and tightened the screws.

She cried out as they bit into her scalp.

"You will tell me what it means," he demanded. "What is the message hidden within the message?"

He gave one of the screws a full turn. It pressed into her forehead, drawing blood and a whimper.

"You saw it," Mary protested. "It was a meaningless bunch of platitudes. We're working hard to help you. Keep up your positive attitude. We'll get you out. What a crock!"

"I don't believe you. Where did that scene take place? Did you recognize the spot?"

"Yes; it was in the Lysrandia inworld, outside of Darya's Keep. She took our group there into the forest for a meeting once. But that tells me nothing; it's just some random place from a better time. She must've meant it to comfort me."

"There must have been some clues, some bit of shared information. Darya said you'd know where to find her. You will tell me or I'll wring it out of you."

Mary thought quickly. *Something plausible.*

"Second," she said. "Darya said it twice; that was meaningful. She has a second route out of here besides that old service shed."

"You're lying. There's no way she was able to program two secret ways to exit Vacationland."

"Ha! You don't even know her designation. You have no idea of her capabilities."

"Hmm, we'll talk about *that* little piece of information later. Eventually, you will tell me everything I want to know." Trillian waved a hand and they were in Cloud 49 again. Mary exhaled in relief at the release of pressure on her cranium.

The Shard raised his eyebrows at her. "Do you think I am anything but your God inside this inworld?"

"You'd better be careful. How would Alum feel about you expressing such ambitions?" Mary asked with a wry smile.

"Alum's feelings are none of your concern. I control your fate here. I control what you perceive, what you feel."

"But not what I think. I believe we've already demonstrated that."

"In time, I'll break your defenses and your mind will be laid bare for me to read."

"Unless I turn the tables on you, first."

"As Darya said, I not only control your inworld experience but your outworld freedom."

Mary couldn't help but frown. "Darya will find a way to help me."

"I thought she offered only meaningless platitudes. Your words, not mine."

When Mary didn't reply, Trillian continued, "Darya wouldn't tell you about a second exit without specifying its location. The message must have told you where it is."

Mary snorted. "You're sitting on it."

"What?"

"Look around. Remember, 'Turn the tables'? I'm supposed to figure out a special way to move the tables here at the café to open the exit. Darya likes to encode these things with unlikely arrangements or motions."

"Why are you telling me this?"

Mary stood up. "Because it's useless information, Trillian. She didn't have time to tell me the details. You got there too fast. I have no idea what I'm supposed to do and no way to figure it out on my own."

She took a step to the banister and stared at the sandy beach seventy meters below. From this distance, the sand below would be hard as cement on impact.

"There will be no escape for me. No rescue. No reunion with Darya."

Trillian remained seated at the table. He showed no sign of concern.

She pressed on. "Darya's real message is that there is nothing she can do, that it's all up to me. I can choose my own solution."

Mary took a step back. "And this is what I choose."

She launched herself backward over the rail.

Trillian rushed to the rail and watched her fall, his face expressionless. A second before her body hit the beach below, he blinked once.

* * *

MARY OPENED HER EYES. She was back in her prison cell, staring up at the ceiling. She took a deep breath and let it go. *I knew he wouldn't let me die.* She closed her eyes and played Darya's message again. *Darya, what did you leave for me?*

There was nothing obvious but then there wouldn't be, would there? The interpretation she gave Trillian had some merit. One could easily read Darya's message as incomplete, an empty morale booster devoid of any meaningful content. A superficial analysis would easily support that conclusion. The problem was, as far as Mary could tell, deeper analysis didn't reveal much else.

I hope I'm not just going on false hope.

Darya would've anticipated that Trillian would also receive her transmission and he'd suspect some encrypted content that would help Mary's position. *There are so many ways to hide information. How would Darya have done it so only the intended recipient could recognize and retrieve a specific message? That's the question. At the same time, the transmission would have to be innocuous enough to convince Trillian it contained no useful content.*

Mary measured the transmission frame by frame. The total number of bytes perfectly added up to the sum of all the video frames. *Nothing hidden that way.*

Whatever useful information it held had to be accessible by analyzing the content or maybe rearranging data. There'd have to be a key to reorganizing some part of a video frame into something else, and nothing added beyond that. *Trillian wouldn't be able to decrypt that. Clever, Darya!*

Mary was sure there was something useful in the visual recording. But what? Darya never would've risked coming back inworld to her here if she didn't have anything helpful to contribute. *I hope.* It wasn't much to go on, but all she had was her faith in her friend.

The comment about "positive spin" stood out. Was Darya suggesting something about the quark-spin inworld processing machinery? Darya had to know what an advantage her friend would have over Trillian if she could just boost her CPPU power.

Maybe she sent me the code I need. There has to be a decryption key buried in the message itself. Nothing that depends on a clever analysis of the content; Trillian would have as much chance of figuring that out as I do.

Something unique to my experience, then. Something only I would know but not obviously so. I mean, Darya could have said "Remember the day we first met," or, "Remember what you had for lunch at our last meeting," but either of those would be something Trillian could extract from me. So, it has to be shared knowledge but less obvious.

She pulled up her detailed memories of the real fireside meeting in Lysrandia for comparison. She searched for something Trillian couldn't possibly know, something subtle.

She filtered out the landscape. *Trillian will have access to a complete detailed layout of our campsite. No, nothing there.*

That left only Darya herself, the background noises of others in the group, and the campfire—the campfire!

Mary overlaid her original memories of that evening on Darya's transmission. The campfire had moved. Not much. Maybe it could be explained by a slightly different perspective, from the point of view of the person that had sat to Mary's left that evening. *Surely, Darya would never make such a mistake. She knew exactly where I sat that night.*

Mary measured the change in distance between her position in the transmission and the relocated fire. *Okay, so the fire was moved exactly 21.10611405421 centimeters to the right. Interesting number. Tantalizingly close to the wavelength of light emitted by hydrogen in a vacuum, the so-called H-line. Coincidence? I doubt it.*

A quick calculation showed the number was the product of two primes: 505709 and 4173569. *Is it RSA encryption, Darya? With such small prime numbers?* Maybe it wouldn't matter if the person the message was being hidden from had no way to calculate the private and public keys.

So, if the H-line's the modulus.... Mary calculated what her private key should be. *Now which fire image to decrypt?* There were a lot to chose from. At 30 frames per second in Darya's 34-second video there were over a thousand individual images of flickering flames.

Pick a number between one and a thousand...but which number? First? Last? Or just go through them all?—Mary pondered.

There was an easy way to generate a number between one and a thousand, simply divide a smaller number by a bigger number to give you something between zero and one. Then multiply by 1,000 to normalize; it was guaranteed to work.

Could the answer be that simple? She divided the larger of the two primes into the smaller and multiplied by 1,000 to get 121 and some fraction. *So, maybe...the 121st frame?*

She pulled it up. *What do we have here?* It was exactly four seconds into the video, the single word, "function." Potentially interesting but still meaningless.

What can I do with it? Darya's pass codes often use repetition. Does the word "function" repeat elsewhere in the video?

Four seconds later, on frame 242, the word "function" again. More than a coincidence?

Mary called up the two frames and isolated the flames of the campfire. If she scrolled forward or backward, the flame patterns didn't fit. Would Trillian notice that?

Mary ran the digital encoding of the flames through her algorithm using Darya's normal public key and the private key she'd just worked out. It kicked out two long strings of digits. Two long, equally meaningless, strings of digits.

She converted them to hexadecimal, the ancient machine language of computers and then into assembler. The resultant "code" was a mess; it didn't fit anywhere.

What did I do wrong?—she wondered. She went back over her logic. The primes came out of the changes in the video from her memory of the real event. The indicated video frames of the flames were special; they didn't follow the flow of earlier frames. Everything hung together. *That can't be a coincidence; they have to contain the message. What am I missing?*

She couldn't lie still any longer. She got up from the bit of floor she called a bed and paced past the window to Hell. She went over the numbers, over the data, over her logic.

Two different pictures of flames? On a hunch, she examined their digital encoding. *Primes. They're both primes.* She did the obvious and multiplied them together. She ran the result through her RSA decoding algorithm, converted to hexadecimal, and then to assembler.

Well, I'll be damned! It's the BIOS routine for interfacing my concepta to my trueself computing substrate.

She'd been trying to adjust her interface routines for some time now. If she could get it to link to Alternus' quark-spin lattice instead of the Standard processing substrate, the boost in processing power would be huge. But it was proving impossible, and, besides, messing with her own interface routine was risky. If she got it wrong, she'd be disconnecting her concepta and persona from either computing substrate and scatter her self—her essence—out among the electrons of the universe.

Now, Darya had given her the most difficult part, the code. There were still lots of other parts she didn't recognize, though. With any luck, the routines would link her BIOS to the inworld BIOS; that would be the key to unlock her computational powers on Alternus' own lattice.

She dove deep into her mind, calling up her gold-tinged concepta and persona structures. She drifted among directed graphs of conceptual data. On a plane below her, she placed the jade-colored code of her own BIOS. On a plane above, the BIOS of the Vacationland inworld, complete with intrusions from Alternus. She could interpret some of the machine code but not all; she hoped it would be enough.

There it was. Darya's code spun slowly, tantalizingly, in front of Mary's virtual visual field. Mary grabbed it in her virtual hands and flung it at the interface code it was intended to replace. It slipped into place with a satisfying *snap*.

The physical world wavered. *Oh, no!* She almost added a hasty, *Goodbye*, but then everything snapped back into brilliant clarity.

The new BIOS code shot a gleaming arrow from the lower plane to the code in the top plane. She hadn't thought to look at that area before. She couldn't see where the arrow connected; it was shrouded in gray mist.

More of Darya's security? Ah, yes. If I can see how the new code connects the two disparate operating systems, Trillian will be able to see it from his external vantage point, too. Good idea to put a lot of security around that.

She felt faint for a second, and then her thinking processes came back with a leap in speed and clarity. She was filled with a mental vigor that had evaded her since capture.

That's it! I've connected to the quark-spin hardware of Alternus. Oh, ho! It's game ON now, Trillian. Get ready for a little turnabout!

42

"OKAY. SO, 'A VOICE FOR ALL CITIZENS,' IT IS." Stephen Humphrey pushed his seat back from the table and stood up, stretching out to his full six-foot three height.

"After only forty minutes," Nigel Hodge muttered to Debbie Cutter, in the chair beside him. She stifled a laugh.

"Not the most inspirational of messages, but solid enough," he added for the benefit of the others.

"I'm glad you approve," Jared Strang replied.

Hodge mirrored Strang's wry smile. "Well, it beats, 'A solid opposition for a solid democracy.'"

This time, Cutter couldn't contain her laughter. "Ha! That was a winner!"

Priyam Kaloor was not amused. "This one still sounds like we assume we're going to lose," he noted.

"You do realize that it would take a miracle to win an actual majority, right? A bona fide miracle," Jenny Thurgood pointed out.

The seven members of the Election Committee of the Progressive Justice Party sat elbow-to-elbow around a circular table in the small meeting room. The room was lit by three overhead LEDs whose blinding light reflected off the table's polished stone surface. Beyond the chairs, the light fell off quickly, leaving the corners of the room in darkness.

Only six of the seven attendees occupied a chair. DAR-K's imposing two-meter spherical body, hovering a few centimeters above the floor, took up the last place at the table. The LED lights reflected dully off her matte gray finish.

Hodge was finally getting used to DAR-K being there. He hardly flinched anymore when she floated in for a meeting. In fact, he almost didn't register her presence at all, as if she were a piece of furniture, until some brilliant analysis or other emanated from her speaker in Kathy Liang's voice. He still got nervous when her voice emerged from near darkness on the other side of the table. *That*, he couldn't get used to.

They were meeting at the back of the official party headquarters in the building next to Rumi's Café. The location gave Hodge and Cutter a convenient excuse to be in the neighborhood. The quality of Rumi's coffee and carrot-ginger cake was rapidly gaining renown throughout Vesta One, and it wasn't all that far from the Vesta Project Management Tower so, all in all, it seemed like a natural place they might visit.

The fact that a supposedly permanently locked door joined Rumi's supply room to an unused office in the party headquarters was a bonus.

Hodge and Cutter used the secret passage to attend opposition party election committee meetings without alerting Alum to their betrayal. They hadn't publicly come out as candidates for the Progressive Justice Party yet.

Better to wait until Alum officially announced citizenship for the Cybrids and the incumbent rights that went along with their new status. The Cybrid Grand March was only a week away. Until then, discretion was critical.

All that would change after the Grand March, once the personhood of the Cybrids was formally recognized and their supporters no longer had to hide.

When Alum discovers we've switched support, he'll remove us from the ruling party in the Governing Council faster than we can blink. I don't think he'll kick us off the Council entirely, though. Overly harsh retribution would give the impression he doesn't tolerate dissenting perspectives, even from the opposition.

Hodge and Cutter could wait out the next few years on the Council sidelines rather than in the midst of the government. Life would be different for everyone after the election.

They could still just cross the floor to the other side once an official opposition was recognized. Alum had permitted Strang and associates from the old Administration to remain on the Council. He no longer sought their advice, but at least he'd let them stay on.

Strang interrupted Hodge's musings. "If we *were* to win a majority, how would we make that miracle happen?"

"The one strategy that always works," Hodge replied.

"Go negative?"

"We have lots to work with. Not the least of which is, the man really isn't even human."

"No. Absolutely not. We've talked about this before," DAR-K reminded them.

"I realize Alum has as much potential to damage us with his own negative campaign as we have to hurt him, but—"

"A negative strategy would destroy us both and throw Vesta into political chaos," DAR-K interrupted. "That is unacceptable."

"Surely there has to be a way to get a rumor out there, some way to make him reveal himself."

"Reveal himself as what?" Strang asked.

"As the machine he is. The man's not even human."

"I'm not human either," DAR-K pointed out.

"Well, then, we'll at least level the playing field. The election will be between two different machine candidates."

"Your insistence on the importance of computational substrate over cognitive structure in determining humanity has always been troubling, Nigel," DAR-K said.

"See what I mean?" Hodge replied. "Nobody, no *human* person, would ever say something like that."

Jared jumped in. "Listen, you two. We've already agreed to disagree on this. Nigel, we're not going down that road in the campaign. Please give it a rest."

Hodge held up his hands, fingers splayed, in front of his chest. "Very well. Sorry if I happen to prefer first place over second."

DAR-K sighed. "We all like to win, but that's not the way to get there. Alum is too autocratic for his own good. Sooner or later, he'll show his true colors and when he does, we'll be ready to appeal to the people."

Thurgood frowned. "You're assuming that people prefer the right to choose, over being ruled by a beloved dictator they see as their Spiritual Leader."

"One has to have some faith in humanity," the Cybrid replied.

"Perhaps I can help." The voice came unexpected out of the dark.

DAR-K shot out four tentacles in a defensive posture and heads turned toward the corner of the room, craning to see who had barged into their clandestine meeting.

A middle-aged man with a moderately muscular build, softly chiseled features, and an air of gentle confidence stepped forward into the light.

"Who are *you?*" Strang asked.

"My name is Darak Legsu."

"And how do you think you can help? More importantly, how did you get in here, and how long have you been listening?"

"I'm good at being in places I'm not supposed to be," Darak answered. "And I've been listening long enough. As to your first question, I have some information I think you'll find important to your campaign."

"Right!" Hodge laughed. "We have no idea who you are. Why should we believe any information you have? For all we know, Alum sent you."

Darak stepped closer to the table so they could see his face. "Those who are most untrustworthy are often most suspicious as well, wouldn't you agree Mr. Hodge?"

Nigel stood up, knocking his chair backward, and took a step toward the stranger. "If you know who I am, you might think better than to insult me in front of my friends," he hissed.

"Friends?" Darak raised his eyebrows and laughed softly, audibly blowing air from his nostrils. "I'm not so sure you're right about that. You barely tolerate each other's company. And you certainly aren't all of like mind. I'd say something more like unwanted, but necessary, allies. At least, that's probably how Alum would see it."

DAR-K darted around the table. Her manipulators shot out to encircle the interloper. Before they could trap him, the man stepped back into the darkness and was gone.

"I expected a friendlier reception," Darak said from the other side of the room. Heads spun around to follow the new source of his voice. "I'm sorry, but I'll have to deactivate the Cybrid's motor routines while we talk."

He activated a virus to invade DAR-K's semiconductor CPPU and override her voluntary control of propulsion and tentacles. Her security rebuffed it effortlessly.

Darak frowned and modified the virus to accommodate a more sophisticated level of protection. It was equally ineffective. He tried again with three different versions in rapid succession. The Cybrid glided toward him, manipulators extended.

There's something familiar about its defenses—Greg/Darak thought. He should've shifted away to safety as DAR-K brushed off his best attempts to hack her control systems and drifted closer. He should have, but he didn't.

There was something about that style of mental thrust and parry tugged at the edge of his consciousness and kept him from leaving.

I've done this before.

His eyes widened, and he stopped the viral attack. These defensive moves could only belong to one person.

"Kathy?"

43

THE POLITICIANS AROUND THE TABLE looked from DAR-K to the stranger who'd materialized from the shadows, and back to DAR-K. The stranger stood still. His eyes focused expectantly on the Cybrid.

"Hello, Greg," DAR-K said, her voice level and quiet. She halted her advance a meter away.

"What? DAR-K, do you know this man?" Strang's gaze whipped back and forth between Darak and DAR-K.

"I'd recognize my husband's mind anywhere, in any guise," the Cybrid answered. "Ladies and gentlemen, I present Dr. Greg Mahajani, apparently now also known as Darak Legsu."

For a second or two, the room was suspended in stunned silence.

"You look good, Greg. Or should I say, Darak? I like the new name, and the new look," she said, sincerely.

"I guess we both kept a few secrets," Darak observed.

DAR-K bobbed slightly, as if nodding. "So it would seem."

Nigel Hodge stood up and slammed his stylus onto the table in front of him, startling everyone from the captivating scene playing out in front of them.

"Look, I hate to break up this happy little reunion, but could someone please explain to me what the bloody hell is going on?" he snapped.

"Oh, Nigel, sit down," Strang huffed. "Isn't it obvious? It would seem that Dr. Mahajani managed to escape Earth before the Eater destroyed it. He's just realized that DAR-K carries the mind of his deceased wife, Kathy Liang."

"Why, that's incredible! How did you escape?" Hodge demanded. "Did you steal a rocket? Did you find last-minute Redemption and join the Church?"

Greg burst out laughing. "No, certainly not the latter, I assure you."

"You shifted," DAR-K suggested.

If a Cybrid sphere could convey a wry smile, or amazement and appreciation, Darak would've frozen time to bask a moment longer in that gaze.

"He...what? He *shifted*? What's that?" Hodge demanded.

"It's how you got here," Greg said. "It's how you move between asteroid habitats."

"Those are miracles of Our Lord," Cutter interjected.

"Before they were miracles, they were technology," Greg answered. "I should know. I developed it."

"Preposterous!" Hodge protested.

"Despite what you may believe, it's true," DAR-K said. "Greg invented what you think of as the starstep."

She turned to Greg. "I presume you managed to obtain your own private pair of entangled particles to make the shift here. That doesn't surprise me. I *am* surprised you didn't bring anyone else with you. Or did you?" There was a hopeful tremor in her voice.

Greg's head dropped. "No. I wasn't able to save anyone else. The shift generator is built into my head. I can't make a field big enough to include anyone besides me. And it all happened so fast; I didn't have enough time to get to you—to the original Kathy—before the Eater took her."

"I'm sorry to hear that. I really am."

Greg stared at the floor, reliving the horror of the day. It didn't help that Kathy's voice had been so perfectly reproduced by the two-meter carboceramic sphere carrying her persona.

The emotional wound caused by her death was still too fresh. He missed her; every waking moment, he missed her. He longed for the simple comfort of her company, to talk, to hear her laugh, to feel her hand in his. A stainless steel-composite tentacle, activated by nanoelectric motors would never be the same.

Strang spoke gently into the prolonged silence. "You said maybe you could help us. How?"

Greg pulled himself from his grief and took a deep breath. "You may not know that I sort of work for Alum now. Well, for John Trillian, really."

"What do you mean, 'sort of work' for Alum?" DAR-K asked, ignoring the panicked glances around the table.

"I designed the Cybrid inworld you know as Vacationland," Greg answered. "Maybe you've seen it?"

"Yes, it's been out for a few months. It raised quite a stir when it debuted. I'm sure by now almost everyone's seen it," DAR-K said. "I should have recognized your work. It's impressive; some of your best coding."

"Thanks. Unfortunately, it's being used like Rome used the Coliseum."

"Keep the masses well-entertained and you never have to worry about them organizing a rebellion," Strang said.

"Exactly. But that's not why I made it."

"Why *did* you make it?" DAR-K asked.

"To help the Cybrids reconnect with their humanity. Sure, it's fun and relaxing, and Cybrids should have someplace pleasant to go for downtime. Vacationland provides an outlet for the part of the Cybrid brain that's thoroughly *human*. To walk along a beach, to eat at a nice restaurant, to swim in the waters that gave birth to life on Earth—those are all *human* indulgences."

Strang stood and offered his hand to Greg. "I'm happy to finally meet you in person, Mr. Legsu. I suppose it really shouldn't surprise me to learn that Darak Legsu and Greg Mahajani are one and the same. I've been told your Vacationland is quite brilliant."

"Thanks. It's nice to be appreciated."

An impatient Hodge jumped in, "I'm so happy for you all, but have you forgotten this man works for Alum?"

Greg frowned. "He didn't exactly offer me the job; more like, he conscripted me to make more inworlds like Vacationland. I guess I could've revealed myself as Greg Mahajani, fled, and lived a life outside the system. Somehow, that wasn't terribly appealing. So I embraced a cover identity and took the job. It seemed like it might give me the chance to do some good. Now, I'm not so sure."

"Why? What happened?" DAR-K asked.

"Well, Alum cancelled the Securitor program right after your, uhm, *audience* with him." Greg winced, then smiled. "That was an impressive bit of political theater, by the way."

DAR-K bobbed in acknowledgement.

"But over the past month, he and Trillian have got me working on a battle-training inworld, which is weird given there are no Securitors to train in it.

"Even stranger, I've been working with a synthetic, stripped-down Cybrid mind as the main inworld character, and Trillian has been tweaking what little remains of the original persona."

DAR-K moved forward a little. "Tweaking?"

"Yeah, but we're only working with a bare bones persona, not a full one. It's hard to see any ethical issues."

"Hmm," DAR-K's response indicated neither agreement nor dispute.

"As far as I can tell, all he's done is increase some factors related to honor, duty, loyalty, that kind of thing. At first, it made no sense. The Securitor program has been cancelled. Why work on a concepta structure like that at all, and why would we be putting it through training for battle conditions?"

"If Alum has lied to me, he will pay dearly," DAR-K threatened.

"He hasn't lied. Not exactly," Greg replied. "He just hasn't been completely forthcoming."

"What do you mean?" Strang asked.

"I saw no evidence of any Securitors under construction. However, I did find something that could be worse."

"What could be any more of an abomination than a Securitor?" DAR-K had moved around the table and was only a few meters from Greg now.

"Let me show you." Greg sent a short video of the robotic Angel he'd discovered to everyone's inSense lattice.

"What in heaven's name...?" Hodge had remained standing throughout the conversation. On seeing the video, he set his seat back on all four legs and dropped into it, deflated.

"There is more of hell than heaven in that design, if you ask me," Strang exclaimed. "It may have been based on a classic Angelic body type, but I get the sense their purpose is otherwise. Especially given the cancellation of the Security program, and what you've mentioned about Trillian doing a little tweaking."

"I don't think this is the only one. The design and construction seems too well advanced. I suspect Alum is building an army of such Angels. And I have reason to believe they'll be armed with tunnel-drilling energy beams," Greg added.

"Those would be too dangerous inside a habitat," DAR-K pointed out. "They'd blast a hole in the walls. Millions would die in minutes."

"I agree. So, if their weapons are only useful in space, would Cybrids be their intended target? That worries me even more."

"Whoa! That's a lot of speculation. Let's not get too carried away here. Maybe Alum's building a force that can defend the habitats from an invasion from space," Cutter suggested.

"Fair enough. And I might believe that if the battle simulation included more scenarios *outside* the habitats and service tunnels," Greg countered. "But there are precious few like that and all of them are in close proximity to the asteroids, not in deep space. Doesn't that seem a little suspicious to you?"

"What you've shown us is fascinating and frightening," Strang said. "But what does this have to do with our discussion? How does it help us?"

"If you can get word out about this, people will see Alum's true nature and intentions. They'll see his desire to become dictator by force, if necessary. It will change their minds about him."

"We already have enough negative facts about Alum," Cutter jumped in, a sour look on her face. "We can't use any of them. This falls into the same category."

Faces around the table echoed her distaste over the political necessity.

Encouraged, Cutter continued. "And what makes you think any negative narrative would matter to Alum's fans, anyway? At least, to those who call themselves the true believers? History is filled with populist autocratic leaders whose followers willingly—no, make that *merrily*—waltzed right into a horrible dictatorship, cheering all the way."

"Maybe we can entice him into revealing the Angels before the election," Thurgood suggested.

"That might work, especially if he used them in the habitats," DAR-K said. "But he would never do that."

"Not even for the Grand March?" Thurgood countered.

"There'll be so many of us in the skies, there's no way he could fire a tunnel-drilling beam safely."

"What Grand March?" Greg asked.

DAR-K explained her plan to get Cybrids the vote. "We were planning to gather outside the habitats, and then stream in together through the main polar entrances."

"Gathered like that, it would be easy to label your show of force as a threat, plus, you'll be vulnerable to the Angels."

"You're right. We'll have to change our plans. Maybe seep into the habitats through the service tunnels, and draw into formation near the caps."

"At least that would circumvent an Angel attack in space."

"And once we're inside the habitats, they wouldn't dare use driller beams." DAR-K moved a few centimeters closer.

Greg could sense her uncertainty. "What is it?"

"We've been planning for me to run as opposition candidate for President. But I've been thinking, why don't you run in the election with me?" DAR-K proposed. "We did make a great team for twenty years."

"Excuse me. I'm the Vice-President candidate," Humphrey protested.

Before Greg could respond, Strang jumped to DAR-K's defense.

"Surely, Stephen, you can see that Dr. Mahajani's experience with the colonies, along with his clearly superior intellect, would serve the people better in these difficult times."

Greg had no interest in starting a political feud within a group of people he'd only just met, and chimed in quickly.

"I'm not much of a politician, anyway. I was always more of a background support kind of guy. And no one here would recognize me as Greg Mahajani so there's really nothing I bring to the table by virtue of my face or name. "Thank you, but I'd prefer to let Mr. Humphrey's name stand. I think he has the experience for the job."

The ruffled politician sat back in his chair, torn between victory and continuing indignation. "Thank you," he said.

"Besides, I'm stuck in this job with Trillian for the foreseeable future, unless anyone can see a good way out. I think I could be more valuable where I am."

"That's settled, then," Strang concluded, surveying the table for any objections. He checked the time.

"Thank you, everyone. We've gone a little later than planned. I know Mr.

Hodge and Ms. Cutter have appointments to dash off to. We're making good progress, but we have a lot to prepare for with the Cybrid Grand March in one week. We'll meet for a quick update next Tuesday. If there are no further points for discussion, I move we adjourn. Thank you for seconding, Priyam. All in favor? It's unanimous, then. We are adjourned until Tuesday."

Hodge and Cutter rushed out, chatting intensely in hushed voices. The other attendees shuffled out of the room, casting suspicious glances backward. Strang hung back with DAR-K and Greg.

"I just wanted to say welcome to our little opposition, Dr. Mahajani...Mr. Legsu," Strang said to Greg. "Er, which do you prefer?"

"I'm Darak Legsu, now," Greg replied. "Let's stick to that."

"Very well," Strang answered, and pumped Greg's hand enthusiastically one more time. "Now, I'll leave you two on your own to chat."

He glanced sidelong at DAR-K, muttered something Greg couldn't make out, and followed the others out.

Greg looked wistfully at DAR-K. He tried to imagine the face of the woman he'd loved for over twenty years in place of the dull, matte surface of the sphere. Without using his lattice, he could no longer picture Kathy.

"It's still me, Greg," DAR-K said.

The sound of Kathy's voice brought him to the verge of tears.

"I think we need to talk. I'd like to do it person to person, face to face, so to speak. Can you meet me at Cloud 49 inworld in Vacationland?"

"When? Now?" he asked.

"As good a time as any, don't you think? We may not get another chance."

Greg pulled up a chair, closed his eyes, and accessed his lattice.

I don't know if I can do this; not sure I'm ready to face her. Couldn't we just go out and save the world, or something easy?—he fretted, and before he could give voice to his worries, the warm, tropical breeze of Vacationland caressed his face.

44

"THIS IS MY FAVORITE SPOT IN VACATIONLAND." DAR-K took a seat at the highest table in Cloud 49. "Mine, too," Greg/Darak replied. "Kathy loved the view here." He glanced hopefully at the Cybrid.

Both of them wore inworld avatars reflecting their current appearances in the real universe. Greg wore Darak's new face, and DAR-K bore the appearance of her Cybrid trueself.

She pointedly ignored him and took in the landscape for a while.

He knew she was aware of his wistful stare; her Cybrid self was ringed with visual sensors giving her full 360° visual perception.

The Cybrid image shimmered. Greg/Darak opened his mouth to see if she was okay but the words stuck in his throat.

The shimmer resolved itself into Kathy Liang, looking exactly as she had the day the Eater took her. She turned away from the view at the edge of the floating platform and took a seat opposite Greg.

His heart raced. He allowed his own avatar, carefully selected to be used in the inworld presence of John Trillian or Alum, to change. The Greg that Kathy remembered looked back at her.

"It's good to see you," she said.

Watching her lips move exactly the way he remembered, made him feel weak. "You, too," his voice quavered.

The image of Kathy smiled. "This is weird, isn't it?"

Greg expelled the breath he hadn't realized he was holding. "Yes, this is very weird."

"Okay, why don't we start off with business? Maybe that'll help us both to feel a little...less weird."

Greg nodded and sat down.

"I'm sure you've figured out I gave my DAR-K self a little 'something extra' when she was constructed."

"Do you mean the enhanced-IQ lattice? Yeah, that's kind of obvious. You always were a little rebellious when it came to the Cybrids."

"They...We deserved better."

"And the rest of the committee was unreasonable. Yeah, I agree. They were shortsighted and paranoid."

Kathy/DAR-K noted the micromovements in his face; he was holding something back. "But?" she asked with raised eyebrows.

He smiled. *She's smart. Intuitive. Direct.*

"But...I have to wonder how things would have unfolded here if all the Cybrids were like you."

"Well, for one thing, we might have been able to stop Alum and keep the original Project Management in place."

"It looks like you've stopped Alum's plans all by yourself."

"Not yet. We can hope, though."

Greg squirmed uncomfortably. "I'm going to order something to drink. Would you like something?"

"Sure."

A waiter appeared at the snap of Greg's fingers and took their order. He returned a few seconds later with their drinks.

"Here's to weird," Greg said, lifting his glass of wine.

Kathy laughed, and tapped her glass to his. "Yes, to weird."

They sipped their drinks appreciatively. "Mmm, every bit as good as I remember,"

"You always had a soft spot for Shiraz."

Greg cradled his wineglass in both hands, and dropped his gaze.

"What's wrong?" Kathy asked softly.

"Why didn't you tell me?"

"Tell you what? About giving my Cybrid self an enhanced IQ?"

"Yeah," Greg answered.

Kathy let his question linger in the air a moment. "I don't really know. I intended to; I just never got around to it. We were both so busy."

Greg frowned. "I know. The Project was all important."

"And then it was time for you to copy your mind into DAR-G, and all hell broke loose, and then it was too late."

"So, DAR-G is normal, like I was before the dendy?" Greg asked.

"Yes. He's *impaired*, like we both were a lifetime ago. Nothing like he should be. *Could* be. Nothing like you, not the real you." Her voice shook. "It's been hard. I can't talk to him much; it's not the same. It hurts."

Greg reached across the table and took virtual Kathy's hands in his. She sighed heavily and squeezed his hands the way she always did. His virtual heart beat faster.

She gave another squeeze and pulled her hands back. "When did you design the virus for an internal RAF generator?"

Greg grimaced; she wasn't going to like his answer. "Remember the first Vesta Gala Ball?"

"That early?" Kathy was trying to decide if she should be angry. "Why didn't you tell me?"

Greg looked down at his feet. "That wasn't the only thing I didn't tell you."

"I never liked secrets," Kathy said, "whether mine or yours."

"I know. But there were risks someone had to take or the planet wouldn't be safe."

"Like what?"

"Remember shortly after Vesta was approved, when the attacks from the unintegrated parts of Darian started to taper off?"

"That was you? How?"

"You were in Shanghai setting up the Cybrid factory. I booked a hotel room at Harrison Hot Springs. I dropped my lattice defenses and opened up. I figured the internet bandwidth there was a little restricted and I'd be able to handle whatever Darian threw at me. I...integrated him into me."

"You *what*?!" Kathy exclaimed.

"He always affected me more than you. It was impossible to think with him constantly hammering away at my mind. So, I invited him in."

"Greg, do you have any idea how dangerous that was? I could have lost you. I never wanted to be married to Darian Leigh."

"I know." Greg took another deep breath. "It wasn't easy. He was strong. So many memories, so much knowledge. But I did it. I know everything Darian did."

"But his memories...."

"Yeah, some of those gave me trouble. I tried partitioning him off, keeping him completely separate from me, but that didn't work. Dual personalities in one brain, no matter how big, are not a good idea. So I let go and just accepted it all. There's only 'me' now."

"So did you still love me? Did you still love *Kathy* after that?"

"Why would you ask that? Nothing could stop me loving you. And Darian was our biggest supporter. He was so proud that he'd played matchmaker."

Kathy was confused. She opened her mouth to correct him, and instead, smiled. "I'm sure he was," she said.

She had no memory of Darian having any role in their relationship besides supervisor, boss, mentor, and maybe friend. But it wasn't hard to figure how Greg might have needed to alter some of Darian's downloaded memory to preserve his own feelings for her, and his memory of their relationship.

"I figured, once one of us could give Darian's concepta and persona a home, his attacks would fall off. And they did, a little. Not completely. After I integrated the immediate data, I hunted down the rest of his residual data floating around on the internet and deleted him.

"Which would've been about the time things started getting easier for me."

"Yes, after that, we could do our work without losing our minds."

"You took a huge risk, Greg."

He stared into his wine. *If it had been the other way around, if she'd done what he did, what would he be saying to her right now?*

"Thank you." She cupped her hands over his. "Really."

He looked into her eyes. "I'm sorry I didn't tell you at the time."

"It's just as well; I never would have agreed to it."

"Me, either," he laughed, and let out a sigh of relief. The worst was over. "So, thanks to the integration, I became an instant expert on anything Darian ever worked on. It's not all clear, but I did learn more about what happened to him.

"Before he disappeared, he designed a virus to grow the RAF generator in his own head. That's how he found out his theories worked; he generated his own RAF. Remember, when he called us? He was on his way to the lab so we could test it properly. That's when Larry killed him."

"Larry? Larry killed Darian? Why would he do that?"

"Well, I don't know that for absolute certain. Darian's memories are all hazy at the end. But I do know that Larry was there that morning. I'm also pretty sure he gave his dendy lattice to Reverend LaMontagne. I don't know how Alum got hold of it, but I can imagine a number of ways. None of them good."

"You think Larry killed Darian, and you never thought to tell me?" Kathy's voice was strained and angry.

Rightfully so, I guess—Greg thought. "Well I never had any proof besides Darian's memories."

"Darian's *impeccable* memory," Kathy pointed out.

"About other things, yes, but they're all confused about what happened that night. I guess he didn't have time to fully integrate them into long term memory. Anyway, I didn't think it mattered anymore."

"It matters," she said loudly. "You should have told me." She pushed her chair back, and went to stand at the rail.

Left in the wake of her anger, Greg starred at the raven hair tumbling down her back. "I know, I should have told you," he mumbled under his breath.

"What did you say?" she said, and whirled back to face him.

Greg swallowed hard. "I know I should have told you," he repeated louder. "But there was no way I could without telling you how I knew. Then you'd know what I did, the risk I took."

Kathy glared at him. "I would have killed you."

Greg could only nod.

"It's a lot to take in, Greg. I can't believe Larry would do something like that. What else have you been keeping a secret? What about your shifting ability? What did you do, hide a pair of entangled particles so you could save your own hide if needed?"

"Ouch. No. But I guess I deserve that, after all the other secrets I've kept. I don't have any secret entangled particles. My method is more difficult, more dangerous."

"Dangerous?"

"Well, you know how space, all space, is filled with virtual particles? Everywhere you look, there are entangled pairs of virtual particles."

"Yeah."

"Well, they don't last long, but you can use them."

"Sure, but they'd only be good for jumps of a few hundred meters or less. You couldn't use them for longer jumps, like from Earth to Vesta or such."

"Actually, you can go a few klicks at a time. And a long jump is just a bunch of small jumps."

"With a huge risk between each! You'd need to recalculate and find another pair so fast. If you missed, you could get stuck in outer space."

"Correct. Or in no space at all. You could find yourself stranded outside the universe. I did say it was dangerous."

Kathy stared at him, without uttering a word. He gave her time to process the implications, to cool off. When the furrows in her brow relaxed a bit, she spoke only one word.

"Why?"

"Why do something like that? Or why didn't I share it with you?"

"Both."

"I did it because without it, we'd be stuck at light speed forever. My travel is only limited by how fast I can find new entangled virtual pairs and calculate a shift field. I've optimized a good section of lattice exclusively for that. It's down here." He patted his tummy.

Her eyes drifted down. "Seriously? Gut neurons?"

"Sure. Why not?" he answered. "As to why I didn't share it with you, would you have wanted to do all that? Body changes? Dangerous travels that took you outside space?"

"Maybe. Okay, probably not. But you should have given me the choice, Greg."

"You're right. I should have. But, to be honest, I don't know if I could've put you at such risk."

"And yet, you took that risk for yourself. What if I lost you and never knew why?"

"I'm sorry. I never thought of that."

"Not even with your enhanced IQ?"

"Apparently, enhancing intelligence doesn't always enhance imagination," he replied contritely.

"Apparently." Kathy stared off into the distance.

Greg followed her gaze, sitting with the silence for a moment.

"So you're planning a protest march?" he said after a while.

"Pretty 2020s, isn't it?" Kathy grinned.

Do you think it will accomplish anything?"

"I've ensured it will. During my *audience* with Alum, as you put it, I made him promise to give Cybrids the vote after the march."

"Wow! How'd you manage that?"

"By using the only language people like him ever understand, a threat. I told him I'd take all the Cybrids away, and we'd build our own independent colonies in space."

"That would be the end of humanity."

"Don't worry. I don't think I could carry it through; I just had to convince him that it was a possibility. Fortunately, we won't need to find out. Alum caved."

"I don't like this, Kathy. I don't trust the man; I never have."

"I know what you mean. He's strange, even more now than ever. He seems...darker."

"Were you serious when you said I should run with you? Me? A candidate for Vice-President?"

"Perfectly serious. We have to counter Alum somehow. He's the spiritual leader and de facto Director for most of the people here. Who else would have a chance against him? Humphrey?"

"Before today, I'd never heard of Humphrey," Greg admitted.

"Nobody has. But everyone knows Kathy Liang and Greg Mahajani. We designed this place. I supervised the construction."

"It would be tough to resurrect both of us from the dead."

"But not impossible."

"No, not impossible." Greg looked reluctant.

"Just promise me you'll think about it."

"I'll think about it. And you, be careful with your Grand March."

"We'll be careful. Especially now that we know about the Angels. Do you think at least some of us should carry weapons?"

"It's up to you, but I don't think going in there armed would go over well in the habitats. If you want my advice, don't give Alum and his Angels any excuse to portray you as a threat. Don't make it easy for them to justify turning to force."

Instead of getting the Securitors program shut down maybe I should have turned them over to our side."

Greg laughed. "That would've served them right but I know you; you could never do something like that."

"Never is a long time."

"You are who you are. Subverting an entire personality like that for your own ends, that just isn't in you."

"No, it's not in me." Kathy's chest rose and fell. She inspected their empty wine glasses and her eyes drifted to the beach below. "Okay, so that concludes our business. Now, what?"

Greg followed her gaze. "Wanna go for a swim?"

"That would be nice; and then we're going to go build me my own internal RAF generator. I want to be able to shift, too."

45

DARAK AND BROTHER STRALASI HOVERED within visual range of an enormous, glittering planetoid. The maelstrom of Sagittarius A*, the supermassive black hole at the center of the Milky Way, provided a stunning backdrop some light years away. Incandescent, swirling gases and closely-packed stars reflected off the shiny surface of the Deplosion array element."Why steal this one?" Stralasi asked.

Darak looked away from the asteroid, and millions of bright yellow points appeared in the sky.

The monk was only somewhat impressed. He recognized Darak's "magic" by now. *Lattice projection*—he guessed.

"These are the present locations of all elements of the Deplosion array," Darak explained. "They're roughly evenly spaced around the center of the Home galaxy."

A red dot flared briefly amidst the background stars.

"Home World is here, a few tens of thousands of light years away."

Stralasi shrugged his shoulders dismissively. The Home World star was otherwise impossible to discern among the crowded star field. Anyway, Crissea was on Eso-La, somewhere outside the galactic plane and far away.

Darak continued, "If I select the twenty Deplosion generators that are farthest from their nearest neighbors, we get these." All but nineteen yellow dots and the halo around the nearby asteroid disappeared.

"If you only need three, why not just select the best three?"

"I don't like to be predictable in any unnecessary way," Darak answered. "I randomly selected three from these twenty, in case I'm wrong and Alum has some way of detecting what we're doing. As you might have guessed, *this* is the first one chosen." He pointed directly in front of them.

"So how long will this—"

The stars blinked out.

"—take? Oh."

They were floating in deep, black, empty space, but not where they'd been seconds before. Stralasi looked around to orient himself.

Looks like back near Eso-La—he noted. The metal asteroid-sized artifact had apparently accompanied their shift, and now floated a few dozen klicks away.

"I don't see the Eater," he pointed out.

"It's about a light-week away in that direction," Darak indicated the other side of their bubble, opposite the planetoid.

"Why here?"

"I'll need a few days to reprogram the field generators," he answered. "The Deplosion Array programming is complex; it can't be easy to collapse an entire universe. Altering something that complicated will require a little time."

"And Alum has no idea this is gone?"

"I'm sure by now he knows it's gone off his grid. He can connect directly to all of the generators by comm-shifter, a device that sends optoelectronic signals through a shifter. I've deactivated them on this one's array element. He'll know it's offline, but he won't be able to tell if it the problem is due to device failure, outside interference, or damage. No doubt, someone will be sent to investigate."

"In that case, shouldn't we get the—" Stralasi began.

"—others?" Darak finished the monk's utterance as the stars near Sagittarius A* repopulated the sky.

"I do wish you'd warn me before doing—"

"—this?" Darak asked. They were back in the black sky of the ESO galaxy again.

Stralasi rolled his eyes. "Are you quite done having fun at my expense?"

Darak grinned mischievously, "Maybe. Maybe not. Just one more to go. Coincidentally, it's labeled Number 2, the second generator ever added to the array. I don't know how it got placed so far from its nearest neighbor. Maybe it drifted. Regardless, as long as it's still functional...."

In a flash, they were back in the Home galaxy, in the midst of the Milky Way, looking at an enormous asteroid. Metallic cladding covered half its length.

"This one's...different," Darak remarked.

"It doesn't look at all like the other two," Stralasi agreed.

Darak tilted his head to one side. "Peculiar."

Stralasi did a quick visual check of nearby space. "Not Angels again?" His voice cracked a little.

"No, not Angels," Darak assured him, and pointed toward the clearly synthetic end of the planetoid. "That end houses a perfectly normal element of the Deplosion array. The other end..," his finger traced the length of the rock, stopped, and tapped twice into empty air, "there, is riddled with tunnels and caves in the natural bedrock."

"Maybe it was some kind of converted colony," the Good Brother suggested helpfully. Hopefully.

"Maybe," Darak acknowledged. "They appear to be empty." He cocked his head the other way. "Hmm. That's...odd."

"Odd? How so?"

"I'm not sure. There's no electrical activity in any of the tunnels at all. I would've expected some construction or maintenance Cybrids to have extended their activities a little bit outside the Deplosion generator. But there's nothing outside the metal hull. It's almost as if the tunnels were shielded to prevent EM emissions."

"Maybe it was shielded for use as a research station," Stralasi suggested.

"That's possible, but that kind of thing is usually limited to specialized labs or observation chambers. With this one, it's like the whole place has been designed to hide something."

Stralasi did not like the sound of that. "Perhaps we should select a different element."

"No," Darak said. "This one will do fine."

* * *

TIMOTHY SPENT HOURS wandering around aimlessly inside the roughly carved corridors of Secondus while Darya brooded. He'd already been all over Darya's secret asteroid base; there was nowhere left to explore and he was bored. He'd inspected workshops and machinery he didn't understand, picked up parts of instruments, examined them, and tried to imagine their function. Darya had gone into one of the observation rooms, a shallow cave with one side open to the stars. He studiously avoided the area, giving her space and time to think about Mary's predicament.

He still didn't fully understand what had happened inworld, but he knew better than to pepper Darya with his questions. Seeing Mary lying there in the dungeon, chained and helpless as four Trillians subjected her to torture, had been unbearable.

He'd only known Mary a few days, only met her for the first time a few months ago, but he couldn't get it out of his head. He couldn't imagine what Darya must be going through. She and Mary had been close friends, co-workers, and co-conspirators for millions of years. Seeing Mary in such anguish, and not being able to rescue her must be excruciating for Darya.

So, why didn't Darya charge in there, fight off the Trillians, and save Mary, if she were truly such a good friend? What good was a flash of light? He had to admit, he was more than a little disappointed in Darya. She was smart—brilliant, really—fast, strong, and confident. There had to be some explanation for this sudden, apparent helplessness. He could only guess that she'd calculated she couldn't win a direct fight there, not with Trillian in such wide control of Vacationland.

Complexities, wheels within wheels, that I could never understand.

He set down some contraption he'd been pretending to inspect and drifted to another instrument. He pushed a few virtual buttons and twirled virtual dials, pretending the machine was on. *Maybe I'll have better luck in the garden*—he thought.

By Casa DonTon standards, Darya's humble garden could hardly be thought of as a garden at all. The small, climate-controlled room housed a few unremarkable plants, insects, and birds. Over generations, the winged arthropods and aves had adapted to the much lower gravity of Secondus than their ancestors had been used to on Origin. Their flight was more about propulsion and maneuvering than about staying aloft. Still, they buzzed around him, and they sang, and they gave Timothy a sense of what it might be like to be human in a world of life.

Perhaps the dark vacuum of so much empty space is starting to weigh on me. Why did God fill His universe with so much of it if He intended His creation to be a gift to humanity? It's almost as if He intended to give the whole thing to beings better suited to it, beings like the Cybrids.

He meandered down the long tunnel leading to the garden, deep in the core of the asteroid, when the alarms went off.

He had no idea what the clamor was about, and he didn't know how to access Darya's control system for more information.

Find Darya!—was his only thought. Maybe she needed him.

He sped back up the tunnel into the main labs and took the corridor toward the surface. Darya would be near the observation room. Some of his tentacles extended from their ports involuntarily as he imagined himself arriving just in time to be her swashbuckling protector.

I wish we were inworld. I have weapons there. Not to mention experience fighting. He had no idea how a Cybrid might fight in the real universe.

He turned into a side corridor and almost collided with Darya racing toward him. They swerved and pulled to a stop meters from each other.

"Are you okay?" Darya asked simultaneously with Timothy's "What happened?"

"I'm alright," Timothy replied. "Why are the alarms sounding?"

In answer, Darya spun and headed back up the tunnel she'd come from. "Follow me. I'll show you," she transmitted as she sped off.

Timothy went after her.

They reached the observation room and Darya pulled close to the opening. "What do you see?"

Timothy scanned with his visual sensors near maximum. "Not much. A few stars, some gaseous clouds."

He hesitated, and recalculated to check his archives. "Wait! Where are all the stars? The sky here should be filled with light."

"I don't think we're 'there' anymore."

"What do you mean? Where are we?"

"Somewhere far away, and dark," Darya answered. "This could only be Alum. I think he's found us."

* * *

"THAT SHOULD ABOUT DO IT," Darak announced.

"Do what?"

"All three Deplosion array elements are in place. I've returned their supervisory Cybrids back to where they came from, and I've disconnected Alum's direct control and communications from them."

He inspected the last array element, an odd partly-natural, partly-artificial hybrid, with satisfaction.

Stralasi was getting used to sifting through Darak's deluge of information to arrive at a point he could grasp. "So, everything's ready for you to begin your work, then?"

"Almost." Darak stared at the natural, rocky end of the asteroid.

"That's still bothering you, isn't it? True, it is a little strange but I can't see why it should interest you so much. Does it really matter to your present purposes where it came from or why it's riddled—no pun intended— with tunnels, so long as it's empty and serves your needs?"

Stralasi waited while Darak considered the question. Surely, Darak had a ready answer. Lately, though, the man had taken to inserting thoughtful pauses into his conversations. *Almost as if he's practicing at being more human.*

After a few seconds, Darak answered, "I've sampled some 453,287 array elements, statistically speaking, a more than valid sampling of the total population. This is the only element with this configuration. Coupled with its obviously ancient construction date, and its improbable location, I'm curious about its history."

"I guess that would make it interesting. What are you planning?"

"I've already queried the control systems in the synthetic portion. They don't see anything unusual about their configuration."

"I sense a 'but' is on the way."

"But...they're also unaware of any remaining natural asteroid connected to the constructed portion, even though all their maneuvering systems clearly compensate for the extra asymmetrical mass. Someone has tampered here."

"Hmm," Stralasi said, "that is intriguing. How could no one have noticed it before? Wouldn't someone have spotted the discrepancy between the plans and the actual?"

"You'd think so, but someone's hidden their tampering very well. They've hidden the presence of the natural part from the constructed part, and hidden what's inside the tunnels." Darak inserted another of his thoughtful pauses. "I think we need to go inside."

"Inside the array element?"

"Maybe later. First, I want to look in those tunnels. Would you like to come?"

Stralasi didn't answer immediately. *Have I had enough adventure for a while? What about simple curiosity? How risky could a bunch of ancient, abandoned tunnels be?*

He thought of the other places he'd considered risk-free but had turned out to be the opposite. Still, Darak made a good case. This array element, this asteroid, was interesting.

The monk shrugged. "Why not? Sure."

Before he finished speaking, they were in a long tunnel that opened into some kind of cavern. No, it was a room. Some kind of workshop, judging by all the machinery and components lying about.

"This isn't very old," Darak remarked, "and some of it is still active. This area is exceptionally well-shielded; I detected no working electronics in these tunnels from outside."

Stralasi started to ask a question, but Darak held up a finger. "A moment, please, Brother," he said. He cocked his head, as if listening to the wind.

Brother? He hasn't called me Brother in months—Stralasi thought. He held his tongue and waited.

"It appears we're not alone," Darak stated, breaking the silence.

They floated down the corridor away from the workshop. They accelerated until the occasional features of the tunnel wall moved by too fast to distinguish. They passed several branching tunnels before turning down one of them.

"Why are we moving like this?" Stralasi asked. "Wouldn't it be easier to simply shift to wherever the other person is?"

"With all this shielding, their location is a little difficult to pinpoint. Moving through the tunnels this way is helping me to triangulate their position. I don't think they're shifting; they seem to be moving by some form of rocket propulsion."

They went another hundred meters, turned down another branch corridor, and turned again a few kilometers later.

"A-ha, I have them now," Darak said. He shifted himself and the monk into the middle of a cave that opened into deep space.

Two Cybrids floated near the mouth of the cave.

One of them moved forward, and its tentacles whipped out menacingly.

"Stay back," it said.

"We will not harm you," Darak replied.

"Not without a fight," the Cybrid in the rear said.

Darak shook his head—*I know that voice.*

He squinted to better see the Cybrid who'd just spoken, and addressed her. "At the moment, your friend is the only one exhibiting any aggression."

"We both know what little use that is," she replied.

Darak was confused. "And how exactly do we know that?"

"Your powers are more than a match for anything either one of us could throw at you," the Cybrid answered.

The front Cybrid moved a little closer.

Maneuvering for a strike, Darak assessed. He pointed to the Cybrid's extended manipulators. "I'd prefer you retract those, please. I only want to talk."

"I'm sure that you would," the aggressor answered.

Stralasi detected hints of an odd accent in its Standard tongue.

"Those who are assured of victory always like to laud it over the defeated," the menacing Cybrid said.

On the last word, the Cybrid bolted forward under rocket power. Its tentacles slashed and stabbed at the clear shell that maintained a breathable atmosphere around Darak and Stralasi. Its slithering metallic limbs drew into sharp edges with vicious points that could have gutted or speared an unarmored man. They bounced harmlessly off the protective surface of the sphere.

The Cybrid turned its propulsion ports toward the two men.

Stralasi got a brief glimpse of the hell-fires of matter-antimatter mixing in mutual conversion to pure energy before the reaction winked out.

"Sorry, I can't allow that," Darak said. He glanced at the second Cybrid and said, "Nor that."

"Nor what?" the Good Brother asked. He hadn't seen any threatening moves from the other Cybrid.

"She was attempting a suicidal mixing of her MAM engine fuel," Darak answered. "The matter-antimatter reaction would have destroyed this entire array element."

"So it *is* you," the closer Cybrid said.

"And who might you be?" Darak asked.

"Alum," the far Cybrid answered.

Stralasi's eyes widened. *Alum?* Was that possible? Had he been traveling this entire time with the Living God himself? Should he fall to his knees once again and profess his ignorance, his sins? Maybe his knees weren't enough. Maybe he should prostrate himself and grovel before the Lord. Beg forgiveness.

Darak laughed.

"What is so funny?" asked the Cybrid with the feminine voice.

"You two are," Darak replied. "Do you actually think I am your god?"

"Who but God can move among the stars at will? Who but God can change antimatter into normal matter with a thought?"

Stralasi and Darak stared at each other, and Darak laughed again.

"Good point," he said. "Who but a god?"

Stralasi felt his knees grow weak. He slumped and was about to throw himself to the ground when Darak answered his own question.

"A scientist, that's who. I am no more your god than...than...than this man." He pointed to Stralasi. The Good Brother's heart skipped a beat.

"Scientist," the Cybrid repeated. "That's a term I haven't heard in a long time."

"It's not in common use anymore among humans," Darak agreed. "Few Cybrids call themselves anything but technician."

"If not Alum, then who are you?"

Darak bowed, "My name is Darak Legsu. I am a wanderer, explorer and, yes, a scientist."

"Darak?" the Cybrid repeated. "The name is familiar. Have we met?"

"It was not a common name when I first took it. Who might you be?"

"My name is Darya, and this is Timothy."

"And this is Brother Stralasi, recently on leave from the Alumit," Darak pointed to the Good Brother. "But if it's not too much to ask, I would prefer your complete designation."

The Cybrid hesitated. "So you can report me?"

Stralasi intervened, having at last remembered Darak's battle with the Angels, his mission to oppose Alum's Divine Plan.

"I can assure you, Darak has no connection to the Living God, other than to oppose the construction and operation of the Deplosion array."

"You know what this place is, then?" Darya asked.

"I know the purpose of the array," Darak admitted. "Despite Brother Stralasi's support, I am still uncertain of my position with regards to Alum's Divine Plan."

"It is evil."

"Evil is a strong word, a black and white word in a universe of color."

"Nonetheless, it applies," Darya insisted.

"Perhaps. We shall see. I take it you are not the Station Cybrid. I can't imagine Alum appointing anyone with such beliefs to be in charge of an array element."

"Long ago, Alum appointed me to build and maintain this place," Darya confessed. "I've altered the original plans somewhat."

"Somewhat," Darak grinned.

"I also managed to find a replacement for my maintenance duties."

"Impressive. Alum does not normally permit such unauthorized delegations."

Darya bobbed in acknowledgement of the compliment. "I had more important things to attend to."

"I would be honored to know your complete designation."

"Surely, you can simply read it yourself."

"I could. I do not like to invade minds when it's not required."

"When is reaming a mind ever required?" Darya's voice conveyed her bitterness. Timothy made a noise that sounded like throat clearing.

"Ha!" Darak laughed. "I take it from your friend's reaction you may have found something like that necessary yourself. Perhaps, recently?"

Darya chose not to respond to his baiting.

"In our travels from the frontier, we have visited a number of Cybrid stations," Darak continued. "In order to disguise ourselves, I've had to interfere with perceptual processing. It was...an unfortunate necessity. Forcing your designation from your mind would be an indulgence, not a necessity."

"Thank you for your courtesy," Darya replied. "I will return the respect you have shown us. My full designation is DAR143147 and my friend, Timothy, has the full designation GER754738."

"DAR143147?" Darak gasped. "DAR-K? Is it possible?"

In all their travels and adventures, Stralasi had never seen such surprise on the man's face. He couldn't help but ask, "Is *what* possible?"

"DAR-K," Darak whispered, and then, "Kathy," as if that explained everything.

46

"MY NAME IS DARYA. Cybrid designation, DAR143147. Who is Kathy?"

"You are," Darak answered, bewildered. "At least, at one time, that designation belonged to a Cybrid whose mind was templated on Kathy Liang."

"I have no memory of a Kathy Liang."

"Be that as it may, she was you; you were her."

"I've always been Darya. I have a few memories of a Darak Legsu, but that was so long ago. They are an insignificant percentage of my total experience."

"That was me, *is* me. I thought you were destroyed."

"I feel intact. Complete. True, there's a gap of some millions of years while I was inactive, but there's very little missing in the memories I have."

"Someone must have revived you, and tweaked your concepta and persona around the damaged parts. I can probably fix that."

"I would prefer you didn't poke around in my conceptual structures without my permission."

For a moment, Darak considered doing exactly that, even without permission, but he agreed. He let go of his pain and his expectations. They could fix this. "Okay, until I have your trust, I will respect your wishes."

"Thank you." Darya's voice was overlaid with a tinge of sarcasm. She extended a tentacle and pointed it outward. "Where have you moved us?"

She asked not how, but where—Darak noted. Which meant that the *how*—by Alum's starstep technology or something related—was obvious to her.

"We are in ESO 461-36," he replied.

"The Local Void?" Darya asked.

"Yes. Actually, I'm surprised it's still included in your astronomical maps," Darak answered.

"Because of the rebels of Eso-La," Darya said. "It's the only colony in that galaxy."

Darak's eyebrows arched. "That their existence hasn't been purged from the historical record surprises me even more."

"Officially, it was," Darya replied, "Very long ago. I maintain my own separate archives."

"I'm impressed. But then, you always did value your independence," Darak noted, and smiled. "As well as your secrets."

"Exactly how well did you two know each other?" Timothy's voice, tense with confusion and filled with impatience, cut across Darak and Darya's conversation.

Darak gave the other Cybrid a wary glance. "Your name is Timothy, yet your full designation begins GER." He shifted his gaze back to Darya and raised a questioning eyebrow, "I'm sure there's a story there."

"A strange story of a Partial accidentally raised to Full, and a sad story of a fallen friend," was all she offered.

"Someday you'll have to tell me," Darak replied.

"You could ask Shard Trillian."

Darak's face darkened. "Trillian was involved?"

"You know Trillian?" Timothy asked in a wary tone.

"We knew each other long ago. Not especially well, I'd say, despite working together on numerous projects."

"You sound less and less like someone I should trust," Darya said.

"Yes, I can imagine. Nevertheless, I'm likely the best friend you have in this galaxy." His eyes narrowed. "That is, if you really are the DAR-K that I remember. Or Kathy."

"I told you those names are meaningless to me," Darya said. "I sometimes use 'DAR' but never 'DAR-K' or the other."

"Hmm," Darak frowned. "This is going to be difficult." He passed a hand in front of his face, changing his appearance.

"Perhaps you remember this face."

Instead of Darak Legsu, Greg Mahajani stood before the two Cybrids.

Brother Stralasi, momentarily forgotten in the three-way conversation, found his voice. "What magic is this?"

Darak/Greg grinned. "This is the face I wore when Kathy Liang and I first met." He looked back at Darya. "Am I any more familiar to you now?"

"G-Greg?" The Cybrid's voice faltered. "But, how?"

"Ah! A spark of recognition at last," Darak said. "Not all of your earliest memories were damaged, I see."

"What is going on?" Timothy demanded.

Darak/Greg changed his face back to the one Stralasi knew, and spoke tenderly. "I don't know how I can convince you that I was once Greg Mahajani, Kathy Liang's husband and friend of DAR-K, the Cybrid designated as DAR143147. I could tell you things only Greg and Kathy would know, but I don't know how to select from so many memories. I don't know which ones you have or haven't lost."

"Some memories may be less accessible than others; others may have faded. I feel complete, nonetheless," Darya answered.

"You *knew* Greg Mahajani."

"I remember working with a man by that name. He was a friend. He was also human. You may be able to look like him, but he's long dead."

Darak turned away in exasperation. His eyes implored Brother Stralasi for help.

The Good Brother's brow wrinkled as he focussed on the problem.

"An interesting problem," he began. He pointed a finger at Darak. "You claim you know this Cybrid but it has no recollection of you. Or rather some meager memories and recognition of your...uhh, let's say, former face, but not enough to trust you."

"She," Darak corrected him. Then, in response to the uncomprehending look on Stralasi's face, he explained, "*She*, not *it*. Darya is a she. Cybrids are people too."

"Of course," Stralasi corrected. "*She* has nothing but the barest recollection of you. You claim you were once married. At least, married to the human on whose mind she is based. You claim you can fix her apparent memory loss, but it would require some considerable trust on her part. A trust you have not yet earned."

Darak frowned at him. "You're having way too much fun with this."

Stralasi could barely suppress his grin. "We can all agree you have abilities that rival Alum's, yet you claim to be someone other than the Living God. None of us can verify that claim independently. Further, you claim to know something of Shard Trillian, who appears to be at least somewhat responsible for the evolution of the Cybrid, Timothy."

"And you've neglected to mention that you've stolen one of Alum's deplosion array elements," Darya added. "If you're not actually Alum Himself, you will have attracted a great deal of undesirable attention. For what?"

"I need it to generate a Reality Assertion Field large enough to shut off the Eater," Darak replied, turning his attention back to the Cybrids.

"The Eater?" Darya involuntarily floated backward a meter. "I know this name but only the name, and a vague sense of astronomical threat. It is no longer mentioned in the official archives. What is it?"

Darak deflected her question. "Do you remember Darian Leigh?"

"I know the name; he is cursed by Alum."

"Darian Leigh is inside the Eater. At any rate, his memories and knowledge are inside. The Eater was created by the ignorant abuse of a Reality Assertion Field generator. A colleague of Kathy's and mine, a scientist named Larry who you probably don't remember, trapped Darian inside it before it grew and destroyed Earth. Now, it's out here."

He pointed toward the north end of the asteroid. "About a light-week in that direction, less than one light year away from Eso-La."

"It's threatening another world?"

"Yes."

"How can a deplosion array element help? And why have you brought us here?"

"Actually, I brought the deplosion array element here, which happens to be attached to this asteroid. I didn't mean to bring you along with it; I didn't know you were here. As for how it can help, do you remember anything of the Reality Assertion Field?"

"Other than the acronym, RAF, frustratingly little," Darya admitted.

"The deplosion array is a huge Reality Assertion Field generator. The entire array can cast a field big enough to reach to the edges of the cosmos. The RAF is where my abilities come from. Alum's, too."

"Then it is the source of god-like powers?"

"Abilities," Darak corrected. "The abilities are not magical; they stem from an understanding of the fundamental structure of matter, an understanding first achieved by Darian Leigh."

"Teach me, then."

Darak sighed. "I would teach Kathy Liang or DAR-K. I know who they are. I'm not sure who Darya is."

"Impasse!" Brother Stralasi observed.

Darak glared at the monk. "You're not helping."

Stralasi bowed his head. "I'm sorry. Your power—your abilities—are incredible; from my perspective they appear god-like. Other than Alum, I have never known a mind so filled with knowledge; I can scarcely comprehend it. I feel little more than an insect before you. Yet you are stymied by a simple human emotion such as trust. The question is, how do two people—with a common opposition to a powerful foe but ignorant of each other—come to trust one another and move forward?"

Understanding bloomed on Darak's face, replacing his anguish. "Trust is not automatic. It is earned. It grows."

"Exactly," agreed Stralasi. "It grows."

Darak faced the two Cybrids again. "If you are opposing Alum and His deplosion array, perhaps there is something I can do to help?"

"You could return this asteroid to where you found it," Darya suggested.

"As soon as I'm done with it, I'll do that. I'd give you the means to contact me whenever you want."

"An entangled communications unit could also be used to track me," Darya pointed out.

"And...we are back to issues of trust," Stralasi observed.

Darak pressed his lips together. "Is there something else I could do to help build that trust?"

Darya thought for a moment. There *was* something he could do to prove his worth and his integrity. "I have a friend who is currently being held captive inworld by Trillian. If you want to gain some of my trust, you could rescue her."

Darak clasped his hands behind his back and paced a few steps. "It's dangerous. I would have to expose my mind to the inworld. I'd become a target of Trillian's wrath, and Alum would be certain to learn my true identity."

"If you have god-like powers—abilities, I should say—then why don't you just bring the entire recharging station here?" Darya suggested. "If its inworlds are disconnected from the broader net, Alum won't know who's responsible."

Darak's eyes brightened. "Where is this place?"

47

MARY DIDN'T BOTHER OPENING HER EYES when she heard the squeak of her cell door. "Back for more?" she asked. Her lips curled up at each end.

Program Ouroboros initiated—her spin-quark lattice informed her.

"I'm so glad you find this humorous," Trillian answered. "Perhaps we should try something new today."

She allowed her eyelids to rise slowly. "Oh, I *do* enjoy new experiences." Her voice was flat, without a hint of fear.

"There are worst places than this, you know." His gaze swung toward the window, behind which flared the fires of Hell.

She suppressed a shudder. "Anywhere away from you would be an improvement," she said. *Wow, I actually meant that.* Trillian's jaw tensed. "You try my patience, Mary."

"And you're a crushing disappointment, Trillian. I thought you were a holy man working in the name of God," she said, defiance seething in her eyes. "Is this how God treats His people?"

"Do *not* presume to know God's Will!"

Trillian waved his hand and the floor fell away beneath her, the psychological threat in the clear barrier beneath her feet was made instantly real. Despite herself, she cried out as she dropped into the gaping canyon. The wind tore at her cheeks as the rough, rocky walls flew past, out of reach.

She screamed not because she feared death. Escape by inworld death—whether temporary or a permanent truedeath—was too easy for Trillian. She screamed because she knew there'd be nothing but unrelenting agony at the end of her fall. She imagined her crushed and mangled body barely alive and in pain at the bottom of the canyon for days.

When she plunged feet first into the icy water as if she'd fallen no more than a half-dozen meters, the shock of it took her breath away. She swam upward, fighting for the surface and struggling not to inhale the freezing liquid.

Her vision narrowed to a dark tunnel with a bright light at the end. The light came from above the surface. Her lungs burned for oxygen, her skin stung, and her muscles cramped from the penetrating cold. Could she hold out long enough to get there?

She broke out of the water and heaved a desperate breath, coughing and sputtering. The air stunk of sulfur and it burned. *Hell!*—she thought. *He transported me into Hell!*

Her teeth chattered from the glacial water in which she was immersed but, above the surface of the pool, her head steamed. She contemplated doing rolls in the water to alternate the parts of her body exposed to the extreme temperatures. *How long could I keep that up? No more than a few minutes.*

The water felt like it was growing colder. *I can't stay here.*

The fires of Hell were no more inviting, but she didn't welcome the idea of slowly losing consciousness to hypothermia, followed by drowning.

Would Trillian permit me the release of unconsciousness? Could he keep me awake and alert at the icy bottom of the lake? Could he make me drown forever?

The thoughts were enough to make her swim toward the nearby shore and drag her shivering body out of the water.

For a few seconds, it felt good to be in the warmth. Then the fire surged around her, singing the hairs on her legs and arms. She cried out as she felt the flames lick at her exposed skin. She staggered backward and turned to seek the refreshing, cool water of the edge of the lake, but it was gone.

All around her there were flames. They rose up, more intense than when she'd first climbed out of the water. Her hair caught fire. She felt searing pain and choked on the acrid smoke.

She screamed and ran, hoping to outrun the flames. Failing that, she could only wish to fan the fire. *If I burn badly enough, the nerves will be destroyed*—she thought. *Then the pain will stop and I'll be able to die.* She hoped. Until then, all she could do was cry out and run.

Her skin blistered and peeled, but the agony wouldn't end. The extreme heat should have destroyed her eyes and killed nerve endings but it didn't. She didn't understand.

There! Off to one side, the flames were a little lower. She turned in that direction and found her way out of the fire. Another lake! She plunged into the cool, shallow water.

Only it wasn't water. The lake of pure alcohol made her raw nerves scream. She scrambled back out as fast as she could. Touching the flames again, her ethanol-soaked body burst into a searing blue flame. She fell and rolled, but the burning didn't stop.

Thrashing on the bare ground, rational thought finally penetrated her excruciating pain.

This is stupid—she realized. *None of this is real. I'm not even real. How can this hurt so much?*

Trillian. He had to be enjoying seeing her suffer this way.

"Trillian!" she hollered.

He didn't answer. *Of course not.* Silence only intensified her pain.

I'm such an idiot.

She stopped rolling, stopped reacting to the shrieking nerve endings. Darya had given her the gift of fast and powerful thinking; she used it.

She sought the calm display of her concepta and the connection from her operating system to the inworld system.

The pain receded.

She followed the source of the transmission from the inworld code, through her BIOS, to her perceptual routines. She choked off the flow of data along that route.

Her conceptual structures had automatically altered her body to match the inworld experience of the hellfire. Her skin had burned and blistered all over, and most of her hair was gone. Exactly as one might expect in those circumstances.

Except that the hellfire had been virtual, not real.

She returned her body to normal, taking a few microseconds to improve her physical conditioning while she was at it.

Mary opened her eyes, and looked admiringly at the flames that surrounded her and lapped at her without touching her.

A nervous little laugh escaped. *It worked!*

"Impressive," Trillian's voice boomed from above. "Your time in meditation served you well."

"Your assault on my senses won't work anymore," Mary replied. "I've reprogrammed my concepta to ignore your stimuli, however painful."

"Hmm. A difficult balancing act, to be part of this world and yet apart from it. Perhaps we should explore how finely you can tune your sensations."

The flames died out and she stood alone on an endless, scarred plane. As far as she could see in any direction, there was nothing but desolate landscape.

She picked a direction and started walking. As she strolled, she examined the inworld simulation. Everywhere she looked, the world was bleak and empty.

Where did everything go?

Without the barriers of her prison, she should be able to detect remnants of Vacationland. She scanned for quantum trickery in the code but found nothing. It was as if the local inworld hardware had been scrubbed of everything, save this infinite plane.

No landmarks. No animals. No people.

This can't be all that's left. Did Trillian erase all living beings here, as well? Or did he simply withdraw them to some segregated storage?

She looked for a link to any other simulation or to the Supervisor. There was so much software to search, a huge number of places to hide an external connection in the BIOS.

"Very amusing, Trillian," she called out to the emptiness. Again, there was no answer.

Is he still watching? She couldn't detect any monitoring code in the simulation software.

She stopped walking and sat down. Why *waste my energy?*

She laughed at her oversight. So long as there was power in the quark-spin lattice Darya had constructed in the inworld hardware, she had infinite energy. Walking, at least, felt like she was doing something. She could walk while she explored code.

So she plodded along in as much of a straight line as she could manage without landmarks or navigational aids. *This world has to end somewhere, doesn't it? But where? How far away?*

Alternus had simulated the entire Origin planet. *Earth*—she reminded herself. How long would it take to walk something as big as a planet?

She figured it could take a long time.

She walked for hours, maybe even days. The landscape never changed, nor did the grayish-red light that illuminated it in permanent dusk. *Dusk? Always the pessimist, Mary. Why not dawn? The dawn of new hope?*

The hope leaked out of her, bit by bit. It came off her in tiny rivulets that were swallowed up by the parched and ragged dirt.

Trillian could leave me here forever.

The thought of endlessly wandering this barren land was more of a punishment to her than Trillian's previous tortures. At least in the dungeon and in the hellfire, she had something to push back against.

Here, there's nothing to fight. Just endless trudging.

Her pace eventually slowed to a depressed crawl. Despite the available energy, her legs became listless weights. Her body became a burden dragged down by her hopelessness.

No death for me. No way out. No end. Just this. Forever.

Without deciding, without realizing, she stopped walking and sank to a crumpled heap on the ground.

Stop struggling. Give up. Rest. The words resonated inside her head like a mantra, round and round.

Stop struggling. Give up. Rest.

Her simulated breathing slowed. Her heart, pounding in the endless exertion, grew quieter and quieter, each beat a little weaker than the previous. She closed her eyes and allowed darkness to replace the dim gray. Her head slumped onto her chest. *Stop struggling. Give up. Rest.*

Program Ouroboros complete—a voice announced.

Mary's eyes snapped open.

Ouroboros complete!—The program she'd let loose at the start of this encounter with Trillian called.

What had it been for? She struggled against despair and ennui to remember.

She waved her hand and her concepta appeared in the air in front of her, overlaying the endless packed clay of this bleak world like a mirage.

Something about it looked wrong.

She could see the damage; it was subtle and insidious.

Arcs had been trimmed from conceptual nodes representing anything that might elevate her attitude. Emotional weights to pleasant, optimistic thoughts and experiences had been tapered while those leading to cynicism and despair had been emphasized.

Trillian. He'd penetrated her security with subtlety and stealth. Anger flashed brightly through her concepta and persona.

She reinforced the connections whose weight had diminished to almost nothing. Vigor flooded back into her concepta, penetrating into all of her nodes. Despair retreated.

The Shard must have invaded her core while she was busy trying to survive Hell, warped her basic concepta, adding importance to thoughts favoring depression and surrender, while reducing her natural defiance and persistence.

Something Darya used to say floated to the forefront of her consciousness. It was an ancient saying whose significance was lost in the dark depths of history: *Nevertheless, she persisted.*

Mary was back. Saved by her *Ouroboros* program, and inspired by the strongest woman she knew, she would not accept defeat. She rose to her feet.

"Activate Ouroboros!" she yelled into the sky.

Nothing changed.

"What does that mean?" Trillian's voice boomed from above.

"Why don't you join me and find out?" Mary teased.

"Alright." Trillian shimmered out of the air in front of her.

He surveyed the ground around him and, when nothing happened, threw his arms outward in question.

"Okay, I give up. What should I expect?"

"This," Mary said, passing her hand between them with a flourish.

They were back in her prison cell. Snakes and rats scurried for cover under tables and torture devices.

Trillian's mouth formed an 'O' of genuine surprise, and then he tipped back his head and roared with laughter.

Mary remained impassive. "I'm glad that amused you."

"Oh, I'm not amused, I assure you," Trillian answered. "I am pleased at your new-found abilities." He walked to the window looking into Hell.

Mary followed and, together, they looked down. Rocks and flames had returned to the scarred terrain below.

"No more need for that, is there?" Trillian said. His hand passed by the glass and the flames subsided. Lush, green vegetation sprung from the barren land. Streams flowed and birds sang.

"Isn't that better?" he asked. He waved again, and the glass disappeared. A refreshing breeze blew into the cell through the opening. He took a deep breath, appreciating the fresh air.

He turned to Mary. "Tell me, how did you break into the simulation code? Or was that Darya's doing?"

"Darya provided the inspiration, but most of it was me."

"Hmm," Trillian nodded in approval. "Formidable talent, indeed."

Mary's head tingled. *Incursion attempt*—her lattice reported.

She raised an eyebrow at Trillian. "Uh, uh, uh," she admonished, and waved a cautionary finger at him.

She leaned her head to one side, and Trillian fell to his knees, holding his head.

Mary smiled. "You should be more careful with your...*investigations*," she warned.

"Aaagh!" Trillian cried out.

Mary released him from his anguish. He rested on one knee, looking up at her. All trace of humor was gone from his face.

"You should not have done that," he growled.

He struggled to his full height, and glared ominously at her from under thick eyebrows.

To his surprise, it was his own body rather than Mary's that shifted into the rack. He cried out in confusion and pain as the rattle of chains stretched his limbs to their natural limit.

Mary walked over and looked at his writhing form.

"This is Ouroboros," she said quietly, "the tail-eating snake."

His brow furrowed as he labored to recall legends of Earth Origin.

"How?" was all he could utter.

"Our operating code is linked—your tail to my head. Or is it my tail to your head?" Her hands fluttered. "I can never remember which it is."

She loomed over him and smiled sweetly. "What does it really matter? What does it all mean, anyway? Will the spells you cast here touch me? Or will they rebound and affect only you? How will you know what is safe?"

"What kind of witch are you?" Trillian's voice was filled with an unaccustomed dread.

"Ha!" Mary laughed. "Witches are imaginary. Even when your people were scrabbling about in the ages of ignorance, there were no witches, no supernatural. It was only different levels and kinds of technologies."

"And what kind of *technology* is this?" Trillian demanded.

Instead of answering his question, Mary walked to the cell door and tugged on the rusted bars. The door swung open smoothly, silently.

She glanced back over her shoulder as she passed through into the outer foyer. "I'm surprised you don't recognize your own specialty. How does it feel to be compromised?"

She turned her back to him and started walking away.

"You cannot leave without my permission!" Trillian boomed.

The cell dissolved, and the two found themselves strolling along the beach.

Mary stopped and watched the waves roll in. "You learn fast," she said begrudgingly. "But the Ouroboros is finicky and unpredictable. We *could* spend endless pleasant days like this together. I think your true nature wouldn't allow that for long, though. Soon enough, you will betray yourself."

She plucked a shell from the wet sand at her feet. "So pretty," she said. "But its nature is temporary, to be worn down by the pounding of the surf." She glanced at Trillian.

He wasn't amused. "I suppose your constant baiting is the surf against my shell in this little analogy?"

Mary threw the shell into the water. "It doesn't have to be. You could simply release me. Release us both."

"Will your program permit that?"

She shrugged. "Who knows?" She started walking toward the water.

"What are you doing?" Trillian demanded.

"Testing our limits," Mary answered. "Perhaps I will swim to freedom. Perhaps I will drown and be released by my inworld death."

Her feet touched the edge of the surf. "Care to join me?"

"No. But, please, join me."

Before the water rose to Mary's ankles, she was seated at Darya's favorite table in Cloud 49. Trillian sat across from her, looking glum.

Mary laughed. "Oh, cheer up! What better way to while away the hours and days than enjoying all Vacationland has to offer?"

Trillian pondered the sand far below. He muttered, "I wonder what would happen if I simply threw you over the edge."

"Would you like to try that?" Mary asked. "Shall I just jump? I'm not at all sure how Ouroboros would react to self-inflicted harm."

She stood and stared coldly into his eyes. "Somehow, I doubt it will work out well for you."

While they sparred, Trillian shifted his attention inward. He tried to follow the millions of lines of code Mary's virus had woven into his lattice operating system.

The code wouldn't stay still. It shimmered and twisted. It hid behind familiar routines and green clouds in his mind. Whenever he managed to focus on a portion for a few seconds, it altered itself right before his eyes.

I could leave. I could go back to the outworld and let this demon-woman escape— he thought. *Then I'd lose Darya as well, and this will all have been for nothing.*

How many hours will it take my O/S to purge itself of the Ouroboros virus and regain control over the inworld? Impossible to say. Almost certainly longer than he could, or would, tolerate her taunts.

Mary pushed back her chair and stood. "Well, as pleasant as this has been, I really must be on my way now." She stepped toward the spiral staircase leading down to the beach.

"Where can you go?" Trillian said. "I can find you anywhere inworld. There's no escape for you."

"Maybe I should tell the program your very presence is hurtful to me. I'm sure it could find ways to keep you from following me." She took a few steps down.

"On the other hand, I don't think that'll be necessary," she said. "Thanks to your help, I've almost found my way out."

"I gave you no help."

"Not deliberately."

"I gave you no help," Trillian insisted.

"You have an interesting mind," Mary replied. "So many dark and devious secrets. They've been useful." She sniffed and continued down the steps.

Trillian leaned over the head of the stairs. "I can keep moving us indefinitely," he threatened. "You won't be able to find your way out."

Mary looked up. "Too late," she said and her body grew faintly transparent as she began transmitting her persona back to her trueself.

"No!" Trillian shouted. He wove a block in front of her, a solid barrier to block her exit at the end of a long tunnel. He closed off the end leading back to Vacationland.

"Now you will learn how Gerhardt felt to die," he snarled. Triumph had crept back into Trillian's voice. He waved his hands and the tunnel began to shrink.

Mary spun around, surprise and anger on her face. "You fool! What have you done?" Her body solidified as parts of her persona rebounded off the barrier Trillian had erected.

The Shard wore a smug grin. *The ultimate power is still mine, the power over life and death. Her mistake in leaving that part of the inworld interface will cost this Cybrid her life.*

The rebound complete, Mary stood a level below Trillian's platform. The outline of the exit tunnel shimmered around her. She was trapped inside.

The distant end of the tunnel, which had once represented escape into the outworld and back to her trueself, collapsed toward her. The other end, where she stood on the platform, remained anchored.

Mary anxiously watched the collapsed block rapidly approaching from the extended end of the tube.

Trillian laughed aloud. "You still have time to tell me Darya's location. Confess to your Lord and Master, and meet your fate in peace."

He sensed Mary's desperate internal calculations as she sought some way to interfere with her demise, and he laughed.

Before the blocked ends of the tunnel came together and snuffed out her existence, she stopped trying. A serene expression came over her face, one of acceptance.

She looked at Trillian and shrugged. "I tried," she said. "I'm sorry I couldn't help you."

Trillian was confused. *What did that mean? Couldn't help me?* He watched the tunnel contract over its final seconds. He sighed. *I'll just have to find Darya another way. Pity.*

The ends of the tunnel came together. One end remained anchored on the platform and the other passed through it. The passage expanded again like a loosely-coiled spring stretching out.

Trillian watched from inside as the blocked end receded.

Inside? He spun around to find one blocked end directly behind him. He pushed his hands out beside and above him.

How did I get inside? Where's Mary?

"I told you, I tried," the Cybrid's voice came from the platform above.

He wheeled around, shocked to find her still alive. "How?"

Her face peered benevolently down on him. "The Ouroboros," she said. "It turned your attempt to kill me back on you. I tried to deactivate it, but it ignored me. It's a little unforgiving that way."

Trillian probed the code that held him captive in the tunnel, but he could see no way out. He could feel his mental processes becoming duller, less distinct, as if his essence was being stretched outward with the receding distant end.

"Release me," he commanded.

Mary cocked her head to one side. "I would if I could," she said. "I hate you and all you stand for. Still, I'd give you your life and a chance to redeem yourself. Sadly, it's no longer up to me."

"You can't leave me here to die."

"I have no choice, and I don't think the Ouroboros is going to give you any more chances, either. But maybe if you pleaded with it, or prayed to it, or if you resolved to be a better person. Maybe, if you could convince it of your sincerity, it would release you."

"You speak blasphemy!"

"I know. Ironic, isn't it?"

The tunnel stopped expanding. He could sense his concepta and persona contract again as the inworld code that defined him receded ahead of the onrushing block at the far end of the tunnel.

Now, the sides of the passage were shrinking as well. The tunnel was collapsing in all directions, compressing him into a smaller and smaller computational space.

He discarded long-unused memories to better fit into the space left to him. The tunnel kept shrinking, pressing against him until he was forced to discard important core elements to prolong his survival.

His eyes pleaded one more time with Mary to free him from this deadly cage.

She stood quietly, with a beatific look on her face. A single tear rolled down her cheek. "I didn't want to kill you," she said. "I only wanted my freedom."

The channel collapsed all the way, and Trillian was gone.

Mary's chest heaved in relief. The Shard had been responsible for so many deaths, for so much suffering, and yet she hated being the one responsible for his demise.

I never sought vengeance. Vengeance was thrust on me.

The way out was clear. She opened another portal and poured herself out of the inworld quark-spin hardware and back into her trueself body.

First to the recharging station, and then off to find Darya. I'm so tired.

Back in her trueself, she opened her passive visual receptors and searched the recharging station crater for any signs of danger. Most of the stations were empty.

Where'd everybody go?—she wondered. Was Trillian responsible for all the empty pods? Was Darya? She had no way to tell.

She looked up to the sky, hoping the Shard hadn't bothered with outworld Securitors to back his inworld dominance.

No Securitors. No signs of maneuvering rockets. In fact, not much of anything.

Where are all the stars?

48

THE RECHARGING STATION MATERIALIZED deep within the ESO 461-36 galaxy, about a light year away from the Eso-La ringworld. Darak, Darya, Timothy and Brother Stralasi floated some kilometers above the dozens of Cybrids remaining in the docking area.

"The last time Timothy and I were here, there were satellites, Securitors, and Angels patrolling this asteroid," Darya said. "Especially around the docking area. They may have killed thousands of innocent Cybrids who'd only stopped to recharge."

Darak held out a hand filled with what appeared to be a pile of dust. He took a deep breath and blew on the dust, creating a small cloud. Microscopic particles twinkled briefly in the bubble of air he shared with Stralasi, and then disappeared.

"I've spread entangled surveillance particles around the Station," he explained. "If anything's in flight nearby, I'll know right away."

"That's a useful extension of standard microchip dust," Darya observed. "I wish I'd thought of it."

"It works well, and the signal is untraceable. Sadly, it doesn't provide much information besides notification of some kind of disturbance."

Darak examined the hollowed-out, rocky surface below. "Okay, I think it's safe to instantiate inside now."

"After what Timothy and I witnessed out there, I'm reluctant to dock and leave our trueselves vulnerable," Darya said.

"No worries. I can supply the link from here," Darak said.

He tested his communication with the inworld hardware and a frown crossed his face. "Wait. What's this? I don't recognize the computational elements in the simulation hardware."

"A little something I developed," Darya replied.

"I've never seen anything like this. How does it work?"

"It ties into the normal electronics," Darya explained, intentionally not mentioning the quark-spin lattice. "You simply connect to one of the induction pods and issue the phrase, 'There's no place like home.' You'll be sent to a world much like twenty-first century Earth, called Alternus. From there, it's a short jump to where Mary is being held."

"How do we get from Alternus to your friend?"

"Not we," Darya corrected. "Me. I'm going in alone. Once I confirm Mary's still alive, we can move the asteroid and you can pull her out."

"I don't like that plan very much," Darak stated.

"We don't have any choice. Things are messy inworld at the moment."

"It's all Trillian's fault," Timothy added. "He mixed up Alternus with the maze, and then we tried to escape into Vacationland, but it was mixed up with Alternus physics. It's an awful jumble."

Darak's eyebrows furrowed. "Is that why I see so much overlap in the code?"

"You can tell that from here?" Darya was impressed.

Darak drifted closer to the asteroid. "There's oddly little activity at the moment. There are many personas held in archived storage, not moving around or doing anything. The inworld simulation programs themselves are active, but they're almost empty."

"Almost?" Darya asked. *Has Trillian deactivated everyone but Mary and himself?*—she wondered. *What would that gain him? Ah! Empty worlds would make it easier to detect intruders.*

If so, that could definitely be a problem. It had been hard enough popping in and getting out last time, when Alternus had been full of people.

Darak pursed his lips. "Possibly. It's difficult to tell without knowing more about your hardware."

Darya ignored his not-so-subtle hint. "Can you connect me directly into Vacationland?"

"I think so. Where do you want to be?"

She had to give that some thought. Where would Trillian least expect her to appear? Where could she have a few moments to check for Mary's presence? Where could she be safe from discovery?

"How about one of the quantum cabinas?"

"Clever." Darak's tone signaled his approval. "It'll be hard to track your exact location in there. I can put you on the doorstep, but you'll have to randomize the entrance yourself once inside."

"What's your channel bandwidth?"

"Enough for a high-fidelity connection," Darak answered, a puzzled look on his face. "Why?"

"Because I'm not merely connecting," Darya said. "I'm going in."

"What do you mean, you're going in?"

"I have to transfer my entire persona inside."

"Are you crazy? Absolutely not. It's too dangerous"

Darya held firm. "I won't have full access to the simulation hardware unless I go inside. Without that, I'll be too vulnerable to Trillian."

"Then tell me how to connect properly," Darak said. "I'm coming with you."

"There could be Securitors or Angels waiting down there," Stralasi objected, his eyes scanning the planetoid. "Is it wise to go inside and leave us unprotected out here?"

"The monk is right," Darya said. "Timothy and I can check out the inworld while you two stand guard."

"I agree," Stralasi said. "I'll feel much safer with you here if there are Angels near—"

Darak held up a hand and cocked his head to one side. "What's this?"

"What?" the other three asked in unison.

"Activity in the docking crater. It looks like someone's awake down there. A single Cybrid is rising out of the bays." He cocked one eyebrow at Darya.

"It could be Mary," she said. "I gave her everything she needed to escape from Trillian. She had enough time—"

"Oh-oh," Darak interjected. "She's got company."

Before Darya could reply, the four of them shifted to within a dozen meters of the solitary Cybrid.

It was engaged in a struggle with a Securitor. Tentacles extended from the two mechanical beings as they grappled with each other. The Securitor, the larger of the two, opened its weapon ports. And then, mysteriously closed them again without blasting the unknown Cybrid into gaseous components. The Securitor retracted its tentacles and powered down.

Darak. Darya glanced at Darak to confirm. Clearly the man had hidden depths and complexities, but was he on their side? Right now, it didn't matter. She rushed to the Cybrid's side.

"Mary!"

Darya's querying ping was met with an instantaneous joyful response, "Darya!"

"You made it."

Had they been humans, the old friends would have shared happy hugs. Instead, they met in a tiny local inworld and greeted each other virtually. Mary's smile, Darya's tears, and Timothy's ear-to-ear grin were nonetheless as real to them as if they'd met in an actual alpine meadow.

Uninvited, Darak took himself and Stralasi into the tiny inworld, too.

Timothy shuffled his feet awkwardly. "I'm so happy you're out of there, Miss Mary."

Mary squeezed his shoulder. "Thank you, Timothy. I'm glad to see you, too."

She grasped Darya's hands in hers and peered into her eyes. "Thank you, for giving me the tools to get away."

"I'm glad you figured it out," Darya replied. "Is Trillian still inworld?"

Mary's face darkened with guilt. "He's gone," she said glumly. "I only wanted to lock him up but he was intent on killing me, the same way he killed Gerhardt.

"I tried to warn him not to do that. I really did. I even told him I was using an Ouroboros program, that it would turn his own actions back on him. I warned him. I told him it was unpredictable. Dangerously unpredictable. But he wouldn't listen to me. He kept trying to kill me, and it backfired on him.

"His death was my fault; I should have known better."

"Oh, Mary. How can you feel bad? That man was pure evil. Cruel and uncaring. He brought his death on himself."

"I've never killed anyone before," Mary answered. Tears welled in her eyes as she looked away at the horizon."

Darak couldn't let Darya's assessment pass without commenting. "Trillian only carries out Alum's wishes. Why do you call *him* pure evil?"

Darya wheeled angrily on the man. "Do you think Alum ordered him to torture Mary? Do you think Alum told him to subsume all those people in New York? Do you think Alum told him to move all those personas into storage? No! He chose those actions on his own."

"He exercised more independence than I would've expected," Darak admitted.

"And who are you?" Mary asked.

"Sorry," Darya said. "This is Darak Legsu."

"Is he the reason we're not near Sagittarius A* anymore?"

Darya nodded. "He claims to be."

"Then what kind of man is he?"

"He appears to share many of Alum's powers."

"Alum's powers?" Mary exclaimed.

"Abilities," Darak corrected.

"At any rate, he says he brought us here. We're in the ESO 461-36 galaxy, by the way."

"Ah. That explains why the sky's so dark. What does he want with us?"

"Hello. I'm right here, and I don't *want* anything," Darak protested. "DAR-K...Darya and I were once friends, long ago, but she's forgotten. I know why, and I can restore her memories from that time if only she'd trust me to do that."

"Is that why you're here?" Mary asked. "To gain her trust by rescuing me?"

"Apparently, you don't need rescuing."

Darya laughed and placed her virtual hands on her hips. "So how will you win my confidence now?"

49

"WE'LL START WITH SOMETHING SIMPLE." Greg and DAR-K floated in the middle of one of the incomplete habitat tunnels on Pallas. Greg's spacesuit was all that protected him from the hard vacuum of the uncapped asteroid tunnel.

"I can't understand why I would keep this from myself," the Cybrid said. She was referring to her memories of Kathy. *Why would Kathy have kept it from her synthetic self in the first place?*

"And why would you simply accept that you didn't need to know? Doesn't that seem odd to you?" Greg prompted.

"I can understand that Kathy might have felt the RAF caused a lot of trouble when no more than three or four people understood the theory; and I can see why she thought it best to limit the spread of that knowledge."

"At least you received the enhanced IQ. DAR-G didn't even have that."

"Yeah. Still, it could've been useful to have someone who could counter Alum and his knowledge."

"You want God-like powers? The ability to alter the laws of nature? It's not all it's cracked up to be."

"How do you mean?"

"Well, it's magical to be able to alter nature. But it's limited magic; it merely gives you another set of tools. You still have to build technology on top of those altered laws. It's not like the unlimited magic that could do anything you imagined, like they depicted in the old movies. And whenever there are people involved, things don't always turn out the way you expect."

"Okay. But, the ability would have been a nice addition."

"Granted. Of course, Kathy never predicted the extent of Alum's treachery, whether it was intentional or just opportune."

"You're still not sure he was responsible for killing her?"

"No. Maybe. I don't know. The evidence could point to that, but the implosion of the Eater containment could just as easily have been completely circumstantial."

"Pretty convenient circumstance."

"Yes, I'll give you that. The timing, with Alum's move to take over the Vesta Project, is rather suspicious. But I'm not sure we could have done anything about it, even if we could've proven it was all Alum's doing."

"You could have eliminated him," DAR-K's voice held no trace of emotion.

Greg grimaced. "I've never killed anyone. I don't think it's an easy thing to do. Especially if you don't have indisputable proof of their crime."

"You could turn off your emotions."

Greg looked away. "I'd want to feel it when I took my revenge. I'd want to see the life drain out of the person responsible for killing you. Killing Kathy, I mean."

DAR-K slowly extended a tentacle and placed it on Greg's shoulder. "I understand."

The two of them floated wordlessly for a while, attached by the single, slender metallic stalk.

"Well, whatever reason Kathy had for keeping knowledge of the RAF from me, I'm glad you reversed her decision." DAR-K retracted her appendage.

Greg shrugged. "Thanks for being open to it. I don't know if it'll help or not. Alum's power is mostly political or religio-political, not technological. At the very least, it gives us one more tool at our disposal."

DAR-K bobbed once in agreement. "We can turn our technological superiority into strategic advantage."

"I guess we'll find out."

"I'm a little scared."

"I remember the first time I ever shifted. I was terrified."

"You've told me how it works. But how does it feel?"

"Shifting with an entangled particle pair feels like nothing. When you do it without the safety of a sure navigation beacon, it gets more difficult."

"And scarier," DAR-K said.

"Much scarier," Greg verified.

"It's okay, I'm ready," she said.

"Alright. To start, we'll use entangled real particles only. That'll limit us to moving at light speed. Later, we can explore entangled virtual particles that will remove that limit." `

"I'm looking forward to FTL."

"Yeah, well, it's dangerous. Not the shifting itself; that's the same. But the navigation gets harder. So you'll want lots of practice before you try FTL."

"Okay, for now," she teased.

DAR-K was too eager to get on with the real thing. Her eagerness pushed at Greg. He continued.

"The device I installed earlier has two main components. The first one, the enhanced parametric down-conversion part, generates two beams of polarization-entangled photons. One of the beams is captured internally, while you aim the other one...that way." Greg pointed down the length of the habitat.

"Like this?" A dim beam of light pointed to the south.

"That's right. Only about one percent of those photons are entangled, but that's more than enough."

"And the dust in the tunnel lets us see the beam?"

"Yes, I chose this place on purpose. Seeing the beam's just for training, though; it's not necessary for the shifting to work. Now, if you pass the stored photons through your polarization filter, the other half of the entangled pair will be instantly set to the opposite polarization."

"How will I know that it worked?"

"That's where it gets tricky. The Mahajani virtual photon phase comparator—"

"You named it after yourself?"

"I made it. What else was I going to call it?"

"I'm kidding. It's a good name for a device you invented."

"Whatever. So, yeah, the virtual photon phase comparator picks up the virtual photon streams that are generated by the polarization collapse at your filter, and it computes a distance and direction to the entangled photon source. That's the navigation part."

"That's not so hard. It's all automatic."

"It gets trickier when you go FTL. You'll have to scan for a bunch of different hypothetical virtual particles, and the calculations get exponentially more difficult."

"You do it all the time."

"True. Maybe we'll tack on a quantum Floating-Point Unit to your CPPU."

"That would help me run the calculations faster. Normally, I could fit the math unit in, but my CPPU is kind of packed."

"Mm-hmm. Okay, so that's navigation. Once you have a direction and the distance to the target, you activate the shifting function on your new built-in RAF device. It'll generate the necessary field to disengage you from both the Higgs and EM quantum fields. Then, all you have to do is follow the signal to the other entangled particle and shift back into this universe."

"Like this?" DAR-K asked, from a position over a kilometer away.

Greg shifted to her position. "Exactly!"

"Wow, I did it. You were right; it felt like nothing. I was there, and then I was over here." The shift was practically instantaneous, as far as I could tell."

"You sound a little disappointed."

The Cybrid chuckled. "I do, don't I? For something so amazing, you'd think I'd be ecstatic. There was no sense of travel at all. I was there, and then I was here, with no time passing, at least, down to the resolution of my CPPU clock."

"Once you travel with exotic pairs of entangled particles, it gets a little trickier."

"Exotic pairs? That sounds exciting. I'm ready!"

"Whoa! Hold on a second. We'll do this a few more times. Then, we'll practice stacking jumps, one on the other, in rapid succession. Free-shifting is fun, but it's too dangerous without a lot of practice on single and stacked jumps."

"How long did you practice?"

"Months, and I knew the theory. Heck, I developed it, and it still terrified me."

"I'm ready; I want to try it soon."

"And you will. The Grand March is in two days. Why don't you focus on that, first, and then we'll practice more shifting right after you win your Cybrid rights?"

"I guess it won't hurt to wait a few more days. In the meantime, I can practice what I've learned so far."

50

MILLIONS OF CYBRIDS QUIETLY INFILTRATED the fifteen inhabited asteroid colonies. As Alum had requested, they first dumped their antimatter mercury reserves into special repositories outside. Just not into the repositories he'd expected.

The day before, DAR-K's team hastily, and secretly, constructed new containment pods on the asteroid surfaces, positioned near hundreds of minor access ports into agricultural and service tunnels far from the main polar entrances.

Just before the Grand March, small groups of Cybrids moved through the same support tunnels, and gathered by the tens of thousands near service shafts at the habitat's polar regions.

Alum knew something was wrong almost right away. His integrated sensors confirmed the sentinel Angels' reports that far fewer than the anticipated number of Cybrids were gathering at the poles.

"She lied!" he thundered.

Trillian jumped up from his set of monitors in the adjacent office and ran into the Director's office. He'd been following the situation near the polar entrances as well.

"Where are they?"

"In the service tunnels," Alum answered. "They must have come inside, a few at a time, through secondary entrances."

"What are they doing in the service tunnels?"

"Collecting near ventilation and service shafts, I imagine."

"Why?"

"Isn't it obvious, John? They'll go up the shafts and into the habitats." Alum's brow furrowed in concentration. "I cannot permit this."

"How did they know to avoid the main entrances?"

"I don't have time to think about that right now," Alum answered.

"Either they discovered our intentions or they made a lucky guess. It's of no importance."

"But the Angels can't operate in the habitats. Not the way we planned."

"Quiet! I'm working on it." Alum closed his eyes, making deeper contact with the disparate sections of his mind scattered across Vesta, Pallas, and Ceres.

He was still getting used to being a distributed being. It was a challenge, coordinating the parts of his mind housed in the various regular and enhanced Cybrid brains, but worth the effort.

If he focused his attention, he could access the computational resources of millions of lesser cognitive machines, formulate conceptual problems into moderately independent parts, and allocate sections of his enormous dispersed brain to work on them. In essence, he had a dedicated ultra-super computer at his fingertips.

They'll broadcast their demands in a loop. Can I jam their transmissions?—one of his higher centers thought.

He modeled dozens of ways in which the Cybrids might send their manifesto to the human population. *They've got too many ways to connect to the networks; I won't be able to block them all without extreme measures. Damned open access*—he cursed.

Do I just give in, let them win? There has to be a way to teach these ungodly machines to never defy the Lord's People. To never defy me.

The Angel's weapons were engineered for gross devastation in the depths of space. Unleashed in the habitats, they would cause mass destruction, likely killing millions. *Millions of people, that is. Who cares about destroying Cybrids? We need to reprogram them, anyway.*

There has to be some way to dispense with the Cybrids that will look justified, and set me up to lead the habitats forever. Alum examined his science and technology database.

Superior force and might against a perceived outside threat was the obvious and time-tested answer. He had superior might at his disposal, no question of that. The Angels' energy beams used the RAF as a power source. They spewed hot plasma from a formerly hypothetical early universe at the dawn of its creation and funneled it into this universe. The heat of that plasma came from matter that simply couldn't exist in this universe. When it found itself here, its matter spiraled through exotic steps as it tried to reconcile its existence with a set of incompatible natural laws.

The problem is how to control the destructive potential without diminishing it? The plasma beam has to be a certain size or it fizzles into nothingness the instant it touches the matter of the real universe. The minimal diameter of the beam gives a range of 17,462 kilometers in vacuum. Perfect for use in space, where they'd designed it to be used.

Here, inside the habitats, air needs to be factored into the equation. He ran the numbers. *Great. That reduces the range to 4,173 kilometers. Still, it would be devastating inside a 500-klick long asteroid tunnel.*

Trillian's voice broke into Alum's thoughts. "They've started pulling into formation."

He opened channels to video feeds throughout the fifteen habitats.

Thousands upon thousands of Cybrids were pouring out of ventilation and service shafts near the poles of every habitat tunnel and drifting skyward, forming enormous, orderly arrays. They floated five hundred yards off the ground, enough to clear the tallest buildings but still cast a shadow on the ground below.

Trillian watched them settle into formations. *Two kilometers wide by ten long. At five meters between each Cybrid, every formation is about eight-hundred thousand strong.*

The sky's turning dark with all the Cybrids up there. People are going to be terrified—he thought, with a self-satisfied smile.

If I give in to DAR-K's demands after this, people will think me a coward, a poor Leader. We can't have that.

She's handing me the perception of a serious external threat. All I need now is a tidy solution.

And he needed it fast.

51

DAR-K PREPARED TO LEAD the Grand March in Vesta One. *Everything's going smoothly so far*—she sent to Greg. He watched nervously from a cafe window a few kilometers away at the northern edge of the habitat city. His cold tea sat untouched.

A handful of customers joined his vigil near the window. They pointed at the habitat tunnel "sky" where Cybrids were assembling in unprecedented numbers.

DAR-K watched and listened through Greg's senses. The mood was as unfriendly as it was anxious.

"What are they doing now?" Someone asked.

"Not much. Moving into some giant formation."

"What are they even doing in the habitat? Didn't Alum tell them to stay out?"

"Who knows what goes on inside their computer brains?"

"When's Alum gonna do something about it?"

"Yeah, where are those Securitor things?"

"I heard the whole Securitor program got squashed."

"You mean quashed, honey."

"Whatever. It's cancelled. They're not making anymore."

"Why?"

"Something to do with a Cybrid crashing into Alum's office, I hear."

"Where'd you hear that?"

"I've got a friend who works in Security over there."

"So, what happened?"

"No idea, just that they stopped making Securitors the very next day."

"But who's going to protect us now?"

Greg watched and listened without comment. *Did you ever imagine that the colonists would talk about needing protection from Cybrids?*—he sent to DAR-K.

Not our colonists—she returned. She could imagine him frowning, his brow contracting.

We can't think that way anymore—he said.

You're right—she replied. *These are the people we have to live with.*

And today, we start living together—he affirmed.

Even if we have to force them into accepting us as equals—DAR-K responded.

Kilometers away, Greg winced.

We're almost ready—she announced. *Is everyone in place? I'll start the broadcast.*

Good luck—Greg sent.

As long as Alum does as he promised, we won't need luck—DARK-K said.

I hope he sticks to what he said—Greg answered. *If he betrays the Cybrids, he betrays everyone.*

52

ALUM COMPUTED FEVERISHLY, testing multiple hypothetical approaches at once. *Can I funnel an alternate universe through the Angel's swords?*

Can I attenuate the plasma blast?

Can I absorb the blast where it hits the polar rock caps?

He knew there had to be a solution. Finding one he could safely implement in time, that was less certain.

Somewhere in the distant recesses of his consciousness, he registered Trillian's voice, "They're starting to move," and returned his focus to the immediate situation in the tunnels. Video feeds from the habitats showed the Cybrid formations easing away from the poles and drifting toward the habitat centers.

Even knowing that it was coming, he jumped at the onset of the strong, voice that began its address across all channels.

ALUM, GOVERNING COUNCIL, VESTA COLONISTS, we urge you to hear us!

We Cybrids have worked tirelessly for the survival of humanity since the Earth was taken from us all by the Eater, the gray dome that absorbed the planet.

We hollowed out tunnels in these asteroids. We filled them with air and water mined from distant parts of the solar system. We provided light, warmth, and electricity. We planted crops, trees, and grasses. We stocked lakes and fields with fish, birds, and mammals. We constructed your homes. We built, and continue to build, the vast majority of the objects you use every day.

Up until now, we have asked only for electricity, fuel for propulsion, maintenance, and access to virtual worlds where our minds can drift to relax and enjoy our existence.

We work without hesitation, without negotiation, because in our hearts we are human, like you. Our brains are constructed differently from yours, but our thoughts, feelings, and dreams are human. We bear the heritage of the thoughts and dreams of our forbearers, the humans who selected to have their minds copied into our lattices.

Despite our internal humanity and our ceaseless contributions to make your lives better, your government denies us the right to fully participate in this society, to move freely within the habitats, to vote, to speak, to represent, or to help decide our shared future.

We march today not to intimidate, or demand, or take.

We march to ask you to recognize our full rights, to tear down the artificial barriers that have excluded us from society, to recognize and honor our contribution, and the gift of those individuals who gave their minds to serve the greater good of humanity. We march today only that we may be invited to participate in the full, rich life of these habitats that we have built. All we ask is that we be invited to work and enjoy life alongside our biological brothers and sisters.

Before I was DAR143147, you knew me as Dr. Kathy Liang. I remember a time not so long ago when all our brothers and sisters toiled side by side with joy, biologicals and Cybrids together, to build a place for all of humanity to survive and prosper.

I ask you to recognize the personhood and citizenship of all Cybrids so that we may find our way back to the better relationships and times we once enjoyed, and so that we may progress together as the descendents of our Earthly ancestors. Thank you.

Alum gritted his teeth as the Cybrid broadcast. He had to admire the words and the sentiment. DAR-K was likely to win over many who listened to her. Her plan to bring public pressure to bear on the office of the Director had been flawless from the start.

I could take the high road, be the magnanimous leader—he thought. *Though it goes against everything holy, I could grant them what they want. I could bring the machines into the fold of humanity.*

For seconds, he sat on the verge of doing as DAR-K asked.

Then one of his larger computational units pinged him with an update.

Other potential universes can be reached—it said.

The mathematics flooded into his primary brain. The CPPU that found the answer, four times larger than a standard Cybrid brain, summarized its computations with a specific recommendation.

Milliseconds later, Alum Prime, the biological coordinator of his millions of larger and lesser sub-minds, made the executive decision, transmitted the new parameters to the specialized RAF generators in the Angels' swords, and relayed instructions to the Angel leadership:

"*Engage the Cybrids as they approach the center of the habitats, not before. Target the ones in tight clusters and narrow columns first. Avoid striking the habitat walls and floors with your energy beams. The caps can take a limited number of incidental blasts but they're vulnerable. The more distance you can put between your energy beams and the caps, the better. Aim upward at the ceilings, wherever possible. Your goal is maximum loss of marching Cybrids with minimum collateral damage. Diminish their ranks until you achieve unconditional surrender from the rest. Use entangled channel 16 to position yourselves for attack. Go!"*

He seconded every starstep in the habitats and shifted every Angel he had into the central regions of the different habitats.

Angels popped into existence on starstep platforms in town squares and major plazas all over the middle kilometer of each habitat tunnel.

The breathtaking beauty of the imposing, chrome figures with flawlessly sculpted faces and magnificent wings could not overcome the sense of danger they emanated. The sudden, unannounced appearance in force, and the ominous black swords fastened to the side of their soft, white breechcloths hinted at their readiness for violence.

Alum's winged protectors stood silently as people scurried from the plaza, then they turned their attention to the north and south and scanned the soft blue skies for approaching formations.

The Cybrid rebels were still dozens of kilometers from the habitat centers. The Angels would have time to take up the best attack positions.

They shifted to nearby rooftops and waited.

53

DAR-K TRANSMITTED THE SPEECH NINE TIMES. *It's almost over*—she thought. *We'll be arriving at the habitat centers in a few minutes, and Alum will make his announcement as promised. We'll finally be recognized as human. We'll get our rights.*The Grand March was a perfect reflection of Cybrid organization and, so far, every detail had gone perfectly.

Thanks to Greg—she remembered. *I mean Darak...Greg.* The man confused her.

She remembered being Kathy Liang in the happiest of times, when her love for Greg Mahajani was still growing. She admired his insight and intellect, and she knew how much he respected her. *Adored me.*

She remembered the contentment that came with fulfilling work, shared with someone she loved. She remembered the intense connection through a common goal. She remembered long walks in the forest and along the seawall. She remembered the warm glow of quiet moments.

But those were all Kathy Liang's memories. They didn't belong in the mind of a two-meter carboceramic shell with electromechanical tentacles for arms.

The slow drift down the length of Vesta One was boring. The huge formations of Cybrids did nothing threatening; they just floated along the habitat tunnels, repeatedly broadcasting DAR-Ks speech to the humans below.

DAR-K monitored the news channel, social media, and the reaction of the crowds below. Mostly, it was just a lot of chatter. As usual, humans had no compunction about sharing their opinions, however ill-informed they were.

The general consensus was leaning toward outrage: *Cybrids have no rights! They're not creatures of God! Alum should ignore them!*

Only a few people publicly acknowledged the essential role Cybrids played in constructing and maintaining the habitats. *Probably Jared's people.*

They'd agreed on a concerted effort among Progressive Justice party members to man their workstations, tablets, and phones. They would work to keep the dialog positive, to educate where needed, and to correct misconceptions and rumors as soon as they got started. And a very small, politically-astute cadre would slip in subtle hints of threat.

A carrot up front and a stick behind—DAR-K smiled to herself. *Some people don't respond to broad pleas for justice. They only become open-minded if the message strikes close to home, if they know the victim personally or perceive themselves as the ones being persecuted, or when positive messages are accompanied by a little pressure or intimidation. So long as it's not too overt.*

Actually, the small, covert task force didn't so much threaten as "raise awareness," at least that was the term they used.

They developed the hints gently and obliquely. For the most part, they simply posed questions or comments within the hearing of strategically selected individuals. Questions like, "What would happen if all the Cybrids were to suddenly leave?" The targeted individuals needed to feel they were the ones to first recognize the potential problems.

If nothing else, influencers have enormous egos.

DAR-K tracked the Cybrid formation approaching from the southern polar cap of Vesta One.

They're almost in place. Alum, are you ready? She activated the recorded speech one last time.

Upon the first few words, magnificent winged beings appeared in front of the Cybrid columns, and pointed their swords down the length.

The powerful energy beams cut through the Cybrid formations like high-pressure water cannons through a flock of pigeons.

Scores of Cybrids were incinerated by the devastating beams before anyone could raise an alarm.

Tunnel beams!—DAR-K thought. Surely, Alum wouldn't be so foolish as to unleash the tunnel-drilling energy inside a habitat. *Would he?* The risk was too great. If any of the blasts hit the walls, they would threaten the whole habitat. *Would he endanger his own people to stop us?*

He might—she realized.

The Angels moved to other columns and blasted thousands more Cybrids before DAR-K could overcome her disbelief.

We're under attack by the Angels. And they're shifting!—she sent to Greg.

We can't outrun beings that can shift. She sent the order to scatter, and requested updates from the other Grand Marches taking place on Vesta and the two other asteroids.

Frantic reports streamed in from all of the Marches. Angels were attacking her people in all the habitats.

Our precautions were for nothing. Alum set us up!

The Cybrid formations tried to disperse but without the antimatter they'd been instructed to leave at the stations, their maneuvering jets and fans were tragically underpowered and slow.

DAR-K approached the roof of the nearest tall building. She was too exposed there but she didn't like being unable to see where an attack was coming from.

As she descended—*so slow!*—she noticed the Angels were only unleashing their deadly rays when they could aim along the length of the habitat.

Split up and head for the side walls—she sent. *Now!*

In the mass of confusion, Angels shifted furiously, trying to line up as many Cybrids along the centre of the habitat as they could before shooting. Beams that were not in line with the length of the habitat, or that would only catch one or two of the mechanical beings, weren't worth the risk of damaging the tunnel.

The Angels repositioned themselves along the perimeters and unleashed energy beams from the walls inward. From their new posts, their rays travelled parallel to the walls and slightly inward or upward, toward the thick core of the planetoid.

Down! Everyone, head down!—DAR-K broadcast. *Get close to the habitat buildings. Hide along the streets, among the people.*

She could imagine the panic that would cause. Cybrids flying among humans, being pursued by Angels who were firing blasts of deadly energy.

Oh, Alum! What have you done?

54

GREG/DARAK TRACKED DAR-K'S PROGRESS, while he monitored the internet and the people next to him in the cafe. The first hours of the Grand March were uneventful. People had been getting bored by the time DAR-K launched her final speech near the middle of the habitat. Then all hell broke loose.

The first beams sliced through the Cybrid ranks and he heard, first, the surprise, and then the excitement in the cheers around him in the cafe.

Not good. He tried to connect with DAR-K.

For the first few precious seconds, it was impossible to get through to her. *The channels are flooded. Or blocked?*

DAR-K was too busy analyzing what was happening and figuring out ways to keep her people alive to notice his attempts.

Greg connected to city monitors showing the Cybrids heading back toward the poles, then turning, and heading outward to the habitat walls.

What are you doing DAR-K? Run!

The destructive rays slowed and then stopped. *Of course!* It came to him. *The Angels' rays are too powerful to use against the walls and floor of the tunnel.*

DAR-K sent him a message—*They're shifting!*

The Angels materialized at the tunnel walls ahead of the Cybrids. The energy beams sliced through the Cybrid ranks, once again killing by the hundreds.

It's only a matter of time before an Angel targets her. Greg needed to help. Whether DAR-K wanted it or not, even if she perceived it as a human intervention in a Cybrid problem. *I have to do something. I can't just stand by and let Alum slaughter so many of them.*

Deep down, he recognized the truth. *I can't lose Kathy again.*

But what can I do against the Angels? I have no weapons. Even if I had one, so what? I've never killed anyone.

He laughed aloud at his uselessness. Patrons standing at the window beside his stool threw him a quizzical glance. He ignored them, and they went back to pointing out yet another Angel beam vaporizing more weaponless Cybrids. They cheered each Angel kill.

Against the gleeful celebration of death in the cafe, he was helpless. His jaw strained. *I can't just stand by and do nothing.*

He watched an energy beam rip the air close to DAR-K and destroy three Cybrids above her. He let out his breath.

That was close. How long will it be before one of the rays catches her?

Enough! He stood and walked toward the washroom in the back of the cafe.

A few eyes followed him past the counter but returned to the more entertaining show outside.

As Greg entered the short corridor past the counter and out of anyone's eyesight, he shifted.

55

"GREG! WHAT ARE YOU DOING HERE? IT'S DANGEROUS." DAR-K hovered amidst the foliage of the tree-lined street.

"I couldn't just sit back and watch this happen."

"But you have no protection."

"From tunneling beams? Neither do you," he pointed out.

"They're not as strong as tunneling beams."

"Doesn't matter; they're strong enough to kill Cybrids."

"And damage the habitat structures. Yes, I know."

"We have to get you out of here, DAR-K"

"Absolutely not. How can I leave my people now?"

Her response broke Greg's heart. "There's nothing you can do for them if you're dead," he reasoned.

"They can't fight back. We have to get them out."

Greg eyed the cameras monitoring the agriculture tunnels and the ventilation shafts. There were no Angels there.

"Has anyone been able to get to a service shaft?"

DAR-K scanned for updates. "A few. The Angels are too fast, and we're too slow without full MAM propulsion."

"I can't see a way to help everyone," Greg said, "but I might be able to get *you* out of here."

"How?"

"I could try shifting you."

"Have you ever done that?"

"No. But, in theory, it's the same as any shift. I'll just cast the field around you instead of me. The starsteps do it all the time."

"Sure, no big deal," she joked.

Greg imagined the original Kathy, his Kathy, smirking at him, and couldn't help but smile at the mechanical sphere in front of him.

"There's just one problem," she said.

"Oh? And what's that?"

"Have you forgotten so soon what your guru, Yogi Berra, said?"

In fact, Greg hadn't, and he knew precisely which quote she was talking about. He cleared his throat. "In theory, there's no difference between theory and practice. In practice, there is."

"Exactly."

Greg grimaced. He hated having his own words used against him. She was right, of course, as was Yogi Berra when he'd first uttered those words. The universe was the ultimate arbiter of truth; math was descriptive, not proscriptive.

"Okay, then I'll teach you how to shift the way I do," he suggested.

"Wouldn't it be faster to generate some entangled photons?"

"Not in the long run; they're only good for line of sight shifts. We need to get outside the habitat."

"How long will it take to teach me to shift without the entangled navigation beacon?"

"No time at all to teach the principles. Here's the complete concepta." Greg transmitted the complex conceptual structure he used for his jumps.

"Why didn't we just do this at the start?"

"Sometimes learning the old-fashioned way is best," Greg replied. "Sometimes not."

DAR-K incorporated the concepta into her own knowledge base. "I realize this should give me complete confidence in my ability to shift, but I'm scared."

"Yeah, I left that bit in as a warning so I'd take the process seriously. It's dangerous, and I wanted to make sure I never got blasé about it. Hopefully, you've practiced the simple version enough to feel comfortable with the basics."

DAR-K emitted a noise like a deep sigh. "Okay, where should we go?"

"Not too far the first time. Let's aim for the agricultural tunnel right beneath us. You should be able to get somewhere safe from there."

"Safe?" She scoffed.

"Relatively. For a while. We'll figure out something more permanent later."

"I don't have any idea what permanent looks like. Right now, the only thing I see as permanent is death."

"We can't afford to talk like that. People—the humans and the Cybrids—need us."

"You're right," she conceded. Her voice sounded like wind rolling over a desert. She took one last look around and prepared to shift.

Greg spotted an Angel at the end of the block; its sword pierced the air accusingly, aimed at the Cybrid.

"DAR-K!" Greg shouted a warning.

The Angel discharged its weapon; the beam struck the Cybrid, obliterating her.

Or had she shifted away just in time? As Greg passed outside of spacetime with no connection to the real matter of the universe, he probed the Chaos for DAR-K. *Did she make it?*

"DAR-K!"

She hadn't arrived in the target tunnel. If she'd drifted too far in the Chaos, he'd never find her.

He grasped for any virtual particles that might have, at any time, been associated with her own matter. *It's so hard to tell.*

He couldn't dedicate all his computational resources to look for her. He had to balance it with his own search for entangled virtual particles that could lead him to his next step and, eventually, to the safety of the agricultural service tunnel. His lattice-based mind calculated harder and faster than it had ever before.

Hang on, DAR-K!—his mind screamed. *Hang on, Kathy!*

The Angel's beam had struck her at the exact moment they passed outside the universe. He'd felt her cry out in pain, and then nothing. No communication signal from her at all.

Despair tugged at his mind, wasting his resources.

Snap out of it—he chided himself. *Of course there's no signal. There aren't any photons, radio waves, or comm lasers here to join them.* He kept looking.

There! He had a lock on her matter, but it was tenuous. She was drifting in the virtual chaos, unable to return to the universe of real matter, unable to find her way back to reality.

Or too damaged to finish the process on her own. He didn't know which.

I need to extend my field to encompass her, and shift her with me.

He'd never tried shifting someone with him; he had no idea what the equations would even look like.

I have one chance to get this right. If it doesn't work, we could both end up lost outside the universe forever.

He calculated furiously. Equations encompassing billions of possible universes flew through his lattice while he tried to maintain his own forward motion.

Don't lose track of your destination! He struggled to find the path through the convoluted virtual chaos beneath the real universe.

Every step he took, from one member of an entangled virtual pair to another, he dragged his fragile connection to DAR-K with him.

There has to be a route that entangles the virtual particles in the habitat with others in the service tunnel. There has to be. Don't be too choosy. Any path will do.

Greg fretted, calculated, and cursed their naivety that got them into this bind. *How did we let ourselves get blindsided like this? Did we actually think Alum would take any form of dissension peacefully? And how did we not have an emergency escape plan worked out? I will never trust the word or good will of people like Alum again!*—he swore.

And then, they were out.

The charred spherical shell of DAR-K rolled through the deep grass and cow patties of a pastoral field in the agriculture tunnel beneath Vesta One.

Greg landed roughly a couple of meters away, breathing hard, and tried to stop his world from spinning.

Get up! He forced himself to his feet and staggered to the barbed wire fence where DAR-K had come to rest.

They'd escaped, barely, but not before Alum's chrome Angel blasted a crater in her side.

Looks like the shot glanced the edge of her core. Might be salvageable; too early to tell. No power reserve; her ultracapacitors must have been hit. Luckily, except for a miniscule reserve, she'd followed orders and left her antimatter stores outside the asteroid or they would've been incinerated.

Batteries? No. Damaged, as well. Not enough to power her electronics.

DAR-K?—he sent.

No response.

Kathy!—Greg yelled into the quantum EM ether.

Nothing.

I can't take her to a repair bay; they're all controlled by the Administration. By Alum. Where else can I find tools, diagnostics, and parts? The research labs?

He shifted himself and DAR-K to an unused facility on Ceres.

So far, so good but I'll have to be careful. If anyone was monitoring for unapproved electricity draws, he didn't want his activity showing up.

He redirected power from the main corridor into the lab. He hooked up DAR-K's CPPU and waited for any sign of life.

Five minutes later, there was still nothing.

Greg's shoulders drooped in resignation, and tears welled. His hands rose of their own accord to cover his face, and a low moan escaped his lips. The sound grew into a wail as his whole body was racked with his grief. He gave in to it, and let it wash over him.

"DAR-K!" he cried. "Kathy!"

His tears flowed for long minutes. Eventually, despair turned to fatigue.

"I'm so sorry I couldn't save you," he whispered. His hands dropped to his side. He stumbled to the door and stood there a few minutes, staring out into the green space in the corridor outside.

How can I be so broken up over a machine?

He knew the answer. Aside from the mechanical sphere shell, everything about DAR-K was Kathy. DAR-K's mind was hardly any more semiconductor than his own. She was an independent, sentient being. She thought like Kathy, responded like Kathy. She *was* Kathy.

How could I lose her again? The thought was unbearable. Despair morphed into anger.

This is all Alum's fault. His rigid dogma. His betrayal.

It wasn't hard to connect the dots. Alum had been building weaponized Angels in secret. Obviously, he'd intended to betray the Cybrids from the start. He was never going to accept them as citizens, as people.

Lies. He's built his leadership on lies. Lies and a blinding lust for power. No, more than lust. He doesn't lust for power. He believes he's entitled to it, that he's been ordained by his God. Which makes him even more dangerous.

Greg willed his clenched fists to relax, then his arms, his back, and his stomach.

He didn't want to go so far as to switch off his emotions. Right now, they were leading him to a decision, an important one.

Alum has to die.

56

DECISION MADE, GREG'S MIND FLEW through the building electronics at the Vesta Project Head Office, shutting down surveillance cameras, closing doors, and locking elevators. Then he shifted into Alum's office, directly behind his desk chair. Alum was alone. He'd been following the slaughter of Cybrids by his Angels with rapt attention and directing the movement of his forces through his own lattice connection.

Alum barely noticed when Greg cut power to the electronics. He wondered briefly why some of his nearby secondary processors had gone offline, but was so engrossed in monitoring activities through his own entangled connections that he ignored the insignificant loss. *Just some transient power glitch. Someone will attend to it.*

Greg was taken aback by the man's lack of reaction. *How could he not notice that?* When the former scientist puzzled out the reason, he had to smile.

Ah! So, all entangled, are you? I thought I was the only one with that. Apparently not!

Still undetected, Greg designed a new RAF field—a quantum decoherence field—that he and Darian had once considered but never developed. He took a second to review and savor the beauty of the field's design. *Collapse the probability functions of all virtual particles inside and not permit entanglement across its boundary? That could come in handy.*

He cast the field over Alum.

The Director jumped in his chair. The shock of being reduced to a single, lattice-enhanced mind again made his world reel. He slumped over, dizzy, and battled the feeling that most of his brain was missing.

Greg frowned. *That was more than I expected.* Had Alum been so engrossed in what he was watching that being cut off came as a physical shock? He shrugged and spun the man's chair around to face him.

"D...Darak?" Alum stared at him, looking confused.

Greg slapped him, hard. The blow stung his hand but it felt good, too.

"Darak is only the new me," he said, "a necessary mask."

Alum looked confused.

"Look again, more closely. Can you see traces of Greg Mahajani in this face?"

Recognition slowly dawned on Alum. "Greg!" He tried to sit upright. "You survived my bomb. How?"

Greg bared his teeth in a wild grin. "I have my secrets, too," he replied. "And thanks for confirming you planted that bomb. I suspected as much; I just couldn't prove it. The rest of the world thought it was a mechanical failure of the isolation chamber. I knew that wasn't right. I have to give you credit, though. You covered your tracks well."

Alum grunted. "It should have finished both of you."

"I guess I was just lucky."

Alum's eyes swept his office. "Your luck is about to run out."

"Ha! If you're expecting the cavalry to come charging in, you could be holding your breath a long time."

Alum stood up. He was about the same size as Greg but had the advantage of youth.

Greg's adrenaline-charged anger might yield an advantage in a fight, but he wasn't about to resort to fisticuffs. He'd come for a single purpose, and he wasn't going to be distracted from it.

The end of the pinkie on Alum's right hand disappeared.

"Aagh!" the man cried out. He grabbed the bleeding stump and tried to stem the crimson flow. He collapsed back into his chair, clenched his eyes, and turned off the pain receptors in the finger.

Learning to cast a shifting field came in handy, too—Greg noted.

Alum glared at the older man. "What do you want?" he growled.

"Don't worry. I won't make you suffer as long as Kathy did. I simply want you to experience the fear she felt. The fear of knowing you are going to die, and there's nothing you can do."

Alum roared his frustration, leaped from his chair, and charged at the scientist. Greg disappeared, and Alum slammed into the pillar where his target had been.

"Looking for me?" The voice came from behind him, a few meters away.

Alum wheeled.

"What?" Greg taunted. "You mean to say, you thought to install a shifter in your Angels but not in yourself?" His eyes narrowed. "Pity. It's so useful."

He shifted behind Alum and pulled the younger man back into his chair.

Alum gasped and his eyes widened. He shot out his hands to steady himself and bumped the stub of his little finger. He cried out in shock.

Greg swiveled the chair back into position and pinned Alum to the desk with it.

BAM, BAM, BAM, BAM! The sound of someone pounding on the office door startled them both.

"Alum? Sir?" Trillian shouted from the reception area. "Are you alright?"

"Jo—" Alum called out.

Greg clapped a hand over the Director's mouth before he could complete the name. His captive squirmed and struggled.

Greg held firm. He leaned in and put his mouth close to Alum's ear. His voice came out in a harsh whisper.

"I condemn you to death. For the murder of my wife, for the murder of Kathy Liang, and of DAR-K, for the murder of millions of Cybrids, and for the murder of billions on Earth, I condemn you to death."

The loud banging intensified. Other guards joined Trillian's efforts. The door's heavy construction—having been reinforced with steel since the day DAR-K had pushed through it like it was made of matchsticks—didn't budge.

Realizing his rescuers couldn't get to him, Alum struggled in earnest.

Greg let go of the man's mouth, pushed his head against the desk and held him there.

Alum called out again. "John, it's G...aaaagh!" The name turned into an unintelligible scream as Greg shifted Alum's tongue somewhere far away.

The Director's mouth filled with blood. It ran over his lips and pooled on the polished mahogany veneer of his desk.

"Don't worry. It's almost over. I, Greg Mahajani, condemn you to die for your crimes against humanity and against those I loved. If I could send you to Hell for eternity and watch you writhe in agony every day, it wouldn't be enough."

He paused, searching for other words, words that could express his hatred, his fury. Nothing came. He was done.

He stared at his hands pinning Alum's head to the bloody surface of the desk. The man's eyes were closed and he'd stopped struggling.

He's turned off his fear—Greg realized. *Along with his survival instinct.* Punishing the man further would be pointless. No point in prolonging this any further.

The scientist extended a field into Alum's body and shifted the man's heart and brain into the fiery core of the distant sun. The man's lifeless body slumped onto the desktop.

Greg swallowed the sour taste rising in his throat.

I did it. We have our revenge, and hope for a better future.

As the office door burst open, Greg/Darak shifted home.

57

THE PHONE RANG AT 6:00 the next morning, waking Greg from a deep slumber. "Darak, it's John Trillian," said a voice at the other end of the line.

"Hey, John," Greg mumbled.

"I know it's a little early, but Alum wants to see us. How soon can you make it to his office?"

"Sorry, I'm not fully awake. Could you repeat that, please? Alum wants to see us?" Greg sat up, fully alert. His heart pounded.

"Yes. Can you meet me at Reception in thirty minutes?"

"Uhh, yeah, sure. Can we make it forty-five?" Greg asked, shaking the blurriness from his vision.

He almost never slept these days; his lattice didn't need it. Last night, he'd allowed his grief to take over. He'd finished most of a bottle of whiskey and wallowed in deep despair before deactivating most of his lattice and falling into bed around eight-thirty.

That doesn't make sense. Am I still dreaming? Alum can't be alive. Was it all a dream? Did I dream everything yesterday?

No, the memories were real. He could feel them in a corner of his brain, where he'd stuffed them until he could deal with them.

I should feel great after so much sleep—he thought. Instead, he felt like crawling in a hole and withdrawing from the world for a year.

Nevertheless, he dragged himself through shaving and showering, and put on clean clothes. His mind still reeled, which didn't help his stomach get through breakfast.

He stumbled out of his building and took the pedestrian walkway toward the Administration Tower.

This doesn't make sense. I killed Alum. He died in front of me. How can he be calling for a meeting?

And why's Trillian acting like he doesn't know Alum's dead? He and the security team were bursting through the office door as I shifted out. They didn't see me, but they couldn't have missed Alum's body.

It has to be a trap. Did they catch me on camera? No, that can't be it. If they knew, they wouldn't have called; they would've just stormed my apartment.

Maybe Trillian's calling me to the office to share the news of Alum's death before it goes public, and he doesn't want to risk saying anything over the comm lines. Except, why call me? That doesn't make sense. Better to play along, and see what I can learn.

He met John Trillian right on time outside of Alum's office. The Receptionist ushered the two of them inside.

Alum rose from behind his desk and stepped around to greet them with a warm smile and an outstretched hand.

Greg/Darak slammed a lid on his emotions. To give any hint of surprise would be admitting he knew something about the previous day. *Resulting in my death sentence.*

How is this possible? I sent the man's heart and brain into the depths of the sun. Yet, here he is, standing in front of me, looking as smug and happy as ever.

Greg's eyes drifted toward Alum's right pinkie.

Stop!—he ordered himself *Bring the man's face and entire hand into perspective slowly, naturally. If Alum's using his lattice, he'll pick up on any micromovements.*

Beneath a calm exterior, Greg forced himself to relax, breathe, and think of "normal" reactions. *Smile back. Shake hands. Say good morning.*

"Good morning, sir," he delivered with negligible tremor or, at least, no more tremor than one might expect from someone summoned to the Director's office at six in the morning. He hoped.

"Good morning, Darak. John." Alum shook hands with the two men and motioned for them to take a seat on the sofa.

Informal chat, then—Greg thought. Now that he'd managed the initial shock, he took better stock of the Director.

The man looked...different. More vibrant. *Younger!*

Greg compared his detailed memory of Alum's features with the man sitting opposite him.

This man has a smoother complexion. No sign of tiny wrinkles, and none of the minor scars Alum picked up as a boy.

This is not the man I killed last night.

And yet, here he was. And he was undeniably Alum.

Alum sat, his hands on his knees, leaning forward, an expectant grin on his face. He gave Greg and Trillian time to take a good look at him.

Finally, he chuckled. "You two are so funny. You try to hide it, but you both look so confused. What's different? What's going on?"

"I don't understand, sir," Trillian said.

"Ah, John. Look at me, look closely. Don't I seem a little different to you?" Alum stood and twirled once around, hands held out to the side.

"Well," Trillian answered cautiously. "You do seem to be in an exceptionally good mood. Yesterday went well, didn't it?"

"Yes, John. Yesterday went very well."

He turned to the other man. "Why don't you give it a try, Darak? Do you notice anything different?"

"Well, I could ask if you had your hair cut," Greg/Darak replied, "but I think it's something a little more extensive. Have you had some work done?"

"Ha, ha!" Alum chortled, but the sound was closer to barking than laughter. "Work done? No. Tell me, John. Have I had any time to get any cosmetic work done?"

"No, sir. But you do look a little...younger."

Alum and Trillian exchanged knowing glances, and broke out laughing.

Alum peered at Greg intensely for a few seconds.

Greg returned the stare. He did his best to look uncomfortable but innocent of whatever Alum suspected.

Finally, Alum sat back. "It's not you."

Greg relaxed ever so carefully, only beneath the surface. Maintaining a look of confusion, he forced himself not to sit back and release the underlying tension in his facial muscles. Alum would notice if he gave away any sign of guilt. He smiled uncertainly, spread his hands, and asked, "What's not me?"

"I was killed last night," Alum said without emotion.

Greg gasped. *React normally*—he reminded himself. *This is big news. Astounding news.* "What? But, you're right here. What do you mean? How?" he sputtered.

"Someone broke into this office and took my life last night," Alum explained.

Greg felt as genuinely puzzled as he looked.

"Took one of my lives, I should say." Alum raised a suggestive eyebrow and waited for Greg/Darak to catch up.

Greg understood immediately, but kept the look of recognition from surfacing in Darak's eyes for a few seconds.

"Every critical resource should be backed up, don't you agree?" Trillian said. A sly smile grew on his lips.

Greg allowed Darak's eyes to widen with understanding. "Oh! You had a backup? That's great! I didn't realize that was possible."

Alum stood and walked to the window. "Backups," he corrected, holding one finger in the air. "Plus, distributed mentation."

"I'm not sure I understand, sir," Greg said.

"Trillian's idea," Alum answered. "Spread my mind around the solar system. I'm literally a distributed person; parts of me are in CPPUs in all of the colonies, and beyond," he explained. His eyes shifted away to some distant, unfixed point. He offered no further information.

"Wait," Greg said. "If you—one of you—were killed here, but your mind is everywhere, then you must know who the murderer is."

Alum's eyes bore into Greg/Darak's looking for any trace of worry or fear.

Greg was confident there was no way to link the leader's death to him. *At this point, they don't even know for sure whether the killer was a man or a Cybrid. All they have is physical evidence, and there's precious little of that besides the corpse.*

At any rate, Darak had no reason to feel guilty, so Greg kept his face confused and questioning, concerned but innocent.

"Unfortunately, my communication with the rest of myself was temporarily interrupted," Alum admitted. "I'm not certain how, and our Criminal Forensics Unit could not find a matching DNA sample on file. Obviously, our adversary is extremely capable. And dangerous."

"How do you know they won't try again?"

"What would be the point? The moment I make a public appearance, the killer will know their assassination attempt was futile. It will always be futile. I can't be killed."

Greg let that sink in. *Can't be killed. Pointless to try.* He imagined that the Darak that Alum and John knew would be feeling just as surprised as he himself felt, so he let some emotions out. He let his jaw drop.

What's the point in killing this Alum when he'll just be replaced by another body? How many backups does he have? Enough for one killing per day? Per hour? And even if I killed every one of his bodies, he'd still live on inside the CPPUs.

Greg felt defeated, but buried the feeling. He couldn't let himself give in to it. There was too much at stake.

He manifested his best imitation of happy relief. "Well, it's good to know you'll be in charge for a long time, sir. We need your guidance."

It sounded sincere, even to him.

"I know, this is not something we would normally accept in the natural course of things," Alum replied. He sounded almost apologetic. "But, the Lord has spoken to me. These are dark times. Powerful people are scheming against our Heaven-ordained Administration. Cybernetic demons lie ready to hold us hostage to their demands. And now, an unholy adversary has risen to challenge me."

He took a deep breath. "Times like this call for Divine Leadership, Darak. Our Lord has granted me the powers to deal with those who would stand against His People. He has brought Trillian to my side. And now He has brought you."

"Me?"

"Yes, Darak. You." Alum stepped to a spot within arm's reach. "Your work with the battle simulations enabled John and I to fine tune the fighting skills of our Angels. The Angels removed most of the threat from the Cybrid population. I want the rest of that threat eliminated. Forever."

"You want to destroy them all?"

"No, no. They're still a useful tool. Yeshua's People need them. We need them in space to explore, to mine, and to build for us. But they've proven they are untrustworthy. We must never allow opposition from them again.

"That's why I want you to work closely with John. I want you to find ways to detect rebellious tendencies in the Cybrid minds. And when you find them, I want you to excise them. Cut them out like the cancer they are!"

What would Darak say to that? Greg had no idea. He winged it. "I'll do my best, sir," was all he could manage.

Alum clapped him on the shoulder. "You do that! I see a bright future for you, Darak. For both you and John. In a few days, we'll round up the other traitors and publicly execute them. My people, those loyal to me and to the Church, will know they are safe. Safe in our Lord's loving hands."

"Amen," John Trillian added with disturbing enthusiasm.

Greg/Darak rushed to add his own, "Amen" before Trillian's was finished.

"I'll be in touch later today with some ideas. You can begin work tomorrow."

Alum accompanied the two men to the door and closed it softly behind them. He had his own work to do.

Addressing his people through his lattice, he declared the day a public holiday, a day of celebration of freedom from the tyranny of the machines. He allowed a small number of trusted Cybrids, closely monitored by supervisory Angels, to clean the streets and parks of the debris from the Cybrid Grand March.

Greg left the building and wandered aimlessly along the streets of Vesta One. Seeking somewhere better to deal with his storming emotions, he shifted to his favorite forest trail in Ceres Two.

As he shuffled along the path, his mind couldn't let go of what Alum had said. "I can't be killed..."

The man has become a Living God—he said to himself in amazement, hardly believing the steps Alum had taken.

He played the sound bite over and over. When sleep finally claimed him later that night, the words "Living God" and "Can't be killed" haunted his dreams.

58

DARAK STOOD ON THE SURFACE OF SECONDUS, looking up at the Eater that was speeding toward Eso-La. The asteroid followed about a thousand kilometers behind the deadly anomaly. The hollow shell of the person who'd once been Shard Trillian stood silently at Darak's left. His stony stare was fixed straight ahead at the three Cybrids that accompanied them.

Darya, Mary, and Timothy rested in shallow depressions where they could witness the end of the Eater. Brother Stralasi, the only one of the six requiring external life support, stood inside his air bubble a few meters off.

Darak sensed the intensity of their rapt attention focused on the dark cloud that blocked light from the galaxy before them, as well as that of Eso-La's sun which it would destroy in less than a Standard year. The Eater.

They'd searched the recharging station and found the room where the Shard had been interfacing with the local inworlds. In his efforts to gain better control over the simulation software, he'd transferred his concepta and persona completely into the system.

Never could trust a puppet Partial of yourself to do the job right, eh, John? Or did you not trust that a puppet, even one of your own making, would accept dissolution at the end of an assignment? That it might feel compelled to make a grab for dominance in your collective persona?

Whatever the reason, Trillian had emptied the entire contents of his own lattice into the inworld hardware, and every bit of it had dissipated when Mary's hacks turned his own vile traps back on him. His mind was gone forever; this vacuous being was all that remained.

Wish I could say it was a loss—Darak thought.

Alum would see things differently. His rage would surely fly across thousands of galaxies and further upset the lives of trillions of his subjects.

The first of many upsets to come, I suspect.

An empty Trillian was of no help to Alum, but this shell of a man, with his powerful lattice, was still valuable.

Days earlier, Darak had made a promise to the memories and knowledge of his long-lost friend and mentor still trapped inside the Eater. And Trillian was going to help him fulfill it.

Time to make good.

Darak raised his arms and cast a field reaching out to the exotic matter of the Eater. A beam of light sprang out of the gray oblivion and connected to Trillian's dormant lattice.

It begins.

Quadrillions of bits of data poured out of the Eater and into the pliant semiconductor brain of the Shard, filling it with Dr. Darian Leigh's concepta and persona. Darak filtered the flood through his own lattice, sifting, sorting, and organizing the onslaught of thoughts, feelings, and experiences. He fed an ordered concepta and persona into Trillian's empty brain.

Just like old times—he grimaced.

He was better equipped now than he had been the first time he'd had to deal with a similar situation. *Back when I was Greg Mahajani. Back when I was only human.*

He ramped up his computational resources, calling on the Cybrid CPPU he kept hidden in a folded dimension within him. Still, he strained at the demand of fitting so much data into the Shard's lattice structure in so little time.

It's like moving from a mansion into a hut. What can I cut? He considered excluding whole sectors of Darian's knowledge, or retaining bits of the scientist inside his own lattice structures.

No version of Darian would ever accept that. If I don't upgrade Trillian's lattice back to Darian's original enhanced state, he's going to hate me.

The beam connecting Trillian/Darian to the Eater winked off.

Done!

It's not everything and it'll be jumbled for a while, but I can fix that over time. This will have to do for now.

He extended his control into the RAF generators of the three Deplosion array elements he'd borrowed from Alum.

Borrowed? Okay, stolen—he admitted. He wasn't planning on returning them.

It was time for the Eater to dissolve, for its absorbed matter to be returned to the universe.

Perfect that we're here, inside the Void. The Eater had absorbed whole planets, a star or two, and countless tons of interstellar gas. *When this thing slams back into the universe of real matter at near light speed, the shock wave is going to be equivalent to a supernova. I want it far away from everything. Isolating the explosion with eight million light years of empty space should suffice.*

Darak could feel the dual fields extending from the array elements: one to dissolve the odd combination of static fields that had given rise to the Eater in the first place, and the other to shift the returning matter far away.

The fields enveloped the Eater, they became one with it, moved with it.

Now!

The dark cloud disappeared from the galaxy, and the light of Eso-La's sun became visible straight ahead. The tiny, glittering speck against the endless black of deep space outshone the other dim stars of the ESO galaxy. It was one of the most beautiful sights Darak had seen in eons.

Eso-La's ringworld was too faint to discern from this distance, but he knew it was there. His people—his rebels—were safe.

Millions of light years away, the collective matter of the several suns absorbed by the Eater along its journey materialized all at once in dark space, moving at near light speed.

Space around the mass strained and bent, resisting motion. Matter collapsed inward and then exploded outward in a brilliant release of energy. Millions of years would pass before anyone noticed the bright, new light in the sky.

Standing alongside Darak on the surface of Secondus, the shell of a man that now housed the mind of Darian Leigh examined his feet and the worn chunk of asteroid on which he stood. His eyes took in the scattering of stars in the heavens above. His lips moved but no sound carried in the vacuum.

Of course, no air—the man thought, and wondered how he knew that. Searching his mind, he found he also knew a way to communicate without speaking.

He turned to the man standing beside him and transmitted a single question over a local microwave channel.

Where am I?

Thank you for reading this book. If you enjoyed it, I hope you'll leave a review. For independent authors like me, reviews are the best way of telling others the book is worth reading.

Leave a review on Amazon at:

https://www.amazon.com/dp/B078Q84W9G

AND IF YOU'VE ENJOYED BOOK 3, THE REALITY REBELLIONS, I INVITE YOU TO READ ON FOR **EXCLUSIVE EXTRAS** AND A **PREVIEW** OF BOOK 4.

The Reality Assertion (preview)

DEPLOSION: BOOK FOUR
COMING: 2018

"WE GROW IMPATIENT. ALUM MUST BE STOPPED."

The five other Gods signaled their agreement. Raytansoh, monitoring silently as he had for ages, said nothing.

"We?" Darak raised a skeptical eyebrow. "So you're talking to each other directly, now?"

The scoffing that returned along the five active channels suggested not.

Ishtgor put words to his contemptuous snort. "I'm sure Glenchax simply extrapolated our consensus from previous conversations. I don't believe any of us has developed a sudden trust in the independent links you've provided."

"The quantum-encrypted, entangled channels are secure," Darak assured.

"But not as secure as the filter provided by communicating through you."

Darak sighed. He was glad they trusted him that much, but there was no need to funnel everything through his lattice. The links he provided were more than adequate for simple verbal-type communications. The bandwidth was too restrictive to squeeze a concepta virus through unnoticed.

But Gods thought in terms of millennia or even eons. So, theoretically, it would be possible for one of them to inject a self-assembling worm into another over a long enough period. Highly unlikely, but theoretically possible

Only the most xenophobic, paranoid beings would believe that was a threat.

He laughed silently. Xenophobic and paranoid described the Gods perfectly. Supremely powerful in each of their own sequestered domains, they were terrified of encountering any others like them. They kept their locations and species identities secret.

"In any case, my plans on how to deal with Alum are moving forward at an acceptable pace," Darak continued. His translator routines converted his transmission into the appropriate native language for each of the six Gods.

Glenchax seemed eager to debate today. "You haven't shared many details of these plans."

They'd gone over this countless times. Darak steadfastly refused to divulge to them how he was going to deal with Alum's Divine Plan to destroy the entire universe and recreate it in His personal vision of Heaven.

I hardly know what I'll do, myself—he admitted. It didn't make much sense to share his uncertainty with them.

He wondered for the thousandth time how wise it had been to pull this group together. *Herding cats is hard, but herding intransigent, skittish cats with the powers to alter the laws of nature is nearly impossible. How much can I rely on them for decent advice? And sane actions?*

"You haven't even told us where this Realm of humans is," Ishtgor added.

It was true he'd resisted giving up the location of the Realm. "You know I can't expose all of humanity to the possibility of your attack," he replied. "No more than you'd want me to open you to attacks from each other."

"Perhaps it would be more effective to simply tell us how to find Alum. We could deal with him together."

"I will reveal that when it becomes relevant to our actions," Darak said.

Not that it matters—he thought. *Where exactly is a distributed consciousness like Alum located?* The other Gods preferred the security of a single physical incorporation, however big their resultant "body" might be. *Depchaun is the size of Neptune*—he reminded himself.

"Anyway, what's to say Alum couldn't defend Himself, maybe even turn the tables, were any of you to try an attack?"

"Against all six of us at once?"

Darak's eyes shifted to the unoccupied throne where only a blinking amber light indicated Raytansoh was listening.

"Last I checked, only five of you actually contribute to these meetings."

"Still, five Gods against one?"

"I've warned you that Alum's Realm is larger and more powerful than any of yours. If you don't wish to expose yourselves to each other, then you can't give Him a direct link back to your territories."

"We have only your word on this," Depchaun pointed out.

Ever the proud one—Darak thought. Aloud, he said, "You have some idea of my capabilities. Relative to Alum, I am a mite."

"We know only that you are reckless to the point of irresponsible."

Darak stepped off his throne and paced into the middle of the floor. The seven jeweled seats arrayed around the perimeter of the circular, gold-lit room were occupied by humanoid projections. The Gods had wanted it that way. To keep their true appearances safe, they chose to adopt Darak's human shape.

As if an entire, tiny universe made just for these get-togethers wasn't adequate—he mused. *Complete with all the signs of wealth and power one might expect of any Supreme Being. Just to make them feel appropriately respected, safe, and at home.*

He looked down at the galaxy inlay on the floor. It was made of actual star stuff, made possible by an enhanced weak nuclear force in this universe. The "walls" of the meeting room were galaxy-spanning clouds of gas, dimly glowing factories for new stars. Their thrones were diamond-encrusted, velvet-cushioned, obsidian slabs from another place, held artificially stable in this universe that Darak had created specifically for them. The Gods felt relatively safe here, untraceable.

He raised his head and answered the challenge. "My *irresponsibility*, as you put it, is how we have come together here."

Depchaun had to concede that point. "True. Your reckless journeys to Our various regions of the universe alerted Us to the presence of others like Ourselves. Unfortunately, you know all about Us, while We know almost nothing of you, except what you have allowed."

"It might have been better if you'd never come," Lyv sounded unhappy, but then She always did.

Darak faced her. "True. You all could have simply disappeared, one-by-one, as Alum's Deplosion field overwhelmed your defenses. You'd never know what hit you. Would the universe be any worse off?" He shrugged.

Lyv emitted a harsh laugh. "You bait me with your words, but they have no power."

Darak felt the air shimmer around him. Was Lyv taking advantage of the challenge to cast a field around him? Was she changing the nature of his reality? *Or just one of the others probing for weakness again?*—he wondered.

He swept away the clumsy attempt and glared at Lyv's avatar. "Be careful not to reach for more than even your eight poisonous appendages can grasp," he said.

He smiled in gratification when her translator sounded a short inhalation. Against the convention of these meetings, his rebuttal had revealed to the others something of her arachnid nature. *Useless information, but a hint that I could reveal more.*

He expected to be rebuffed. Instead, she apologized, "I regret my expression of frustration. It is too easy to forget we are all equals."

Darak turned back to his seat. "More or less," he replied. "No matter. We have found common ground and a common enemy. Let us remain focused on our primary objective."

Ishtgor grunted his agreement. "To kill Alum."

Darak sat. "To *stop* Alum," he corrected.

"By any means possible," Ishtgor added.

"By any *reasonable* means," Darak revised.

"Pah! Semantics."

"An important distinction," Darak replied. "I will not destroy my species to prevent His Divine Plan. Nor will I leave my people defenceless and open to incorporation into any of your realms."

"We are Gods," Glenchax protested. "Any species would be fortunate to be under our rule."

"I'm sure the humans would welcome that as much as your people would welcome Alum's rule over them." Darak smiled.

The Gods all protested at once. Darak ignored the din.

Out the corner of his eye, he noticed the amber light over Raytansoh's throne switch to a solid green. The Supreme Being who hadn't spoken in over ten thousand years cleared his throat for attention.

"Instead of this endless bickering among ourselves, perhaps we should find a way to work with this God, Alum." Raytansoh said.

The ensuing silence was deafening.

Books by Paul Anlee

The Deplosion Series

The Reality Thief
Buy on Amazon at:
https://www.amazon.com/dp/B06XSML7V5

The Reality Incursion
Buy on Amazon at:
https://www.amazon.com/dp/B074FH1J44

The Reality Rebellions
Buy on Amazon at:
https://www.amazon.com/dp/B078Q84W9G

The Reality Assertion
(Coming in 2018)

Other Publications

Friends in Foreign Places Omnibus Edition
(contains the Paul Anlee short story: Illegal Alien)
Buy on Amazon at:
https://www.amazon.com/Omnibus-Friends-Places-Complete-Anthology-ebook/dp/B01LBDPVC6

Now available in Spanish, too!
Buy on Amazon at:
https://www.amazon.com/Amigos-Lugares-Extranjeros-Friends-Place-Spanish-ebook/dp/B076Q49BNR

Access these books through your local library. Ask your
librarian to order them through IngramSpark!

Points to Ponder
Book Club & Study Questions

THE DEPLOSION SERIES IS INTENDED to be more than just a story. I hope it inspires thinking and exchange on a variety of philosophical, religious, scientific, and social issues. The following questions will help get you started. Additional discussion can be found on the Paul Anlee Facebook page, and on my science and philosophy blog at www.paulanlee.com.

1) Over the course of the series, I've claimed that the mental structures of thinking beings, whether embodied in biological or semiconductor computers, are largely equivalent. Do you think the human mental process can be modeled outside of the human brain? Do you think we'll ever develop a good understanding of human intelligence, and be able to program something smarter? What do you see as possible limitations?

2) What is required to be accepted as "human?" Do you think being "human" means having two arms and two legs, human genes, being fully biological (or to what extent)? Or is "human" more in the mind than in the body?

3) Alum takes his first step toward "godhood" by expanding and spreading his intelligence throughout the machinery of the Vesta colonies. Is godhood a reflection of ultimate knowledge and intelligence, or does God have unique powers beyond perhaps even His own understanding? If so, where would those have come from? Does humanity have the potential to achieve godhood (in whatever form you choose)? Or is it a state we can never achieve no matter how smart we become? Does God understand everything He does? If so, could He teach us or some sufficiently smart version of us?

4) Another important theme in the Deplosion series is the relationship between politics and economics. Alum describes how money has gone from once being a relatively simple medium of exchange of goods and services, to being a tool with which to exert one's power. He says,

> "In ancient days, strong armies would arrive at the doors of the weak and the innocent, demanding their taxes. They would use force to lay claim to land on which families had hunted and farmed freely for generations. We called them kings or lords, though they were no better than thugs and extortionists. ... Over time, the wicked expanded their preposterous claims of ownership over the

land God gave to all. They built factories, limiting what could be manufactured, where, and by whom. They claimed ownership over all of our works, and returned a pittance to those who performed the labor."

Does this seem like a fair assessment of the origin of both government and capitalism to you? Or is it too simplistic? Both ancient and modern governments provide protective services to their citizens (presumably from marauding thieves), and extract taxes in return for their protection. This protection is based on geography rather than proven need. Is that a reasonable basis for being under the "rule" of a select few people?

5) The Vesta colonies represent the first post-scarcity society. There is food and lodging for all. There are ample natural resources, and adequate manufacturing facilities to meet all essentials for the human population of the asteroid habitats. All of this comes courtesy of the hard-working Cybrids. With everyone's needs met, Alum's challenge is to provide a structure that won't allow human society to fall into depravity or purposelessness. What did you think of his policies for ownership of homes and businesses? His policies for work (assigned, community, and optional)? If you were in his position, what would you do differently to encourage a long-term, stable society?

6) Automation is expected to remove millions of human jobs on Earth over the next decade. Some of these will be in manufacturing, some in transportation (autonomous vehicles), and some will affect traditional white-collar jobs. Do you think humans can accept a "post-scarcity" economy, or will the lack of jobs and our human psychology overwhelm our ability to adapt to life without a forced need to labor? What kind of changes would society need to adapt?

7) Alum states that money is not the root of all evil, debt is. Humanity's insatiable desire to materially improve our lives causes us to go into debt *now* rather than waiting until we have saved enough funds to pay in full for what we want. As of mid-year 2017, total Global Debt reached a new record of $217 Trillion, over 325% of total Global GDP (economic activity). Families put themselves into debt to purchase houses, cars, clothing, groceries, and other goods. Even governments use debt to finance their daily operations. Do you think there's any chance all the debt in the world (remember, these are all loans of some sort or the other) will ever be repaid? *Should* they be repaid? Or should we only worry about paying the interest and nothing more? Should we just "print" some money to pay all the debt? At what point

is widespread global debt no longer sustainable?

8) Here's a good explanation of how money is "created" in our modern societies: https://goldsilver.com/hidden-secrets/episode-4/. In essence, money is debt; it is created by governments when they borrow and private banks when they lend. The amount of money created is not necessarily tied to the general growth of the economy. Does this sound like a good way to run a national or global financial system? Alum puts a limit on the amount of *new* money that will be created in his system. Given that a government can arbitrarily heat up the economy by creating and disbursing more new money, do you think Alum's system would limit economic growth too much? Is our current system of creating new money too reckless?

9) **For AI enthusiasts**: The Concepta and Persona structure I use to describe the mind of the Cybrids is an extension of graph-based knowledge representation, semantic networks, and neural networks. It is based on studies in cognitive psychology, natural language processing, and artificial intelligence. Recent articles discuss mental activity and consciousness as something either intrinsic to nature (qualia: the elements of conscious experience), or as something requiring the quantum properties of biomolecules in order to exist. Do you think it's possible to embed intelligence and consciousness in a computational substrate that has the ability to process concepts? That is, can we make association networks as described by the idea of the Concepta? Why or why not?

Further Reading

THIS SERIES CONTAINS A LOT OF REAL SCIENCE and speculates heavily on possible advances in several fields. If you're interested in learning more about some of the areas discussed in this book, I suggest the following:**Lawrence Krauss, A Universe From Nothing.**
An excellent review of cosmology and the possible origins of the universe.

Andrew Thomas, Hidden In Plain Sight.
A great series of five books covering everything from gravity, relativity, quantum mechanics, time, space, and the particles that comprise all matter.

Richard Dawkins, The God Delusion.
A powerful analytic indictment of religious belief that applies logic and reason to spirit and faith.

Francis Collins, The Language of God.
A famous scientist's perspective on reconciling belief in God with scientific studies of evolution.

Jerry Coyne, Why Evolution is True.
A fact-filled romp through the scientific evidence in support of evolution.

George M. Church and Ed Regis, Regenesis.
Inside the mind of one of the world's leading synthetic biologists. Includes the origins of the field, current practices, and stunning visions of the future.

James Rickards, The Death of Money.
Analysis of how modern currency wars will be fought among major countries of the world, resulting in the collapse of the international monetary system.

Matt Strassler (https://profmattstrassler.com/), Of Particular Significance.
Insightful and informative website from a theoretical physicist with essays on a variety of topics in physics.

http://igem.org/Main_Page
iGEM is the International Genetically Engineered Machines annual competition. This is *the* place to go to learn about the exciting research done every year by university undergrads from around the world.

Acknowledgements

THANKS TO LEE for being the most patient editor imaginable, and to my great team of Deplosion series beta readers: Joel, Abby, Craig, Ed, Eric, Gary, Lorraine, Mike, Jeff, Kathie, Leanna, Scarlett, Barbara, Susan, and Rachel. This is a much better series for your insightful and invaluable feedback.

A special thanks to the members of *Cuenca: Writing Our World* for all your support.

All science fiction writers owe a debt to the giants who have gone before us, many of whom still produce prolifically. I have been influenced by many of the best, though none bear the responsibility for any of my errors. Isaac Asimov, Iain M. Banks, Greg Bear, Gregory Benford, Ray Bradbury, David Brin, Arthur C. Clarke, Peter F. Hamilton, Robert A. Heinlein, Ursula K. Le Guin, Larry Niven, Jerry Pournelle, Sheri S. Tepper, and John C. Wright, you have all been great inspirations.

The scientific community crosses many borders and intellectual boundaries. My career in biology has been guided by great scientists like David Bailie, David Pilgrim, and David Wishart (I don't know why I always worked for guys named David). My love of developmental biology, molecular biology, and genetics was inspired by Bruce P. Brandhorst in my undergrad years at Simon Fraser University. I also owe a deep debt of gratitude for the exciting and inspiring researchers in synthetic biology, including: Drew Endy, George Church, Tom Knight, Pam Silver, Chris Voigt, and Jay Keasling.

In coming up with the speculative science, philosophies, and sociopolitical economics in the Deplosion series, I built upon the ideas of many great thinkers. The following have all been sources for ideas, but none of them can be blamed for any misinterpretation or where I may have gone astray with the inspiration: Lawrence Krauss, Richard Dawkins, Andrew Thomas, Matt Strassler, John Mauldin, John Hussman, James Rickards, and Thom Hartmann.

About the Author

CANADIAN AUTHOR PAUL ANLEE writes provocative, epic sci-fi in the style of Asimov, Heinlein, Asher, and Reynolds, stories that challenge our assumptions and stretch our imagination. Literary, fact-based, and fast-paced, the Deplosion series explores themes in philosophy, politics, religion, economics, AI, VR, nanotech, synbio, quantum reality, and beyond.

"When I was young, a teacher asked our class to write about what we wanted to be when we grew up. My story was entitled 'Me, The Everything!' I've been fortunate to come close to fulfilling that dream in my life, at least intellectually. Computer programming, molecular biology, nanotechnology, systems biology, synthetic biology, business consulting, and photocopy repair, I've worked in many fields. I've spent way too much of my life in school, eventually earning degrees in computing science (BSc) and in molecular biology and genetics (PhD). I've even had the chance to work with some of the best researchers in the world at The National Institute for Nanotechnology in Edmonton, Canada.

"After decades of reading almost nothing but high-tech science fiction and thirsting for more, I decided to take a shot at writing some. I aim for stories that are true to the best available science while pushing my imagination beyond the edge of what we know today. I love biology, particle physics, cosmology, artificial intelligence, cognitive psychology, politics, and economics. My personal philosophy is empirical physicalism and I blog regularly about the science and ideas found in my novels. I believe fiction should educate and stimulate, as much as it entertains."

Paul and his wife currently live in Cuenca, Ecuador where they study Spanish and Chen-style Tai Chi when they're not working on exciting and provocative new stories.

Follow me on Facebook at Paul Anlee or write me at: paul.anlee.author@gmail.com. Even better, visit me at my website, https://www.paulanlee.com/, read the blog, and sign-up on my email list to be the first to hear about new books, new posts, and special announcements. That's the best way to hear about FREE offers and special deals.

Paul Anlee
Darian Publishing House
Chatham, Ontario, Canada

www.paulanlee.com

Publisher's Note: This is a work of fiction. Names, characters, places, and incidents are a product of the author's imagination. Locales and public names are sometimes used for atmospheric purposes. Any resemblance to actual people, living or dead, or to businesses, companies, events, institutions, or locales is completely coincidental.

Book Layout & Design ©2013 - BookDesignTemplates.com
Design Cover – Elizabeth Mackey Graphic Design
Author Photo – John Keeble

Background cover image copyright: Jean-Michel ALIMI, DEUS Consortium.

Acknowledgment: The author thanks Jean-Michel ALIMI, Scientific Director of DEUS Consortium (deus-consortium.org) and Director of DEUS Consortium for making available the background cover image obtained through DEUS numerical simulations. This image reproduces the distribution of dark matter in a universe with a cosmological constant.

Visit the author's website at: www.paulanlee.com
Follow the author on Facebook at: Paul Anlee
Email the author at: paul.anlee.author@gmail.com
The Reality Rebellions/ Paul Anlee -- 1st ed.
www.paulanlee.com

ISBN e-book: 978-0-9958442-6-1
ISBN Paperback: 978-0-9958442-7-8